T0357040

The Drifting Moments

Also by Paddy Carroll

Glassdrummond

Borrikeen
Unmasking Patrick Kavanagh

ISBN: 978-1-917242-19-6 (Hardback)
ISBN: 978-1-917242-20-2 (Ebook)

Published in association with Choice Publishing, Barlow House, Narrow West Street, Drogheda, Co. Louth, Ireland.
Trade enquiries to – www.choicepublishing.ie

The Drifting Moments

"...coming through the rye."

A Novel by Paddy Carroll

Tour and Judith,

Hope you enjoy the read.

Paddy Carroll

To Jerilynn, Leona and Patrick

Part 1

Prologue

A loft apartment in Tribeca, Manhattan, NY - Thursday evening, 20th June 1968

*I*f you love me let me go,' he blurted out, knowing their hearts were bound by invisible ties.

He knew she loved him. But is it a selfish love he asked himself. He saw a panicky look spread slowly across her face, her complexion grow deathly pale, her lips bloodless. Holding her gently by her upper arms, he looked long and deep into her tortured brown eyes masked by tear-tangled eyelashes.

'No! I can't,' she cried, a searing moan that ineffaceably scarred his soul.

Scalding tears trickled down, mascara streaking her cheeks. Subdued by unreflecting emotions provoked by the calmness of the surroundings, self-conscious of time leading to this inevitable parting, he finds himself unable to speak. Wordlessly he embraced her trembling body for what seemed a soundless eternity, but for what was but a brief moment. In the midst of her tears, he hunkered between her legs and clasping her closer still he could feel her nervous energy dissipate, rippling through her body.

'You must let me go,' he heard himself say, pitilessly, the blood throbbing in his brain. As if hypnotized, she folded like a toy doll filled with beads as she let her head drop on his shoulder, her streaming hot tears dripping onto his shirt.

'I love you Steve. I love you. More than I felt possible,' she whispered, clinging to him, her raw voice breaking in unbearable wretchedness, unable to express the emotions she felt.

'I'll love you all my life...but I can't be with you anymore. It's a dead end. Let me go,' he said, trying to contain his ardour, his body aching as every sinuous nerve tightened in his want to crush her to him so that he

1

might never have to let go of her, tears welling up in his bloodshot eyes. He kissed her passionately, tasting the salt of her tears on his lips burning and stinging, amid mingling tears their sniffling noses pressed hard against each other's cheeks. The intense intimacy of this moment pulses through him as he hungrily caressed her, their ineluctable passionate want of each other surmounting the scorching pain; his pain knowing that after this night he would never make love to her again, never be with her again; her pain knowing she had lost him. Her soft murmuring words filled him with fervent sensations realizing he would never hear those words again. In the searching, impregnable silences, their night of last togetherness was poignantly ravelled.

1

Stephen MacAlindon's earliest emotional memory is of trundling to Sunday mass at Saint Peter's with his mother, holding on to the decorative stanchion of the perambulator in which his baby sister Monica lay sleeping, hearing the reverberative tolling of the cathedral bells that filled the air with sound. He could not have been more than four or five at the time and readily recalled the smart hand-me-down polycotton jacket he was wearing, a reversible blue and grey with the head of a growling tiger imprinted on the back of the grey side which he insisted on wearing out for show, the blue side boringly plain. Traipsing along Clonard Street in new plimsoles, kicking pebble stones and then heeding his mother's rebuke – "stop that there now coddy for you'll ruin them new gutties of yours". On entering Percy Street, as they approached two women heedlessly barring the way as they stood chatting, both attired in floral-patterned aprons, one with a headscarf covering hair curlers, the snidey comment was heard – "Are yis away to bless yerselves with the Pope's piss. Why don't youse go to the Free State for yer kind's not awanted here." His mother, holding her head high, lengthened her stride causing him, as he peered back over his shoulder afraid the meddlers were following them, to lose his footing on the uneven pavement. Tumbling, he scratched his knee and began crying as if the sky had fallen in on him, his distress waking baby Monica in a yowling chorus. What brings this memory so vividly to mind is the felicific calmness of his mother's voice as she picked him up and wiped his snotty nose with her perfumed handkerchief, gently stroking his grazed knee with her gloved hand, his tear filled eyes mesmerised by her looming blood-red lips as she kissed his trembling mouth, sending a tingling sensation down his spine. All through mass, in a strange thrilling tenseness, he let his tongue trace the concoction of her lipstick on his lips redolent of his favourite raspberry jam, and something else he then had no word for.

He well remembers his first day attending Saint Mary's Primary School. He was four years and five weeks old. The week before this milestone in his rawly childhood, his mother bought him a new canvas satchel, sky blue in colour, and on opening it he found a colouring book of The Brothers Grimm Fairy Tales, a box of five colouring pencils, a lead pencil topped with an eraser held vice-like by a brassy knurl, and a jotter. So excited was he that he could hardly wait to start school, his mother and father thrilled for him, their pleasure in his excitement imbuing him with the confidence of a daredevil. The satchel was not permitted to be out of sight, he opening and closing the snib fastener, inhaling the strange chemical odour of its newness, checking and rechecking the contents as he unloaded them, again and again, barely able to resist scribbling on the jotter. Pleading to be allowed begin colouring the faintly etched fairy tale characters Hansel and Gretel led to a scolding by his mother who chided him – "Ah coddy! that would be unfair to yer teacher who can't wait to see yer handiwork in action." And so to school that lively day, lopping along Clonard Gardens, practically pulling his mother by the hand in his haste to get there. On entering the school vestibule, a hugely winged figure rushed toward them seemingly primed to grab him in its witchy claws. He let go of his mother's hand, turned on his heel and ran for life, the satchel slipping from his shoulder to the ground (he gave its loss not a second thought – he could run faster), not daring to look back despite his mother's frantic calls. Not catching up with him until he had turned into Clonard Street, on her hunkers, she held his shaking wiry frame and espying his face turn a chalky pallor, breathlessly quizzed him:

'What is it Stephen? Why did ye run off like that there?'

4

'Bat… the bat mammy,' he said in a barely audible blubbering voice, 'did ye not… not see… the big black bat.'

'The what! That's yer teacher ye silly codger. That's Sister Marie Louise.'

'The bat snatched at me, wanted to take… take me away and gobble me up,' he whimpered, giving her a gormless look.

Her mind's eye envisioned the panicky scene as Sister Marie Louise had made her approach in a flurry of impetuous authority, soundlessly gliding forward as if on skates, raising her arms in welcome, the inner folds of her black cassock webbed like the wings of a bat in full flight. The conjured up picture lead her to a gladdening recognition of the reason for her son's bolt for freedom. Nevertheless, he would not, and did not, return to the school for another year, by which time he was persuaded to be brave in helping his baby sister Monica make her start. Monica, a petit three year old, had been sent to school at such an early age so the MacAlindon parents could coax their roguish son to make his belated reappearance.

He did not like the nuns: their grotesque black and multilayered garb; the wimple adornment of bone-like headdress shaped like the wooden press frame of a tennis racket, making it impossible to behold the human personality underneath; the beaded rosary, like a chatelaine belting the waist, the length of a skipping rope with a brassy crucifix dangling at the knee, clacking unnervingly as the nuns swished about the classroom; their suspect kindness hesitatingly dispensed, more often than not alloyed with an unhealthy measure of austere control and a frighteningly rigorous discipline. Sister Marie Louise was not averse to pinching his cheeks, pulling his ears and giving him the odd cuff about the head, berating him for a numbskull, and every so often ignominiously making him stand like a dunce by the blackboard with his back to the class. Most humiliating were the occasions she demanded his younger sister Monica be fetched from the infant's classroom to help drum into "that blockhead of yours" the sequence of the letters of the alphabet, or, how to count his times tables. By mid January, perceived by the nuns as being physically too big and educationally too disruptive for the high-infants class, he was moved into first class and had to make new friends all over again.

Sometimes after a particularly trying day, in tearful hissy fits he would bawl out his mother about how much he hated school, disheareningly throwing his schoolbag on the hall floor. The only learning he really enjoyed was religious instruction which gave leeway to his vivid imagination while listening to *picaresque* stories about Herod, summoning up quaint images of the birth of Jesus in a stable in Bethlehem and the coming of the Magi to visit the holy infant. It was his grasp of such New Testament stories that won him his only best-in-class star prize – a scapular bearing an effigy of Saint Teresa of Lisieux.

One day, Sister Marie Louise was particularly abusive to Yvonne Mulcahy, the girl sitting beside him in the two seater desk, bellowing out, amongst other things – "you should stay at home Yvonne and not be wasting my precious time", the outburst causing this waif of a girl to quail feebly, tears coursing down her cheeks as she wet herself. When the urinary discharge seeped to the floor, Sister Marie Louise whacked him on the back of the head practically dislodging him from the seat, clamorously declaring him – "no better than an untrained mongrel dog". In spasming fear, gobsmacked by the unexpected blow and stinging invective, he took refuge in silence. By the time he had recomposed himself, an altruistic impulse decided him not to plead Yvonne had been the culprit, taking the blame in hope of preventing the nun dishing out more punishment to her. That seminal moment proved the first occasion he found himself treated as a hero by his peers, glowing with pride, the glow that only self-satisfaction can bring, and, despite his tender age, he felt good about it.

*

Sitting by the Modern Mistress cooking range, the firebox now radiant red-hot, he watched his older sister, Eileen, as she stood at the table cack-handedly arm muscling in a canary-yellow basin the ingredients for a Christmas pudding, his mother finishing off the mix in a large Spode bowl, Monica whinging because she wasn't allowed be all fingers in the mess. Teasingly, Eileen would time and again stick out her tongue at him and then lick the wooden spoon, knowing he was finicky about his food. He wanted to wipe the moue of disdain off her mouth; but how? Such irksome antics he did his best to ignore. Earlier his mother had, with manic concentration on the task the whole family must help with, shifted him from the scrubbed pine table where he had been busily colouring in a cartoon of "Pinocchio" to make room for the pell-mell undertaking and ordered him to fill the coke scuttle and bank up the stove fire. Trepidatiously he had braved entering the coal shed outback next to the jakes, afraid of rats rumoured to be the size of tomcats, the smell of cat shit turning his stomach (a bottom panel of the shed door had broken-off by having been routinely dragged over loose coals and had yet to be repaired by his father despite his mother's constant nagging, the resultant gap attracting snoopy felines from all over the neighbourhood in use of the coke stack as a shithouse). By the time his father returned from work extolling their industry, the pudding was slowly steaming in a linen bag suspended over a pot of boiling water, the seasonal aroma pervading the house. Next morning he watched with amusement his mother pour an egg-cup-full of whiskey over the pudding, now moulded like a leather beaten pug ball on a fancy plate, strike a match and set light to it.

'Why are ye burning it?' he begged of her as he eyeballed in a commingling of horror and excitement the blue flares rise and turn into orange-red tongues that licked, glistened, and blackened the skin in a crackly combustion.

'Ah shure 'tis no good. May as well burn it,' she tauntingly replied, tongue in cheek, as she blew out the acrid dwindling flames.

Just then a knock came to the front door and his mother, hastily wiping her hands down the front of her apron before slipping it off, retreated from her splendiferous creation. He, his fingers tapping arhythmically on the table top, looked upon the charred and still smoking husk and grew disillusioned at the futility of all that effort in producing such a pig's blowout. Venturing to touch it, the sizzling heat scorched the pads of his fingers, and rapidly withdrawn, he mopily awaited her return – what's keeping her? The wooden spoon lay within easy reach and overtaken by quirkish mischievousness he ploddingly plunged the weapon into the pudding until it crumbled, dollops falling from the table to the floor, leaving him satisfied with a job well done. The hair on his head statically pricked-up on hearing his mother's envenomed screech as she re-entered the kitchen.

'What've done?' she bad temperedly squawked.

Observing her panic-stricken look, her red face distorted with rage, he blanked out in timorous confusion, suddenly afflicted by pins and needles in his feet and hands.

'Jesus Mary and Saint Joseph what've ye done to me pudding.'

'But ye said... said 'twas no good.'

'I said what?'

'Ye said 'twas no good, that's why ye burned it.'

'Well doesn't that just take the bleedy biscuit.'

She saw the affrighted innocence in his face and moving to cuddle him vowed never to tell "a mocking white lie" to any of her children ever again.

*

Because he continued unhappy at Saint Marys, his parents enrolled him in Colaiste Ris, the Christian Brothers Boys School on Glen Road, for the start of the second class term. Although located more than a mile from his terraced home on Bombay Street under the tower of Clonard Monastery, the move was made all the more exciting when his father presented him with an oldfangled inky bicycle, red paintblobs daubing the rust spots piebald. On his cycle run to and from school he adopted the vigilant tactic in evading the menacing attentions of snarling street dogs that seemed to have an inordinate hunger for the delicate tissue of his calves and ankles – he carried a stick. The Christian Brothers who taught him also carried a stick about their person and made liberal use of it: tapping sleepy heads; rapping knuckles incorrectly shaped in the holding of pen and nib; sanctioning punishment for unsatisfactory homework, or, breach of any school regulation. All suchlike infringements authorized a brother's exertion in the meeting out of up to six slaps, the more serious transgressions entailing six on each hand. One winter morning, Samuel "Mugsy" Dixon had failed to present Brother Xavier ("Monkey" the boys nicknamed him) with the required completed homework and was marched to the front of the class for a condign caning, Mugsy pleading lack of time due to exhaustion in having to rise every morning at five o'clock, hail rain or snow, to help his father with his milk run:

'Hold out your hand like that there now.'

'Sir! Sir! Don't hit me there.'

'No more of your oul guff Dixon, or you'll get six on the other one to boot.'

'Please Sir, I'm scalded with chilblains.'

'Where?'

'There Sir, there.'

Brother Xavier, to the mantra of "IF NOT – WHY NOT" with each strike, gave him six of his best, rarely missing the chilblains, every flensing hit jerking out an agonised grunt from Mugsy who refused to snivel, his free hand chafing the numbed mitt as he returned to his seat cursing Monkey under his breath.

In fourth class, the year Maca made his Confirmation, Brother Daniel ("Drac" the boys nicknamed him because of his prominent

9

eye-teeth and ash-grey pallor) catechized the boys and would playfully slap them on the cheek (as the Bishop would do on Confirmation day) whether they got the answers to his questions right or wrong, but if wrong the slap had a sting in it. On the morning of the ceremony, togged out in a grey short trouser suit (his first suit), a white rosette with a medal of Our Lady of Perpetual Succour adorning the lapel, his father's gift of a spanking new ballpoint pen proudly exhibited in the breast pocket, he felt apprehensive, consumed by a sense of self-importance yet fretful of what catechismal article of faith the Bishop would question him on. The family gathered at the front door impatiently awaiting his wilfully defiant sister, the mother leaning on the newel post and shouting up the stairs – "for heavens sake Eileen what's keeping ye", she chivvying her daughter that she would make them late, of how unfair and selfishly she was behaving, causing them to arrive at church at the last minute on such an auspicious day. Eventually Eileen, cool as a cucumber, came down the stairs sheepishly fingering the thick ringlets of her hair.

'Are ye all right Eileen for yer looking a bit peaky. Yer not sick are ye?' enquired her mother as they exited the front door.

'Fine, I'm fine mammy. Quit fussing will ye.'

'Ye look like ye seen a ghost,' gibed Maca.

Eileen made to give him a clip about the ear but he ducked and weaved like a flyweight boxer.

'Quit don squabblin' this minute the pair of yis. Can youse not behave yourselves like Christians for this one day. Come here to me Stephen till I straighten don tie on ye.'

In Saint Peters Cathedral, whilst nervously awaiting his turn before the bishop amid the assembly of novices, he insensibly began to chew the plastic clasp of his new ballpoint pen, finally snapping it off. By his turn at the altar rail, when moving to kneel, he unwittingly swallowed it and was immediately convulsed by suffocating hawking that brought tears to his eyes.

'Are you ready to become a soldier for Christ my son,' the night-marishly attired bishop earnestly asked, touching his forehead with a hoary forefinger. All he could do was nod his head in assent, his face transmuted puce, sweat tickling between his shoulder blades.

'Can you name the three divinities of the Holy Trinity?'

'God the Fattthhheeerrr… eeeegggghhhh –'

'Yes my son. God the Father. And the other two?'

'Eeeegggghhhh… God tthhee Soossoooonnnnn.'

'Very good my son. And the third divinity?'

'The eeeegggghhhh… Holy eeeegggghhhh –'

'Yes yes. God the Holy?'

'Eeeegggghhhholy shit. I'mmmm chokkkin'.'

As the bishop caressed his flushed cheeks, an incandescent Brother Daniel, having observed the escapade, rushed to drag him away, censuring him for his tomfoolery, and marched him back to his family, by which time the choking pen clasp had snaked to his stomach. Abashed, he watched a bodeful scowl spread over his mother's face, while Eileen and Monica fought to stifle titters of laughter. With the hustle and bustle of the day that was in it, his mother did not make enquiry as to the cause of his shenanigans until they had gathered with other families afterwards for a celebratory meal in the Roma Café. On hearing his tearful explanation, she gave him a big cuddle saying – "Well little blue eyes, nature will just have to take its course." However, all that morning she had remained worried by the sickly visage of her daughter and suddenly spotted the reason for Eileen's pallidly weird physiognomy:

'For the love of God Eileen what did ye do to yer eyebrows?'

'Nothin'.'

'Nothin' is right for you've nothin' where yer eyebrows should be.'

'I… I shaved them,' answered Eileen nonchalantly.

'You what?'

'I shaved them with daddy's razor.'

'Christ Eileen, you looked a sight all mornin'. I didn't know what the hell was wrong with ye. What possessed ye to do a thing the like of that there?'

'Dunno. Musta been bored.'

*

Alfred, his father, considered himself an accomplished musician and in pursuance of his foiled ambition played the piano at week-ends at the Felons club, a pastime which helped ease the drudgery of his manual working week, albeit his playing signified unpolished honky-tonk syncopations. Alfred's form of relaxation at home was the playing of an old, much dented, tenor saxophone, and Maca, imbued with the sense of music by the pentatonic rhythms he heard his father play in the parlour, would spend hours alone in his bedroom messing about on the unwieldy instrument, quickly mastering it, creating and developing his own style, a corruption of popular and jazz classics all achieved without music lessons or sheet music, just a good ear, practice, and impromptu footle. Alfred's genial serenity in the home (they played cards, snap being a favourite, he letting his children win by turns) did not preclude him from being the final arbiter of family quarrels and discord, dispensing righteous punishment which often included the use of his belt, his wife's threatening admonitions to the children of – "just wait till yer father gets home", or, "when yer father gets wind of this", quelling them into matriarchal obedience. However, reminiscence ordained that Alfred's most exemplary role was that of storyteller, particularly in the telling of ghost stories which he narrated with a macabre pungency. On long winter nights, chilly drafts ruffling the net curtains, he would gather the children round the banked up orangey-red picture flames of a coal fire that flickered across the surrounding darkness, holding them spellbound in trembly dread, his wife occasionally upbraiding him as she sat in her armchair knitting:

'Myself and the lads, I was a lump of a fella at the time not much older than yerself Stephen, used go proggin' for apples up at the Wyndham estate above the Glen Road. 'Tis all built up now but then 'twas in the heart of the countryside. And one day be the hokey but didn't we come across a ramshackle mausoleum at the far end of –'

'What's a mauso… mausoleum daddy?'

'It's a big showy tomb only important people get to be buried in. Anyway, this mausoleum was at the far end of the orchard close to the manor house, the rickety gate into which was rusted rotten but unlocked. We left the progged apples at the entrance and into the creepy death house we ventured like three brave musketeers, holdin' on to each others coattails, kickin' skeleton bones and skulls out of our way. By the time our eyes adjusted to the darkness, Hawkeye Mulligan was about to step into the unknown where a great big hole opened up before us. Like roped together mountain climbers we managed to pull Hawkeye back from the precipice and what do ye think we saw risin' out of the great big hole?

'What did ye see daddy. Tell us tell us.'

'As we peered into the bottomless pit we saw a great big wooden coffin, as black as the ace of spades, blacker than don soot in the chimney there, with the lid slightly ajar. Oh we were the brave fellas then I tell ye. With all the strength we could muster we lifted the creakin' lid of the coffin till it stood at a tilt, makin' a horrible sound, eeeuuuggGHHH, like the noise the big door at Saint Peters makes on Easter Sunday morning, only so so much more spooky if yis can imagine that there now. And there starin' at us was the terrifyin' sight of, of –'

'Of what daddy?'

'No no, 'tis too scary to tell.'

'Tell us daddy… please please tell us.'

'An oul hag of a woman, her claw nails worn to stumps from scratchin' at the lid of the coffin, her jaw bone fixed in an eternal scream.'

'How did ye know daddy, know 'twas a woman?'

'Because Stephen me boy, 'twas as plain as the nose on yer face to see that her shredded cobwebbed shroud was a bottle-green velvet dress and there were tufts of scraggly long hair hangin' from atop her skull. Oh what a grisly sight hhaaAGGGHH, gives me the creeps just thinkin' about it. 'Twas like a scene outta hell. She had been buried a…alive -'

'Freddie! Would ye quit scarin' the livin' daylights out of the childer with yer oul codology,' the mother crossly piped up from her armchair by the fire. 'If Monica starts bawling in the middle of the night 'twill be yerself that'll have to look after her.'

'Then Runty said,' continued their father, 'yis know Runty O'Driscoll who lives beyond in Whiterock, the fella with the… the gammy leg. He was me best pal at school –'

'Yeah! We know we know. What did Runty say?' asked Eileen, bemused by the horror-struck faces of her younger siblings.

'Runty says "What's that on her finger?" We looked and saw on the middle finger of her left clawin' hand a gold ring with the biggest, the hugest red ruby stone, glintin' in the dark, glimmin' like the treasure of Monte Cristo, worth thousands 'twas. Hawkeye grabbed her clawin' hand and made to take that ring by pulling it off her finger when of a sudden a gust of wind went WOOSSHH, rose up outta nowhere and terrified the life out of us, as if we weren't scared enough. Me and Runty scampered from the pit as fast as our legs could carry us to jibes from Hawkeye callin' us scaredy pants. As we ran toward the light we heard an unmerciful bang, an unmerciful BHUUMPP that would waken the dead. Sounded like it came from another world, and his screams made every hair on me head stand up – "LET ME GO… let me go… I won't steal yer ring if ye let me go". The coffin lid had slammed closed snarin' Hawkeye's jacket. Poor Hawkeye thought the oul hag had hold of him by the coattail and made his escape by givin' it up to her lethal grip. We scarpered off home, shaken, not a word spoken between us, the apples forgotten and left to rot. We never went proggin' at Wyndhams again. Be that a lesson to yis now, never ever try to steal or take what doesn't belong to ye.'

*

One day, when he was in sixth class, Mr Van Gerssael, a war *émigré* from Belgium, organist and choirmaster at Saint Peter's Cathedral, called at Colaiste Ris during a tour of the city's Catholic schools seeking suitable choirboys. Brother Daniel had selected ten pupils (all junior members of the school choir in which Maca was a reluctant participant) as potential candidates. Escorted to the assembly hall for a trial session, they were gladdened to have most of the morning away from their lessons, Maca particularly delighted to miss the mathematics class not having done his homework the evening before. Mr Van Gerssael was a small frail balding man, sartorially dressed but for the tobacco burns and ash stains bedecking his waistcoat and the lapels of his charcoal grey suit.

'Who's the stick insect,' Mugsy Dixon mumbled as they entered the assembly hall, resulting in uproarious laughter among the unlikely recruits.

'Behave now boys. Mr Van Gerssael has a busy schedule and requires your prompt and full attention,' said Brother Daniel, as they mounted the stage where a long wooden bench was already in situ. 'Dixon, MacAlindon and you three… stay in front please. Murtagh and the rest of you up on the bench… stand up on the bench,' he peremptorily commanded.

Maca observed Mr Van Gerssael scrutinize the group with beady simian eyes, then place a pyramidal case on the rostrum from which he extracted a metronome, and take a tuning fork from his jacket pocket.

'I vood like at least one of you boys, perhaps two of you, to join my choir,' began Van Gerssael. 'It vill depend of course how gooot singers you are. Dat is vhy I am 'ere, to discover if any of you are gooot at the singing, or gooot enough. I take it dat you vould like to join the choir at Saint Peters.'

'Well boys. Answer Mr Van Gerssael,' glowered Brother Daniel after a kind of fuddled silence.

'Yes Mr Van Gerssael,' they chorused.

'Velly gooot. Furst the scale.'

'Doh…Ray…Me…Fah…Soh…Lah…Te…Doh.'

The fixed doh scale was repeated several times in a diapason of chortles and groans.

'Ve vill begin vith Adeste Fideles. Dis hymn you are familiar vith at Colaiste Ris no?'

'Yes Mr Van Gerssael,' an antiphonal chorus hurls back.

'Gooot. Tank you. Ve vill have no music as I vish nothink to detract my ear. I listen to voice only, okay. Is dat okay?'

'Yes Mr Van Gerssael.'

'You vill begin on the fourttthhh beat,' the motley crew heard him enjoin as the metronome ticked and the tines of the tuning fork hummed.

'A…des…te fi…del…es…lae…ti…'

'Stoup stoup! Harmony is everythink. You must all, must all of you begin on de fourttthhh beat. Dat is ven my index finger, dis finger is pointing at you. Again now please.'

'A…des…te fi…del…es lae…ti…triumph…antes veni…te ve… en…i… te…in…Be…eth…'

'Stoup stoup! Dare are some of you who are singing and some who're not.'

Maca floundered in uncontrollable giggles at the double entendre, the others in schoolboy asininity caught-up in the contagion of his laughter. Van Gerssael, primly a-hemmimg, stood before them in startled amazement yet the patience he demon-strated was in stark contrast to the twitching grimaces that suffused Brother Daniel's ash-grey face.

'MacAlindon… Murtagh… the lot of you. Stop acting like a pack of hyenas. You're not at the circus now you know,' Brother Daniel barked. 'Behave yourselves and concentrate, concentrate or you will have me to deal with afterwards.'

Following further disharmonious and boisterous renditions of familiar hymns over the next hour or so, nine of the budding choristers were dismissed by Van Gerssael as not being up to the mark, none of the nine too put-out by this result. Noisily exiting the assembly hall, they could hear Billy Galligan being put through his boy-soprano paces in the singing, with nasal tremolo, of Panes Angelicus.

*

Towards the end of the sixth class year, his mother, who loved her only son with an acquisitive passion, prevailed upon him to sit the scholarship examination for Colaiste Ris High School. Two scholarship places were up for grabs, for which fourteen boys applied. The examination was held in the assembly hall and Maca was puffed up by his efforts on the History and English papers but found himself struggling to make headway on the Mathematics paper. Billy Galligan, seated closest on his left, seemed to be reaming off the answers to what Maca perceived as insoluble conundrums. In his mind he thought – if I signal Galligan to move his answer paper to the edge of his desk, I could cog from it. Having stealthily done so, Galligan did not, or was convincing in posturing that he did not, understand the semaphoric gestures. In desperation, he wangled similar overtures for help to Sammy Dixon on his right, and when Mugsy showed him his paper, he saw that he had barely filled out half a page. Growing more panicky, he once again made a pleading appeal to Galligan for help which was, as far as he was concerned, insensately ignored. Being somewhat careless in his predicament, of a sudden he found the invigilator, Brother Alphonsus, a plump man with a bald head and a craggy grin (Grumpy the boys nicknamed him), kneeling on one knee beside him, picking up his paper and peering myopically at it, the repulsive tufts of hair curling out of his nostrils and ears on close view, the stubby fingers of his right hand all the while caressing the aspirant's thigh underneath his short trousers.

'Having some bother are we MacAlindon?' Grumpy drawled.

'Sir,' he replied with a sheepish grin.

'Only an attempt at answering two questions as far as I can make out. You have written in all the questions, in a very neat hand I might add, leaving space for the replies but you have only taken a shot at answering two of them, erroneously if I'm not mistaken. What happened ye lad? You're not a complete ignoramus are you?'

'No Sir! Dunno Sir,' he reacted with a shrug of his shoulders.

'You've done all these sums before without any difficulty, as homework for Brother Daniel. So what's the bother now?'

'Dunno, dunno,' Maca mumbled as he sat glued to the seat apprehensively eyeing Grumpy's wandering hand, shrinking from enlightening his interrogator he had cogged that homework.

'Come now, stop the shilly-shallying and out with it,' said Grumpy, his fingers pinching the soft flesh of his thigh.

'I'm feelin' sick Sir,' he blurted. He couldn't even think straight, some atavistic instinct motivating him to lie.

'Uh-huh! And what ails thee.'

'I'll be kilt Sir, kilt. Between me mother's rosaries and novenas beseechin' Saint Gerard to help me pass the exam, if her prayers aren't answered she'll skin me alive for skivin' Sir.'

'And are you... a skiver MacAlindon?'

'No way Sir! No way.'

Brother Alphonsus rose wearily off his knee, levering himself up by leaning on the desk, and walked slowly back to his station at the stage end of the assembly hall. When the allotted examination time was up, and all papers collected, the disencumbered scholars noisily pushed back their chairs in haste to depart.

'Well done boys. You have a long summer ahead of you so make the most of the holiday. And remember Almighty God always watches over you so be of help to your parents whenever, a bit of hard work about the house won't kill you. Strengthens the body. You know what they say – a healthy body maketh for a healthy mind. God bless now and cheery-bye. You lad, MacAlindon, stay back. I want a word in your ear.'

Maca slumped back in his seat, watching in trepidation as Grumpy painstakingly sifted through the collected examination papers, and on retrieving his paper hold it close-to in careful inspection and then shuffle to his desk.

'Well well MacAlindon, on this performance there'll be no scholarship for you. You don't want to end up like the other dolts being the smart lad you are, the sharpest pencil in the box I'd say. Did you not understand the questions?'

'I told ye Sir… not feelin' the best. Me head's spinnin'.'

'Spinning like a top eh? Me thinks your're a bit of a trickster. You got them right before so why not now?'

'I got confused Sir,' he said, nervously clearing his throat.

'The answers are immutable,' said Grumpy as he pulled up a chair and seated himself beside him.

'They're what Sir?'

'Only the format of the questions has changed. Instead of twenty horses in a field we have here twenty pigs in a farmyard. Easy as pi. So let's revisit some of these confusing questions. We'll start with the pigs. A farmer has twenty pigs in his farmyard. One day he takes five pigs to market and is successful in the selling of four of them. On his return to the farm how many pigs does the farmer now have left in the yard. Well lad?'

'Sir… fifteen Sir.'

'And what about the pig the farmer couldn't sell? He left fifteen in the farmyard and came –'

'Came home with one Sir. Sixteen… sixteen pigs left.'

'Well put it down lad, write it down on your paper.'

His eyes narrowed as he concentrated on writing in the answer, tongue purling between his teeth. Again he felt Grumpy's hand on his inner thigh. Grumpy, with adrenalized deliberation, brought him through the other unanswered questions in similar fashion. By the time he was writing in the answer to the final question, Grumpy, with salivating grin, was fingering his pecker.

'That's a grand wee rooster you have there lad.'

In panic he dropped the pen without finishing writing in the answer and ran from the hall. Retrieving his bicycle from the cycles shed, he sped off to his father's place of work at uncle Peter's coal yard which was closer to the school than home. Breathlessly re-counting him what had occurred during the maths examination, he bemusedly looked on as his father doffed his cap, threw his leg over the bar of the bicycle and sped off in the direction of Colaiste Ris, calling out:

'That's teachers for ye – "A man amongst children, a child amongst men". Be off home with ye now son. 'Tis but a short walk. And not a word to yer mother. Or anyone else for that matter. Do ye hear me now, this is one for yer old man to sort out.'

Maca was honoured to be one of three successful candidates to win a six-year scholarship at Colaiste Ris High School that year.

His proud mother made a whole palaver amongst the neighbours about his success at the exams – "hard work always gets the right result".

2

That summer, Maca's parents packed him off to his maternal grandparent's house down country. As the only boy of three siblings, it was prescribed by his father that the rupture to boyish routines would prove beneficial to him, his grandfather needing help on the farm (summer being a busy time for farmers), and if found to be of some use he would be rewarded with a weekly wage from which he could make savings towards purchase of that Raleigh three gear racing bicycle he always hankered after. The intimations at the time suggested his parents thought of him as growing into a somewhat unruly chisler in need of disciplinary workaday practices and a healthy pastime, and where better to have some degree of sensible behaviour inculcated in such a dawny chisler than on a farm.

Prior to this foray, his first venture outside the confining sphere of existence in Belfast, he knew his grandparents only from the infrequent visits they made to their daughter's home (and even then having endured the usual perfunctory greetings and cringe-making messy kisses from the old crone, he and his sisters were herded into the kitchen with a warning from their mother to be good and stay quiet as mice – "Grandpa doesn't like noisy children"); and once when the extended family members met at the wedding of his father's youngest sister aunt Rose. On the latter occasion, grandpa gave him a shilling after ruffling his hair with a gnarled hand saying – "Be the hokey but isn't he a cracking lad". To his child's eye they were old, repulsively old; grandma always dressed in sombre black, her hennaed hair tied up in a bun held tight to her head with countless hairpins that only emphasized her mottled complexion; grandpa of shambling gait, stiff in the joints, grunting every time he sat into or effortfully climbed out of a chair, constantly complaining of arthritic pain, his rufous hands meshed in liver spots and bulbous blue veins like tangled shoe laces. He didn't like his grandpa then: the peculiar smell like an addled hen egg that wafted in his lumbering wake; the flecks of blood that blotted his face from careless shaving; his plummy nose (too much whiskey his father opined); the oily bronze-grey strands of hair he hand-swept across his bald pate on removing his hat in a vain attempt to hide its stark polished whiteness; the ambiguity of his smile as Maca wondered whether he pleased him or was just another thorn in his flesh. But that was before he grew to know him, to know things about him.

His mother and Eileen walked him to the bus station, his face still blotched red from tears of woe after the prolonged loud outburst to his "uncaring" parents about the unfairness of the world and his place in it. Eileen resentfully bawled at him to stop being a crybaby that it is she who deserved to go on holiday, not him. Her pique stiffened his resolve to brave it out and make the best of things. Having reluctantly arrived at the farm that first summer, grandpa waiting for him at the bus station to drive the four miles or so in a gleaming black Volkswagen with a mullioned windscreen and rear window to the isolated hills that comprised the sixty-five acre sheep farm, the mountainy summits of which were common land. This encounter began ominously; his grandparents if anything seeming older than his memory of them, looking even more senescent dressed in their shabby everyday clothes. Grandma's tousled hair, loose strands falling about her reddened ears, as she stood on the stone flag kitchen floor on bony legs with yucky blisters of psoriasis, grumbly gabbling over the pots on the cooking range, or, scrubbing with hennaed hands the vessels and pans in the sink; the quirky way she had of carphologically rubbing the palms of her hands across her bust at the first sign of stress. Grandpa skeletal, worn and wrinkled with bags under his eyes; his propensity to freely break wind, noisily, albeit outdoors in the main, a cause of hilarity among the smart alecs within sniffing range ("practising for a shite are ye boss?"); his habit of undoing his trouser-fly buttons as he sat cumbrously spreadeagled of an evening by the kitchen stove, launching globs of sputum to sizzle on the blazing turf. Such boorish characteristics mortified him until he got used to their idiosyncratic ways.

The farmstead encompassed a ramshackle stone farmhouse at least twice as large as his parent's house, with two annexes of more recent construction in breeze block; the smell of wet dog permeating the living space; the whole interior a network of shadowy nooks and crannies (particularly wraithlike at night-time). The outbuildings and rank dung smelling byre a ruckle of white-washed rubbly stones that had not been licked by a distemper brush in donkeys' years (Maca did the job during his second summer stay); and at its gable end a lean-to wooden hayshed with sheets of rusted corrugated iron roofing. The whole melange subsumed him in a prospect of ghostly terrors, a dread not alleviated when that first evening over supper his grandpa related how he came to buy the place:

'Your grandmother knew nought of my intentions. I was fed up workin' in Coburn's hardware store, wanting to do me own thing, wanting to get away from the townies. I heard over time some of the customers talkin' about the Murdoch place being up for sale for so long 'twould appear nobody was interested, but thought little of it till Nellie here one day suggested the change to sheep farming would do me a power of good – "Aren't you always talkin' of changin' your way of going" were her very words to me. So that same evening I drove out to the place to have a chat with Ben Murdoch, no certainty in me head of buying. No indeed! 'twould depend on what money he was lookin' for it. 'Twas a fine winters night, a gibbous moon in all its glory casting a bright silvery light, so I had no problem finding me way along the narrow meandering roads. The house was in darkness as if nobody was home and havin' made the trip out I climbed from the car determined to have a look about the place, no sense in a wasted journey. Presently I heard the creaking hinges of the hall door and a young gimlet-eyed lassie of about five or six stood there in the opening wearin' a long pink coloured frock, her fair hair braided tightly to her head. "You're in the dark I see, not the candle or lamp lit the yet. I was hopin' to have a wee chat with your daddy about the sale of the house and farm" says I, to which she made no reply, simply pullin' the door wider to invite entry. The moonlight flooded the hallway as she led me to what I took to be the dining room, a moonbeam streamin' through the window spotlighting a layer of dust on a lavishly moulded thick-legged mahogany table. 'Tis still below in the room. "Is your daddy about a'tall?"says I and my enquiry meeting with such a bodeful silence set me thinkin' how strange the whole scene was. Yet being preoccupied with sizin' up the place I passed little remark. She then headed for the stairwell and I thinkin' she wanted to show me the upstairs rooms made haste to tag along behind her. However, when we arrived on the upper landing, she unlatched a narrow door that led to a cramped stairway. "A candle to light the way would prove serviceable," I suggested, clambering in the wake of her silent footfall, hearing the thud of me own footsteps on the bare tread boards as I kept the head down to mark my step. A gust of cool air pinched me cheeks as I realized we had reached the roof, the night sky under the moonlight hung with a shroud of preternatural mist. Stealthily, she moved to the granite parapet and with her index finger pointed to something below. I, it goes without sayin', had my heart in me mouth lest she slip and fall and earnestly sought her to back away from the danger. Persisting in pointin' at whatever 'twas she obviously wanted me to see, I tentatively placed my hand on the parapet and peered over, the rippling moon reflected in a duck pond winkin' back at me. Just then the misted beams of headlights of an approaching car blind-spotted me and the image evaporated into the surrounding darkness. "Is it your dad do ye think? I'd be happy to have a word with him now" I said, turnin' for affirmation from my elfin hostess. She had gone. No doubt racing back down the stairs to greet her father I was thinkin' as I began cautiously retracing my steps. At the foot of the staircase I heard voices as a key turned in the door lock and the door pushed in.

'"Christ Almighty! What the hell are YOU doing here?" came the startled voice of Ben Murdoch as he rushed to flick the light switch.

'"I've come to have a chat with ye Ben, about the sale" says I, somewhat taken aback by the unfriendly tone in his voice.

'"How in the name of jaysus did you get in?"

'"Well not seeing a light I did think no one was home but yer daughter kindly showed me round. I did ask to –"

'"Me daughter? What kind of a bleedy prank is this?"

'"No no! We were on the roof when we saw the lights of yer car approach. Yer daughter was just showin' me the pond. She's a friendly wee lassie, a lovely girl altogether and a credit –"

'"Will ye houl yer whisht man!" he then barked, throwing his arms about the shoulders of a very upset Bridie Murdoch. "There is no pond. Our daughter drowned in a pond, ten year ago now. The pond has long since been filled in."

'Well, as you can imagine, there was no talk of a sale that night. But I made it me business to meet up with Ben Murdoch soon after. We walked the land and struck a deal more than fair to both parties. That's all of forty years ago and 'twas the best decision I ever made. Yer mother Stephen, and the rest of them, had the happiest of childhoods in this place.'

At such an impressionable age, Maca found himself mesmerized at the rich vein of story telling that poured out of his grandpa, and petrified by the thought of there being a ghost in the house, however benign. Thereafter, he was permitted to keep a light on in his room at night, despite the old man's caustic rebuke that it was "a shockin' waste of electricity". A few days later, Nellie set up for him a small reading lamp with a low wattage bulb, her consideration gladdening him and appeasing grandpa. Some evenings, particularly when neighbours called, the radio would be switched off and grandpa would relate phantasmagoric stories that made the hairs prickle on the back of his neck. Whether suffering an overactive imagination, or, due to the eerie atmosphere in that house, weird sounds occasionally penetrated the walls of his bedroom, tormenting his juvenile brain with spectral images of an imminent brutal death. He was there but a few days when he realized that his grandfather and grandmother slept in separate rooms.

*

Nellie, having been twice mentioned in these drifting moments, should now be introduced to you, as she played a most enigmatic part in Maca getting to know his grandpa and learning about the man's chequered past. He had no previous acquaintance with her having never heard mention of her name by any member of the family, nor had she ever travelled with his grandparents on their family visits to Belfast. Being encouraged to call her auntie Nellie, intuitively he knew she was not really his aunt. How did she come to be living with his grandparents? Reckoning she was many years younger than his grandma, he astutely perceived that it was she who, to all intent and purposes, had the run of the house. He sometimes got the impression that grandma felt intimidated by her, without hesitation doing as enjoined (always urged with persuasive suggestion rather than fiery demand), and content to leave it to her to make the normal household decisions of a *bean a ti*. His grandma would spend most of her time kowtowing to the tyranny of farmyard chores looking after the pigs and chickens and the like (chores he willingly helped her with once he had mastered the farrago of feeds) when she wasn't preoccupied in preparing and cooking the main meals. Unlike her, Nellie came across as a free spirited character, their personas as different as chalk and cheese, grandma being so doddery and her reticent conversation peppered with malapropisms. Whereas Nellie retained a youthful feminism and interest in fashion emphasized by the clothes she wore enhancing her svelte figure and bulging bust (held in precarious bondage). He found her a lively and impetuous woman, her expansive chatter spilling over with the latest gossip. She could drive, and twice a week would trip to town in the Volkswagen to do the shopping. He quickly discerned that she was his friend and confidante, always looking out for him, and if harsh words were spoken by the old man (sometimes accompanied by admonitory blows) regarding his failure to perform, or perform correctly, some designated task, she would give him a chummy wink as if to say – "not to worry, 'twill blow over soon enough". One such episode was the day he was set the task of thinning turnips in the garden field being instructed to leave the robust seedlings six inches apart by pulling the unwanted seedlings in-between. Kitted out with cut squares from an old potato sack bound at the knees with straw rope, he scrambled up the drills ever vigilant about exact spacing and would replant off target pulled seedlings to maintain the symmetry. The job put him to the pin of his collar. That evening his grandpa smacked the back of his head while hollering – 'Ye bleedy galoot! Half the bleedy crop's been lost.' – Nellie's cosseting rescued him from a tearful outburst, stimulating his reliance on her mollifying assurances that grandpa's bark is worse than his bite.

His other reliable friends were the sheep dogs, Shep and Rocky, black and white collies who to begin with seemed shy of him, nervously scampering away as he made to pet them or lowering their heads afraid he was about to beat them. In a very short while they grew to trust him and their frisky welcome each morning gave him great heart at the start of the working day. That first summer the help expected of him was a source of quiet satisfaction, the ephebic tasks being light and exciting in their novelty, consisting mainly in joining grandpa and the dogs in the daily rounds trampling the hills that rose steeply behind the farmhouse checking on the livestock, particularly the sheep as they grazed where the tenacious tussocky grasses, criss-crossed with rabbit-runs, gave way to gorse and bracken, the prickly burs clinging to his trousers. On these long walks the old man indulged his endless boyish enquiries – "Just like a young fellah to ask so many questions" he'd say. Why do the sheep have splotchy blue dye on their backs? Why do ye let them mix with other farmer's differently colour-splodged sheep on the mountain? How did ye train the dogs to recognize and round up your sheep only? When did ye buy the Volkswagen? How much did it cost? Then one day amid an ababu of curiosity he cheekily asked of him – "Is auntie Nellie really me aunt? How long has she been livin' here?" Tiring of the prattling interrogation, his grandpa thumbed his nostril expelling a bolus of snot, telling him brusquely to – "Quit yer aul gibberish. Life's tough enough without prying bleedy questions".

If a ewe or lamb was found to be sickly or injured, the old man would hoist it on his shoulders, holding its tethered legs either side of his neck, and lodge it for the duration of its convalescence in an old tea chest by the side of the kitchen range. Over time, Maca began to carry orphaned or rejected lambs for similar treatment, it then becoming his sole responsibility to bottle feed the maturing pets (he came to love them so much he found it hard to part from them).

Friday afternoons became the highlight of the holiday when he journeyed with Nellie to the town to lend a helping hand with the weekly shopping, a goodly part of his wages splashed out on chocolate bars and the comics kept for him under the newsagents counter. The recognition of his name penned on the top corner of the front page of each comic gave him a vivid sense of himself – it was his first realization of his singular identity. On the drive back, they would stop off at The Market Bar where Nellie partook of a glass of porter ("Guinness is good for you" she'd say), buying for him an orangeade and potato crisps.

"What's don yokey-me-bob hangin' there beside the till?" he asked her one day, noisily munching the crisps.

"'Tis a bull's pizzle," she chirped mischievously. "Any shindy in the house and Bill makes good use of it. Isn't that right Bill?"

"Right ye are Nellie. The aul pizzler's always at the ready."

She appeared to be on more than friendly terms with Bill (later he set about deciphering the gist of their *risqué* banter).

Toals, a house-shop where you were served through a hatch having asked for or pointed to the item wanted, owned by an elderly childless couple (she a local – he a thick accented Scot), was a handy outpost when the essential foods of everyday living ran low being just a stone's throw away from the farm. Discovering Mr Toal sold cigarettes singly was when his habit of smoking was triggered, inhaling like his grandfather as he toddled home in a dizzy tobacco haze.

Some evenings, grandpa and Nellie drove away in the Volkswagen, or, in sunny weather marched off arm in arm along the bosky daisy carpeted back lane, the embankment on either side teeming with wild flowers - bluebells, anemones, irises and the ripening reds of honeysuckle weighty with drowsy bees, birds warbling the sounds of summer. He never knew where they were going and more often than not was fast asleep by the time they got back. Nevertheless, now and then the following morning he would overhear grandma sardonically make enquiry such as –"How's Kathleen", or, "Did Big Michael buy the whatchamacallit…the new tractor yoke yet", and listen to the old man's mordant remarks about the people enquired of. Maca could only but assume they had been visiting neighbours or friends in the parish, and felt sorry for grandma being left behind (initially feeling guilty that it was because she had to stay and look after him). Yet on such occasions she appeared content to sit in grandpa's chair by the fire reading Irelands Own and back copies of Old Moore's Almanac, allowing him free rein to listen to his favourite programmes on the radio (Dan Dare and the like), safe and sound from Grandpa's usual desultory comments (the news and weather forecast were all he was interested in) of –"don't go fillin' yer silly head with the likes of that kinda rubbish. 'Tis all a load of boloney."

Now and then of a balmy evening neighbours would arrive at the house carrying their own speciality musical instruments (some crudely home-made), the performers accompanied by mothers, spouses and offspring, and a cracking session of melodic enter-tainment in the kitchen would endure into the small hours, albeit of a bungling calibre, a myriad of bum notes vibrating the musty air exuded by the sweaty players amid a miasma of tobacco smoke. Dinny Nash played his self-made wooden flute that had a cracked tube necessitating a dip in the water barrel outside the back door every thirty minutes or so to tumefy and close the split. Each time on his rejoining the session, those occupying adjacent chairs to his high-spirited playing were showered with spurted sprays of water. That was about the time Maca took to playing the tin whistle (had he the saxophone he'd have showed them), and fell madly in love with Dorothy Ryan as he watched her graceful fingers delicately caress the keyboard of her accordion.

*

The following summer he was keen as mustard setting out for the working holiday on his grandparent's farm, his fledgling ardour for Dorothy being a compelling incentive. Having diffidently watched her from afar, they became kissing friends the day he showed her his new Raleigh racer bought with his own hard earned money. Garrulously confident, she relieved him of the care of coming up with something new and interesting to say. If anything, he adjudged her a little too sure of herself, making fun of his tendency to blush on casual meetings (infatuation forgives all).

Perhaps, he supposed, she being the only child of the principal of the local primary school, a lack of self-esteem had no place in her make-up. He found her to be a well practised kisser making him jealous, poisoning his mind with images of townie fellows chasing and pawing her, his ever increasing sleepless nights dominated by angry thoughts of the choice things he would say in challenging such a one should he catch him in her company. At every opportunity he would set off on his bicycle to Dorothy's house, being with her or close to her fast becoming an all consuming obsession.

Of course the work on the farm went on apace. However, his period of stay did not include the busy times for sheep farmers: the lambing and shearing seasons, but by now did involve the hullabaloo and excitement of dagging and dipping for parasites. The latter activity necessitated the coordination of all farmers with sheep on the common, and on the day as many as ten, including farmhands, would gather for the effective functioning of the undertaking. The sheep were rounded up and penned the evening before, those to be dagged separated and the dags cut from them by working well into the twilight. Next day from dawn to dusk the sheep were herded toward the narrow exit from the pen and manhandled, thrown, and submersed two or three at a time into a dyke three foot deep filled with foul smelling chemicals. Whilst turns were taken about in exchanging roles, most of the men did not let up until the job was wrapped up. Maca, on learning to grab a sheep firmly, but gently, afraid of hurting it, felt a manly pride in rarely letting the wilder ones buckleap out of his grip. That day at dinner, all seated outside on threadbare chairs at trestle tables covered in a check-colour-patterned oilcloth, his grandma determined (in that assertive wont of grownups) he should have extra helpings of bacon, cabbage and potatoes saying –"a growing man needs plenty of grub", plying his plate to excess (he hated cabbage), his cheeks flushed red in response to a ravishing knowing look from

Nellie.

Agreeing to spend the full summer break from school on the farm his grandpa, having recognized his maturing interest and ability in carrying out the necessary work (so much so the old man took to rising late most mornings), was happy to rely on Maca's youthful enthusiasm in the knowledge that if an emergency arose the boy would report the full nature of the problem and help rectify it as best he could; and knowing the dogs liked his juvenile exuberance and did the boy's bidding.

Then two events, by happenstance on the same day, brought about calamitous consequences for all concerned. The old man had taken to his bed some days before with a severe chest infection and Maca, rather than redoubling his efforts to carry out the workload, turned lackadaisical, daydreaming of being with Dorothy. Each day in slapdash haste he would check on the sheep, the dogs padding at his heels, and help grandma with her chores, then speed off to town on his bicycle to be with her. By midmorning of his grandpa's fifth day abed, having scrambled on foot to take a dekko at the sheep, he was puzzled by the reluctance of the dogs to follow him back to the farmyard, but overcame their recalcitrance by commandingly whistling and beckoning them. He then hot-footed to the house for a quick change of clothes, looked in on grandpa to assure him everything was fine to find him in a deep slumber, and, charged with moony intensity, sprinted away on the bike to meet up with his sweetheart. They had agreed to go to the cinema matinee show starring Marilyn Monroe in "Niagara". In the darkness of the cinema, she let him kiss her which elicited guffaws and sniggers from some of the rougher boys from the town, their loutishness unsettling him yet seeming only to encourage Dorothy to bouts of prolonged necking (he had had to come up for air several times). Afterwards, he bought her lemonade out of a roiling tank in Sam's café where some of the yahoos from the cinema escapade made glaring eyes at them, one burly looking fellow brazen enough to impudently ask her for a lip-smack. Maca was chuffed by her haughty dismissal of such a crude approach yet held a sneaking suspicion she might have enjoyed it. On the way back to her house they stopped at the summer vacated school and shared his last cigarette while lolling shoeless on the grass in a current of cool air under the refreshing shadiness of the tarpaulin covered bicycle shed. On flicking away the butt end he stretched to kiss her supinated foot, but she leaned away, her legs asprawl, and out of the blue said she would show him her "thingy" if he showed her his. Without waiting for a sign of assent from him to the pact, his face encrimsoned in jittery anticipation, she slowly removed her knickers letting him feast his eyes (for what seemed an age but was probably less than twenty seconds) on the moist incarnadine lips of her fanny crowned with a hint of gingery pubic hair. Every muscle in his body twitched with adrenalized energy as he rested on benumbed arms, gawping, his legs intertwined in the air behind him. She quickly pulled up her knickers, and intoned triumphantly –"Your turn now". Overcome by mind-numbing shyness, scrambling to his knees, he timidly unbuttoned his fly and with awkward hesitancy extracted a flaccid penis at which she stared intently before light-heartedly holding its drooping head as if to feel its weight, her fingers inducing a semi erection, her ticklish touch freeing the shiny purple conker from its prepuce. In panic on hearing her frenzied giggle his badge of manhood quickly retreated and, grinning foolishly, shoved it back in the fold of his underpants. Back outside her house, she asked him to stay for tea. However, knowing her mother would be there he began to lose all semblance of rational behaviour, a sense of abasement hanging over him, and made his excuse that his grandpa remained sick in bed and regrettably he had to go check on the sheep for him.

Standing on the bike pedals to aid him in the climb of the first gradient of the stony hill road to the farm he could hear the dogs frenzied barking and then saw his grandfather above at the house leaning out of the bedroom window, still attired in his red and white striped pyjamas, wildly gesticulating, and over the ever shortening distance hearkened to a thundering row going on between him and his nearest neighbour, Peadar Murphy, who was hammering the side of his fists against the front door and threatening the devil and all if he got his hands on the miscreant. The *contretemps* of imprecatory abuse continued unabated on Maca's approach, he quickly discerning its cause; the sheep had broken into Murphy's field of cabbages and ruined the crop – "What's not eaten by the buggers is so trampled as to be inedible", he heard Murphy bellow. Murphy was shouting at the top of his gravelly voice demanding compensation, his truculent protest provoking Grandpa to make raucous retorts:

'You can fuck off with yerself for 'tis yer own fault for not proper fencin' yer field as should be. I know me law when it comes to the like'a that.'

'Why you're nothing but the two ends of a mare's tit. I'll have the polis on ye if you don't make good me losses.'

'You're the one obliged by the law to fence out. There's none the bit of onus on me to fence in. That's the way of it Peadar, sorry and all as I am for yer troubles. So you may take yerself the hell off my property and not be annoyin' the face of me and me crocked abed with a bad chest.'

Maca pulled up the bicycle behind Murphy who said, fidgeting his fedora from hand to hand – 'Ah there ye are now avick. I ran dem bleedy sheep to the upper meadow. You'd better take a look at them for there's some badly bloated fit to burst with the gas.'

Consternation then broke loose when Nellie was heard yell from grandpa's window that he had collapsed on the floor and, in an emotional outburst, begged Peadar to send for the doctor. Maca felt weighed down by inner guilt, on many counts, moping about in bewilderment amid the bombination of activity surrounding the unfolding drama. Later, a mood of sullen resignation crept over him as he watched grandpa sitting canted over in the front passenger seat of the Volkswagen driven by Nellie on route to hospital, tears streaming down her cheeks; Dr O'Reilly in close pursuit in his mud spattered Hillman Hunter, a look of profess-ional concern creasing his conventionally serene face. Grandma, in their absence, evinced a scheming countenance as she, with her habitual senile inquisitiveness, fossicked through every drawer in the house with not a word to him while they awaited Nellie's return with the grim news, save her pungent command, she assuming a sly malicious grin, to join her on bended knee in a recital of the rosary (the succour to her misanthropic hebetude), she crouched on a hassock by the fireplace humming out the prayers. Maca had, in the interim, traipsed the sodden dun grass hills below the rocky scree turned bleak and grey under a mantle of low cloud, spits of rain gathering way in runnels of muddied water, checking on the sheep, some caught-fast in a tottery barbed wire fence. The big gate at the top of the meadow-hill stood open. He felt sure he had closed it. Four sheep were lost to the gasses, including the bell-wether. Agitated, he removed the bell, his woes coagulating in a lather of sweat – how to explain the loss to the old man. Nellie on her reappearance advised the boss had suffered a stroke rendering him unable to speak, "aphasia I think the doctor called it", his left arm and leg a deadweight of emaciated muscle. She told Maca not to get in a tizzy – "We've more important things to worry us what with your grandfather being so ill an'all. Say nothing of it for the poor man has enough to contend with", she said behind a pellucid smile, her calming voice easing the tension in the house.

And so it was that on the invalid's return home to convalesce, during some long nights when Nellie and Maca sat with him as he lay prostrate in bed, he learned from her something of the old man's days as a freedom fighter during the war of independence, and how her life came to be entwined with his. With time the patient could, in vexed frustration, say a few words out of the corner of his mouth, but only Nellie understood what was to Maca incomprehensible gibberish expectorated with grievance. Grandma did not, to his knowledge, darken her husband's bedroom doorway (although she cooked for him liquid foods like broth and porridgy soups for ease of consumption), she seeming to grow even more morose with the passing days and weeks as if vegetating in her senescence, and occasionally he thought he spied what he took to be a vengeful grin spread across her hapless face.

On one of those nights Nellie related how, when she was about Maca's age, she lost her much loved father. It was years later at age seventeen that she learned the cause of his death. Her father had been a sergeant in the Royal Irish Constabulary and, unarmed, had been brutally shot in the back of the head by a unit of the IRA. She determined to know more and, while researching the incident in her local library newspaper archives, discovered that his grandfather had served time in jail for the murder, being freed in 1922 when the treaty between Great Britain and Ireland leading to the establishment of the Irish Free State was enacted. Embittered by the heartlessness and, to her mind, the cowardly means by which this man had taken her father away from her, she decided to track him down and confront him with her outrage:

'When eventually I got to meet him, I was so keyed up with indignation and bitterness toward him that I thumped and thumped him with my fists, telling him how much I hated him, how he was the scum of the earth to do such a dastardly act, that I hoped he would burn in hell. I became so hysterical that before I realized what was happening I found myself in his arms being comforted, he holding me tightly to him, not saying a word, just holding me till the impotent rage subsided in me, replaced by a sense of utter embarrassment owing to my erratic behaviour toward this stranger. He didn't say he was sorry. Didn't try to explain it away. He just looked at me with an expression so grave that told me all. That told me he understood my torment. Yet I wanted to know more, perhaps reach some understanding. And so he agreed to meet me again. I kept thinking how strong he had been that first meeting. How dignified in the face of my resentment. Well! No doubt you've guessed what happened. Yeah! We became an item. I couldn't forget him, had no wish to forget him. I knew he loved me, the way he took charge of my life. I fell in love with him, only later finding out he was married with children. One time he told me he loved me even more than his own children. And then, at twenty three, my mother died. I had nowhere to go in this topsy-turvy world, except the boat to England. Joining that exodus and the break with my lover was avoided by my becoming a member of his household. I was I suppose like a governess to his children. Your mother loved me, at least as a child she loved me. You can ask her about me some day, maybe when you're a bit older. And here I am, still in love with this man, despite his crippled body, and what others might see as his selfish ways. Your grandfather's a good man. I'll share his days to the last.'

Three nights following on from Nellie's astonishing revelation Maca heard, in the early hours, a heavy thud coming from the old man's room. Still maintaining the foible of leaving his reading lamp on to ward off ghostly apparitions, he turned over in his mind what could have caused it – Had grandpa fallen out of bed? No, surely that wasn't probable. Yet it did sound very much like a sack of spuds falling to the floor. If hapless grandpa was lying on the floor he wouldn't have the strength to haul himself back, or grab a blanket for cover as he lay there helpless in the cold. Why did he not call out for help? Is he able to call for help? Nellie must have heard it too. Yes. Nellie would see to him. But what if she's in a deep sleep and didn't hear that thudding noise? Oh God. I'm afraid to walk the dark passageway to his room. If I put the lights on I'll wake the whole house. Leaving his bedroom door ajar to shed some light along the long corridor, he made his way gingerly to his grandfather's room at the front of the house, the grandfather clock in the main hall below striking the half-hour as he noiselessly turned the door knob and entered the gloomy space. There in the halation of mellow light diffused from a bedside lamp he espied Nellie in silhouette standing sedately by the bed, her large breasts freed from the bodice of her nightdress pendulous as she leaned over the old man whose good hand caressed the soft flesh, his brindled skin like a half cooked pancake hanging on his arm, she cupping a breast to his greedy mouth. Enervated by the shock of this, to his nescient eyes, revolting scene, not knowing the ways of the world, he watched, dazed, his legs gelatinously truant, nerve centres trembling out of control, his mind melting, uncertain, unable to think. With moist palms, he silently closed the door and tip-toed back along the shadowy passage to the comforting spilling light from his room and throwing himself on the bed buried his face in the pillows. He did not sleep a wink that night.

Before returning home and back to school in September, he told Nellie of his concern for her and grandma – "How will youse work the farm without the help of a man about the place?" At which she smiled graciously, saying – "Don't annoy your wee head worrying about the like'a that. We'll manage well enough with the help of God... and the neighbours of course".

That winter his grandfather died, and his mother took command of the funeral arrangements. It was Maca's first experience at close quarters of the holy fanfare of a wake and funeral. Surrounded by numinous spirits, he stared in stupefied astonishment at the old man's cinereous shrunken corpse laid out in an open coffin, rosary beads melding in waxen fingers, the cerecloth visible under the collar of a loose-fitting shirt, shrouded in his best, now oversized, suit. 'How can they be sure he's dead?' he fretted. Family members, neighbours and friends came to the farm from far and wide, filling the house with motley insufflations of pious sentiment whilst sipping tea, and late into the night swigging neat whiskey, tipsily relating rollicking anecdotal tales, some irreverently humorous. Nellie behaved not at all like her normal pragmatic self, slinking into the background, having left it to grandma and her daughters to make the appropriate decisions (she had not been consulted). He told her of his fears – 'It's awful to be dead.' 'Well,' she replied, 'your grandfather lived a good span and was ready to go.' 'I can't cry. Why can't I cry?' 'You'll cry when you're minded to cry.'

A crowd thronged the house next morning, Maca affrighted on hearing the thumps of hobnailed boots on the stairs as the pall-bearers grappled and levered the coffin this way and that in vain. Defeated, grandfather's shaken remains exited through the bedroom window. At the church a tricolour flag bedecked the coffin, removed following a volley at the graveside, a cloud of gunpowder lingering in the air, ceremoniously folded to the plangent strains of the last post, and handed to his grandma, the mourners mechanically repeating the funerary litany. It was a time when the consolations of religion made up for the desolations of life.

A few days later the solicitor arrived at the farmhouse to read the will, wherein, after the customary proviso that all debts, funeral and testamentary expenses be first paid, the house (including all contents) and farm (including all stock) were left, to the profound shock of the family, to Nellie, his grandmother to enjoy a right of residence for her lifetime and a half-share of the farm income. A hasty departure by the disinherited and their self-righteously offended disenfranchised dependants occurred that very evening. Despite Maca's protests that Nellie and his grandma needed him now more than ever, his mother insisted he return to Belfast with them –"ye must finish your schooling" she scolded. Indeed, as he made plans to spend the next summer school holiday on the farm, she refused permission, her decision reluctantly supported by his father. That ruling, at the outset gut-wrenching (he would no longer get to see Dorothy), conveniently clashed with the rite of passage of angsty teenage exposure and neurosis and, truth be told, his pell-mell charge into adulthood left him not giving a fiddler's curse about grandma and Nellie, being solipsistically self-occupied.

Almost a year to the day of the anniversary of the old man's death his grandma died and the family, his mother to the fore, refused the old dear a lyke wake at the farmhouse, despite Nellie's whole-hearted pleading (perhaps she dreaded a repeat of the distress on her father's removal), she collecting and removing the deceased's exiguous personal effects with demonstrative competency, the coffined remains indifferently held overnight in the sombre surroundings of the town funeral parlour. Maca and his sisters, Eileen and Monica, stayed at the farmhouse with Nellie for the duration, their parents and other family members pointedly availing of bed and board accommodation in town.

Having overcome the initial shock of Nellie's visible aging, caused primarily, he believed, by a broken heart in missing the old man, he noticed how dapper and nimbly she continued to comport herself. Sitting up late with her on the eve of the inhumation, he made clear as best he could how the family alienation of her was not of his doing or liking, indeed that it was beyond his com-prehension. She appreciated his candour, and went on with a good heart to satisfy his curiosity respecting the management of the farm. The land had been let out on conacre – "Farmers are always hungry for more grazing opportunities" she said. Asking how she dealt with Peadar Murphy's claim for compensation, she told him he had been the first of the neighbours to rent the land, even nom-inating the amount he was prepared to pay for it which she didn't haggle over, and he failing to make the annual payment (which she had suspected was likely to happen) she didn't pursue him but let the land the following year to Robbie Goss at a higher return, and Robbie kept everything in good order. "Peadar didn't come next nor near me knowing he owed me, so that settled matters between us" she concluded.

Later, lying contented in bed, no longer in need of a comfort light, he revisited in his mind that daunting bedroom scene forever branded on his brain, and pondered the nature of the relationship between Nellie and his grandfather. How could she love the man who killed her father? How could she love a man so much older than she? Why did his mother hate her so much? Why did he feel closer to her than he did to his own mother? His sullied innocence remained revolted by the starkness of that image, an image that now flooded his consciousness and kept him from sleep. It would be many years, long after his first experience of passionate love, before he appreciated the real nature of the relationship being one of pure love, a relationship that only those who have loved, truly loved, at least once in a lifetime, can empathize with. He marvelled then at how the childish affinity he felt for her back in the day had grown, over the time of compelled estrangement and absence, into a bond nurtured by a mature awareness of the human condition and non-judgmental understanding.

3

By his third year at Colaiste Ris High, Maca began to enjoy school, the pupils being treated like young gentlemen rather than as rowdy hooligans in need of a good caning to keep them in check, resulting in the symmetries of mathematics dawning on him and no longer puzzling. History, probably because his favourite teacher taught it, was his best subject. John Shevlon (the pupils nicknamed him "Gudgy" and he was fully aware of the sobriquet by which he was known behind his back), who was one of five laymen in the school and the oldest teacher, was a kind, caring and pragmatic instructor of young men's minds, albeit of an eccentric disposition. An example of such eccentricity was the holding up of a small mirror when writing on the blackboard, so permitting him keep an eye on the mischief-makers in the four rows of five desks each behind him.

One morning after yard-break between classes, Maca and his fellow classmates returned to the classroom to see chalked in an artistic hand on the blackboard a sheriff's star badge above an epigram written in extravagant curlicue:

> *I am the long arm of the law and shall not fail to catch*
> *The hoodlums who believe they can prevail against the*
> *Righteous justice seeking of a God fearing man.*
> *The time is nigh to meet out a befitting punishment*
> *To those who, for gratuitous amusement, flout the law.*

When the pupils had clamorously taken their seats, Gudgy drew an asymptotic chalk line from the back wall of the classroom to the bottom of the blackboard, so isolating by this demarcation the outer row of five pupils at their desks from the rest of the class.

Advising the pupils occupying the remaining three rows to take out their book – "A History of Europe Part II" and begin reading Chapter 4 titled "France under Cardinals Richelieu and Mazarin", he then targeted the victimized five by relating the following incident with sagacious sincerity interspersed with hierophantic virtuousness:

'Last evening after school whilst walking unperturbed up Rice's Lane on my way home, minding my own business, striding at my usual leisurely pace, for the bones be weary though the spirit be strong, in contemplation of the simple things in life which feed the soul and help determine one to battle on, two boys from this class, seated in this very row, committed a foul and ignominious act. They well know the nature of the foul deed they perpetrated against my person and by their perfidious characters shall we know them, for guilt is indelibly stamped on the pusillanimous faces of these scoundrels in crime before even I take heed to challenge them. By what right I ask, by what perverted sense of puerile amusement, the doing of something simply for the fun of it perhaps, by what twisted thinking I should like to know do the executers of such a villainous act believe they will evade the sanction of the law. Escape justice they most assuredly will not! For we all must learn, each and every one of us, that our every action has a consequence and the offenders in this particular wickedness must learn that lesson. And learn it they shall.'

All in the classroom hung on his every word, watching him pace to and fro in front of the blackboard, as they tensely awaited the revelation of the nature of the blackguardly act complained of and the names of the culprits. Gudgy became aware of the edgy groans that welled up amongst some of the pupils.

'Let me come to the kernel of the matter then,' he continued in sententious sonority. 'These two cretins, unprovoked and without due cause, stole milk bottles from the door of Daly's grocery shop and flagrantly rolled said bottles, three in number, albeit empty of content, down the slope of Rice's Lane in my direction, blatantly, deliberately and with malice aforethought in my direction.'

A communal sigh of relief was audible throughout the room. Some of the pupils had imagined a bodily assault or some such grievous offence had been committed. Most were now certain of the identity of the perpetrators who could be seen squirming in their seats in abject discomfort. Gudgy hastened to the front of the isolated row of desks and, planting his feet four-square with hands on hips, exclaimed in rarely aroused fury:

'To what intent you may well ask? Undeniably with the intent of causing harm, harm to my person, the said act wantonly abusive of my person. At any rate most decidedly with the intent of belittling my good name and character in this community. Stephen MacAlindon, yes you, stand now before your prosecutor. Michael Murtagh, on your feet also. Up front the pair of you and face your peers.'

The culprits, sheepishly, stood facing their classmates, Mossy Murtagh feigning tears that failed to flow, Maca giddily uptight.

'Now gentlemen of the jury,' continued Gudgy, striding centre stage and turning to address the class. 'See what shame hangs from their repugnant countenances. What shall we do with the miscreants? You, MacAlindon, were the main offender. Yes! it was you who sent the said milk bottles on their maleficent course. You Murtagh aided and abetted the said MacAlindon in the nefarious deed with boisterous encouragement and total lack of due respect for your elders and betters. For punishment you Murtagh will write out Chapter 4, word for word mind, thrice and present it to me by class next Monday. Likewise for you MacAlindon, and in your most legible handwriting mind, but by way of discriminating punishment you will stand outside this classroom door for the time remaining and see President Keaveny in his study at two o'clock sharp. Be off with you now.'

Maca made heavy work of gathering himself in readiness for

departing the classroom, his demeanour betraying neither swagger nor apology.

'Mr Shevlon Sir, I may've done some wrong things in the past and been justly punished for it,' he said, pushing his hands feep in his pockets as he sidled to the door, 'but this time ye've got the wrong man.'

'Nil desperandum' he tsked, his teacherly denunciation thawing in an exultant grin knowing he had run the fox to ground – 'Well now Mr MacAlindon, until I find the right man you'll have to do.'

Part of John Shevlon's modus operandi of teaching included the spontaneous nomination of one of his pupils to act as tutor during class. He would encamp in a particular student's seat, directing the ousted party so selected to the front of the class charged with the task of enlightening his peers with his knowledge of a particular subject or personage in history. Towards the end of third year, Gudgy, having forgotten, or, having chosen to forgive Maca's indiscretions earlier in the year (he was not a man to bear grudges), so directed him to counsel the class on his knowledge of Gustavus Adolphus, one time King of Sweden. Maca had not been attentive in his study of the warrior king and began hesitantly to pronounce on the subject. Observing Gudgy's apparent keen interest in his ad-lib spiel, vigorously rubbing his bristling jaws with nicotine-stained fingers while intensely studying the stuccoed square panels of the ceiling, he continued, extempore, growing more confident and expansive in his rambling presentation. He deliberately avoided quoting dates knowing they could trip him up. But the facts relating to the king's celebrated battles he spoke of with great dexterity, even going to the trouble of drawing a map of the king's dominions in Europe on the blackboard, highlighting battlefields. Apart from an occasional snigger from some of his classmates, all in all, he was pleased with his performance in concluding and handing the baton back to Gudgy.

'Well well MacAlindon, that's your water-down version and a

more rigmarolish, apocryphal recital 'twould be hard to come by. No! I should temper that remark. There was some vivid imaginative discourse in there right enough and that's a fact. But which king you spoke of and in what period of European history it related is a mystery to me, and presumably will remain a closed book to all scholars reliant on your guidance on such turbulent times. Your gift for cartography however was most illuminating. Gustavus would have, no doubt, been pleased to have been gifted Eastern Europe as far as the Great Caucasus. Now you'll have to learn the proper version, about the real Gustavus Adophus and the true extent of his kingdom and dominions by writing out chapter seven three times. Have it on my desk by Monday.'

*

Two weeks before the break for summer holidays, all third year students were obliged by the Christian Brothers to attend a three day religious retreat with two nights stay over at Saint Joseph's Redemptorist Monastery in Dundalk.

'That's in the Free State Sir, isn't it?'

'The Republic Murtagh. Dundalk is in the Republic of Ireland. The twenty six counties has been a republic since '49. Dundalk is but a few miles south of the border in County Louth. Who can point out Dundalk's location on the map here?' asked Brother Martin (Chippy they nicknamed him), looking keenly at the upturned faces of his charges. 'Is there not a one among you who knows where the largest town in Ireland is?' No one volunteered.

'Hands up how many of you have visited or spent holiday time in the Republic.'

A high-spirited show of hands in response represented approximately half the pupils.

'Those of you who have never been to the South have a wonderful trip ahead of you.'

'I live close to the mon'stree in Clonard Gardens Sir,' Maca said. 'They're Redemptrists so why are we goin' to Dundalk?'

46

'Adventure MacAlindon. Adventure. It is to be hoped the expedition will open up your vacant minds and give you lads a taste for the freedom enjoyed in that part of this wee country of ours.'

Maca had never been south of the border. Filled with eager excitement he could barely wait for the venture to begin. Yet he had mixed feelings about the retreat itself, the compulsory element arousing suspicion that in addition to the spiritual indoctrination associated with such an enterprise, the process would be utilised by the clergy as a screen for sifting out suitable candidates for the religious vocation – "Many are called but few are chosen". When he was ten or eleven years old, his ingenuous dynamism lead him to believe he was predestined to become the first Irish Pope, the panoply of resplendent papal vestments and the exotic pageantry displayed at the Vatican being the main stimulus for such wishful thinking. Now aged fourteen his burgeoning antipathy to the clergy and celibacy in particular proved a major stumbling block, his every nerve and sinew growing attuned to the baffling appetite of adolescent sexuality. He had no intention, no Sir-ee, of spending a lifetime in furtive wanking having discovered the purpose for which girls had been put on this earth. Sceptical about the significance of religion, and distrustful of the motives of those who practised it, he was intent on making the best of his first stay away in a "new country", in discovering what goes on outside his own ghettoized ambit, determined to forget for the while the dull drudgery of his juvenile existence.

Meeting up with his fellow travellers at the school that Tuesday morning, his pyjamas, spare shirt, change of underwear and socks, and his toothbrush rattling around in his father's battered cardboard suitcase, he was all of a doodah at the prospect of the long bus ride to Dundalk, the old charabanc out of Joe Meaghan's bus depot parked in the schoolyard gleaming in the early morning sunlight. The school principal, Brother Keaveny, escorted the boys on the journey and had them solemnly recite, ploddingly, five decades of the rosary and the prayers of the faithful, and then portentously remind one and all the triduum was a silent retreat and that apart from praying, singing hymns, and the confessional, they must remain mute, obey God and his priests, and respect the rules of the monastery. He then led with gusto the school trippers in the singing of sacred chorals, any lingering enthusiasm for devotion petering out on approach to the border. Brother Keaveny shuffled off the bus and spoke with a black coated customs official for what seemed an interminably long time, handing over some papers, some of the more inquisitive boys pressing their snouty faces against the windows for a better look. The officer then boarded the bus and silently marched the length of the gangway sternly scrutinizing the journeyers, then retreated backwards while inspecting the incongruously varied array of luggage on the overhead racks, and disembarked without a word. "Does he think we're the IRA" someone jested, raising guffaws. "Wait till he gets us on the way back" Maca retorted. The Irish customs waived the bus through.

On arrival at Saint Joseph's and on sighting the forbiddingly cold black-grey granite stones that make up its pastiche gothic architecture, an eldritch blue light on the slate roofs giving the place an arcane eeriness, he felt downhearted, a disquieting pre-monition of trouble sending shivers down his spine. From his bedroom at home, he could see the illuminated twin spires of Clonard Church and the monastery with its warm redbrick glow that seemed to welcome pilgrims, he and his sisters spending dreamy nights there hallucinating about castles in the sky. Comparatively, the austere façade of the monastery in Dundalk gave him the heebie-jeebies. He among the hellion group contin-ued to babble in a rollicking manner as they rushed pell-mell off the bus, being quickly reminded of the rule of silence by loud shushes from a grim looking monk hurriedly walking towards them in chilling foreboding rebuke. Ordered to line up in rows of twos they were marched in phalanx into the building and corralled in a cheerless entry hall reeking of camphor and carbolic soap. The welcoming monk, now standing three steps above them on the staircase under a pendulous brass candelabra the better to oversee the unruly brood, bellowed instructions at them: each boy would have his own room which would shortly be allocated either on the third or fourth floor; in twenty minutes they would hear a bell ring and on hearing this bell they must return immediately to the ground floor and gather at the base of this staircase; they would then receive further guidance for their stay. Maca's accommodation on the fourth floor was a dim cubicle eight by six feet in the attic space, with eczematous patches of whitewash peeling off the walls and a canted ceiling that restricted headspace, a dormer window the only redeeming feature as it overlooked the gardens and gave him a bird's-eye view of the grass and clay courts of the local tennis club on the other side of the boundary wall. A pilgrim's comfort comprised of a cast iron bed with a slither of horsehair mattress and a coarse grey woollen blanket. No sheets, no pillow, no light-shade; the only adornment a black wooden crucifix with a luminous body of Christ in his death throes anchored to the wall. The mattress on closer inspection had a blotchy stain of dried piss or semen the size of the Isle of Man (per the scale in his atlas). On turning over the mattress the stain was the size of Australia. He left the map of the Isle of Man side up. There's no fucken lock on the door, he mutely cursed, foaming at the mouth, so I can't even wank in peace.

'You are very welcome one and all to Saint Joseph's Monastery. I am Reverend Father Matthews, Abbot of this sacred congregation,' enunciated the head honcho in sonorous echoes, the boys now gathered in the church. 'May I remind you that this is a silent retreat. You will remain silent for the duration of your stay here. You will not converse with each other. You may only speak when spoken to by one of our brethren. You are not to commune with

49

each other in the cells. Under no circumstances whatsoever are you permitted to leave the confines of this monastery. Your time here is to be spent in devout contemplation of the living Christ, his blessed mother the Virgin Mary and the communion of His saints, especially our very own Saint Gerard Majella. In finding the true Christ you will find yourselves. Let Christ in His mercy come into your heart. When not at church or in communal prayer you may retire to the community room or take walks in our pleasant peaceful gardens and say your own prayers. You may select books and instructive socioreligious pamphlets from the extensive range you will find on the bookshelves in the community room. I urge you to avail of this reading material. Its guidance and Christian ethos if adopted will help make you a better person in the eyes of God. Morning mass is celebrated at seven o'clock. All of you must attend, washed and civilly attired and ready to receive the holy sacrament of the Eucharist. Breakfast is served in the refectory after mass. All meal times with menu of the day are notified on the blackboard outside the refectory. Be on time for your meals. At half past ten, you will return to church for religious counselling given by myself or one of the brethren. Evening devotions and worship is held here at seven o'clock, attendance is optional but encouraged. Confessions will be heard between two thirty and four thirty each afternoon' he said waiving his arms and pointing out the four confessionals. 'During unscheduled hours you are expected to spend the time in prayer, in tranquil contemplation of your sinfulness, and in enlightening reading. Are there any questions?' The Abbot's goggling eyes panned the silent gathering. Maca snidely observed the angelic expressions on some of the gaums faces already imbued with an evangelical fervour, so intent were they on making a good retreat. 'Oh! I should emphasize, there is no smoking, just like in your own school. NO smoking permitted anywhere including the garden areas. Any questions? Well if no one has a question. But do remember, if any boy has a concern, if anything is worrying you, you may approach myself or any one of the brethren who will be pleased to help you. Any boy with a personal problem may seek individual counselling. All you need do is ask. As Christ said – "ask and it shall be given unto you". So! No questions? Then kneel for a decade of the sorrowful mysteries.'

After a leaden recital of the rosary, the Abbot enjoined all to bow their heads and reflect upon their sins, man being born a sinful creature, and to earnestly beg God's forgiveness. In the intense silence a raspberry fart could be heard. The Abbot's eyes glacially scanned the pews seeking out the culprit, seeming to settle on a group of boys quaking with suppressed laughter. Removing his biretta as he rose from the abbatial throne, he dronely demanded:

'Who did that? This is the house of God. Who amongst you dares defile the house of God?'

There being no response, the Abbot steadily marched like a pious turkey cock down the centre aisle, moving ever closer to three boys making piggy snorts amid others chortling heh-heh-hehs.

'Own up before God for God knows who you are.'

Mossy Murtagh got to his feet, a sweaty panic causing another slippered fart to further test the stitches of his trousers, arousing widespread giggling.

''Twas me Father.'

'Are you a Christian? Have you no respect for God's house?'

'I didn't mean it Father. 'Twas me nerves, me stomach has a bad dose of the nerves.'

'You may all go now,' said the Abbot, turning on his heel and clapping his hands so filling the church with resounding echoes. 'Dinner is at one o'clock sharp in the refectory. Jump to it when you hear the bell. This afternoon one of our returned priests, Father Doyle, will enlighten you on the great humanitarian work being carried out by the missionaries in Equatorial Africa. On how through education and medicine the light of Christ is shining bright for our Negro brothers and sisters. Then I expect to see each and every one of you at evening devotions. What time does evening devotions commence?'

'Seven o'clock Father,' most answered in unison.

That first interminably long stygian night, lying on the penitential back-breaking bed listening to the coded knocks ringing out on the central heating pipes and radiators, he felt the stab of hunger as time itself moved at snail's pace. Tap-tap-taptap-tap was knuckle rapped on the door. Quietly opening it he found Mossy in his pyjamas standing in the impenetrable cavernous darkness, his bare feet like suction pads squelching on the wooden floor as he walked woozily into the room, mephitic air breezing in his wake.

'Me fucken head's melting. I feel sick Maca.'

'What's wrong with ye ye girny bollix. 'Tis probably that crap dished up for dinner. Don't know what it was but I've stood in it many a time,' he replied, his senses dulled by monotony.

'Nah! Belly's in shite all day. I'm afraid to let a good fart in case I mess meself.'

'I've nothin' to give ye for it Mossy. Go dump in the crapper.'

'I'm scared stiff to go to the lav. 'Tis miles away at the end of don fucken corridor. Not a light kind could I find. Never know what you'd bump into in the inky blackness. Not that I'm afraid of the monks, fuck 'em. 'Tis the chance of meetin' the dead ones on the stairway that bugs me. God only knows where they bury the bodies in this place.'

'I'd no idea ye were such a pissy scaredy-pants. Will I go with ye?' he offered, prepared to face the ghouls with equanimity.

'Nah! Fuck it, 'twill pass. Did ye bring any fegs. I'd kill for a feg.'

'Fegs! Were ye not listenin' to the bossman's spoof?'

Standing at the window looking through the pitch-blackness out beyond the stone perimeter walls, they could see distant car light beams, like cones, snake by under the dingy street lights. The communications racket grew louder so they joined in sending coded raps on the radiators, the diversion lasting well into the early hours.

The next day went by creeping slow, beginning with cold showers at dawn endured by the lazy stragglers, inclusive of Maca and Mossy, the hot water used up by the early birds, Maca being furiously inspired to masturbate under the chilly spray. The shock of an early rise left most with sleepyheads all day, dampening any enthusiasm for high jinks. A day of fervid religious observance was encountered. After evening tea the indolent three shirked the religious devotions and, in an aura of feigned reverence, rambled the Stations of the Cross pathway in the Calvary garden. The throaty song of a robin could be heard nearby.

'Would ye look at the red breast on don fella. The blood of Christ spurtin' his lanced side so they say,' regaled Maca.

'Here's a grand hole for a game of muga,' said Mugsy Dixon, making it deeper with the toe of his boot. 'Have youse any marleys on yis?'

'Fuck that for a lark, I'm dyin' for a feg,' said Mossy. 'Let's go over the wall and find a shop. Or maybe there's a pub nearby.'

'Jaysus that's a different ball-game altogether. What if we're spotted,' pleaded Mugsy.

'Well I'm not hangin' about. Are yis game,' urged Maca.

They identified an area of dense shrubbery close to the boundary at the far end of the horse-shoe shaped Calvary garden and easily climbed the wall bedecked with the nacreous spoors of snails and splotchy birdshit and dropped onto a pathway. Misgivings about the smell of rain in the air, they wandered along the potholed way in hyper-freedom, like escapees constantly looking over their shoulders to see if a posse of clerics had been sent to track them down, crossed a rusting railway line and traipsed through a residential area before stumbling on a cluster of shuttered-up shops. The newsagents remained open. Mossy demanded they divvy-up the cost of the cigarettes – 'youse are great at smokin' OP's', and having collected asked the elderly shopkeeper to recommend a brand. He was handed ten "Sweet Afton". Maca bought a packet of five "Woodbines", Mugsy a two pint bottle of "Taylor Keith" orange. Standing with their backs to the shop under the awning that flapped in the blustery breeze, crepitant thunderclaps distantly rolling in the thick of roiling clouds, smoking fags and guzzling the orange drink, they heard music and laughter round the corner and on investigating came upon two old codgers swilling pints of stout outside a public house, a ceili in full swing inside.

'Mossy, you look a lot older than Mugsy and me. Go you on and get a pint of lager. We'll settle up later.'

They waited in great expectation for Mossy's return with the alcohol and were soon confronted by his silly grin. It being a no-go, Maca approached one of the old codgers:

'Can I ask a favour, would one of yis get us a pint of Harp. Here's the money.'

'Did Joe refuse yer other fella there?'

'No! He's just not feelin' the best and we haveta look after him.'

'Go way outta that. If I ask Joe for lager he'll know it's not my drink. I'll get ye a Guinness if yer fit for it?

'Sound! A pint of Guinness so.'

Some minutes later the desperados were swigging from the one pint glass, spitting and guffawing as they competed for the ugliest grimace. Sham brio emptied the glass to the last drop. Hearing the peal of distant thunder they headed back by the newsagents and were surprised to spy Billy Galligan and Fergus Lynam sauntering towards them. Briskly skulking behind the side canvas awning, they waited for the two blimps to enter the shop before scarpering back up the road in a sudden downpour of portentous rain. Maca was first to drop on the monastery side of the slippery-wet boundary wall and on the spot was grabbed by the Abbot who had sprightly moved from behind the cover of a mulberry bush. Mossy and Mugsy stood like guams before running harum-scarum as if each had a hot poker up his arse.

'So I didn't spell it out enough for you me boyo. What part of the rules did you not understand?' Father Matthews, under a black umbrella its shelter not extended to his prey, held Maca by the scruff of the neck, drawing his shirt suffocatingly tight around his throat. 'Did you hear me say 'twas forbidden to leave the monastery grounds?'

Maca appeared to be taking his vow of silence seriously, being half choked and unable to speak.

'Well did you me boyo?' demanded the Abbot. He nodded, his face flushed borderline blackpurple. 'Nevertheless you decided to pay no heed to that warning. Have you been drinking? There's a whiff of the drink off ye,' shouted the Abbot with a feral snarl, dropping the umbrella and hitting out with his free hand and landing a stinging slap on Maca's by now rainsoaked face.

''Twas just… a pint Father,' he gasped with adenoidal intensity.

'A pint! You've been to a public house. A pint! That's more than ten cups of tea. Would you drink ten cups of tea in one sitting?' asked the Abbot, energetically kneading his cheek with his fingers.

'I didn't… drink it all meself Father. We shared it.'

'You and those other two. Empty out your pockets,' he barked, retrieving his umbrella and retaining exclusive protection from the elements, sheet lightning now filling the turbulent sky.

Maca fumbled around the pack of cigarettes in his pocket and produced the other contents – a handkerchief, hair comb, and some loose change.

'All of it,' snapped Father Matthews. The pack of cigarettes with three Woodbines remaining fell to the ground.

'What's this we have here? Pick it up. Show me that there. Ah! Woodbines, the poor man's addiction,' the schoolmarish tone now set by his scything comment. 'You're in bi-ig trouble young man. Bi-i-g trouble. What's your name?'

'Stephen… MacAlindon Father.'

'And the names of the other two ruffians?'

'I don't know Father.'

'You don't know. What do you mean you don't know? They're your school pals aren't they. You're digging a hole for yourself and it's getting deeper by the second.'

'No Father, they're at me school all right but not in my class. I don't know them from… from Adam.'

'Right smart Aleck… 'tis home you'll be going now.'

He was dragged in parabolic buck-leaping across the Calvary garden, rain water rilling down his face, being released from the Abbot's vice-grip only when tripping on the stoop at the monastery door. Ordered to his room he was terrified on hearing the Abbot's heavy footsteps behind his own squelchy climb up the staircase. On arrival in the room the Abbot said:

'Right Master MacAlindon, pack your bag.'

'What? Now Father.'

'No! Next week. Of course now, you're on your way home I tell you,' he re-emphasized.

'But how will I get home Father? I've no money,' he cried out in panic, his heart thumping, his temples throbbing.

'Spend it all in the pub did you? Well that's your problem then isn't it,' said the Abbot with demeaning humour. 'Now pack that bag. I'll be recommending the school expels you. And I'll be writing your parents via your school advising that the whole wretched business stems from your wilful disobedience, your dishonourable delinquency.'

He made a ham-fisted job of packing his case. Nervously looking out the dormer window, the cadaverous light of the naked bulb in the room causing the evening twilight to appear pitch black, neck hairs prickling, his papulous face erupting in a rash as spasms of panic convulsed through him; dread of the stormy night and the long trek home; fear of the consequences at school and the possibility of being expelled; the backlash when his parents found out.

'Forgive me Father Matthews. I didn't mean to disobey ye. The mother 'ill kill me when I –'

'Give me the names of your two accomplices?' a cruel scowl pored over the Abbot's face.

'I don't know them Father. I swear to God I don't know them,' he tremulously intoned.

'Blasphemer! How dare you use God's holy name to hide your vile lies.'

'I swear on the Bible I don't –'

'Look me in the eye boyo when you tell barefaced lies. What class are you in at school?'

'Third Year… Blue Father,' he blubbed, his mouth so dry he could hardly get his tongue around the words.

'I can find out what class those other two are in. Where will your lies land you then?'

He was numbed into silence, his legs trepidatiously truant.

'Well me boyo, answer me that and stop this lying.'

The boyo kept shtum.

'Come with me,' the Abbot brusquely ordered as he stormed out of the room. He had difficulty keeping pace with him as he was conducted to the community room and told to stand by the door, his school mates looking with sidelong glances at his reddening agitated face, some grinning in undisguised spiteful glee.

'This boy is being sent home in disgrace for leaving the confines of the monastery by climbing the boundary wall in unholy search of gratification of his nasty habits, drinking alcohol and smoking, Guinness and Woodbines no less. Such defiance of the cardinal rules of this sodality, clearly and painstakingly explained to all of you on your arrival, merits severe chastisement. He was caught red-handed so the punishment befits the transgression. I know there are others among you, at the very least two others, who have also breached these rules. I want those boys to examine their conscience, take a deep breath, and step forward. Come now, God is watching, this is the moment of truth so do the right thing.'

In the stilly silence consequent on the Abbot's ultimatum, all that could be heard was the unabated drum-beat of rain on the roof and the mechanical motion of the bell tower clock as it struck the three-quarter hour. For a wearisome few seconds Maca kept his eyes fixed on a scuff mark on the toe of his shoe, only raising his head on hearing the scraping noise of a chair being pushed back on the highly polished wooden floor. Mossy took two steps forward. Mugsy soon joined him. The Abbot's face broke in a broad triumphal grin as he made to move towards the recognizable wrongdoers. Then Fergus Lynam stood forward, and Barry O'Reilly, briskly followed by Dan Cronin. The disaffected mood quickly spread and soon half the boys of Third Year Blue had stepped forward. Others from Third Year White came next. At a count of seventeen boys standing in solidarity, the Abbot rushed to exit the community room banging the door forcefully behind him. Mossy was aware that Billy Galligan had remained cowardly in his seat – 'What sort of a chicken-livered shit are ye? We saw you with Fergie below at the shop. Most of the fellas who stood up didn't climb over the wall but you did.'

Those who had stepped forward, and some who had remained seated, now ran to Maca and hoisted him on their up-stretched arms passing him along a line of vulpine howling heads. Others audaciously began to remove the hortatory posters to prayer and a life in Christ from the walls. A monk, alerted by the pandemonium stormed in, loudly clapping his hands, enquiring what the rumpus was about, and, admonishing the boys for their clamorous behaviour, ordered them to their rooms.

Next morning the bus bumped over the cobbled courtyard, arriving a few hours earlier than scheduled for the homeward journey. Maca was scared shitless on boarding the bus when confronting Brother Keaveny who gave him a cadaverous frown and grimace, exhaling pietistic insufflations coupled with a long exophthalmic stare. No words were spoken between them. Nor were any prayers recited on the trip home. A timorous babel broke out as Brother Keaveny opened a large box of Lemons Emerald toffees and went up and down the aisle of the bus offering them to his charges.

During the last week of school term there did not appear to be any repercussions from the escapade at the retreat. Nor did his parents seem to hear of anything about it, leaving him much relieved that he would not face the threat of expulsion. However, fate played a new card when dealing him a brutal hand.

4

'Give her more diddy there Maca or we'll never get to the fucken hooley,' said Mugsy from the front passenger seat of the car they had just nicked from off Donegall Road in central Belfast. They were of the same mind, amid recoiling gasps, the car must be owned by a cat woman on account of the overpowering smell of cat's piss they inhaled on their adrenalized dart into the vehicle.

'Will "Jugs" McClintock be there do ye think lads? Jeez I'd love to screw don one till she begged for mercy,' said Mossy, sitting forward in the back seat to ensure he was heard above the dinning engine noise, the nescient sexual connotation filtering through his bluster. The three desperados were on their way to a carnival dance in Bangor and had just missed a directional fingerpost.

'You wouldn't know what to do with her Mossy,' Maca guffawed.

'And why the fuck wouldn't I. 'Tis not for stirrin' me tay I'd be usin' it.'

'Don't be talkin' the like of that there about the girl Mossy. But listen here now, if Joanne's with her yer on,' said Mugsy. 'Youse know me lads, any port in a storm, eh! eh! I don't like the cut of your ride Maca. Are ye chasin' a bit of skirt tonight?'

'I'm hopin' Dede will show up for herself and meself do be gettin' on like a house on fire. She promised she'd do her best to be there... with her girl friends.'

'Jaysus that could be jammy. Ah! 'Tis a bucket of water we'll be throwin' over ye by the end of the night yer so hot for don one.'

'Fuck off Mossy ye lump of dried cowshite. What with yer nailed-on rides 'tis you'll need the coolin' off as well we –'

Beams of torchlight arced above the middle of the road, being waved frenetically and then directly at the oncoming car, momentarily blinding the occupants.

'Fucken hell! 'Tis the peelers,' shouted Mossy in alarm.

'Nah bejaysus! 'Tis the B Specials. Put the foot down Maca. Dem fucks will do us over if they get a howld of us,' said Mugsy, frantically wiping the murky windscreen with the back of his hand.

Maca, just into his fifteenth year, did not have sufficient driving experience or expertise to control the speeding vehicle and crashed through the check point. He struggled to steady the car, now veering from side to side of the road in an uncontrolled skid, the engine vrooming. Gunshot smashed through the rear window sending splinters of glass in a mushroom cloud blasting through the interior with ear-splitting din. The car careered across the road and came to a shuddering halt atop a banked ditch. Dazed and leaking blood, he leaned out of the burst-open car door.

'Get out. Get out yee Fenian bastards,' a brusque voice bellowed from behind a blindingly penetrating shaft of torchlight.

'Watch out they're not… not carrying George,' another voice breathlessly commanded. 'Don't rush them for the scumbags were ready for us.'

He could hear Mugsy making guttural noises and on looking over saw he was slumped over the dashboard. On exiting the car, suddenly conscious of an excruciating pain in his chest, he felt a stream of thick warm gore trickle down the back of his neck. Attempting to wipe it clean he fingered pulverized bone and bloody brain tissue on the collar of his jacket. Mossy lay crumpled like a bean bag behind the driver's seat, half his head blown away. Maca's body went into spasms of shock, an abrupt alertness to his vulnerability making it difficult for him to catch his breath.

'They're hurted. Me friends is badly hurted. Get a doctor. For God's sake get an ambulance,' he pleaded as he felt the heavy blow to his left ankle of a well directed boot.

'Spread the legs you piece of shit. Wider. Hands on roof.'

Maca then bore the brunt of a rifle butt to the small of his back. He staggered but stayed on his feet. Bending over in pain he splayed his hands for support on the car roof.

'Please! For God's sake help me friends. Hang in there Mugsy,' he yelled above the whirring sound of the hissing engine, dipping his chin between his outstretched arms. 'Help's on the way.'

'You caught one of ours you fucking scumbag. He's in bad shape back up the road there. You'd better start praying he makes it or you're dead meat.'

Fleetly looking back up the road, Maca could see two auxiliaries attending a casualty on the shadowy roadway screaming to high heaven.

'Stand up on your feet like that there,' another B Special snarled at Sammy as he pulled him from the vehicle. 'Nothing much wrong with this fellow George, looks out of it though... probably the drink. Did you check the boot?'

'Some blood from the head on this one Harry. The glass I'd say. Open up the boot you fucking pope-head.'

With tremulous hands, his heart hammering against his ribs, Maca opened the boot of the car and was ordered to stand aside. He spotted an envelope on the ground and when the B Special had turned away, he pocketed it. A torch was shone into the boot and one of the B Specials then cautiously searched the space under the rubber mat covering the spare wheel.

'Nothing here George, save a woeful stink of cat's piss. Otherwise she's clean.'

'What the fucking hell were yee pope-heads up to,' said George, 'stolen car no doubt. Would I be right about that there now?'

'We was on our way to the dance in Bangor. We didn't mean nothin' by it. We meant no harm. We'd have left it back.'

'Did ye hear that Harry... they'd have left the car back,' the auxiliary said sneeringly. 'I'm sure the owner will be pleased to see the state of it now. They have the cut of young-bloods about them

Harry, up to no bleeding good. Your man in the back there looks in bad shape. Better radio in for a second ambulance.'

On this Saturday night of August 11, 1956, his best pal, Michael "Mossy" Murtagh died ignobly from a bullet wound to the left temple. Sammy "Mugsy" Dixon suffered multiple lacerations, severe bruising, and temporary concussion having hit his head against the windscreen. Maca sustained multiple lacerations from flying glass and bruising to his upper torso caused by impacting the steering wheel. During the Black Maria ride to custody he had a peek at the envelope. It was addressed to Corporal George Roberts. Tossing it on the floor, he memorized the name.

*

Earlier in June, Maca had met for the first time the pulchritudinous Deirdre Desmond at a summer hop in the Clonard Community Hall. Unlike with other girls, who tended to gather in clutches like chickens clucking in a coop gabbling nonsense, and with any one of whom he had no uphill having a banter and the odd bout of French kissing and heavy petting, his whole being trembled at the sight of Deirdre, she being so drop-dead gorgeous in a febrile kind of way. He spied her sitting, smiling demurely, sipping lemonade, feminine charm personified as she inclined her head sideways revealing a slender alabaster neck, her face graced by high cheek-bones, she seemingly captivated by the devoted attentions of the smoothie Frank Connolly, who, he later discovered, rarely left her side. Even when she danced with other guys Connolly would join them on the floor in a threesome, waving his arms up and down like a yo-yo, and if a slow smoochy tune was played would excuse her partner and be with her by himself. Maca ventured to dance with her, transfixing her with his eyes as she seemed to shimmer and fade in front of him, yet found himself tongue-tied and imbecilic in his attempts to interest her in small talk, his sense of humour all but dried-up by the unnerving weightiness of his nascent feelings for her. She appeared aloofly farouche and indifferent to his approach which only spurred him on to make a conquest of her. Smitten, he judged her the most haunting spectre of female beauty he had ever seen, with her fine long blonde hair, her ice blue eyes and her full kissable, slightly sensual, mouth. The heady smell of her perfume and the velvety jolt of the soft cool touch of her hand made him swoon with adolescent chutzpah, yet diffident as to how to win her over. Frank's bully boy interloping broke the spell. However her lissom, ethereal image proliferated in intense thoughts of her thereafter disturbing his sleep and affecting his appetite, so much so that his mother, espying his lack of alacrity, teased him about his being touched by the insanity of love. But what would she know, he brooded. He determined to shift her, make her his girlfriend. The chase entailed him, on tenterhooks, in turning up at the most likely of places at the most likely of times, including cycling by her imposing home, contriving to run into her as if by chance. All such attempts proved fruitless, and although he felt giddy with nervous energy, the depressive bouts of failure he endured in not meeting or seeing her left him drained. He had confided his blues to his friend Mossy:

'For fuck sake Maca just ask her out. Go to the house and ask her out. Or 'phone her. Connolly'll give ye her number.'

'Nah Mossy. I can't risk her turnin' me down. She's so stand-offish. I need to be as cool as she is, like it's no great shakes if she doesn't want to go with me. I can't let her see how fucken wired I am for her, how fucken mad I am about her.'

'What makes ye think she won't go with ye? Ye said she gave ye the glad eye. And maybe being wired for her is no bad thing. Shows her yer feelings are genuine, that yer not just another bullshiter.'

'Yeah right! Anyway, don't know what the fuck I'm doin'. 'Tis fucken wearin' me down all this chasin' after her. Backin' off when push comes to shove. Sometimes I wish I'd never clapped eyes on her.'

By and by, one evening cycling home he caught sight of Deirdre as she lithely walked amid a throng of whooping, laughing factory women wending their way from the early shift. Hit by a dopamine rush, he doubled back, heart in mouth. She was carrying a shoping bag.

'Hey! How's it goin'?'

'Hi Steve,' she said, her lips parting in a smile or grimace, he could not tell which.

'Want a hand with the bag? Looks kinda heavy.'

'Mum sent me out for milk and some other odds and ends.'

'Here, let me hang it on the handlebar. I'll walk along with ye.'

They walked on in silence, he so happy to be in her company, yet tortured by the blankness that filled his mind causing him to react archly bashful. Farcically, they began to speak at once, eliciting an exchange of shy chuckles.

'I was just going to ask if ye enjoyed the hop,' he said, a tenuous quiver in his voice.

'Crikey, of course I did. I love dancing.'

'Me too. I enjoyed dancin' with ye, short an'all as it was.'

An embarrassing silence broke again between them.

'There's a hop next Saturday at the AOH Hall. Kicks off at eight. Would ye be on for goin' Deirdre?'

It was the first time he had called her by her name and as he heard himself say it he found his thoughts enjungled by uncertainty. Was he too impetuous in cutting to the chase?

'Aahh! My mum probably won't let me go.'

'Why... why not?'

'She always wants to know who I'm with and who'd be there and... and things like that.'

'I could call for ye at the house Deirdre.'

'No. Better not,' she said as she nimbly tucked a loose strand of hair behind her ear.

Subdued by her brusque response, he felt the deadweight in his legs as the heels of his boots clacked along the pavement.

'Maybe I could ask Frank to call round and take me. Mum likes him and I'd love to go.'

Heavy of heart, his stomach turning queasy with envy, he asked inside his head – Why is she talking of Frank taking her. Hadn't he just invited her. Is she playing hard to get?

'And if Frank takes me I could meet you there.'

'That'd be great Deirdre,' he chirped, now elated on hearing those last three words, aware he was musing on her name with every unspoken plea. Deirdre DD Dede. It sounded like wind chimes in his befuddled head – Dede.

'Thanks Steve. I'll take it from here. No need to come the whole way.'

As he helped remove the shopping bag from the handlebar of his bicycle, she reached out a bare arm unveiling tiny gold hairs that impassioned him, her hand briefly touching his sending an adrenalized shock wave to his enfeebled brain.

'See ye Saturday evenin' then Dede.'

'About eight you said. Hope to see you then Steve.'

It seemed to him Saturday took ages to come round. Arriving at the AOH Hall at half past seven, Mossy in tow helping boost his waning bravado, he was uneasy as to what to do about Frank Connolly, Deirdre's ever present companion, and what the evening's frolics might bring about.

'Ye went a bit heavy on the Old Spice there Maca. Spill the bottle did ye?'

'Too much eh! Should I wash it off?'

'Nah! But I could smell ye half a mile off ha! ha! Only slaggin' ye pal.'

'These pants is very baggy Mossy, the arse damn near down to me knees. What do ye think?'

Mossy mimicked Maca's lopping walk, bow-legged, with such droll gestures that they laughed till the tears rolled down their cheeks.

'They were the only clean pair I could find in me hurry to get out of the fucken house.'

'Truth to tell there's a touch of the dropped crotch all right,' Mossy snickered. 'Quit flappin' like an oul woman ya header.'

They were standing at the entrance door of the hall, the hooley inside in full swing with live band music blaring from loud-speakers out onto the street. Hankering for her and not trusting his eyes that Deirdre might have slipped in unbeknownst to him, he impatiently scanned the floor for sight of her. Two minutes shy of eight o'clock the blood-red lipsticked hoydens Joanne Johnston and Madge McClintock, dressed like the cat's pyjamas, approached them accompanied by Eddie Atkinson, a Protestant from the Grosvenor Road who now and then attended Gaelic football games in Casement Park with his Catholic neighbours (nonchalantly standing for 'The Soldier's Song' it was tattletaled). Mossy's face lit up on gurneyeing Jugs's heaving bosom – 'a firm handful there' he purred. Maca had, on occasion, the pleasure of heavy petting sessions with Joanne, she thrilled to let him tongue-examine her tonsils, and he, frustrated by onanistic abuse, electrified to accompany her to the back row of the cinema where in darkness, his jacket thrown over his lap, she would fondle him to erection and with enthusiastic nimbleness wank him off. Such stimulating dalliance proved an enigmatical gratification to forgo, but her shrill gossipy harping about anything and everybody weighed the balance, so he kept his distance.

'How yis. Long time no see,' said Joanne, batting her eyelashes.

'Up she flew and the cock flattened her. What are yis up to,' said Mossy, counting on enjoying the charge of a hard-on during a smooch dance with one or other of the vamps later in the evening. Maca, anxious not to miss out on Deirdre's arrival, ignored them.

'The band's great don't ye think,' Eddie enthused.

'Aye! They're hot enough all right,' Maca granted.

'Any chance of an owl jive Steve?' Joanne avidly invited.

'I'm not dancin' yet Jo. I'm waitin' on someone.'

'Feck me! She must be somethin' special for you to have yer tongue hangin' out like that there. Who ye waitin' on anyway?' she retorted with impish mockery, provoking a cynical smirk on Eddie's face.

'He's waitin' on Deirdre Desmond,' Mossy smugly butt in.

'Ach, he's not is he? Don snooty bitch. Thinks she pisses perfume that one she's so la-di-da,' she hissed real snarky.

'Shut yer trap Jo.' And turning to Mossy he barracked him – 'did ye hafta blabber that there… ye blithering eejit.'

'Ooooch! touchy… smarty-pants,' she jeered.

'Fuck off Jo… go crucify yerself,' he barked, giving her a fixed and angry look.

'Come on Madge, let's leave them to her nibs. There's plenty more fish in the sea. God only knows what cesspool these feckers crawled out of,' barked Joanne with a sneering strabismic glare as the hoydens sashayed off, Eddie scurrying after them.

'For fuck sake Maca, ye've a face on ye like a cut cat,' said a chastened Mossy watching the hornbags strut away. 'That pair are itchin' for it. Ye done me out of a nailed-on ride with yer messin'.'

'Don one's a fucken nutter… a few screws missin'. Wise up Mossy… you can't be an ignoramus all yer life. There's lots of hot biddies in the place from what I see,' he retaliated. 'Ten past eight… no sign of Deirdre. I'll bet don fucker Connolly took her on a long walk by the Lagan bank.'

'Don't break my balls… jaysus. Here… have a feg and calm yerself. If she said she's comin' she's comin'.'

'Nah! I told ye I should'na pushed it. When I got the chance I pounced instead of takin' her easy. She's not comin' Mossy. I can feel it, like an itch I can't scratch.'

'Quit talkin' shite Maca… yer a glutton for punishment. What of it if she doesn't show tonight? Ye'll get a run at her again.'

'Not fucken likely. Arse-face Connolly rules the roost there… should'a known better.'

Just then he spied Frank sauntering into the hall, alone, and grimly swaggered over to him in a kink of emotions.

'Deirdre not with ye Frank?' he asked in an aggressive tone, knowing she had eluded him once again.

'Maca! Hell no. The mother wouldn't let her come.'

'Why not?'

'Ah! She has something against the "bowsies", as she calls them, that hang about the place. You'd never know with her. She's a bit of a snob. Scots and a fucking prod to boot. She can be a right pain in the hole I tell ye.'

'And where's Deirdre now?'

'At home. That's where I left her anyhow. She told me she was to meet ye here and I did me best. But the mother wasn't having any of it.'

'But she said she was comin' with you. I thought you were her steady?'

'Me fuck sake! Wish I was… jump at the chance. No Maca… you're barking up the wrong tree on that there.'

He was mollified on hearing this and tempered his aggression.

'So what's with all the escortin' Frank? What's that all about?'

'Just so, es-cor-ting. My mum's very chummy with her's, seems Mrs Desmond trusts me to see the girl right, to look after her like, and sure I love lookin' after her. She's great craic ye know, once you get to know her.'

'Does she want to see me Frank do ye think? For a date I mean.'

'Well that would be tellin'. Here, give her a buzz tomorra.'

Frank passed him a slip of paper with a telephone number scrawled on it. 'About eleven… when her mum's out at church. Nothing like findin' out for yourself.'

He was bright-eyed and bushy-tailed on returning to Mossy.

'Jaysus! Ye'll never believe it. Yer man's not her boyfriend a'tall. He's only lookin' out for her he tells me.'

'Lookin' out for her is right the bollix. So where is she then?'

'The mother wouldn't let her out of the house. I'm to 'phone her tomorra. Fucken hell, a hullabaloo about nothin'… can ye believe it? Come on. Let's grab dem rides and get jivin',' he wound up.

Next day, on tenterhooks, he called her from a public telephone box on the Shankill Road, praying he wouldn't run out of pennies.

'Sorry I couldn't be there last night.'

'That's okay. I'd really like to see ye. Maybe go to the flicks.'

They agreed to meet outside Clonard Monastery the following Friday at seven o'clock; the Redemtorist's were holding their annual charity bazaar over the weekend and her mother would not object to her presence there unescorted. The days of waiting passed torturously slow, hour by hour. Wanting to impress her he visited the barber's shop and had his first crew cut. Finger combing his new hair style he felt it bristled like grass, the upshot of which left him self-conscious, believing he looked more like a hoodlum mugshot than the hotshot he set out to be. Humbled, he marched off in the tawny sunlight of a wet June evening to meet her, dressed in his best garb of green cargo corduroys, white polo shirt, black leather jacket, and peak cap. Restlessly strutting to and fro the well worn pavement outside the monastery amid the rank smell of damp leaves, a scabrous looking dog unwanted company, all of a sudden his heart aflutter as he watched her approach with a friend who knowingly batted her eyelashes at him, rebooting his self-assurance thinking Deirdre had been giving her some pointers about her feelings for him. Then, on removing his cap they broke into a girlish fit of giggling, leaving him deflated again.

'What did you do to your hair?' she asked cheekily, running her fingers over his crown.

'Don't ye like it?'

'It tickles. You're like a hedgehog. I preferred it long. But sure 'twill grow back.'

Despite his diffidence, his inkling was that all was positively fantastic between them, especially when the girls linked him while walking into the community hall. Once inside, her friend went off with others leaving the love-birds to fend for themselves.

'Did you hear on the news… there's going to be another world war?' she said with a parodic smile.

'Nah! I don't bother listenin' to the news.'

'Well you should. It's very serious by all accounts.'

'What is?'

'The threat of a third world war. Dad says it's inevitable.'

'What's inevitable about it?' he peremptorily asked, camouflaging his ignorance.

'That fellow, the president of Egypt, Nassa or Nasser I think his name is, he nationalized the Suez Canal. Dad says the semiotics of war is there for all to see. Israel, Great Britain and France may declare war.'

'What's so great about Britain?' he snorted.

'Don't be facetious Steve. It's no laughing matter,' she haughtily replied, a slight moue of vexation creasing her lips.

Suitably reprimanded, he made a mental note to look up the meaning of semiotics and facetious in the dictionary, never having heard the words before. They moseyed around the bazaar: she of farouche demeanour spending on trinkets saying how cute they were; he miserly keeping the few bob he possessed deep in his pocket so he could splash out on buying her a soft drink and some titbits. Later, while spooning ice cream soda from plastic cups and nibbling chocolate muffins, Frank Connolly approached with a bemused beam in his eyes calling out – 'So the pair of yee got together then?' They stood in awkward silence, unresponsive, Deirdre's cheeks pinkening, Frank's bumptious advance an unwanted intrusion. Maca, observing her closely side-on, grew more and more aware how special this girl is: her incisive mind; her effortless unaffected loveliness; how alluring the shy and quiet harmony of her face; a girl he could not act the braggart with, who chided his foolishness and spurred his curiosity. Favoured by her company, he supposed he was in love with her. He gave Frank a discreet sign to bugger off.

Walking her home that night in the glimmering twilight along the rainswept pavements dappled with caducous cherry blossom petals tinged rusty-pink, gently draping her shoulders with his jacket, she linked his arm with affectionate prehensility as they talked of school, sharing whimsical stories about teachers. He related some humorous anecdotes about Gudgy Shevlon's eccentricities at which she heartily laughed, and at some of which she expressed fevered incredulity. She told him of how bored she was at school; of how dejected she felt at not being in control; how she could not wait to get to college, her elder sister doing law at Queen's University. She would like to follow her there and do medicine. He replied parenthetically that, as yet, he had no idea what to do with himself, having no ambition or fixed direction for the future, but expressed a passing interest in the law, that history was his favourite subject, that he really couldn't say what he might do, having at least another three years to do at Colaiste Ris. Arriving at the bottom of the road where she lived, she turned to face him and he immediately cottoned-on that this is where they would say their goodbyes. She let her hand linger in his as they dallied awhile on shifting feet.

'Will we go to the flicks tomorra night,' he tentatively asked. She agreed, and they made arrangements to meet outside the cinema. He kissed her shapely mouth, her lips warm and responsive. Intuitively, he knew not to French kiss her. That thrill would come in good time following their getting to know each other better.

'Toodle-oo Steve.'

'See you tomorra then.'

He watched her saunter away, her comely nylon stockinged legs gleamy-crimsoned by the incarnadine illuminating street lighting. Mentally he begged her to turn and wave to him, the blood pounding through his veins, promising himself that if she did so he would marry her. And she did, her smile radiant. Shambling home he felt iridescently happy, heartened by the silky scimitar moon and scintillating stars that glittered in a by now cloudless sky.

*

There had been nothing untoward in the fourteen years of Stephen MacAlindon's life until that horrendous night of mayhem that led to the death of his best friend Mossy. Now, arrested and charged with causing grievous bodily harm to the B-Special, his future prospects had taken a turn for the worse. His relationship, or potential relationship, with Deirdre had been summarily terminated by her implacable mother, who, on hearing of it, redoubled her protective efforts in having her daughter chaperoned on every outing while his trial was pending in the juvenile court, and by removing her from the scene altogether having placed her in a boarding school at the start of the autumn term. All utterly changed: his life force wasted moreover in thinking of Deirdre and how things might have panned out; his lonesomeness consumed by bitter regrets for the loss of his best pal; bittersweet memories increasingly outweighed by fantastical schemes of avenging retribution against corporal George Roberts who had so callously shot Mossy.

In December the trial was heard in the Minor's Court of Her Majesty's Criminal Courts of Justice. The accused were convicted on all counts, sentenced to detention at Her Majesty's pleasure, Maca for a minimum of three years and Mugsy Dixon for one year, at an industrial school for the reform of delinquent boys. He begged his father to let him take the saxophone, pleading he would master the instrument, that it would help while away the wearisomeness of his incarceration. His interest in brass and big band music had been magnetized by the popularity of Eddie Calvert who had a huge number one hit that summer with "Oh My Papa".

The Principal of the borstal, Reverend Thomas O'Malley, imposed a puritanical discipline with a regimented dreariness the inflexibility of which reminded Maca of the rigorism ordained by the retreat at Saint Joseph's Monastery, except now there was no escaping it. In accepting his punishment and the forlornness endured away from home, he lost himself in the petty preoccupations of borstal routine and endeavoured to be well-behaved: cooperating with the teachers and the supervisory staff; complying with the house rules no matter how austere or unfair he perceived them to be; keeping his bed and clothes neat. Good behaviour, Father O'Malley had trumpeted, could result in early release back to the care of family and friends, and this became his goal. He and Mugsy quickly adapted to the diurnal rhythms of the place, alerting each other to the dangers of associating with certain types ("watch out for don fella he's fucken psycho, told me the other day to quit tootering the bleedy sax or he'd shove it where the sun don't shine"); mastering the art of survival by staying within groups, and if isolated when confronting one of these thugs by holding an averted gaze. In those first weeks he acquired a new friend, Johnny Cassidy, who hailed from Ballymurphy, a hail-fellow-well-met, finding himself riveted by his wise guy antics, and who turned out to be an inveterate provider of smut by bartering "necessities": two fags traded the use overnight of a skin magazine; five fags and a bar of chocolate got you a well thumbed copy of "Forever Amber", or some other such stimulating doorstopper for a week. The relief of a needful wank was greatly enhanced by such reading material. Demands of his mother that additional luxury items (especially cigarettes) be sent with the permitted monthly parcel quickly escalated ("madcap extravagance" she complained,

74

accommodatingly), accumulating a stash the better to service his growing avidity for erotica, as well as dole out favours.

One day intent on exchanging "necessities" with Johnny in the latrine, they were accosted by Father O'Malley as to the nature of the transaction being conducted between them. Being unforthcoming with a satisfactory explanation and a plausible reason for missing class, suddenly he saw stars cascade before his eyes in result of the unison upswing of the Principal's arms clashing their heads together. 'Don't let me catch you clodhoppers out of class again,' he reprimanded as the malefactors dizzyingly shambled off.

Remembering Deirdre's stated intent and focused ambition of going to Queen's University to study medicine, he diligently applied himself to his studies. Considering himself the shrewdest in the class, he was perplexed by the low standard of tuition, obviously adopted to suit the dolts who either could not or would not grasp the advantages of enlightenment: the scope and boundaries of geography; the warning lessons of history; the symmetry of English prose and verse; the symphonic mysteries of simple geometric and algebraic equations. All anathema to his moronic classmates. Desultory attention to learning, despite urgings from him, had seen Mugsy relegated to manual and technical classes such as woodwork and motor mechanics.

Gaelic football being the main sporting outlet for expending excess energy, all internees were encouraged to participate. A tyro at the game, Maca's versatile fluidity on the ball had him playing full-forward for the Hornets, the best team in the school league. A mixture of ambition and ruthlessness saw him make captain soon after. As captain, he drafted Mugsy into the team at right full-back. The lay teacher who coached the football league, Mr Goodall, was, to Maca's way of thinking, an obnoxious, aggressive butthead, constantly bellowing from the sideline boorish admonitions such as – "get the finger out ye wanker", and, "you must have been a grudge baby Maca. Somebody had it in for your father". A deep ditch filled with murky water covered in places with a slimy film of virescent scum ran the length of one side of the football pitch. Keeping a weather eye open, during a match one brumous wintry day, the saucered goal mouths a quagmire, he dekkoed the coach patrolling that sideline spouting the usual inane vulgarities. Gesturing to Mugsy to kick the pug-ball in that direction, in giving chase he deliberately mistimed a tackle and hurtled into the coach with a glancing blow upending him in the pestiferous dyke, water insects frantically pulsing to the edges. Feigning profuse apologies, barely able to keep a straight face, he offered his outstretched hand to the sodden teacher and pulled him out, the jostled victim of the prank spewing viscid ditch-water as he scrambled to the bank. Once again he found himself treated as a hero by his peers. Later that year, Mugsy's release on grounds of good behaviour after serving nine months encouraged him further in abiding by the rules.

In the fifteenth month of his incarceration, Maca's problems at the school began in earnest with the appointment of a new principal, the Reverend Pascal Kearney. The new administration was met with belligerent antipathy, but following installation of a television set and snooker table in the recreation room the boys, for the most part, grew positively enthusiastic. Although of saturnine features the burly shaven-headed Father Kearney seemed a man for the times; the removal of corporal punishment for infractions of the school rules being considered innovatory reformism, substituted by a penalty points system whereby an offender accruing three penalty points or more was deprived of his monthly pass for the cinema, a sporting event, or similar outing outside the school compound. Such ameliorative changes helped engender a more constructive response from most of the inmates, who applied themselves to daily work routines with a renewed energy. The new principal instilled a belief in the worth of each boy's contribution to the better management and running of the institution, leading to greater enjoyment of their time there. Taking a personal interest in the wellbeing of his charges, the cleric interviewed each of them in his study, enquiring about their hobbies and hopes for the future. He readily identified in Stephen a love of books, discerning in him a thirst for knowledge from any available source. Having stumbled on some naïf jottings secreted under his dormitory mattress he recognized an imaginative talent for writing, and wishing to encourage him in that endeavour secured for him a position in the school library. The new job proved a bed of roses compared to Maca's former duties peeling potatoes and general skivvying in the kitchen. It also permitted him more study time. The situation seemed to be improving for the better as Maca grew into adulthood. The first inkling he had that all was not above board was the night Father Kearney, with flashing torchlight in hand, inveigled him to leave his bed and join him in his study for discussion on the progress of his studies.

'You've settled well in the library Stephen. Enjoying your work?'

'Yeah! 'Tis not bad.'

'More time to pursue your reading and writing no doubt. What subject matter takes your fancy these days eh? Something of momentous interest I trust.'

'Nah! Not really. I do like jottin' down me thoughts on things Readin' helps.'

'Indeed. I've read some of your "thoughts on things", insights beyond your impressionable years I believe. I'd like to be of help, give you some direction on your reading material. I often think, walking into a library or bookshop, how disheartening it is to realize that in a lifetime it's not possible to read all the books stacked on the shelves. Not that one would necessarily want to do so of course. But even in a chosen subject, biography or history for instance, the amount of books available seems overwhelming. As Montaigne said "Even if all that has come down to us by report from the past should be true and known by someone, it would be less than nothing compared with what is unknown".'

'Who did ye say said that Father?'

'Michel de Montaigne, the great French essayist. How meagre is the knowledge of even the most curious of men, and how astounding is this world by comparison. And you are curious Stephen are you not. What are you reading at the moment?'

'Well I do like readin' history. And Father O'Flaherty got me hooked on poetry, especially Patrick Kavanagh's "The Great Hunger" which I find intriguin'. And a bit of politics as well. I feel like… reassured in discoverin' things like that there.'

'And learning from it hopefully. So what grabs your attention at the moment then?'

'The American War of Independence. 'Tis interestin' to see how events came about, how things change… democracy and that.'

'Great earth-shattering events Stephen, events that changed the course of history, the course of man's thinking. Good! Such reading gives us a better understanding of where we are today, helps us make the journey of man's all too brief sojourn in this distempered world. You've read Paradise Lost?

'Para what Father?'

'Milton's Paradise Lost.'

'Oh yeah! Bits of it anyway I think. Yeah! We did it at school.'

'Though written a hundred years and more before that great revolution, Milton's eschatological conflict between good and evil weighed as a paradigmatic example of the sublime on the pro-tagonists, all sides keen to claim him as one of their own. As I said I'd like to give you some counsel, merely to guide you along you see. Have you read anything by Thomas Paine?'

'No Sir. Never heard of him,' Maca said, befuddled by the Principal's euphuistic word power.

'Well now here's a book for you I hope… I know you'll find interesting – Paine's "The Rights of Man"', purred the cleric, moving imperceptibly closer behind him. 'It's one of the great books written on the theory of revolution and the establishment of the perfect system of state governance. It inspired those American insurgents you're reading about in their quest for independence from the English Crown. Influenced the French revolutionaries as well. It's my own personal copy. I know you'll take good care of it but… but don't leave it lying about for others to thumb through.'

On showing him the dedication in the book – "it was a gift from a former protégé of mine. Have a look at the graphic prints, aren't they wonderful" – the Principal firmly caressed his shoulders in what Maca accepted as a playful manner, yet was alerted to gather his loose pyjamas about him. Then sitting down beside him, Father Kearney slyly placed his hand on the inside of his thigh and proceeded to gently caress him there. The action so unnerved him, reminding him of the incident with Grumpy at Colaiste Ris, that he burst into a fit of coughing, tightened the drawstring and covered his privates with his hands.

'Off you go now Stephen. I hope you enjoy the read. Let me know what you think of it won't you. If you have any difficulty in understanding it you must have a wee chat with me. Okay?'

Over the ensuing weeks, Father Kearney introduced him, with a degree of urgency for the advancement of his education, to the works of the Greek philosophers – Socrates, Plato and Aristotle. The grooming techniques employed by the harassing cleric in his seduction also acquired an increasingly frenzied urgency, Maca often disconcertedly finding himself embraced and smothered in kisses to his neck and cheeks. During what resulted in being the last session of erudite instruction, he was dismayed to hear the clergyman laically expound the following admonition:

'Do you masturbate Stephen?'

'Eh!' he grunted, momentarily stuck for words.

'Do you pleasure yourself. Not such a hard question is it? Most boys your age do. So, do you?'

'Some… sometimes yeah. 'Tis only natural, holed up in a place like this.'

'Have you ever poked a girl?'

'How… how do ye mean Father?'

'Have you ever had sex with a girl?'

'No Father,' the afflictive loss of Deirdre suddenly flooding his uneasy thoughts. 'Only like… messin' about.'

'Messy business Stephen. Girls cause trouble, make nothing but trouble for boys your age. They bleed, the repulsive matter of all that bleeding. Every month, yuck! The church excludes them when in such an unclean state from entering the sacred grounds. And they are devious, de-vi-ous, getting pregnant in order to escape wretched circumstance. Consider the shame it brings on a family, a son forced into a shotgun wedding to… to someone he thinks he knows. And all this trouble created for want of a little affection.'

If Maca had learned anything from his mother down all the years of his young life it was that women were browbeaten, dominated by a patriarchal church and a political system that exonerated, most certainly ignored, male violence in the home. Alarmingly, he found himself pinned down under the weighty limbs of the principal, whose face, aflame with expectancy and insidious intent, now hovered in close contiguity to his own.

'Affection between man and boy is clean, virtuous, and classically Greek in its innocence Stephen, as no doubt you have gleaned from the reading material I gave you. Trust your instincts, don't fight the corporeity of this God given pleasure,' said the cleric, wheedling away at him, breathing heavily as his hand vigorously rubbed against Maca's crotch, but to his disappointment and chagrin finding his ward's penis remaining distinctly flaccid.

'Nah Father! I'd be too embarrassed. 'Tis not me thing,' he bleated in gut-wrenching astonishment.

'But you haven't tried it. 'Tis a comforting experience. Trust me.'

Panic-struck, he counted on an injection of crudeness into the vernacular to help him escape the clutches of the abusive cleric.

'I told ye Father, 'tis not me thing. Every wet dream I have has tits and fannies in it. I wank to the charms of female flesh. How could I go agin that?'

'No need to Stephen, just go with it. Let me take care of you. Let me teach you about life and its little pleasures. It'll be our secret.'

No longer able to bear such unctuous overtures, he realized a touch of the rough stuff would be necessary for escape. A tactical, forcibly directed knee to the principal's testicles proved conducive to loosening the vice-like embrace, delivering enhanced colour to the cleric's already ruddy complexion. Springing to his feet, relieved to be free of the predator's grip, he ran for the door, shouting as he exited:

'Piss off ye fucken headbanger!'

'You have not... not heard the last of this... MacAlindon,' said the cleric haltingly, an agonized scowl spreading across his rubicund face. 'I'll see to it you pay the price for your insolence... you ungrateful wretch.'

And pay for it he did, for thereafter he was subjected to derisive name-calling, venomous ridicule, and unwarranted punishment by Father Kearney. His inner strength enabled him accept with equanimity and a degree of amusement the clergyman's crabby antics, his sangfroid generating in the cleric apoplectic convulsions, spitting gall and invective in his direction at every opportunity. Maca was saddled with additional duties. A new task he enjoyed was mowing the extensive lawns, inclusive of the manicured layout at the principal's residence, affording him time with his own thoughts in the great outdoors. Alas, when carrying out the final cut of the season the blades of the lawn mower suddenly jammed, and on probing the cause he attempted to remove the twig that had blocked their rotation. On release, the spinning blades entrapped the index finger of his right hand at the top joint. Unable to reach the throttle or switch off the engine with his left hand, he shouted for help. Nobody came to the rescue. In agony, he watched as the powered blade gradually cut through the bone, and on hearing the whirr realized the tip of his finger had been amputated. Pinching the affected finger at the first knuckle to stem the flow of blood, he rushed to the residence and as he frantically booted the door heard sacred choral music loudly playing on a radio. It seemed an age before the door was opened to him by the buxom elderly maid who stood aghast, flushed in the face with copious tears streaming down her cheeks:

'The Holy Father's dead,' she wailed.

'I lost me finger, the top of me finger.'

'The Pope's – ye what? Mercy me what happened ye son?'

'Caught it in the mower.'

Observing the boy's injured hand, blood spurting from the severed joint, his mucky boots depositing cleats of mud on the doorsteps, she told him to stay outside – 'I'm only after polishing me floors' – as she pulled the cotton belt from her apron and tied it in a tourniquet at the base of the mangled finger to stanch the bleeding, then raced to telephone for help. Mr Goodall soon arrived in his car, Maca toppling into his arms in delayed shock. Brought to the local hospital, the wound was cauterized and bandaged. Three days later skin from his thigh was grafted over the exposed joint. In the routine atmosphere of his confinement everybody talked in hushed tones about the death of Pius X11, particularly with respect to his implacable opposition to communism. Back at the school, fascinated by the loss of his body part, he searched for and found the putrefying digit particle in a tuft of grass. Alone with his morbid thoughts, he ritually buried it in the graveyard at the entrance to the borstal compound, surrounded by tilted limestone gravestones roughened by weather, under shadowy trees bearing the meshed rachitic branches of the approaching winter.

His education continued apace although not of the high calibre he had expected to achieve at Colaiste Ris High. Some of the clerics and lay teachers, astutely aware of the gratuitous abuse he was subjected to, made strenuous efforts to alleviate its worst effects by indulging his aspirations and encouraging his voracity for knowledge and betterment. The elderly librarian, Father O'Flaherty, a cleric of gentle disposition who, tired of life, was anxious to pass on to an eager pupil energised by youthful innocence the lessons learned from long experience and disappointment, befriended him and had made a man of him. Recognizing Stephen's zealousness for making a career in the law, this virtuous cleric emboldened him to sit the university scholarship examination, willingly giving of his time in extra tuition, particularly Latin it being a compulsory subject for entrance to the faculty of law. What the old man taught him he absorbed voraciously and stalwartly applied himself to the task. By dint of hard work and natural aptitude, he successfully sat the examination and was awarded a scholarship place in the School of Law at Queen's University Belfast, the accomplishment assuaging his poisonously cynical view of the world. He served the full three years of his sentence in reform school, being released from the nightmare on Thursday, Christmas Eve, 1959.

5

Queen's University Belfast bore a worldly veneer of scholasticism, but under its attenuated skin reposed communal turmoil. Established in 1845 as a non-sectarian institution with the aim of attracting both Low Church Protestant and Catholic students, at the time it was associated with the simultaneously founded Queen's College Cork and Queen's College Galway as part of the Queen's University of Ireland specifically founded to encourage higher education for Catholics and Presbyterians as a counterpart to Trinity College Dublin, then a Protestant Anglican stronghold. Until recent times Catholics were under-represented at Queens.

Amid an agglomeration of buildings that make up the campus today the original castellated building, with its turrets, ogival arches and medieval fripperies, was designed by Charles Lanyon and comprises some resplendent architecture constructed of sunburst brick and sandstone quoins, the shallow tympanums at the entrance supporting a pastiche gothic balcony.

Stephen MacAlindon commenced his studies at the School of Law in this regal college in the autumn of 1960. The academic tranquillity he found there belied the sociopolitical strife lurking within its troubled oasis, caused in the main by the besieged mentality of the governing elite with their cabbalistic adherence to the traditions and praxis of the English Crown, an attachment long dispensed with by the Westminster Parliament. He had entered an intense world of sectarianism and bigotry. His first year there saw the awakening of his interest in politics. The election of John Fitzgerald Kennedy as the thirty fifth President of the United States of America, the first Roman Catholic to hold the honour, engendered in him and most of his nationalist contemporaries renewed pride in what it meant to be Catholic and Irish. Until this time he was not consciously alert to the political shenanigans applied in the governance of Northern Ireland by the political elite: the statutory protection of the manipulated electoral system; housing and employment discrimination applied on socioreligious grounds; identity aided by name and ghettoed address denoting, purportedly, political affiliation; denial of basic civil rights for all. The apparatus of government inflicted these indignities on a nationalist population caught within the gerrymandered boundaries of the artificial statelet, and on the ghettoised Protestant working class. The absence of the universal franchise of "one man one vote" for local council elections had not registered with him as a cause for concern in his youthful years, the electoral franchise for such elections being the property vote. And so the registered owner of one or more properties had one or more votes. This legislatively imposed systemic discrimination favoured the ascendancy class of Unionist Protestants who remained loyal to the English Crown, their obdurate war cries being – "What we have we hold" and "No surrender".

On freshman day when registering at Law School Maca took exception to the question "State your Religion" and had replied "None". He was advised that this was not acceptable on the grounds that, whilst one may hold atheistic or agnostic convictions, one is obligated to state the religion of one's birth. Despite the rebuff, the assistant registrar, a very stout man, florid-faced with bushy eyebrows, in pristine subfusc upon which the university crest was prominently displayed, proved accommodating:

'I'm afraid Mr MacAlindon the college bye-laws direct completion of the registration form in full. No question is to be left unanswered,' he inoffensively opined in a tone as dissonant as that of a gelded hog, pointing out the delinquent response.

'And this I have done Sir. I'm a non-believer.'

'Be that as it may Mr MacAlindon,' regarding him in a quizzical manner, 'one must then state the religion from which one has obviously lapsed, the religion of one's birth. You were born Roman Catholic were you not?'

'I was born into that cult yes, but I'm no longer a member of it. What relevance can it possibly have?'

'Oh indeed it is of major relevance. Is your presence here the result of your being awarded a scholarship?'

''Tis surely.'

'And is that scholarship not paid for by Her Majesty's treasury?'

'Yes yes I know all that,' he impatiently replied.

'Well then Mr MacAlindon, may I respectfully suggest you get over your scruples and complete the form as advised. After all, you do wish to avail of your scholarship funding do you not?'

'Of course. I earned it didn't I? But I don't see –'

'Mr MacAlindon... just put down Catholic with a capital C and that will be the end of the matter,' said the by now exasperated functionary, abetting him with a soupcon of contempt.

His prickly conscience was placated by the assistant registrar's overly polite but forthright manner and so he succumbed and did as enjoined by appending – formerly Catholic.

Eagerly adjusting to the easy-going ways of attendance at university, he found the freedom to come and go as he pleased inspiriting following the harsh years of his incarceration at the industrial school. Self-motivated in his studies, being sated in his hunger for knowledge, he avidly pursued his habit by reading anything and everything off the syllabus he could get his hands on: literary masterpieces; theoretic studies; history and biographies. During the Michaelmas term he met up with his old pal, Johnny Cassidy, now frontman in a traditional Irish band known as The Antagonists. He set out to organise a concert on campus with Johnny's band as leading act, a programme some of the nationalist sophomore students strongly discouraged him from pursuing.

After concert posters had been billed in the neighbourhood, the university's Vice-Chancellor sought a meeting with him in his study, a privilege for Maca, or so he anxiously contemplated.

'Come in Mr MacAlindon,' invited the official holding the heavy oak door ajar. Tentatively shuffling into the funereal space, he eyeballed the leather-bound tomes arranged thematically shelved floor-to-ceiling in the inglenook, the dark oak wainscoting and window embrasures and, cowed and awed in equal measure, sat as directed in the brown leather-covered chair in front of a paperless highly-polished desk.

'Now! how can I be of help to you?'

'You asked to see me Sir,' he nervily replied. 'About the concert.'

'Ah yes! Yes of course,' the Vice-Chancellor said impatiently, removing his glasses and staring at a corner of the ceiling as if studying the antics of a spider marshalling its web. 'This concert of yours, I want a word in your ear about the line-up you've engaged.'

''Twill be great craic altogether Sir,' he mustered, noting the man's starchy lupine appearance.

'No doubt no doubt. Extra-curricular activities we positively encourage, all work and no play and all that. But this band, the what you may call 'em –'

'The Antagonists.'

'Yes yes the Antagonists. I believe none of its members attend college?'

'So! Few of the other acts attend college either. They're musicians, amateur musicians for the most part.'

'But this particular band has –'

'A friend of mine is in the band Sir. I've seen them perform and they put on a helluva show, a great show altogether. 'Tis only for the bit of craic.'

'College doesn't necessarily see it that way Mr MacAlindon. The band is too controversial. Too divisive. It does –'

'Divisive? In what way too divisive Sir?'

'Well far be it from me to put a dampener on "the bit of craic" as you say. I am, however, reliably informed they rather stir things up with their rebel songs.'

'Ah Sir! 'Tis harmless stuff, nobody passes any remarks of the like of that there nowadays.'

'That's not what I'm led to believe I'm afraid. We've never had a band of such kind on campus, formal or informal. And there are those who will go to great lengths to ensure we never do.'

'But sure that's ridiculous altogether.'

'Ridiculous or not, I'm duty-bound to ask you to drop the band's participation,' he sternly pronounced, sitting forward in his chair, finger settling his glasses on his nose and staring fixedly at Maca.

'Ye can't be serious Sir?'

'I most certainly am serious Mr MacAlindon,' he said laconically, pointing his index finger at him. 'Very serious indeed.'

'And what, tell me, happens if I don't drop me friend's band?'

'I can't speak of the consequences for yourself, but it's not beyond the bounds of probability that the concert will be cancelled altogether, or, forced off campus.'

'I don't believe ye. Cancelled because of one act? '

'Because of this particular act. A fiddler or piper of Irish jigs has never been invited to perform at a function in Stormont or City Hall. It may be hard to believe, and college protocol does tend to take a more flexible view. But a band that spouts rebel republican songs is, I submit, taking it a step too far.'

'So we are to have a mono culture here is that it? Aren't there two cultures, two traditions on this island of ours and if this isn't reflected on campus what hope is there for future cooperation, future reconciliation.'

'The future no doubt will take care of itself. I must deal in the present. Regrettably or otherwise, that necessitates your acceding to my request. Do I make myself clear Mr MacAlindon?'

Feeling down in the dumps, having been mordantly alerted to the pessimistic sensitivity of the powers that be to all things Irish, he related the bad news to his friend Johnny, how the band had been unceremoniously excised from the concert programme at the insistence of the Vice Chancellor.

'N'ere to worry Maca, sure them lot up there are nothin' but a shower of blinkered dinosaurs. When was it any differ?'

'Ah! He was nice enough about it mind, but that's not the fucken point. I can't believe in this day and age that this kinda shit still goes on.'

'Nothin' can be done about it anyway Maca. Best leave well enough alone. The band will be doin' a gig in Dempsey's pub on the Saturday night amongst our own crowd and that'll help make up for it. Ye'll come along won't –'

'Why can't we do somethin' about it?' he earnestly asked.

'For fuck sake Maca, better give it amiss.'

'No seriously, we should do somethin' about it.'

'Like what?'

'Like organisin' a protest that's what. Why not?'

A noisy but poorly supported protest march, a lone drummer pounding out an unrelenting beat, took place on the streets abutting the university compound on the eve of the by now officially cancelled concert. The event became a catalyst for further polarization between the majority of students from a unionist background and the nationalists, the latter representing less than twenty two per cent of the student corpus at the time. The college upper-echelons, whether out of concern for security or in a display of unilateral authority, had prohibited the holding of any demonstration within one mile of campus, and had called on the Royal Ulster Constabulary to police the anticipated trouble. The loyalist anti-protesters, easily out-numbering and out-shouting the nationalist "upstarts" with catcalls of malign abuse, lined the pavements. On arrival at the college main entrance gate, Maca and his motley crew of about thirty five marchers found it closed and access blocked by a cordon of RUC constables. "This is an unlawful gathering. Please disperse" bellowed from a megaphone. He approached an officer whom he took to be in charge and pleaded to be allowed deliver to the Chancellor's office a petition signed by over two hundred students objecting to the enforced cancellation of the concert. Feeling a sharp pain in his abdomen, he realized he had been truncheoned by the officer concerned and then struck on the head as he slumped forward gasping for breath. Turning to seek shelter amongst his supporters, he watched agog as they came under attack from the anti-protesters who began hurling stones and other projectiles at the agitators as they scurried for cover. A mini riot ensued. The police, wielding black billyclubs, rushed the student protest lines and randomly lashed out baton blows to any part of a protester's anatomy that came within reach. Those students capable of fleeing the scene did so in terrorized be-wilderment whilst their injured colleagues, some of whom lay incapacitated on the ground, received further truncheon blows in retribution for failing to disband. Horrendous injuries were sustained by some of the unsuspecting marchers, Maca suffering a fractured skull which hospitalised him in The Royal Victoria for over a month, with a further three weeks spent recuperating at home. It was a black day in the annals of the college's history, yet proved a salient portent of the not too distant dismantling of the "Protestant State for a Protestant People", and the disbandment of the B Specials, and, in due course, the reconstitution of the Royal Ulster Constabulary. On his return to college he was counselled by the Dean of the School of Law to confine his activities to his studies – "look out for your own best interests" – as any further transgression of college regulations could well see him sent down. Such emollient cajolery, coupled with dire threats from other quarters, to persuade him to desist from political intrigues fell on deaf ears. Inspired by the embryonal, but exponential, civil rights movement in the southern states of America led by the iconic Martin Luther King, he resolved to be identified with, to be part of, and, where possible, to give lead support to, any protest against perceived injustice at this turbulent time.

*

What to do about Deirdre Desmond? How might he rekindle that relationship? Having diffidently observed her attendance at the School of Medicine, she agreeably engaged in a snooty sorority, he perceived her discreetest intent on distancing herself from him, and spent many sleepless nights rueing his predicament. Notwithstanding the years of estrangement, he still loved her, perhaps now more than ever, even more than during the angst ridden adolescent years when his thoughts of her were dominated by a puerile infatuation. Did she love him? He ardently needed to know, yet struggled to deal with the challenge of winning her back, the challenge circumstance had confronted him with: her mother's unyielding stance in forbidding any contact between them on pain of banishment from the family home should Deirdre succumb to temptation; his besmirched reputation as a convicted criminal (albeit imposed by a juvenile court) to all intents and purposes disbarring him from her polite society. During those early months at college she remained aloof, a few aimless minutes wasted in idle talk on casually bumping into each other, averting eye contact at gatherings in the usual student haunts. However, most telling was her failure to reply to his letters, pleadingly worded, left for her at the Medical faculty. He dared not telephone her home, though desperate to do so, conscious of the probable repercussions for her should her mother put two and two together. The one occasion he did make that call Deirdre answered and after a puzzling silence from her, during which he begged for a meeting, she pretended it was a wrong number and hung up on him. Even the services of her former escort, Frank Connolly, were denied him as earlier that year he had emigrated to Boston, Massachusetts. By the Hilary term, not having succeeded in making meaningful contact with her, out of the blue she nonchalantly sidled up to him in The Phoenix pub, he surmising she had had a drink or two too many:

'Hi Steve.'

'Hey!' he bleated, nervously cracking his knuckles.

'How's the law going?'

'Okay. And med. for you?'

'Great. I love it. Going at it hammer and tongs.'

'Glad to hear it Dede.' His use of the moniker seemed weightily out of place causing him to wince. 'Will ye sit for a minute?'

He made room for her to sit beside him on the low bar stool which she willingly did, pulling up her skirt as she did so revealing her tanned legs, her fingers elegantly bunched on her knees. It was not long before he felt the heat of her thigh against his own. Turning to look into her ice blue eyes, he said:

'Were ye away on holiday or what... ye've such a smashing tan?'

'Yeah! Kitzbuhel.'

'Where's that?'

'Austria. Skiing. You wouldn't believe how hot the sun was though the snow was thick on the ground. Amazing, just amazing. The contrast... sun and snow,' she enthused, shifting her knees a little closer.

'Skiing no less. Glad to see ye didn't break a leg anyway.'

'No thank God. One of the girls in the ski class did, took a nasty fall on the ice mountain that is the Hahnenkamm. Broke her leg. Shocking it was to see her in such terrible agony, her fibula bone jutting through her ski pants. Awful! And she in floods of tears.'

'She was lucky so to have ye on the spot. The medical expert,' he mumbled.

'Absolutely no expertise in that area. Not as yet anyhow. No! the paramedics were there like Speedy Gonzales. Whisked her off the slopes to hospital. When she got back to the hotel, her leg in plaster, the guys were round her like flies, buying her drink, constantly ribbing her about breaking a leg in sympathy.'

They nattered aimlessly of this and that.

'Sorry. Should have asked. Would ye like a drink?'

'No Steve, thanks. Think I'm over my quota. Just came over to say hello. See how you're getting on.'

His mind in turmoil, not knowing how to articulate what was uppermost in his thoughts (when could they get together? when would they make things right between them?), he watched her lustrous eyes shimmering in the diffused lighting of the pub, her toothy smile biting on her lower lip, those kissable lips, as she rose from their shared seating and adjusted her skirt with a downward tug of her beautiful hands.

'I'd better be getting back to the gang.' She gave him a coquettish grin as she unhurriedly turned away.

'Right. See ye around,' he said disconnectedly.

Nothing positive had come of this chance meeting, leaving him shamed by his crippling poltroonery, perplexed by the cretinous blunder in passing up the opportunity of asking her for a date. She had had the courage and the grace to approach him. He had lacked the nerve and the gallantry to broach the subject. A week later on seeing her in the company of a long haired hippy student, boisterously laughing and affecting not to notice him, he ate his heart out, envious of the *savoir faire* with which they strolled as turbid thoughts clouded his mind with emulous images of the good times they manifestly shared in each others company. It proved so debilitating that he took to his bed, his overweening mother, discerning the cause of his malaise ("having wimmin trouble are we? Get that hair cut and smarten yerself up") good-humouredly nursed him back to full health. Back at college, the stand off between them was again on the by now familiar track of edgy politeness. *A contrecœur*, he assiduously applied himself to his studies. Not conversant with the realizable standard needed to gain a pass mark in the examinations, he doggedly pored over with intuitive conviction his books on Roman Law, Constitutional History, Property Law, and Politics & Ethics, his grasp of which improved exponentially, aided by a formidable memory. Actively participating in the tutorial classes, being well prepared in the subject matter up for analysis, he impressed his tutors with his rapid progress, the excellence of his punditry, his masterful retention of legal tenets and reams of historical tracts. Consistently achieving A or B plus marks in his essays germinated in him a growing belief that a "First" was not beyond his capability. On the other hand, he continued to be racked by feelings of inadequacy when comparing himself to the well-heeled, privileged students in his year, an inferiority complex a characteristic shortcoming inhibiting him taking a more active part in the debating society, which was a virtual school for advocacy.

The Professor of Roman Law and Jurisprudence, Maurice Kielty, gave the class some sophistic advice before the summer break, encouraging them to travel and see a bit of the world, and not spend the holiday vegetating in factories in England. Such an annoyingly tactless suggestion may have resonated positively with the advantaged students in the class, but he was amongst those few who had little choice but to "earn a crust". The concession he made to the professor's quixotic admonition was to spend that summer out in the world having secured a seasonal job working in a sausage meat processing plant in Hamburg.

'There would appear to be some error Mr MacAlindon.'

'What? Did I forget to fill in somethin'? Where's the error?'

Maca's application for an Irish passport necessitated him in producing his birth certificate with a certified copy for retention by the passport office. Having queued patiently for upwards of an hour, he now found himself standing before a bungling official in the office of the Registrar of Births, Deaths and Marriages in City Hall.

'The name on your application does not accord with our

records,' said the official, uming and aahing as he fingered his glasses to the top of his nose.

'In what way do ye mean it doesn't accord?'

'Have you spoken to your mother about this?'

'No. Why would I trouble her when 'tis such a simple matter for to get it meself.'

The impolitic official, giving him an inquiring look, turned toward him the well thumbed ledger, indicating with a tobacco stained index finger the relevant entry, wherein he read:

Name -	Stephen Michael McMahon
Date of Birth –	2nd day of August 1942
Gender -	Male
Place of Birth -	The Cottage Hospital, City of Armagh
Mother -	Agnes Mary McMahon
Father -	Not known [Not Declared]

Raging against bureaucratic incompetence, he backed away from the counter in a cold sweat, the blood draining from his face. Peevishly determined to rectify matters, he again approached the official and with quivering voice said:

'There's got to be some… some kind of bureaucratic mistake. My name's MacAlindon.'

'I'm sorry Mr MacAlindon. Perhaps 'twould be best if you had a wee word with your mother.'

'If she is me mother?' he said under his breath as he stormed out.

When confronted by his bewildered challenge, his mother tearfully confirmed that he and his sisters were adoptees; that in his fifth year when fighting shy of attending school his father had had the children's surnames changed by deed poll. The passport office issued him with his first passport in his adopted name following production of a solicitor's letter verifying that being an adoptee the applicant from the age of four was officially named and titled in all matters legal and social as Stephen Michael MacAlindon. Escaping to Hamburg on a working holiday, he pushed all thoughts of his genealogy to one side.

*

The Deutsche Marks earned working in the meat plant more than compensated for the mind-numbing monotony of the job, enabling him save upwards of sixty per cent of his earnings, enough he calculated, to keep him flush in funds during his second year at Queens. He found it difficult to get to grips with the gutturally taxing German language, his indifferent efforts to master it being the cause of much hilarity among his fellow workers who were, in the main, Turkish migrants. The Turks, who kept very much to themselves, seemed well stocked with a plethora of pornographic magazines, the mulling over of which during breaks at work augmented his callow knowledge of erotica and the sins of the flesh. Yet certain of the explicit images (some depicting unsavoury stunts with animals) so repelled his impressionable mind that his unfledged body would break out in convulsive panic attacks, his agitated state eliciting whales of laughter from the Turks who berated him with 'you good Irish Catholic must confess de sins', and, 'you wank like Chinese man tonight eh' as they mimicked masturbatory actions with cartoonish buck teeth and screwed-up slanty eyes. On some days after work, most often a Friday, he would venture with his workmates to sleazy strip joints, no cover charge but the beer costing triple the normal hostelry price, an amusing but costly diversion. As soon as the dancers had stripped naked, the law obliged them to instantly cover their privates and stand motionless till the curtain dropped, which they invariably did to uproarious catcalls and mocking jeers of a rapacious audience. All such antics he found quirkily comical and soon tired of the long drawn out acts of plucky titillation. However, he did acquire a lifelong fetish for the female breast, and a taste for pilsner lager.

He heard on the grapevine about a young rock band from

Liverpool playing in the Kaiser Keller in the Reeperbahn red-light district known as Tony Sheridan and the Beat Brothers. Deciding to check them out, he stravaiged along the Reeperbahn that Friday evening and on finding the club stuck his head in before paying the entry charge and heard the reverberatory tones of a new kind of music blasted from huge amplifiers. Excited by the hubbub, he paid up and entered the cavernous space which was packed to the jack ribs by clued-in revellers. Before long, his senses were bowled over by a sound so different from the hackneyed stuff he was used to hearing pour out of Radio Luxemburg, like the be-bop-a Gene Vincent or the saccharine Ricky Nelson. Catching the eye of the oily haired lead guitarist who, by the look of him, was much younger than himself, he shouted above the din – "hot chording". On hearing the Irish accent, the guitarist pulled him up on stage, where Maca continued gyrating manically to the mimicked tempo of an air guitar. The guitarist was George Harrison, the other members of the Beat Brothers being John Lennon, Paul McCartney, and Pete Best on drums. During a break in the gig, he joined the band at the bar where he was able to cadge a beer, the drink free on the house for the performers. Swarms of sparky women cackled and cluttered around them.

'So where do ye hail from in Ireland?' asked Paul.

'Belfast. Have youse been over?'

'No. But my grandparents are from the auld sod.'

'My grandfather Jack was a Dubliner,' said John, hearing them talk of Ireland. 'He were born in 1858, I think it were '58, in… in. Fuck I can't remember, on the north side. I know he married my grandmother, Mary Maguire, in Liverpool. She were Irish an'all.'

'Don's a great sound I heard out there. Where did that come from,' Maca asked.

'It's the Irish in us. Me dad was a dab hand on the fiddle. Not a fucking book in the house but loads… loads of music. My mother were a one for the singing. Folk songs above all.'

'We make our own sound 'cause we don't have anything else,' said Paul. 'My dad was a band-leader. I used lie on the carpet in the front room as a kid listening to him on the piano. What ye say yer name was again?'

'MacAlindon, Stephen MacAlindon. Me pals call me Maca.'

'Fucking 'ell! With a name like that I'm probably more Irish meself,' said John.

'What brings ye to Hamburg Maca?' asked George.

'Jobbin' in a fucken meat plant for the summer.'

'Fuck! Boring shit like that.'

'Yeah! 'Twould bore the knickers off a nun. Glad to make the few bob though. Badly needed for me college expenses.'

'College boy then?'

'Yeah. Queens –'

'Paying your own way are ye?' asked Paul.

'Yeah.'

'Do ye play?' John inquired.

'What's that?' he asked, barely able to hear above the dinning babblement.

'An instrument. Do ye play an instrument?'

'Another beer anyone?' shouted Pete, a buxom blonde hanging out of him, her slender hand massaging his hirsute chest.

'I'm a dabster on the oul saxophone and the tin whistle, that's about it. And the harmonica, but sure anyone can toot the harmonica.'

'The sax. Listen, we're cutting a forty-five tomorrah –'

'A what?'

'We're doing a recording session with Tony in Friedrich-Ebert-Halle. You should come along. Come along and just hang out. Never know what might go down.'

'Tony's back on stage,' said Paul. 'Probably had a quickie outback. Bring along a bracer for him Pete.'

He followed the Beat Brothers back into the saturnalian revelry of the club proper and positioning himself out front of the stage listened to the mind-blowing music as they blasted away, Tony spewing out German lyrics in a passable German accent – "Mein herz ist bei dir nur" etcetera. It was only when Tony switched to English lyrics that Maca recognised the traditional Scottish tune - "My Bonnie Lies Over the Ocean". What a sassy gig, the sound a blowout for his ears, the women a fillip for his eyes, he airily mused as he found himself jostled back and forth in the free-for-all. In the sweltering humidity of the middle dance floor, swamped by a throng of coruscant women insouciantly gyrating to the ear splitting sound, some flaunting glistening orbs that threatened to escape the sweat soaked material of flimsy bodices, he inhaled a deep drag from a slim cigarette proffered him by a blackamoor sylph dancing in a maenadic-like frenzy. The cigarette left a caustic taste in his mouth, like the taste of charred tea leaves he experimented with as a kid. Unmindful of any infernal comm-ination, he partook of another drag, then another, before passing it back, all the while letting her dewy-eyed pools of prurient lust enrapture him. Inspirited by the phantasmagoric spectacle, he sprouted an erection, an arousal mindlessly unrelenting on seeking out the relief of Adrasteia's nursing hand. A bold hand licentiously groped him, another lecherously caressed the cheeks of his arse, a finger lewdly idling at his bumhole, as he continued to rock, his face betraying raw surprise, his brain addled. If their play made free with his body, he weighed up, he would return the compli-ment. Mounds of soft pliant flesh at his fingertips sent electrifying sensations racing through his veins in a sensual reverie. With heart-pounding foolhardiness, he found himself in blissful nirvana.

Next day he arrived at Friedrich-Ebert-Halle, clear-headed but with only a hazy half-memory of how he got there, dressed in the same clothes, his flushed face sporting black stubble. The stinging rogue between his legs, afflicted with a chafed prepuce, wired his brain, post-facto, that a good night was had. Yet he remained, in mind, a virgin, not having consciously sunk his pecker into the luscious entrammeling folds of the Edenic temptress. If he had done so, he had no sensible image of it. An irrational disgust of miscegenation should have heightened his awareness had he unloaded into the quim of the blackamoor sylph, never having spoken to, let alone been with, a Negress before. He simply could not remember.

'You enjoyed yourself last night?' said George.

'Christ 'twas great. What a gig. Blew me brains out,' he replied gingerly.

'Your brain? Ye must keep it in your pants so. Here,' said George, handing him a saxophone, 'have a tootle on that but keep out of John's way for now. He's in one of his moods.'

'What's the beef then? John said somethin' about a recording session.'

'Yeah! We're cutting a demo forty-five backing Tony on "Bonnie". See what ye can do. Back home we had a sax accompaniment. You'd never know, Bert might slot ye in.'

He had soaked up the sound the Beat Brothers made at the club, and while practise playing became a man inspired. It was not long before he sought out George with his ideas for joining in with a solo intro and a triple-time note playing the chorus. John and Bert on hearing how it blended in rejected the solo intro but agreed the triple-time in the repetitive chorus. The seven inch forty-five vinyl disc was cut after a further two takes, Kaempfert so impressed by his playing that he arranged for him to return on Monday for the recording of the B-side – "When the Saints Go Marching In".

'I have marked the places ver I tink you join in,' Kaempfert said on handing him the sheet music.

'I can't read that!'

'Vy not you von't read that?'

'I haven't a clue how to read sheet music. Not a clue. No need to anyway, I know the tune inside out.'

'Inside out?'

'Off by heart.'

'Ah! By heart ja.'

That Monday was the only day he went missing from work at the meat plant. It proved worth while for he played an even more weighty backing role than in the previous recording.

The following Saturday evening he hunted in vain for his dewy-eyed blackamoor sylph at the Kaiser Keller and the sleazy joints on the Reeperbahn, in the hope that she would fill in the memory gaps of their night of debauchery; perhaps pave the way to consummation of the sexual act when his eyes were wide open, his sensibilities fully alert. Intent, no matter what, on knowingly losing his virginity, he had recourse to the services of a blonde prostitute, Olga, who brought him to a small squalid hotel room. She quickly established her credentials as a genuine blonde on speedy removal of her panties, and her professional prowess by cutting emotionless capers. He self-consciously lost his virginity within ten minutes of meeting her. By way of testimonial, she divested him of a hefty chunk of that weeks wages. He emerged from this giddying gratification with a lifelong passion for the feel of a woman's skin.

*

Come October, he was high-flying on his return to Queens having achieved a "First in Class" on aggregated marks in the examinations; confidently bumming his chat about his summer in Germany, playing-down the plant job and playing-up his super-numerary role on the Tony Sheridan and the Beat Brothers "My Bonnie" record, a copy of the single offered in proof of performance to anyone who cared to listen. Those who did listen seemed unimpressed, most being more into American artists such as Buddy Holly, Paul Anka, The Everly Brothers and the king of rock, Elvis Presley. It would be another two years before the release of The Beatles debut single "Love Me Do", too late to salve Maca's bruised ego. To ease his disenchantment he coughed up a few quid from his savings to his mother to help compose her peace of mind.

The complacency he now basked in at college was in stark contrast to the general feelings of inadequacy he had endured in his first year. A reflective self-analysis ably demonstrated that the problem then had been his lack of self-esteem, he having little sense of self-worth. Now he realized that no one really cared about his religion, his accent, his time at reform school, his being at university on a scholarship. Those he counted as friends and acquaintances, when not caught up in their own petty foibles and inflated pretensions, seemed more interested in his bravura rebelliousness. Enrolling in the Law Faculty Debating Society, his first participation in open debate saw him ad-lib in favour of the motion "That this House Supports the Legalizing of Marijuana". In addition to high-lighting the medicinal benefits of the drug, his winning quip – "taking a drink doesn't make a man an alcoholic so a man who smokes grass is not *a priori* a drug addict" – brought about bouts of raucous cheering and stamping of feet. He quickly got to grips with the art of public speaking.

Having been cerebrally astonished by the ideals of Thomas Paine's "The Rights of Man", and Theobald Wolfe Tone's "Argument on Behalf of the Catholics of Ireland", on November 7 he helped establish with an egalitarian group of friends the QUB Society of United Irishmen, adopting the United Irishmen's symbol of 1791 (the Harp without Crown) and its logo "EQUALITY – IT IS NEW STRUNG AND SHALL BE HEARD". Later he persuaded the Law Faculty Debating Society to put before the house on November 22 the motion – "That no reform of the Governance of Northern Ireland is just which does not include Irishmen of every religious persuasion". At the debate he full-mouthed to rhythmic applause: "We are not a free people. Where is the humanity, the civic spirit, in our governance? On the one side the oppressed nationalists seek justice and fair play. On the other the affrighted loyalists seek to hold what they have, however wrongfully gained and maintained.

With such inherited distrust between our communities we make each other miserable. We… we in this Society demand a fair deal for all – Protestant, Catholic and Dissenter."

These and similar sentiments were tirelessly espoused by the members, helping the society recruit one of the largest member-ships in college, inclusive of a modicum of liberal thinking Protestants. Among nationalists, it quickly became the trendiest grouping at the university. Notwithstanding some unpleasantly strident behaviour at campus meetings, and some ignominious outbursts of inciteful bigotry during debates, the college auth-orities took a sanguine view of events and remained tolerant of the outcome provided the activities were confined to bluster and debate and did not spill over into organised protest; did not threaten, as they saw it, to destabilize the college fraternity.

In the New Year the Society, at Maca's instigation, invited Patrick Kavanagh to give a reading cum lecture at the university. The poet was in superlative form, dispensing barbed comments on the revered poets Longfellow and Yeats and talking-up the stature of Auden, Ginsberg and Spender. All of which was raucously received by a packed lecture hall. At the reception afterwards, Maca and many others were captivated on making closer acquaintance with the "Great Man", riveted by his gravelly voice in the telling of humorous anecdotes. The poet, visibly tiring of the incessancy of the banal questioning by the students, out of the blue threw his whiskey glass at the wall, shattering it, and bellowed – 'I'm doing no more talking till I'm paid.'

In later years he would look back on these "drifting moments" with sentimental hankering, believing his sophomore year to be the high point in his life: finding himself well thought of by his tutors and well liked by his fellow students, some of whom saw in him a talent for leadership; his steadily adapting to the challenges of life and progressing as a high achiever in his studies. It was the year he became a man, the year he began believing in himself and the contribution he hoped to make to society. It was the year of the flame.

Throughout what turned out to be his last year at university, he often caught a glimpse of Deirdre in the throng at student gatherings, or sighted her at the back of the hall during college debates, and found his heart warm-blooded with edgy excitement. There were also painfully surreal times as he watched her in close communion with other men, seemingly oblivious to his very existence. She continued to have a hold over his affections which he could neither dismiss nor advance. Forlorn feelings continued to gnaw at him. Once, and only for a few seconds, he held her under a steady gaze and saw, or thought he saw, a fiery ache in her ice blue eyes as she fixed an immobile stare right back at him. Yet she remained frosty and aloof. So bamboozled was he by her seeming fickleness, he decided to act coolness personified where she was concerned, the mantra – "if she wants to be with me she knows where to find me" parroting in his unsophisticated mind.

Part 11

6

The family's immiserated circumstances did not permit Maca to progress his studies at university, obliging him to drop out at the end of second year without the benefit of a diploma. His father could no longer work being incapacitated by a virulently progressive atrophy; his mother, who bore her hypochondrias like a social crutch, by now chrono-phobic yet obliged to peg away at her job as a cook in Clonard monastery; his older sister Eileen insouciantly plying herself as an accounts clerk at uncle Peter's coal yard; and his younger sister Monica at least showing nascent signs of enterprise and ingenuity in her final year at school. All of which meant he could no longer arrogate to himself the time to profligately be himself. The goal he had set of graduating *cum laude* slipped away irremediably. He was on the market for a job, any job. Despite the advantage of a makeshift education in the law, gainful employment proved impossible to come by. He spent almost all of the summer months in Dempsey's public house, the duties of barman familiar to him following on years of odd work there during his school and college days. Though cheerily engaged by the camaraderie of the pub scene, including Eddie Atkinson and other Protestant neighbours who revelled in the Saturday night music sessions, it offered little advancement of betterment. He detested the washing of empty stout and beer bottles in the lead-lined tanks outback and crating and readying them for reuse, particularly after a night's heavy frost necessitating the breaking up of solid ice lids in the tanks. Consequently, he scouted the usual billboards for opportunities and bombarded local solicitor's offices and government agencies with applications for work as a clerk, having bowdlerized his *curriculum vitae* by dropping any reference to his time at reform school. All to no avail. His mother pressed him to join Eileen at his uncles' coal yard:

'Quit yer faffin' about lookin' for a swanky job and go ask Peter to let ye stand in yer father's boots at the yard.'

'I don't want to work in the bleedy coal yard.'

''Twas good enough for yer father down all the years. He'd still be workin' if a twist of fate hadn't struck him down with that accursed multiple scler... sclerosis. He made a daycent livin' out of it. And Eileen's happy there. If ye got yer foot in the door ye might get a share in the business.'

'That's just what I'm afraid of. If I go work for uncle Peter I'll be stuck there for the rest of me days. 'Tis not what I want.'

'Och ye can't see any further than the end of yer nose. Away on with ye. Why can't ye make a start and if somethin' better turns up... well that's the time to be choosy.'

Eventually he secured a position as a post-sorter with the Royal Mail.

His time at Queens had radicalised his political thinking, engendering in him a keen awareness of the government imposed politico-religious discrimination endemic in the legislated for gerrymandering of electoral districts by concentrating the nationalist population in overlarge wards with fewer electoral seats; restricting the vote to owner occupiers; and by maintaining the property plural vote. This state empowered sectarianism was adroitly defended by Northern Ireland's Prime Minister, Sir James Craig, when he told the gerrymandered parliament in Stormont – "... I have always said I am an Orangeman first and a politician and a member of this parliament afterwards... all I boast is that we are a Protestant parliament and a Protestant state". Believing it was time for change, the status quo no longer sustainable, his dissident thinking more and more thrust him into the realm of seeking peaceful reform, spurred on by the bigoted intimidation he endured at the hands of some of his fellow workers who taunted him for being a "taig" and a Sinn Fein fellow-traveller.

*

On a dull, dark, dank Saturday evening, while partaking of after work drinks in the Pepper Canister Bar with his post office colleagues, tobacco smoke enveloping all in a blue haze, amid flimflammery bluster an altercation broke out:

'We must get reform, "One Man One Vote",' Maca said bullishly, taking a swill from his pint of lager.

'Fat fucken chance,' said Willy with a curl of the lip, a man intolerant of opinions other than his own.

'Why am I one of the disenfranchised? Tell me that now.'

'Too bad aboutcha. You're a fucken taig that's why. You're lucky to have a fucken job like that there.'

'Yeah right. Youse shitheads keep all the good jobs for yerselves. Like at the shipyard, closed shop for the likes of me and my father before me. Needn't bother even applying.'

'I don't have the vote,' interjected Alistair (a Presbyterian). 'It's the property vote. You well know that company director's, the big farmers and the big knobs have six votes. Six fucken votes! 'Tis nothin' but a frame-up by the haves against the have-nots. You're not a ratepayer Maca, that's why you, just like the rest of us, have no vote.'

'Jefferson insisted that all men have unalienable rights and "that to secure these rights, governments are instituted among men, derivin' their just powers from the consent of the governed"', he quoted. 'I work just as hard as anyone else like ye know. Yer in –'

'Jefferson kept slaves for fuck sake,' shouted Willy. 'An unpaid workforce. Only the toffs had the vote.'

'– in the same boat Alistair. As workers why do we put up with it? Why let the fucken bosses get away with it. Look what Castro and Guevara did in Cuba. Got the people behind them and forced Batista and his U.S. unscrupulous backers out. Sure! Batista cleaned out the coffers and gold reserves leavin' the country bankrupt. But the people were glad to see the back of him, glad to be free of big business corruption, free from –'

'They're fucken communists,' said Willy, 'no religion allowed in them there countries.'

'– profiteering capitalism. Maybe dons a good thing Willy,' continued a by now belligerent Maca. 'Religion's a flag of convenience used by the toffs and their henchmen in Stormont to oppress the workers of all political hues. All workers should support the Socialist Workers or Labour Party or the like. We should unite, as the United Irishmen did two hundred years ago, and overthrow the bosses, break up the political cliques and cabals.'

'Don't make me spit. With talk the like of that there you'll be lucky not to have your fucken head kicked in. Bad enough you're being a taig without being a fucken red taig,' Willy bellowed idiomatically.

'With a fucken attitude like that there things will never change. I know we catholics have a lot further to climb than yee prods, but all workers are in the same boat and all boats rise with the tide. The tide now ebbs and flows for change.'

'And what then? Youse pope-heads take our jobs. There ain't enough jobs to go round,' said Willy, his face muscles running riot in apoplectic raving.

'Looka here now,' Maca countered, 'there's upwards of seventy per cent unemployment in the nationalist ghettos. Thirty per cent, mebbe more, in loyalist estates. If workers don't unite for reform, unite to make life better for all by demandin' basic civil rights, the like of one man one vote, jobs for all, there'll be the mother an' father of a flare-up. The anger against institutionalized discrimination is palpable, and spreadin' fast. People with nothin' to lose will lose nothin' by generatin' chaos, by crashin' out of the ghettos demandin' their… fightin' for their rights. Fear… fear for the safety of their wives and families is all that's keepin' the lid tightly clamped on the cesspot of resentments. But believe you me don pot is about to blow. 'Tis so fucken red-hot 'tis about to spew its venom.'

'Fuck off Maca. I keep me head down and get on with me work. Youse pope-heads had better do the same or 'twill be taigs out at the plant,' retaliated Willy with bully boy motility.

'Ease off there now lads,' said Alistair, 'we're not goin' to solve the world's problems with that sorta talk. Let's have another pint and let -'

'No one's talkin' about the world's problems Alistair,' blustered Maca. 'We're talkin' about the problems faced every day, year in year out, in this backwater of ours.'

'I've a wife and five bairns to look after,' Willy spluttered on. 'We take care of our own and fuck the rest. Let them emigrate. Let the taigs fuck off to the Free State an' see if they can get jobs there.'

The squabbling seemed to be interminable.

'Right ye are Willy, have it yer way. I'm away to splash the boots,' he said, rising from the bar stool, hacked off by the argy-bargy and Willy's casuistical bigotry. 'Yer twist Alistair. Mine's a pint of Harp with a shot of lime.'

Standing at the urinal in the tenebrous outhouse massaging the last droplets from his semi-tumescent prick, shallow breathing in a futile attempt to protect his lungs from the ordure-stink of the toilets, he was manhandled from behind, his jacket pushed over his head, a blow to the side of his face felling him to the wet tiled floor. Under a farrago of verbal abuse, kicks from heavy work-boots assailed his head and torso. Stupefied, he managed to crawl into one of the miasmic cubicles, a final boot in the testicles causing him to pass out in shock. On hearing Alistair call out his name he came round in agonising pain.

'What's keepin' ye in there Maca? Will I get a shovel and dig ye out. Your pint's gone flat man. What the fuck! What... what happened ye? For chrissake, look at the state of ye.'

'I was laid into, no doubt by some of yer righteous brothers.'

'Here, give us yer hand there.'

Alistair helped him up on his gelatinous legs and stood him before a handbasin surmounted by a matted cracked mirror where, on languidly checking out his fissured reflection, he doused himself with cold water, washed off spouts of nasal blood and tentatively fingered the erupting shiner that was rapidly closing his left eye. Sickened by the superficialities of the job's daily routines, he grumbled through a clenched mouth of loosed teeth, his life now on nodding terms with violence: 'Fuck Her Majesty's job. I'm headin' for the States to keep me appointment with destiny.'

*

The assassination of John Fitzgerald Kennedy on the one thousandth day of his presidency had been the catalyst for him to take a more profound interest in things American: its culture of freedom and justice for all; its promise of prosperity for those willing and able to work; the opportunities it held out for the fulfilment of hope. Like most people he remembered exactly where he was when he heard the tragic news of Kennedy's death. Having cycled that evening to meet with some of his former college pals at Dempsey's pub where Johnny Cassidy was fronting a gig of traditional music and song, he had noticed people gathered in clusters on the streets, deep in conversation with tired-looking worried faces, and wondered what the hullabaloo was about. On arrival at the pub, he came across Deirdre standing outside with some of her girlfriends, all in floods of tears, causing him even more bafflement. Then on learning the reason behind the consternation he was disconcerted at not being aware till that moment of the great calamity that had been visited upon the free world. Such was his guileless anxiety about his feelings for Deirdre, he was slow to take cognizance of the significance of the tragic event, being apprehensive about her reaction to his sideburns which he had allowed grow, Elvis style. Having dared hope she would be there he counted on impressing her with his modish machismo

112

and trendy gear of drainpipe trousers and winkle-picker cleated ankle boots. Cassidy's gig proved a damp squib, nobody listening to the music, his self-conscious endeavour to rekindle the relationship with Deirdre falling flat, finding her uncommunicative and seemingly disappointed in him for his lack of, what she said was, gravitas. What the fuck does that mean, he brooded. She went home early with her friends leaving him emotionally adrift.

It seemed as if everyone, everywhere, that night talked of the inexorable change that would surely overtake world events, conspiracy theories abounding, including the possibility of an imminent nuclear attack by the Soviet Union. Tossing and turning in bed unable, perhaps unwilling, to sleep, he took up his earphones and tuned to the American Forces Network on his crystal set and through the crackly static listened to *vox pop* which prompted his absorption of the intensity of the moment leaving him in a fever of spiritual fatigue. Next morning he bought his first daily newspaper, scoured the pages, eager to grasp an understanding of the world outside his own limiting enclave, the reports in which shook him out of his scornful indifference to international politics. Kennedy's brief tenure in the White House was written of as a "Camelot"; standing up to Khrushchev during the Cuban missile crisis his "finest hour"; America's seemingly unrealizable endeavour to put a man on the moon by the end of the decade as achievable; his fight on Capitol Hill to grant universal suffrage to all citizens irrespective of colour or creed as an empirical duty; his eloquent espousal of fulfilling the rights proclaimed in the Declaration of Independence, quoting Thomas Jefferson's rousing opening words – "that all Men are created equal, that they are endowed by their Creator with certain unalienable rights, that among these are Life, Liberty and the pursuit of Happiness". Non-stop coverage of the unfolding drama played out on television screens around the globe. Like most working class homes, the MacAlindon's did not possess a television obliging him to satisfy his avid curiosity by standing with others on the street pavement watching the silent black-and-white flickering pictures in a TV rental shop, all screens tuned to the BBC. The images relayed of his widow Jackie aboard Air Force One standing a few feet away from the sheeny metalled coffin encasing her husband's remains, her profile torturously empty, she still wearing the suit bespattered with his lifeblood throughout the constitutional protocol of the swearing in of the thirty sixth President of the United States fomented a susurrus of empathetic agonizing amongst the gathering. Later that night he tuned the crystal set to the BBC Home Service and heard for the first time the mellifluous voice of Alistair Cooke reading his "Letter from America", which so deeply registered in his susceptible mind that he wrote down the broadcaster's concluding words – "This charming, complicated, subtle and greatly intelligent man, whom the Western World was proud to call its leader, appeared for a split second in the telescopic sight of a maniac's rifle. And he was snuffed out. In that moment, all the decent grief of a Nation was taunted and outraged. So that along with the sorrow, there is a desperate and howling note over the land. We may pray on our knees, but when we get up from them, we cry with the poet – Do not go gentle into that good night / Rage, rage against the dying of the light". So taken was he by Cooke's laconic style, thereafter he made every effort to tune in to the weekly broadcast. The Star-Spangled Banner became his favourite national anthem, evoking, every time he heard it, day-dreams about what life for him could be like in that New World. The unalterable reality of these cataclysmic events garnered in him an incipient awareness of his own place in the world, an awareness previously beyond his cares: his antipathetic dissatisfaction with life and where the future might take him; the unanchoring of his roots knowing his father and mother were not his natural parents, Eileen and Monica not his biological sisters; the inscrutable nature of his relationship with Deirdre, his love for her unrequited; the

114

unenviable prospect of holding down a dead-letter job with the Royal Mail; the sense of foreboding that now pervaded his every thought. Such sordid and illiberal circumstances that tangentially infested his consciousness, rendering him unhappy with his lot, now determined him to go to the United States of America as soon as the opportunity presented itself. He would strike out for a new life; escape the clutches of mediocrity. Having intimated to his mother his intention of doing so, she berated him for his selfishness – "Twill kill yer father. He wants ye to have a wee chat with Peter.' Monica kindly advised – 'Do what you think best.'

Following on from the fracas in the Pepper Canister Bar, he wrote his old frenemy Frank Connolly in Boston pleading with him to get him a job doing anything: gardening, painting houses, working building sites, hotel or restaurant waiter, pub barman; anything to get his foot on the ladder of opportunity. Frank's response, received two weeks later, was a hearty – Come on over Maca – that he could get him a job in an Irish owned pub and that he would be better able to suss-out other work availability while holding down a job; he himself working in Morgan Stanley Investment Bank his letter boasted; and there appeared to be oodles of advertisements for office work.

*

Arriving in Boston on March 5, 1964, he set up camp in Frank's apartment, and gratefully settled down to the mundane routine of work as a barman in Tiernans on Hanover Street. Despite having been infected by his father's mischievous carping about "yanks" ("everything but everything is bigger and better over there – they think we still keep chickens and pigs in the tigh"), he was agreeably taken aback by the opinionated Bostonians who effortlessly expounded on any given subject matter. To be in Boston evinced in him the self-possession of being part of the diasporic spread of Irish expatriates. Quickly discovering his sense of self, what it is to be Irish and proud of it, he determined to rip inferiority from his persona. For the first time in his life his place of birth and background was not like a millstone round his neck. To speak with self-assurance in the accent of his nurturing neighbourhood and, although not always fully understood, to be admired and the butt of ludic and casual amusement because of his Irish brogue, rather than the object of a put-down, filled him with a newfound confidence, a confidence he, before long, realized was not misplaced. Every so often he would recall, with cringing resentment, his only visit to London looking for work; how he had found himself schizophrenically camouflaging his brogue because of the baggage of an inferiority complex, and the farcicality on hearing his voice in mimicry of whomever he was talking with; how he had felt a stranger to himself in his struggle to overcome the handicap of being a second class subject in his part of Her Majesty's United Kingdom. Experiencing the Massachusetts elevatory reality check now taught him to respect himself, grow to understand himself, and learn to love himself, realizing he had spent his youth in Belfast in existential extremity yet somehow had never lost his sense of humour. While working in Tiernans' pub, he was many-a-time counselled by well meaning prying customers to not waste his college education on a dead end grind, encouraging him to seek work in some of the law offices or financial institutions downtown. Subsequent to a few unavailing job interviews (not having fully overcome his insecurities), one day Frank thrust under his nose an advertisement in the Business Section of The Boston Globe seeking support staff in the Settlements Division at Lehman Brothers Bank:

'I'm thinkin' of applying myself,' said Frank. 'I'm stuck in Foreign Exchange at Morgan Stanley which is boring as fucking hell. All day pushin' piles of paperwork from A to B.'

'Would I be able for the job do ye think Frank? I mean, what the fuck do I know about Futures and Options?'

'About as much as a pig knows about a fucken holiday I guess.'

'Let's say I get the job, what do ye think'll happen?'

'Look, they'll train ye… You'll be back-room support. Or maybe a runner, not brokering. They won't throw you in the deep end. I suppose the job will involve a lot of shovelling and bundling of paper about the place too. Ah! maybe I'm better off where I am. At the least I know what I'm doin' at Morgan Stanley. Unless of course the dough's better.'

'Do ye mind me askin' Frank what sort of dough yer on?'

'Four hundred greenbacks a month give or take –'

'Phew! Dons twice as much as I'm on in Tiernans, nearly three times as much as I got paid at the Royal Mail. Fuck! Some dosh.'

'This is where it's at Maca. How do ye think I can afford the wheels?'

'Don fucken heapa junk outside the door. Who needs a jalopy in the city?'

'Great for pullin' the broads. Obligatory gear really.'

A stinging envy rushed through his brain. 'Think I'll go for it!'

'Nothin' to lose Maca. Worth a shot.'

'My referees are of fuck all use. Suppose ye couldn't do me a reference on Morgan Stanley paper? Whatya say…'twould be bound to help me along don't ye think.'

Having decided to stop selling himself short by upgrading his qualifications, he applied for the job. With protean conviction, he was up for it. Called for interview, he arrived at Lehman Brothers on Franklin Street in newly acquired spiffy attire (all purchased in Filene's Basement Bargains) of sober dark grey suit, white shirt with double cuffs fastened by black plastic cuff hooks (he had overlooked buying proper cuff links), paisley patterned dark red and green tie, and highly polished black leather shoes, the right-foot shoe hacking at his ankle bone (he dared not limp). Having been presented with an identity pass on a lanyard, he was escorted to the elevator by a loquacious platinum blonde of indeterminate age with dewlaps hanging from her invisible jaw bone, ginormous oscillating breasts that roused in him dark nooky thoughts, and a stratumal layer of gelatinous flesh quivering atop her hypertrophic buttocks (what a grotesque masquerade of American nutritional values he mused). Tagging along behind her he chirpily eyeballed the crude peristaltic lollops of her bum-cheeks; the disinfected, medicinal redolence of a hospital ward that wafted about her causing him to hold his breath momentarily.

'Mr Bart Reynolds will meet you on the fourteenth floor. You'll first be required to undergo an IQ test with –'

'A what test?'

'An intelligence quotient test. Oh not to worry we all go through it. It's just a simple measurement to rate your intelligence level.'

'I'll try not to. Never heard of such a test.'

'You're not a member of Mensa then?' she said with a scrofulous look.

'Mensa?' (table he mentally delatinised). 'What? Like the Round Table or some sort of club. No. I'm not a member of any club.'

'Like Groucho Marx. You wouldn't join a club that would take you in as a member,' cackled the lardass, her high cheeks flushed pink, as the elevator door opened. 'Good luck,' she barked with a parodic smile, her whole demeanour less than prepossessing.

Pressing button fourteen he noted there was no button thirteen, and reasoned either the architect, or, the project manager at Lehman Brothers suffered a severe case of triskaidekaphobia. On exiting the elevator he was taken aback on meeting Bart Reynolds whose endoskeletal physiognomy of protruding cranial bones seemed about to burst through his alopecia skin. The initial sessions of the IQ test were a doddle: completing various conundrums; filling in missing links between the integers; picking up the thread in logarithmic patterns; calculating mathematical equations. What turned out to be the final session flummoxed him when Reynolds placed before him three sheets of white paper stained with inkblots, requiring him to select and tick on each page one box from four possible answers in identifying the image represented, the choice of given answers being:

1. A butterfly [ ]   2. A part of my body [ ]
3. A phoenix rising from the ashes [ ] 4. An ink blot [ ]

Each image looked very much like an inkblot to him, yet he believed that could hardly be right, otherwise why the range of answers. Casting his analytical gaze over the three sheets, he marked the first image –A phoenix rising from the ashes [x]. On scrutinizing the second image it looked very much like the first one but he decided to mark it as –A butterfly [x]. The third image in-tractably failed to metamorphose from an inkblot into anything his imagination could summon up, causing him to lose patience with the test. What did it mean? What did it signify? His inclination was to refuse to complete this last image, but on hearing Mr Reynolds re-enter the office he hastily marked it –A part of my body[x]. Hence he had selected all possible answers except the one he initially believed the images to represent. Reynolds requested him to take a seat outside and await the result of the test. Too agitated to sit down, he strolled back and forth along the open plan floor, hands in pockets, slyly watching the bank's advance guard of female clerks and secretaries, some demurely eyeing him up, and spotting one or two very pretty ones, he ogled them in turn. This most definitely is the place I'd like to work, he told himself, impelling him to perform at his sharpest.

'Mr MacAlindon. Come along to my office please,' Reynolds gestured.

He was aware of the fixed lanceolate gaze of a pretty elf-like oriental girl follow him as he entered Reynolds office.

'Fairly good Mr MacAlindon. Fairly good.'

'Those ink thingamies did for me though. What's that all about?'

'Ah! The Rorschach test, don't trouble yourself about that all right. You scored one hundred and sixty five.'

'Is that good? I'd be interested to know.'

'Above average. Quite a bit above average actually.'

'Phew! Glad to hear it. What's the average?'

'I'd rather not say if you don't mind.'

'Hadn't a clue what to expect never havin' heard of an IQ test before, let alone done one. What's the purpose of –'

'Help's separate the wheat from the chaff. That straight forward enough for you eh!'

'I suppose so. Happy 'tis over.'

'So you'd like to work at Lehmans.'

'Yeah! That's why I'm here ain't it.'

'Take a seat outside again Mr MacAlindon, or grab yourself a coffee. The break-station is on the right far end. We'll be ready for your interview in say –' Reynolds threw his watch arm upwards and folded back his wrist – 'ten minutes. Must marshal the troops.'

As he exited Reynolds' office the broad beam of satisfaction that brought a flush to his cheeks attracted the attention of a few of the staff, some of whom were busily darting about in typical office humdrumness. Rubbernecking over the floor in search of the oriental girl, he focused on her lithe body as she beguilingly leaned over a desk and then, prompted by her colleague, turned to greet him with her chinky seraphic smile. Self-consciously he wheeled around and headed for the break-station but on locating it decided against having a coffee, not wanting bladder-shift to flare up in the course of the interview. Knowing he had the gift of the gab his confidence soared, edgy adrenergic pulses modulating his heightened senses.

The disparate interview panel comprised of two first generation Irish-Americans, including Bart Reynolds, and a Hungarian-American who seemed to hide behind his thick-framed glasses. Comfortably seated, the interview effused:

'What makes you believe you are suited to manage, indeed capable of managing, other people's financial portfolios Mr eh... Mr MacAlindon?' asked the plethoric Irish-American with bulldog jowls.

'The fact that the money's not my own I suppose. No fear of the risk factor,' he answered blithely.

'That's a rather supercilious presumption young man. A double edged sword is it not?

'As long as I don't fall on the sword I think, given time, I can dull the edges.'

'How so?' demanded bulldog, his jowls quivering as he leaned forward.

'By spreading the risk, not puttin' all my eggs in one basket, to coin a phrase.'

'What if the bottom falls out of the basket?'

'Then we're all in the proverbial sh… so I'd hide behind you guys,' he pithily replied with an ingratiating grin that beggars description.

The two Irish-Americans smiled knowingly at this while their colleague sat ruminating on his pencil stub, doodling on a note-pad, and then shifting uneasily in his chair, a deep furrow spanning his brow, seemingly troubled by the interviewee's indefeasible fanfaronade, he gave him a measuring look.

'You have… studied the works of Adam Smith… the Wealth of Nations… for instance?' he asked in a deep ectoplasmic voice, Maca struggling with the vagaries of his accent.

'Yeah! He was Irish,' he boasted defensively, a contrivance deflecting attention from his lack of knowledge of the great philosopher's economic theories.

'A Scot for sure,' he dogmatized, making an irritable grimace.

'Well a Celt then. I'm a Cantillon man myself.' (Back in Belfast he had heard a discussion about Cantillon on his crystal set).

'An Anglo Scot I believe… and Cantillon?'

'Yeah. Richard Cantillon… a Kerry man. Kerry you know… the county in Ireland… he was Irish… the first great economist you know. Cantillon leaves Smith in the ha'penny place… if you see what I mean,' he replied pleonastically amid pronounced pauses.

'He was French,' his interlocutor truculently averred as if talking to a simpleton.

'Irish to the bone. Wrote all his great works in French though. Economic theories, all statistical gobbledegook for the most part, more pukka than makes sense. Banking's all about entre-preneurship and... and risk taking. Cantillon's definition of an entrepreneur is my mantra –'

'And what... may I ask... might that be?' he quizzed, almost aggressively, smiling enigmatically from behind his glasses.

'"One who buys at a known price to sell at an unknown price". If I get this job that motto, emblazoned, will adorn my desk.'

'I don't know much about Cantillon... but of what relevance is he to contemporary banking?'

'The same can be said of Smith wouldn't you agree. In any case we Celts know all about banking,' he replied with an air of defiant self-confidence.

'How's that then? I was not... aware... of a banking tradition emanating out of Ireland.'

'Now that's where you're wrong. We Irish have been so under the cosh, so oppressed by the English over centuries that we learned the hard way. Learned to hide our few possessions well, to turn them to account, turnin' a farthing into a penny, a penny into a shilling. As my mother says – "look after the pennies and the pounds look after themselves"... or dollars in this case. And this all done by stealth and good husbandry as no decent Irishman in bygone days would darken the door of an English banking institution,' he proffered, clutching at straws.

'Decent Irishman? Rogues and... and confidence-tricksters more like. Once again Mr MacAlindon... I fail to see the relevance.'

'The relevance is that parsimony is in our blood –'

'Surely paradoxical... is parsimony not contra to the spirit of banking? Marked purely by prudential motives... if you will.'

Maca took it as a rhetorical question. '"Know prudent cautious self-control/ Is wisdom's root", Robbie Burns said that.'

'I suppose you claim him for the Irish as well?'

'No no! He was a true Scot all right. But his sister married an Irishman, the estate manager at Fortescue's big house. She's buried in the ould sod.'

'You seem to have an answer for everything Mr MacAlindon,' Bart Reynolds interjected, somewhat taken aback by his bragging evasiveness. 'But as William Blake said "Prudence is a rich, ugly, old maid courted by incapacity". What do you make of that?'

'As a student of the law I believe it's my turn to fail to see the relevance,' he replied with dauntless perspicacity. 'As I said, we Celts know all there is to know about banking… about finance. I'm sorta-kinda part of the cute hoor brigade, staying ahead of the posse. And sure is that not what banking is about, buckin' the trend, stayin' ahead of the competition and the regulators –'

'The banking fraternity is hardly a theatre to do battle in Mr MacAlindon,' he confides impatiently.

'Isn't it? Well my services would probably be wasted on you lot so,' he said piquantly, rising in readiness to take his leave from the orchestrated imbroglio. He was pushing out the envelope, believing the interview had ended in abject failure, but remained desperately optimistic.

The Hungarian hostilely smiled, open mouthed, pressing his hands firmly on the desk, seeming on the verge of saying something, but interrupted by bulldog jowls.

'Stephen, I'd like you to meet our Managing Director Harry Iliffe. His office is just down the corridor.'

'Does that mean I get the job?' he said without batting an eyelid.

Bulldog jowls gave him a wry meditative smile.

As they made their way to Iliffe's office, Bart Reynolds said to him as an aside:

'Bit of a whippersnapper. Consider yourself a thinker don't you.'

'Yeah! More than a bit I'd say. Not wantin' to think things out would make me a coward.'

'Smith was more than a mere economist buddy, as a browsing of his Theory of Moral Sentiments affirms,' countered Reynolds, shaking his head ruefully, a supercilious simper overspreading his cadaverous physiognomy.

Maca, not having a clue what he was on about stared at him nonplussed.

7

A week later Stephen started work at Lehman Brothers, nervously at first having bluffed his way through the interview, and not having the foggiest notion of what the job entailed. Luckily, he formed a natural affinity with his immediate boss, Robert Perotti, Manager of the Settlements Division, a suave Italian-American and a great talker, sporting tar-black dyed hair, some fifteen years his senior, who had taken a shine to him and exercised a great deal of patience in showing him the intricacies of the business, giving him chapter and verse on the different roles performed in other departments of the bank and how they interfaced with settlements. Maca, quick to learn, was all eyes and ears. The vivid portrayal Perotti sketched of the multifarious characters who controlled these departments and their minions proved, consequently, of invaluable benefit in enabling Maca quickly differentiate between the big hitters (to whom he would defer and listen to attentively) and the nonentities (whom he could shrug off with impunity unless he found them helpful or amusing). Having brazened out the interview and acquitting himself well in the meeting with the Managing Director, he talking nineteen to the dozen so chuffed had he been to secure the job, he had failed to ascertain the salary commensurate with the position, an oversight which the interview board found intriguing. Flabbergasted on being advised by Perotti that his starting salary would be $500 per month reviewable upwards if he be found to be of good service to the bank after a probation period of six months, he displayed ice cool indifference, behaving like an Ivy League graduate for whom money was not the prime motivator, the challenge being all. Barely able to contain his jubilation he had rushed to the washroom where, contemplating himself in the mirror, he punched the air in irepressible glee, narcissistically examining his countenance as he finger combed his hair, retied his tie and pulled silly faces that only the truly happy psyche can indulge in, dementedly asking – 'who's a clever boy then', his humdrum life transmogrified.

A few months into the job, which he eagerly attended to with sedulous care, he received a worrisome letter from his mother:

12th May 1964

My dear Stephen,
Pride forbade me from writing to you before but things are now so bad here that I feel obliged to take the devil by the horns and beg you to help me. The council are threatening to evict us from the house for non-payment of rent and I'm 2 months in arrears on electrisity. Your father's health is going downhill by the day what with all the other bills. You could paper the parlour with all the solicitor's letters droping thru the letterbox warning that failure to pay within seven days will result in going to court, making me liable for the costs. Eileen helps out as best she can but she hardly has enough money for her own needs. It's not possible to make ends meet on my pay from the monstery. I owe the council £29.3s.7p. and £11.9s.3p on electrisity. If you could see your way to send me some money to get them off my back I'd be forever thankful.
    Are you still working in Tiernans. I know you have a lot of expenses to bear but I'm desprit because of all this stress. So anything you can spare would be a great help. Monica got top grades in her exams and is looking for work. I know she'll help me out when she lands a job, which please God will be soon. If I can settle with the council things may improve. I pray it will be so.
God bless you and take care of you.
Your loving Mum

He mentally converted the sterling rent debt into dollars and next day sent her a money order for that amount together with an additional $50, promising to post her monthly thereafter a cheque for $50 knowing his mother for an indefatigable gossip and prone to exaggerate his abilities, that she would broadcast the gesture as an attestation of his "getting on famously in America – working like a Trojan he is". In writing him after that she never failed to express extravagant thanks, reminding him how difficult it is to make ends meet, she being afflicted with the necrosis of ageing, just about able to hold down her job in the monastery; and of how the family and neighbours said he was a "a topper" for looking after his "aul mum" so well. What a great country America is, he mused, and set about making plans to become an American citizen.

After expiry of the probation period, he was given his head as a house broker with his own portfolio, and had succeeded in persuading Robert Perotti that he be allowed headhunt Frank Connolly from Morgan Stanley as his sidekick. Within a short time he and Frank were moving millions of dollars between banks, securing top overnight rates, and bartering exchanges against sterling and the Japanese yen. His earning power rose exponentially, for in addition to commissions he now commanded a salary of $800 a month with the prospect of an annual bonus of at least $3,000, more than enough for him to be dismissive of Frank's claims of senseless prodigality in agreeing the exorbitant rent demanded when he moved out of Frank's apartment (believing he cramped his style and hacked off by his rifling his food without so much as by your leave) into a sumptuous fully furnished two bedroom apartment in the suburb of Brookline, a brisk twenty minute walk from the bank. With unabashed acquisitiveness, he bought his first car, a second-hand emerald green Ford Mustang with champagne coloured leather seats, chrome steel hubcaps and white wall tyres.

So tired out did he feel in aspiring to and getting to know the ropes of what it took to be an investment banker and in adapting to the role of broker to the obscenely rich, his sex life was proving deficiently dormant, he being reliant on the odd alcohol fuelled lustful fling with connubially demented girls from work following the usual Friday evening adjournment to the pub, or, casual encounters following a night out on the town. Obsessed with the climb to success, a steady relationship was the last thing on his mind. The tchotchke oriental girl, Li (when he had told Frank about her Frank had simulated a bouncing pocket Venus on his lap), whom he was intent on pursuing when first he joined the bank, had turned out to be off limits. Hitting on her in the pub he was muscled out of it by a bulldyke who came to her defence, Li being a tribadic charmer.

One evening a colleague, Brent Fulton (a heavy drinker with all the wiliness and baleful magnetism of an alcoholic who at work habitually waxed uxoriously about his "ball and chain"), asked him for the use of his car for a tryst he had planned with a waitress named Rosemarie from Cirillo's Pasta House on Hanover Street, a restaurant Maca knew well from his time working in Tiernans pub. He cheerfully agreed to the request as he delighted in Brent's anarchic company and dry wit, that is, when he is not making a laughing stock of his wife with his jokey put-downs, or, pathetically drunk. Some hours later on returning the Ford Mustang to Brookline, Brent entered his topsy-turvy apartment in the company of Rosemarie and her humdinger of a friend Julia, both women decked out in minidresses that left little to the imagination. Following cursory introductions, he hastily stacked the autochanger spike of the record player with long play vinyls and popped open a bottle of red plonk as The Beatles blared out "Love Me Do", the burgeoning sound reverberating off the walls of his abode. Meantime, Brent and the girls had heftily pushed aside two cuboidal armchairs and were cavorting in a roisterous dance routine, both girls on high heel stilts. Julia, with arms akimbo and a flirtatious smile on her lips, her lordotic hindquarters revealing the outline of her knickers through her skirt, her coruscating eyes displaying a reckless sensuality, pressed all his orectic buttons in a frisson of lust. He couldn't keep his eyes from the shape of her behind as he joined her in klutzy predaciousness, wanting, needing to get closer. As Buddy Holly crooned "True Love's Ways", Julia whispered that it was her favourite song as they smooched to the slow rhythm, her tongue frenching his ear, her coned jutting kaboobers crushed against his chest, her nailed-on pelvic floor fervidly caressing his rigid penis. His want of her metamorphosed into an aching physical craving as he watched Brent grinning suggestively while giving him the thumbs up behind Julia's back. Following consumption of another bottle of Californian red to blowout pop music and piquant dancing, Brent expressed himself anxious to catch the last train home. Maca dropped him off at the station, and then to his fancy discovered that Rosemarie's flat was his next stop, Julia having coyly climbed into the front seat busily massaging his crotch. Not enquiring where she lived he headed back to his apartment, her pudenda-red lips giving him a mouth blast on the ride there, her studded tongue kneading him to erection anew, her bobbing head inadvertently honking the car horn when stalled at traffic lights drawing prying glances from pedestrian bystanders. Being highly aroused on their return they did not make it to the bedroom and, without osculatory foreplay, ripped the clothes off each other in the hallway. He sucked on her diamante studded nipples with such frenzied intensity that they distended to look like Chinese chequer counters, her delirious moans spurring him on, her svelte legs anchored around his midriff as he pumped into her glabrous juicebox (what an eye-opener), then motionless, held her impaled as he shot his jism, his legs atremble in shagged out lecherousness. Carrying her still speared on his pulsating member, they collapsed in a tangle of sweat-streaked limbs on the bed in satiated exhaustion. Afterwards, sharing grass cigarettes, thick curls of blue smoke spiralling above them, she regaled him with episodes from her romantic travails: how men kept "hitting" on her she being so alluring (owwee!); how men always assumed she was "available", such misogynous assumptions the cause of serious irritation to her (humph!); how she needed the satiety of sex everyday, decidedly as often as possible (bingo!). Her honeycomb lips reinvigorated his flaccid semi-engorged penis twice more that first night. Towards dawn, during another bout of languorous canoodling, she advised him, to his astonishment, not to come, saying it was not healthy for a man to ejaculate more than three times in any one rumpo escapade. Julia's sensuality and ersatz emotion was a revelation, her blithe promiscuousness signalling that some women yearn for uncomplicated casual sex as much as men predatorily stalk it. Sometimes they spent whole weekends in bed, lying on snarled up sheets, each absorbing all the attention and energy of the other in a haze of cannabis induced carnality, with no hankering for others company, no pangs of hunger impeding, entertaining each other with booze, joints, loud music and salacious gossip. His indefatigable appropriation of her body left nothing unexplored, she urging him to lay bare her sexual proclivities and satisfy her predilections. Such ruttish talk should have jarred in his mind like a warning bell but instead only served to make him hornier for her. He had encountered his first nymphomaniac. Julia worked as a hostess at the Fawn Club on Tyler Street and so that establishment became his regular weekend late night haunt, occasionally fetching along a cohort of his carousing work colleagues.

Suchlike hedonistic self-indulgence proved short lived when she began to badger him for a ring. 'Let's get married,' she would seductively suggest as they lay in the serpentine voluptuousness of post coital lassitude. Cognizant of their incompatibilities, knowing she was not the kind of woman he could ever settle down with, he'd be at her every beck and call, little by little he grew bored with her pesky botheration and psychobabble carefree frivolity pre-disposed to ridicule and spitefulness, her cynicism proof of a vindictive frame of mind; a woman born to be fucked, hard and often; a woman whose primary attribute (to his mind) was her pleasure in rough and tumble sex, the rougher the better. The relationship became a burden, weighing him down. Yet hooked on her insatiable carnality, he fought shy of the bleak reality of the situation, floundering in phlegmatic apathy. Then things went from bad to worse when one night she informed him she was pregnant – 'You will marry me,' she beguilingly pleaded. 'I'm keeping the baby.' The cunning bitch, he told himself, had deliberately entrapped him by coming off the pill. How long ago he couldn't guess but he had on recent occasions stayed unmoving inside her, the eyelet of his penis at the well of her uterus, his sperm undeniably douching her to pregnancy. Or perhaps, did she have a casual fling with some stud at the club? 'Abortion is premeditated murder,' she shrieked as she leapt from the bed, alert to his callous indifference. 'Don't you dare plump for that as your prescribed solution?' He remained abstracted and disruptively silent, listening to his own inner spiel.

Heedful of her needs and concerns in the early months of the pregnancy, he played the part of a dutiful partner. However, the yawning chasm of incompatibility drove a wedge between them. He, hollow of desire, with flagging enthusiasm occasionally participated in steamy bonking but over time grew impervious to her seductive charms. He absented himself from the Fawn Club and from nights at his apartment when she would expect to stay there. Such abstinence from her nymphomaniacal athleticism was more than compensated for by his abjuring drugs. He cleaned up his act and became doubly attentive to his work. Irreconcilable estrangement took hold by the time Julia gave birth to a son. Mindful of the circumstances of his own birth, he declined the patrilineal comfort of his name for entry on the birth certificate. Having arrived at the very apogee of endurance, exasperated by her invidious criticism and implacable hostility, he settled a maintenance stipend of $200 a month on her and his son, an allowance he considered more than generous. During baby Gary's first months, he intermittently lavished affection on the child like a doting father, till one day, feeling the worse for wear having indulged in one too many beers, he turned up at Julia's abode carrying a present of a gigantic cuddly bear, and was abrasively introduced by her to the new man in her life. Her odd smile sent a premonitory shudder through him:

'I'm moving out of state,' she trenchantly remarked.

'Oh yeah. Where ye off to?'

'Scott and I are going to California at the end of the month.'

'To join the flower children eh?' his blue eyes cynically fixed her, her face devoid of emotion.

'No! We're going for good. Scott got a great promotion. It'll be a whole new beginning.'

'Well good for him. And Gary?'

'Gary too of course. The whole shebang.'

'Nice of you to let me know. Who the fuck's Scott?' he asked with guileless disparagement, eyeing the dark ovoid sweat stains on Scott's T-shirt each side of his oxters.

'I've known Scott for years, for longer than I've known you. He's more of a father to Gary than you could ever be. Doesn't think you're much of a man by the way,' she snorted, truculently.

In a revanchist mood he observed Scott eyeball him with minatory pugnacity and move closer to Julia as if seeking to protect her from an ogre. With his mind turning this way and that, he said:

'Is that so? ye woolly-minded weenie. Well maybe I can show Scott how much of a man I am by injunctin' ye from abductin' my son out of Massachusetts.'

'You have no right to –'

'Bullshit! I've every right. Amin't I Gary's father for chrissakes.'

'– no right to stop me. No you're not,' she added contemptuously, acerbity in her voice.

'What the fuck do ye mean? You know fucken well I'm his father,' he said, his voice rising belligerently as the confab careened from rivalry to bad blood.

'Not on the birth certificate you ain't.'

'That's got nothin' to do with it? Whatever game ye think yer playin' at had better stop right here and now. Don't fuck with me or we may both regret it,' he reeled off in an endeavour to preclude any deeper rift.

'I was seeing Scott while I was with you –'

'Of course ye were ye lyin' cunt. I'll see to –'

'Hey man! Mind your mouth. Don't talk to Julia like that,' interjected Scott.

'– it you don't take my son… stay out of this fuck-face,' he bellowed, turning to face Scott. 'I'll talk to her any fucken way I like, whatever way I think the situation warrants. This has nothin' to do with you so back off.'

'I'm Gary's father.'

'Oh yeah! And I'm the Pope's son,' he said derisively.

'I'm his father and he goes where we go.'

'Over my dead body. Why are you doin' this Julia?'

''Cause you're a fucking asshole,' she irascibly shrilled, her eyes narrowed with vindictive scorn.

'Right! And you have the intellectual subtlety of a grass snake.'

'I'm Gary's father man. See!' Scott held out a copy of the birth certificate, his moiling belligerence disarming him. Brusquely, he examined it in a desultory way without touching it and saw in the entry under father the name Scott Harrington. In disbelief, he crumpled into a low chair, his thoughts disintegrating.

'So collect yourself and leave now before I throw you out,' Scott said as he unceremoniously lifted him by the arm from the chair.

''Tis a lie, a fucken scuzzy lie. Julia… don't do this,' he pleaded before the mockery of a lovers impasse took irreversible hold. 'You know 'tis wrong.'

'You're what's wrong round here man, so stop putzing about,' said Scott, hauling him towards the door.

A baby's cry could be heard from down the hallway as the door opened, and Maca, stumbling, found himself ejected on to the street, the cuddly bear tumbling at his feet, the decimating effect of acrimony ringing in his ears.

*

Although he held only a superficial interest in federal politics under President Lyndon Baines Johnson, Maca developed a keen regard for the local scene, it being effectually controlled by the

Kennedy, Moynihan and O'Neill clans. Massachusetts had been one of the first States to desegregate education, yet most black students were still obliged to attend schools within or close to their own ghettos, the boards of some schools retaining the wherewithal to fillet out coloureds from their lists, school diplomacy, apparently, having little or no truck with fair play. One Friday afternoon walking back to work in buoyant mood after a liquid, but efficacious, business lunch, he was momentarily distracted by a noisy street demonstration and stopped to watch the antics of the throng of motley student protestors, some wearing pseudo-military uniforms, on the march to the imposing colonnade of the State House. Upfront, an aggressively enhanced bullhorn voice encouraged them to raise their makeshift placards – FREE EDUCATION / FREE CHOICE – and chant rhythmically "Hey! Hey! L.B.J. How-many-kids-have-you-killed-today?" Instinctively, he was filled with regret at not being part of the mass demonstration, their chants pealing in his brain, acutely aware that his work at the bank so monopolized his energies leaving little free time for involvement in the more fundamental principles of democracy. Passing a fountain lion vomiting sudsy water (a student prank), he crossed to Milk Street where a pall of ink-black smoke billowed from an overturned Chevrolet, a wreck of lost motability, perhaps (in his mind) a foretoken of the hellacious loss of Kennedy's camelotic politics.

Arriving back at the office, Petra Flanagan of the backroom support staff had left a "while you were out" note on his desk advising that Robert Perotti and Harry Iliffe wanted a meeting with him at 2.30 pm sharp. He felt the blood throb in his veins as questions raced through his mind as to what the purpose of the meeting could be. Had he made a mistake? Had he lost client's money? Racking his brain he came up with a blank, all expectations of the clients in his portfolio had been met, some exceeded. Of course he knew some clients had sustained losses in the short term, but due to his astute investment intuitiveness such deficits were quickly made up by shrewd placements and overnight deposits, new targets reached and many surpassed. Had anyone from his client-book made a complaint? What was there to complain of? Yes, he did once slam down the telephone when T.K. Tanaka in Worcester had venomously berated him for selling his investment shares in Bank of America for $1.2 million in exchange for a five-day deposit with the Bank of Tokyo. However, when Tanaka saw the Yen rise unexpectedly against the Dollar, he was more than pleased to pocket the $63,000 profit and buy back the Bank of America shares at a deflated rate. In any case, he pondered, that was the best part of two months ago, and Tanaka had more or less given him *carte blanche* since that incident. On entering the MD's office he remained uneasy but soon relaxed on observing the smorgasbord of *petits fours* and other savoury delicacies on Iliffe's desk, Perotti's broad smile through a haze of blue cigar smoke inviting him to partake. He abstained and noisily sank into the smooth grained integument of a red leather armchair.

'Bonus time Stephen,' said Perotti. 'My-oh-my! That time of year again. *Tempus fugit* eh! Of course incrementally there will be a nice little salary hike. You are no doubt aware of the profitability of your portfolio.' Perotti sat forward in his chair, sucking hard on his cigar. 'Second only to mine goddamn it. Are you overnighting at your desk by any chance?'

Having assiduously monitored the commissions and charges he had earned on behalf of the bank ($1.7 million to date with every possibility of breaking the $2 million threshold by the end of the next quarter), he had been considering seeking a substantial raise in salary. This augured well for him.

'Yes indeed, a superlative performance from both of you. You've settled into the job very well young man –'

'Like a duck to water,' interjected Perotti.

'Copacetic with the team. The board is pleased with you,' Iliffe went on in profuse acknowledgment. '

'Thank you Sir. I'm well pleased myself.'

'You're in line for a sizeable bonus,' continued Perotti. 'Close as makes no difference to double your salary.'

He felt a wave of heat pass over him but tried to stay cool and collected, momentarily distracted on noting for the first time the dioramic model of Faneuil Hall behind Iliffe's desk.

'Not getting bored in settlements are we?' asked Iliffe. 'Can become mind-bendingly monotonous after one gets the hang of it.'

'The job's become second nature to me Mr Iliffe. I'm very happy doin' what I do.'

'Glad to hear it Stephen,' said Iliffe, taking a swig from his glass of bourbon. 'Glad to hear it, 'cause I've got a proposition for you… a proposition I believe will excite you. In any case a proposition I want you to give careful consideration to. I'll let Bob fill you in… Bob,' he beckoned, commandingly replacing his tipple on the desk.

Maca braced himself, uncrossed his legs and sat as upright as possible in the sumptuous leather chair.

'Thanks Harry. Head office has a vacancy on the Stock Exchange floor. A different animal Stephen, a different animal altogether believe you me. Even so the board believes you are fitted for the task. How would you like to be a dealer?'

'A dealer! That's my burning ambition, to be a dealer.'

'You're somewhat on the young side for the responsibility,' said Iliffe. 'It's a very onerous placement, requires business acumen, dedication, initiative and –'

'For sure a good eye and the steely balls of a professional gambler,' interjected Perotti.

'– and a strong constitution. Nevertheless, I believe you have the necessary flair. It's a tough grind I'll own you. Talking of dealing being your burning ambition, hope you don't suffer burnout like some. Not too soon anyways.'

'Whatyagotta say for yourself,' enthused Perotti.

'I'd just love to have a crack at it Sir. I believe I have the stomach for it, for the… a challenge like that there.'

'Take the weekend and have a good think on it,' Perotti said, stretching back in his chair, grinning like a Cheshire cat. 'It'll mean a move, bag and baggage to New York. Needless to say I'll be sorry to lose one of my star brokers. But thas-the-way the cookie crumbles. All expenses will be covered by the bank, five star accommodation pending getting your affairs in order. Any furiture or possessions you decide not to take can be stored, again at the bank's expense of course. If you come out as good in the position as we believe you are capable of, the rewards are excellent. All depends on the commissions you earn for sure.'

'This is a wonderful opportunity young man,' said Iliffe, putting a hand on each armrest. 'Your get-up-and-go reminds me so much of my own time starting out.'

'I appreciate your confidence in me Sir,' he exulted, knowing it amounted to another feather in his cap.

'Your indubitable flair will redound to the bank's advantage,' Iliffe paused to look Maca in the eye, 'and to yours it goes without saying. We need your decision by Monday – time waits for no man. Maybe we could pull some strings in your favour,' he said, giving Perotti a searching look. 'Any questions?'

'Well one thing springs to mind,' he said hesitantly.

'Yeah! What's that?' asked Perotti.

'I'd like to have Frank along with me. If I take the job that is.'

'Frank?' Iliffe's face bore a puzzled expression as he turned to Perotti for elucidation.

'Sir, Frank Connolly,' Maca affirmed in an entreating voice.

'What's with you guys? No hanky-panky I trust,' jibed Perotti, making an openhanded gesture as he pushed backward in the chair. 'Of course your personal life is none of the bank's business I know but I'm –'

'No! It's nothin' out of the ordinary Sir. Frank and I go back a long way... growin' up in Belfast and all that. We're kindred spirits. Make a good team.'

*

Shortly thereafter, Stephen and Frank arrived in Manhattan for a preparatory visit with an overnight stay at the Waldorf Astoria, sharing a twin bedroom, the bank providing them with a liberal expense account. Picked up at the airport by a staff car, they dropped off their luggage at the hotel and sped on for an afternoon meeting with their new boss, Jeffrey Robertson, and some of the head office staff. Head office, viewed externally, comprised of thirty-seven seamless floors of blue tinted toughened sheet glass. Internally, floor space was all open-plan with spacious working corals divided by five foot high cushioned screens, except for the executive suites that occupied the thirty fifth and thirty sixth floors. The configuration of the penthouse floor remained unknown to ninety nine per cent of the employees. That evening Robertson, with two of his key staff members and their meretricious wives (flamboyant trophies from their university venatic sprees) volubly entertained the wide-eyed Irishmen to dinner in the Marriot View Revolving Restaurant, their table cluttered with more crystal glass than you could shake a stick at, the top-notch meal marred by Wall Street hubris and streams of fatuous chit-chat – "What do you make of New York? Does it surprise you?"; "Is it what you expected?"; "You too can have all this if you are smart enough and energetic enough to claim it". Bored by the bloviated boasting and palaver, the nettled tyros had an early night, readying themselves for the morrow's primary purpose of their visit, an initiatory meeting with the Lehman Brothers' dealer team at the Stock Exchange.

Next morning, energised by expectancy, he rose early and had a leisurely shave and shower. Dressed in his best suit, he went walk-about on Park Avenue and took a casual stroll to Grand Central Station where, having viewed the grandiose architecture, he picked up a copy of the New York Times. Back in the hotel room, finding Frank oblivious to the world, he awakened him from a deep sleep and Frank, in a stupor, gingerly swung his legs over the edge of the bed and bleated:

'Fuck it Maca! I've slept in school dorms, shared rooms, dossed in hostels in about every state in New England and beyond. In all that time I've never come across a fucker to buzz-snore the like you did last night. You were suckin' in the net curtains, blowin' out the gas. You've got a problem, a real bleedy problem and you fucken gave me a hell of a problem last night. Not a wink of sleep did I get with yer fucken snufflings and snortings.'

The Senior Managing Dealer, Charles Schweitzer ('call me Chubby – everybody else does'), took the neophytes under his wing and initiated them to the codes of practice on the Stock Exchange floor, walking them through the trading pits where dealers bought and sold stocks and bonds face to face with kinetic energy and in staggering volumes.

'Don't try take it all in in one go,' he counselled them. 'In no time you'll get the hang of it. I'll give you guys an easy ride over the first cupila weeks or so.'

Maca warmed to Chubby right off, reckoning he was a regular sort of bloke who would not tolerate bullshitters; the kind of man whose personal hygiene was his business only with a 'fuck you' attitude if it bothered you. When in the job, he recognized Chubby as a one-off, a leader who bellowed his incisive instructions to subordinates with perspicuity and trenchant intolerance of questions ('for fuck sake just do it'). Following close of business, Chubby shepherded the gobsmacked recruits by yellow cab to the Plaza Hotel where, ensconced in The English Oak Bar, Chubby seemed to know, or be acquainted with, half the patrons. The jammed bar was pullulating with drop-dead gorgeous women, undoubtedly a few cocottes among them. Chubby discreetly pointed out certain major league players from the banking and business fraternity, including Chuck Connors, reputed to be the richest man in New York having amassed a fortune from property speculation, and the markets of course. Like many parvenus, Chuck Connors had a mistress, a bottle blonde poseur (bedecked in jewellery that shimmered like a Waterford chandelier) wistfully hanging on every word he uttered and by the look of her at least half his age.

'Everybody knows about Chuck's bit on the side, except his wife. They're always the last to know… the wives,' whispered Chubby. 'Most of the head-honchos at Lehman's have their bit of fluff, some discreetly, some don't give a fuck who knows about it. Too busy climbing the grease pole on the way up, having arrived believe they're entitled to it. Maybe they are. Who gives a shit anyways. Nobody bats an eyelid. It's a badge of honour to keep your trap shut about it.'

He found Chubby's precipitant verbosity mindboggling, relating a mine of information, offering names of his contacts: realtors, lawyers, furniture removals, painters, decorators, the best haunts to hang out; and noted the pages of his pocket diary were chockerblock with contact numbers, the margins holding diagonal entries. All offered by way of helping them relocate.

'I got a fantastic pad in SoHo. A few of the guys picked up awesome bargains there, and in Tribeca. The rundown zones are being developed at a phenomenal rate so it's a good time to get a foot on the ladder. Warehouses, old retail blocks, artisan buildings converted into apartments, studios, lofts, you name it, purchase or rental. Hey! I know. You guys should stay the weekend. Yeah! Why don't ye, let me show you the sights, see how the cat jumps.'

'We've checked out of the Waldorf, one night reservation only and our flight is –'

'No sweat! I've loads of room in my pad if you guys don't have a problem slumming it. My darling ladylove did a bunk on me last week. Called me a schmuck. She'll come running back in jig time. No sweat. Begging… begging me to take her back she'll be. I'm having a ball on my own so let me be your host.'

'We're on the eight thirty out of La Guardia.'

'Which airline?'

'Pan Am.'

'I'll give you a name. She'll change your ticket at no extra cost. No sweat man.'

He adulated Chubby's panjandrum ways and dealings and that Saturday night they painted the town red.

*

Maca was on a high, bursting with the excitement of the move to Manhattan, raring to go face the new challenge, money no object now that his salary had inflated to orbital figures beyond his wildest expectations. The possibility of earning, in addition, huge bonuses based on commissions on contracts concluded to the satisfaction of clients meant his earning power could soar in to the rarefied stratosphere, his standard of living in to the troposphere. Intent on making final arrangements for the move by setting aside for storage his furniture and effects, the necessary boxing of books, vinyl records and bachelor's paraphernalia, and the packing of suitcases for transit to the "Big Apple", he arrived back in Boston and on entering the condominium picked up a telegram from the janitor. Ripping it open his heart thumped against his ribcage - YOUR FATHER DEAD. COME HOME. LOVE MUM. He checked the date – June 9, 1966.

'Jesus! When did this arrive?'

'Thursday. Yeah Thursday. I believe you'd just left for the airport when I signed for it,' replied the janitor. 'Not bad news I hope?'

'My father's dead.'

'Oh! I'm sorry to hear that Mr MacAlindon. Real sorry.'

'Why didn't ye get a message to me?'

'Well I didn't know, I mean, I didn't know your father was dead,' said the janitor sheepishly. 'I left a message, a telephone message for you at the bank. Just to say you had a telegram. 'Tis usual telegrams carry kinda urgent news so I left a message.'

'Righty oh. Thanks Ned. See ye.'

Entering his apartment he suddenly broke out in a cold sweat. Dropping his luggage outside the bedroom door and throwing his overcoat on the floor he headed for the icebox and drank a bottle of beer by the neck. Inwardly he worked out the sequence of events: Sunday the twelfth, nine thirty p.m. eastern time, the early hours Monday in Belfast; if his father had died on the ninth, more likely the eighth, the latest the funeral could take place would be the thirteenth; no way could he make it back home, the interment concluding some twelve hours before he could get there, assuming it had not already taken place on the Saturday. Convulsing in tearful guilt, he retrieved the last beer from the icebox and, heavy-hearted, sank in a simian slouch into the armchair in the television room. An eidetic image of his father's hermetically entombed, death stiffened, waxgrey corpse with a rosary forever clutched, his lively persona never again to be encountered, brought to mind his father's adamantine belief in reincarnation. He wondered what metempsychotical species his father's soul had transmigrated to; whether his blithesome revenant would haunt him. But that was a dark intelligential secret for he knew a necromantic revelation was not on the cards. Wherever his father's soul now rested, he hoped the man was at peace.

Dawdling to the kitchenette rummaging for alcohol he found a half-full bottle of Jack Daniels in the food press, poured a shot, gulped it and returned, bottle in hand, to the armchair. Reconciling himself to the fact that he would not make it home for his father's obsequies, he decided to telegraph his mother next morning explaining the inopportune circumstances. He determined to write her later in the week expressing his heartfelt sorrow; apprising her

142

of how the bank had transferred him by way of promotion to New York; of how he and Frank had spent the last few days there, and, with all the travelling, of how the course of events had thwarted his discovering the sad news in time to organize flights. In this letter, he promised himself, he would tell her how he held her in his arms from across the Atlantic; of how afflicted he is by sorrow and remorse, his heart going out to her, to Eileen, and to Monica in their time of mourning; that they must know that if he could be with them he would be with them. His affinity with their loss and the sorrow he shared with them is easily put into words, he ruminated, but the self-reproach that tormented his soul filled him with a brooding melancholy. Fatigue, prompted by alcohol, over-came his lugubrious thoughts. He fell into a deep sleep where he sat and hours later awoke stiff of limb and aching muscles.

The following Thursday on arriving home from work, he picked out from the clutter of post scattered on the lobby table an envelope addressed in his mother's cuboidal handwriting, a *par avion* label neatly affixed, a line-up of her fucking Majesty's head stamps in the top right corner. Tearing it open he skimmed over the letter, his eyes jumping lines to take the gist in quickly - Your father died - I only left him for a few minutes - behind the door - taken quickly - Eileen tried - funeral is arranged for Monday - Please come home – Phone Alec - and let me know - Alec will get a message to me - I need you - as do your poor sisters - since we lost him – Make that call - Your loving Mum. He checked the date of the letter – June 9. Hastening to his apartment, he slumped in the armchair and charily reread the letter more slowey:

Stephen love,   9th June 1966

Your father died of a massive heart attack this afternoon. God be good to him. I only left him for a few minutes while I ran to the shop for the tea things. I found him behind the door, the weaght of him there blocking me getting back into the house. I pray to God he was taken quickly and did not suffer too much pain.

Did you get my telegram. Where are you Stephen. Eileen tried to phone you. The funeral is arranged for Monday. Please come home. Phone Alec in Dempsey's

Pub 32118 and let me know when you're coming. Alec will get a message to me.
I need you here with me son, as do your poor sisters who haven't stopped crying since
we lost him. Make that call love as soon as you get this.

Your loving Mum.

He did not telephone Alec in Dempsey's public house. Nor did he write the letter to his mother he had promised her in his telegraphed message the previous Monday.

8

The place New York, the buzz Lower Manhattan, get-a-head business a meritocracy, banking the kingmaker, the stock market a behemoth. The players, high above the bleating traffic of the stewing megalopolis in their concrete, steel, and glass-wall skyscrapers overlooking the verdigris copper flat roofs, watch out over a cosmopolis colonized by stick-people hurriedly in pursuit of prosperity and happiness, or, survival and the makings of a square meal. The vertiginous perspective miniaturizes the pedestrian throng to the pointillist likeness of digitalized tickers on the telegraphic tape machines that drone in every mercantile office; those same machines humming contentedly at the success of contracted for, and gambled, returns. The whirring IBM mainframe computer the peripherals technological accumulator of records, the inspeximus of targets achieved and accounts reposited, the harbinger of risk manage-ment in futures and options.

Into this polygonal melting pot gambolled Maca and his sidekick Frank Connolly, hotfoot in adapting to the challenge of the trading pits at the Stock Exchange; Maca, like a dog in the park straining at the leash, sniffing out the competition. At the outset an arbitrageur under the peremptory direction of Charles Schweitzer, within weeks he was shuffling financial instruments in uncounted zeros (counting was the job of the back room support staff) between banks and the markets, daily trading thousands of futures con-tracts by watching the stock indices on behalf of Far Eastern shakers, Mid Eastern Sheikhers, European bagmen, Texas oilmen, providential innovative tycoons, and seedy interlopers of offshore trade. In pride of place on his desk was a woodcut inscription of

Cantillon's definition of an entrepreneur as "one who buys at a known price to sell at an unknown price", a curiosity that lead to convivial discussion at the office.

By a heuristic process he took to the game like a duck to water. On the trading floor he could smell the oleaginous factors in the contracts; he could hear the clamorous screams of the dealers; and he could readily decipher the brisk semaphoric hand signals of the traders in their striped blazers. Futures contracts allowed him to buy or sell at a given future price calculated from the fluctuating value of the Stock Exchange basket of shares index. The futures contracts and the shares index move in basically similar lines, but the time gap permitting leverage in the futures market results in far greater volatility. Futures are more of a gamble. Buying "long" and selling "short"; "low-ticking" and "stop loss"; not getting "hung"; such lingo was the name of the game and he wasted no time in mastering it, the trick being to get ahead of the dealer opposition in any lurch in the market. Chubby was so impressed by his precocity that within months he promoted him to proprietary trading status (trading on Lehman's own account in addition to dealing for its clients). Maca in turn made Frank his primary trader operating the floor, with two other traders and a telephone assistant on his team at the Exchange, and three back room support staff based in head office. Once trading opened, the telephones buzzed with client buy or sell orders, which the dealers signalled to the traders who then semaphored the price. If a seller was on the market to stop loss, Maca could low-tick him by manipulating the price downwards to flush him out and trigger the sale. At the lower price he would then flash the buy price to Frank, or the on the spot trader from his team, and signal the quantity that was usually in the thousands. Buying long on long term investments was low risk for the dealer because it was the client's call and generally guided by five or ten year performance charts. Buying short was pressure cooker trading to be first in line. If another dealer got in first, the adverse price sting in the tail left his colleagues hung and forced to accept a worse price ending up with a lesser return or worst of all, a loss. If Maca got in first the client made instant profit, he earned high commission, and the contract would be concluded within seconds. In any one trading day, he might deal anything between one thousand and seven thousand contracts. He was a rising star player given free rein, watched enviously by the other dealers, his only handicap being not having authority to hold a position overnight (so many things could go wrong overnight). Working at the Exchange was so hectic, often necessitating a change of shirt between morning and afternoon dealing, that when the bell rang for close of trading a trip to the local hostelry for an ice-cold beer was the order of the day, and then back to the office to help the back room support staff work through the thousands of dealer slips to reconcile every trade. Workdays, he traded in futures and options. Weekends, he traded in female flesh, growing even more fatigued by the granularity of casual relationships.

Following the move to New York, Frank lost no time in locating an upmarket two bedroom apartment in SoHo, and had confidently approached Maca with the Lease Agreement for a joint rental. However, Maca had taken Chubby's advice and was predisposed to acquiring an apartment in a less salubrious locale, intending to oversee the renovations himself. He told Frank to go it alone, agreeing to rent from him for the duration pending his own negotiations on a suitable purchase. A realtor introduced by Chubby located for him a rundown loft-studio apartment in need of substantial refurbishment behind Duane Square in Tribeca, with double the living space of Frank's abode. Working with gusto on his first investment in property, he had the interior walls stripped back to the original stone and brick; the woodwork painted a shamrock green, or as close to the hue of shamrock he could get having been subjected to a harangue about colour science by the camp attendant in the hardware store – "blend the colours of the middle spectrum, more yellow than blue, thus maximising the visual light of the paint". Exhaustingly he trudged around the flea markets, often accompanied by a *fille de joie,* hard bargaining for good quality furniture, most of it solid antique, and had the pick of his stored possessions in Boston shipped on. Over one long weekend, he bought the latest accoutrements for easy living in electrical and white goods, and finished out furnishing the apartment with all the home comforts he considered necessary for a charmed existence.

*

He had been caught up in egoistic needs and sucked into the maw of a privileged lifestyle that nothing but an excessive income provides, his good fortune and easy-going personality only to some extent disconcerted by his *coup de foudre* for Martina Amorosino Patterson, Chubby's lieutenant in the back room support staff. Not much older than him, Martina was of such striking beauty that he froze every time they interacted at the office, finding himself dry-mouthed and tongue-tied, and his heart thumping in painful longing. Of dark Latina complexion accentuated by a fiery luminosity, he was captivated by the lustre of her blue-black hair, the playful glint in her brown eyes, the sensual pucker on her lips, and the sheer femininity of her every movement. Availing of any opportunity to unobtrusively watch her, such observations lulled him into a quixotic lustful yearning and a feverish restiveness. As a married woman she was unavailable, social gossip and work chit-chat being the extent of his fervour. Over time meeting at work, especially in the more laid-back ambience of the canteen or amid the hurly-burly of after work booze-ups in Moran's pub, they grew to enjoy each other's company, albeit in the genial presence of their work colleagues, their growing affinity and connectedness toward each other tinctured with nervous energy and playful sarcasm. On most such occasions in Moran's pub, her husband Tom would join the group, oftentimes rushing in late, necessitating Martina to await his arrival before journeying home. Then – *ignis fatuus*:

At a bank sponsored tenpin bowling competition one Thursday evening, he and Martina made a team, and having won the competition (he bowled seven strikes out of ten hurls) celebrated in high spirits back in the pub by buying drinks all round. In that company, Martina stayed close to him, gripping his arm in playful affection as they swooned in togetherness. Later, she asked him for a ride home. Pulled up outside her house, a brownstone mansion in Brooklyn, the engine left idling, the journey there filled with animated prattle, they laughed about the incident when she fell over in the bowling alley having failed a timely release of her fingers from the bowl. He teasingly called her an "eejit", and seeing her quizzical gaze instantly translated "idiot", her reactive lascivious laugh heartening him. She seemed in no hurry to exit the car and, not having invited him in for a nightcap, casually he said he should be heading back to Tribeca, that it was getting late. Leaning toward him as she fumbled to open the door, her rapturous eyes twinkling in the diffused interior light, a seductive moue parting her enticing lips, he gently kissed her, her tongue tantalizingly inviting his to explore more deeply, her fingers softly caressing the hairs on the nape of his neck. Absorbed in tentative passion but not wanting to compromise her should her husband or a curious neighbour observe the indiscretion, he made to drive away from the curb. 'No,' she whispered, warmly clasping his wrist, her honeyed breath caressing his ear, 'not tonight', and stepped out of the car without looking back.

Meeting at work next day it was as though the intimacy had not taken place between them, she nervily avoiding eye contact, he stony-faced. Later that evening in Moran's pub, amid the usual after work revellers, they remained in aloof frisson peering at each other, her brown eyes aflutter under his unblinking gaze. Visiting the washroom, he wrote his home telephone number on the back of a business card and on returning to the bar slipped it into her hand saying – I'll see you anytime. Her husband arrived soon after, appearing anxious to be getting on home, and he dekkoed Martina's fretful reaction in pulling her arm away from Tom's impelling grip. Her espied reluctance apparently overcome, the sparring couple vacated the scene, as did he on finishing his beer, the main reason he was hanging out in the place only to be close to her. Back in his apartment, while readying himself for a Friday night on the tiles with his mostly non-banking friends, the telephone rang:

'Come pick me up.'

'Where.'

'The Sheraton on Seventh. I'll be out front.'

'Ten… fifteen minutes.'

As he approached the hotel in late evening traffic, he saw Martina standing motionless on the steps, and felt his heartbeat pounding in his chest. Wordlessly, she settled into the car and stared off into the distance, anxiety mixed with relief written on her beautiful profile. Multiple unasked questions and misgivings raced frenetically through his mind as they drove back to his apartment in silence, he perplexed knowing she had left Moran's pub with her husband and now she was sitting in his car, alluringly mysterious. At his apartment he made for her a long drink of vodka and coke on ice, her favourite tipple, pouring himself a brimmed tumbler of Jack Daniels whiskey; put the Bob Dylan long play "Blonde on Blonde" on the record player, "I Want You" belting out. Then throwing the rolled futon on the floor sat beside her on the rumpled sink-down sofa. Not questioning each other, being there all that mattered, he kissed her, then kissed her more intensely, tongue deep in her luscious mouth, hands exploring her lean tense body, fingers playing the ridges of her spine, mouth nuzzling her breasts, lips drawing out her nipples, middle finger finding and gently caressing her clitoris, then penetrating her vagina. As if lost to him, seeming deep in a sensory reverie, she went into spasms of orgasmic pleasure. 'Martina,' he whispered, her whetted eyes now fixed on his, 'yer so beautiful'. Standing, leaving their drinks unfinished, he led her to his untidy bedroom, she averting her eyes as if overcome by coquettish shyness or adulterine guilt, he was not sure. He slowly undressed her, and as he moved to undress himself she covered her pert breasts with her arms, almost, it seemed to him, in a virginal gesture, or, maybe she felt cold, her legs now clenched as if to hide her silky bush. As she lay outstretched on the bed, he lovingly caressed her, her body there and then taking on an exquisitely mystical quality. Watching her, sensing her go all of a tremble in roused readiness as he tasted her feminine juices, her eyes glazed and expressionless, he mused – she is mine – that is why she is here. But his cock remained flaccid, the vigour of his desire not blooding him. She made no gesture to stimulate him. Frustrated, he passed her a lighted cigarette, and heavy with fallen hope lit his own, saying:

'Tom's a big man. Maybe that's my problem.'

'It's not a problem,' she sighed, her head nestling on his shoulder.

'I've loved ye from… from afar. Wanted ye from the first moment I saw ye. Now yer here with me and –"

'Hush.'

She seemed surprised he had expressed a secret love for her, a love she had no inkling of, and looking into his eyes, she blew sweet breath lightly on his cheek.

'If that's true you'll find me.'

Looking longingly at her beauty he again fingered her as she began caressing him to erection. A protracted subcutaneous sensation in his penis brought him to the height of passion. She holding, directing, he entered her gently, her labia soon gripping him in noisy sensuousness, eyes locked on each other. He could feel the spasms running through her body. And then she came again with him as he shuddered with orgasmic intensity.

Later, on their hands and knees scrabbling around on the beige woollen carpet under the glare of the overhead ceiling light in frolicsome but fruitless search for a missing earring, holding his right hand in both of hers she probed:

'Your finger… what happened?'

'My stumpy little war wound,' he jauntily replied. 'Nah! Caught it in the blades of a lawnmower… years ago back home.'

'Ouch! You poor thing. Betcha that was painful,' she gloated, mesmerizingly kissing and then bewitchingly sucking the marred digit. He reacted by mischievously pinching her curvaceous rump. Chortling, she removed the remaining ring from her left ear, two entwined rivets of gold, and handed it to him.

Late into the night starting out on driving her home, she jocularly commanded – "Home James, and don't spare the horses". Listening to and lost in the emotive words of Memphis folk rock, he turned the radio volume up when Bob Dylan's "Just like a Woman" came on. They had no need of talk. He stopped short of her house under a streetlight, and they kissed and canoodled till a chink of ethereal dawn light streaked the horizon. On exiting the car, her eyes searched his in a long penetrating look that told him all he needed to know.

Driving back to Manhattan at high speed, he burned rubber in bringing the Mustang to a screeching halt, stopping short of running over a crawling apparition on the roadway. Noticing a crashed car wrapped around a lamppost, the metal folded like an accordion, radiator steam hissing, he rushed to rescue the victim of the accident who emitted moans while mumbling – 'must have fallen asleep at the wheel'. Hearing another vehicle zooming towards the scene, he pulled the casualty to the side of the road. The oncoming car stopped, and as strangers it was agreed that he would deliver the injured party to the hospital, the stranger to report the site of the accident to highway patrol.

His mood on returning to his apartment was one of heady altruistic peacefulness, with only a hint of philander or caddish guilt. The rescue (perhaps saving the casualty from a worse fate) made him feel good about himself. Dragging on a cigarette as he watched the rhomboidal channels of light from the rising sun tangentially pour through the divides of skyscrapers in an ever-widening spread across the gridded streets and avenues of Lower Manhattan, he began to feel uneasy about the torrid illicit romance he had embarked on with Martina, the flirtatious ambuscades now ensnaring him. Retiring with sleepy clumsiness to his tousled bed, the sheets still creased with her form and the attar stains of their lovemaking, he felt satiated by the night's happenings and, self absorbed, fell into a blissful sleep.

Having found her lost earring, he returned the pair to her on Monday by internal mail at the bank with a scribbled note comprising an acrostic poem humorously recounting the incident of loss. Next day on opening an officiously marked envelope, **Strictly Private** heavily underlined, he was pleasantly surprised to receive her typed note of blithesome thanks by the same postal route:

Stephen,   Monday

Your note was a lovely surprise and a thousand thanks for the earrings. I'm being driven mad listening to all the verbal diarrhoea in this place today - so boring.

This morning I was waiting for the elevator on our floor when I saw you driving into the car park and I just wanted to see you – even for a few minutes – so I snailed my way down along the stairs to meet you on your floor. I really enjoyed Friday night. It would be hard to find a place that offered as much as we had at your apartment – Bed; Booze; Chat; Food; etc!! (note the order!). I certainly was very tired all day Saturday as I'm sure you were, but hell it was worth it!! I just lazed around watching TV and listening to records (not at the same time of course) – and…… no, I didn't drink – I wasn't able to!!

Can we do it again soon?? I could see you Friday after work. Drop me a note.

Martina

He dashed off another scribbled message saying he couldn't wait to be with her on Friday, and received one in return apologizing that she could not after all make it on Friday, but could spend all day Saturday with him if that suited. Telephoning around to his buddies, including Frank, he ruefully and with wry humour told them he had to pull out of the ball game that Saturday at the local park.

"She must be hot. Who is it this time?" cracked Frank.

"No one ye know Frank. But yer right... she's hot."

His confirmation to Martina elicited this response:

Stephen   Thursday

Just got your note and am thrilled we can be together at the weekend - I was a little worried in case you had other plans. It's only midday and I'm starving – I always seem to be hungry and eat a lot when I'm bored. I think I will go and rob me some cheese but you know what cheese is supposed to do to you and that could be very dangerous! I might be down to you in a few minutes looking for a "quickie"!! Can you just imagine the scandal? "Excuse me Stephen, any chance of a quickie"!!

How's about I cook us a meal, just for the two of us, candlelight etc. It's my treat - I want to buy the food – I'll leave the wine to you – O.K.? We will have the whole day together and a lot of the night. I may have to go home that night but we can talk about it – don't know exact plans as yet. Dying to see you!

Love Martina

The means by which their tryster communications remained secret had been established and they became lovers. In addition to exchanging love notes, they discreetly discussed plans for rendezvous over the office telephones. Revelling in Martina's ardent adulterousness, he knew that he and she were as one, a conflation which he idealized and feared. Convinced he had found the woman of his dreams, he marvelled at their guessing of each others every thought and response to every emotion. Some months into the relationship, having passed her driving test, she bought her first car, leaving her free to come and go as she pleased, her newfound independence relieving him of the tiresome late-night drives to Brooklyn and back. Not long after this astute purchase, the lovers had their first quarrel. He had planned, with her agreement, for them to stay over a holiday weekend at the Griswold Inn in Essex, an establishment "long on charm but short on plumbing" (he had once overnighted there when journeying between New York and Boston). Having booked a de luxe suite, one with a wood-burning pot-bellied stove, he reserved tickets for "Mourning Becomes Electra" on the Saturday evening in the Eugene O'Neill Theatre close-by. Early afternoon on the Friday of the proposed trip, Martina telephoned him at the Stock Exchange and dispassionately relayed her apologies that she would be unable to travel that day, or on the Saturday due to unforeseen circumstances. He lost his rag and bellowed into the telephone:

'What do ye mean ye can't travel?' he hissed through a fog of disappointment. 'Don't ye realize I've fully paid the inn in advance for the whole bleedy stay? I'd also booked for us to see the play at the local theatre.'

'I can't explain over the phone,' she said, *sotto voce*, so quietly in fact he could barely hear her. As far as he could make out she appeared non-committal and nonplussed. 'Please try to under-stand. I'll tell you –'

'Ye needn't bother yer arse telling me anything. Ye can fuck off with –'

She slammed down the telephone, leaving him steaming at the gills. Finishing work early, indicating to Frank in the pit that he was off, he rushed back to head office to remonstrate with her. She was not there, nor was Chubby, the latter's absence a relief as Chubby would want to know why he had abandoned the trading floor. He wrote her a vituperative note, dropped it in the post room knowing she would not receive it until the following Tuesday, and left for home. In the elevator, he bumped into Myra Johansson from Settlements, a pretty blonde who exuded libidinousness. They exchanged friendly banter and on exiting the building he applied the general criterion of a whim – 'why not'. And so it was that he and Myra spent a glorious Indian summer weekend secluded in bed at the Griswold Inn playing sex games, the performances liberated and athletically enhanced by prodigious quantities of alcohol, they not bothering to attend O'Neill's play on the Saturday evening; the Sunday torpidly spent by the debauchees bathing and soaking and nursing their shagged out genitalia.

Wednesday's internal bank post delivered him a stinging rebuke from Martina:

Stephen   Tuesday

What the hell has gotten into you – you really pick your days well. I don't know why the hell you are so reproachful of me. I tried to phone you two times earlier on Friday from Chubby's private line to explain the circumstances but your line was hot. I had to leave early and took a chance on phoning you from my own extension as I left, and then you started. You know very well that sometimes I can't talk openly on the phone. I felt like a right idiot. There you were asking questions, very loud and aggressively I might add, and I had the office gang listening to the whole bloody conversation. Can't you ever tell when it's difficult for me to talk?

It seems to me there are times you are not happy, unless you are fighting about something – usually something imaginary or unimportant. Is our situation not difficult enough without this? You tell me you are "pissed off", "you are a fool" – well, how do you think I feel when you say things like that? – or does that matter at all? I am mad now – I am pissed off. I don't mind us fighting over something important but to let fly for nothing I can't take.

You know I see you when I can, as often as I can – but that is not enough for you and when I can't see you, you get mad and say things that are not true and take out all your frustrations on me – seems we can only be happy when everything is going our way – there is little understanding on your part, at times. I know you were disappointed – as I was, but you wouldn't let me explain and then I couldn't explain because you blew up and I had to drop the phone. You are being totally unfair – suddenly you get something into your head and that's it – you let fly.

So! Where has all the understanding gone? And where does it leave us? We need to talk. There are certain things, I think, we should sort out.

Love Tina.

As far as he was concerned, that was the end of the whole affair. Conceptualizing the nature of their relationship, his role as her *innamorato* coalescing in a leechlike obsession leaving him immersed in self-torture, he sophistically determined to have no further truck with her, perceiving her behaviour as selfish and uncaring. Her manumitting note had not proffered any explanation or reason for her pulling out late, very late, from their excitedly anticipated away weekend, any hint of which might have surmounted the deadlock. Mulishly, he declined to bear the brunt of the blame for the lover's impasse and parried her telephone calls. He did not join her that Friday evening in Moran's pub in the usual company of their work colleagues. Believing the right decision had been made, his feeble efforts at enjoying himself that weekend away from Martina proved ineffectual. Everywhere he heard her footfall, her infectious laugh, her soothing love talk echoing in his memory; he saw the mischievous sparkle of her brown eyes in the eyes of other women; he smelt her essence deep in his nostrils. At work, he remained morose and aggressive. The following week he received another missive:

Stephen   Monday

If anyone is feeling confused and hurt at this stage, it's me. How can two people be so happy and think they understand each other one week and then last week - wham – total confusion? I don't understand why you seem so bitter and annoyed – I can hardly type this my hands are shaking so much.

I decided to write you this note, which you may never get, but I have so much to say that I thought it best to put it in writing, as if I come face to face with you I will more than likely forget half of what I want to say. Besides, it will make me feel better getting it off my chest!!

I tried to phone you last week because I wanted to talk to you, to sort things out. Your attitude, to say the least of it, has taken me very much by surprise. I had no choice but to pull out of our weekend in Essex – I have already apologised and to be honest with you the reason is no business of yours. You said in your note that because of me you are "losing contact with your friends". You always seem to be complaining about this, that or the other. I rarely complain to you about anything because, I think, if you want to see someone you must make some bloody sacrifices, especially in a situation like ours. For that matter, I haven't seen much of my friends of late, as whenever I can manage to get out on my own, I want to spend my time with you. I have often broken arrangements, inconvenienced myself, etc. to see you. But I don't complain because I'm doing what I want to do and I can be with you for a few hours.If we decide to go on seeing each other, there will have to be changes made, not just by you but by me too. I have never asked or demanded anything of you, as you have with me. I have often gone home late, very late, and have found myself in the "dog house" because of it, but I have never bothered you about it – I dealt with it myself and felt that for the few hours we had together, it was worth it.

I could give you many more examples, but what the hell, as far as I am concerned, it all boils down to the fact that I want to be with you and am prepared to put up with these ups and downs from time to time. But, on the other hand, you don't really help here, there is never any problem unless I arrive home late and you never throw me out on time!!

Sorry I banged down the phone, I was so annoyed – I had to pluck up the courage to phone you last week, afraid I might have said things I would later regret, and now I am confronted by your sulky silence. I don't want to see you unhappy or miserable, I want you to be happy; I want us to be happy when we are together, as we know we can be, and could be, if only we could cut out all the bullshit.

Don't treat my feelings so lightly either, throwing them aside whenever the mood takes you – you did hurt me by what you said in your note. I don't use or abuse your feelings as you say I do. If you know me at all, even just a little, you should know better. God! at times, I would love to kill you – lucky thing I didn't go down to you last Friday and grab you by the scruff of the neck and give you a piece of my mind!! I was really tempted to – can you imagine the tattle that would whip up?? Sorry if this note is a little "hard" on you but as I said I may never send it and having said all that I feel a lot better now. Those are my feelings, you can take them or or leave them. I want to see you - right at this moment I can't wait to see you so that we can straighten this misunderstanding out. Let me see you on Wednesday night – drop me a line.

Love Tina

The sparring lovers got together on Wednesday after work and resolved their differences, straightened out the misunderstandings, and fell into an earthy embrace, their lovemaking hungrily intensified by the thought of having almost lost each other, by the dread of losing the love they both wanted and now needed to hold on to so badly. The following Saturday, they drove out to Coney Island and he presented her with a ruby stone ring (her birth stone). All barriers to the relationship, misconceived and otherwise, fell away as they pledged undying love for each other, Martina promising that no matter what happened, no matter for whatever reason they might part, she would never forget him. Late on Tuesday on his return to head office from the Exchange, he received a note which seemed to undermine their equilibria, the plateau of placidity their liaison had so recently arrived at:

Tuesday

You say you can always judge people by their reactions; so can I and I must say you reacted very peculiarly yesterday on the phone when I asked you about yesterday morning. I don't often lose my "cool", especially not after such a day as we had together on Saturday, having opened up to you in a way I never did before, letting you know my feelings etc., just for nothing.

You told me on Saturday night when I was leaving that you would be worried about me driving home so late etc. You were so worried that you didn't bother your ass phoning me on Monday morning because you thought I wasn't in because my car wasn't in the car park. "You didn't want to drop the phone ......" – that never prevented you from phoning before. It is also quite clear how "concerned" you must have been. As you well know, I don't always drive my car to work. I didn't come down in the last shower nor am I easily fooled. You were not in yesterday morning and is it just mere coincidence that a certain lady on your floor was not in either until after lunch?????????? Just how long do you think you can get away with treating people the way you do????????????????????

I have always said we would have to be honest with each other if it were to work, well, you certainly haven't been honest with me. The fact that you are with other women is your business and is not the point. It is the lies I can't and won't stand. I am glad I can see more clearly now what you really are.
Enclosed ring which, naturally, is very beautiful but which I cannot accept.

No salutation, no valediction, just sentences barrelling along in raw mistaken jealousy. Hastily, he scribbled a note emphatically denying having wronged her in any way; confirming he had gone directly to work at the Exchange having dropped his car that morning at the garage for a tune-up; accusing her of deliberately fabricating an excuse to leave him; and offering to stay away from her if that was what she wanted. Next day he received her response:

Steve   Wednesday

Well! I don't feel very happy or proud of myself right now. What can I say? I'm sorry to have caused you unnecessary hurt and pain, and ask you to forgive me. In the past, you have made similar accusations, wrongly too, and I could never understand it, and here I am doing exactly the same to you. Your explanation was that it only confirmed your feelings for me and that is the only explanation I can give you too – for, if I didn't care so much I wouldn't have bothered saying anything. I am not looking for an excuse to leave you, if either of us want to do so we have agreed to be honest with each other. I don't want to leave you – I never have.

I was so happy on Monday and was looking forward to your call. As the morning passed and when I didn't see your car in the car park, a combination of disappointment and hurt led me to believe as I did, and then one thing just followed another. All I can promise you is that if anything like this happens again, I won't jump to conclusions without talking to you first, and ask you to do likewise. I promised this time I would be different with you and I have been, up to now that is. No! I don't want you to stay away from me, you won't feel hurt and lost – I promise you if you stay away I will feel that way. I remember once I criticised you and told you to see a psychiatrist, well, maybe I had better see one, or better still, let's see one together!!

I want to see you happy and smiling again – you are lovely when you smile and it is the way I love you most. I miss you and think about you all the time.

Please forgive me and love me again – I love you and I need you.

Love Tina

*

Their liaison was in its second year, the year in which he became an American citizen. Not only did Stephen and Martina feel inextricably bound to each other, but out of the petty jealousies and misunderstandings endured in the past grew a new confidence. All the precautions they took to hide their love only strengthened it. That commitment, and their awareness of the invidious situation they found themselves in, drove them to behave with the foolish pride of contentment and take risks above and beyond the tolerance of the calumnying busybodies and mordant gossipers that represented a menacing minority of the workforce at Lehman Brothers.

About this time one Friday afternoon over beers after close of trading, Chubby had cause to take him aside and apprise him of some scuttlebutt he had picked up that day in the canteen.

'Perhaps I oughtn't to tell you, but you're pissing on my patch! You know my thinking on this kinda fuckery,' he said. 'I know it's nobody's business but your own, but using Robertson's office for a late night booty call with the lady is bad karma.'

'Whatdoya mean? That never happened,' he countered, staring slack-jawed at Chubby.

'I don't givva shit whether it happened or not. I'm just telling you what I heard. And if I heard it then it's out there in the oozing mire for everyone to put their own slant on. Look around ya kid… you can bet your bottom dollar before you know what's what everyone will be talking about her having your baby.'

'Whoa! We're just good friends,' he chuckled, taken aback by Chubby's directness.

'Good friends? Stick with me here now. What you do in your spare time is no matter. What fucking matters is that her husband is a big noise at Citibank. If he gets wind of it there'll be a shitstorm, maybe curtains for you at Lehman. You with me on this kemo sabe? You ain't in the club… not yet anyhow. And these guys pull rank, ruthlessly close ranks, and back each other against the outlier, against the interloper,' Chubby seethed in steely elucidation.

'I hear ye, I hear ye. I don't care. I –'

'That's a bunch of horseshit, you don't care. Kamikaze horseshit. You'll end up the scapegoat, giving smug people a lot to be smug about. And don't think I haven't noticed your dereliction of duty, skiving off from the floor. Frank's not you Steve. The clients want you. Get your shit together man.'

Maca's stellar performance on the Stock Exchange floor had continued unabated, his boss Jeffrey Robertson more than praiseworthy of his dynamo achievements, a vote of confidence supported by Chubby, and ably demonstrated by the substantial increase he had received in his annual bonus. Nevertheless, he had taken chances, roping Frank in to cover for him as dealer when he and Martina had other things on their mind. Having listened to Chubby's reprimand, he ruminated on whether or not he should talk to her about the possible repercussions of such gossip for both of them. Her husband knowing, or not knowing, was never discussed between them, and he had not been inclined to ask. What purpose would it serve? Moreover, finding out Tom knew would inevitably complicate matters. In Moran's pub later that evening, troubled by Chubby's revelation, he kept his distance from her, aggressively fending off with trite off-the-cuff remarks any discreet approach she made. Amid the crescendo of babblement he could not think straight about the possible ramifications should their relationship be uncovered, and needing his own space to think things through he left without saying adios to anybody. Stomping back to his car in the head office car park, he had just fired the engine when Martina sat into the passenger seat beside him. Gunning the accelerator pedal and burning rubber on exiting the bank premises he brought her, in spiteful silence, to his apartment. Not offering her a drink, he gulped a bottle beer by the neck, sprawling in his armchair, a "fuck you" attitude permeating his responsive gestures as she stood hurling put-downs: "What is it… what the hell is wrong with you" – "What in the fuck am I supposed to have done wrong now… you mad selfish bastard" – "It's all self self self with you" – "What in the fuck brought this on", her lambasting words cursing him shrilly, sputtered with sibilants, her nostrils quivering. 'Go on slanging me! Pile it on!' he jeered.

Then listening in subdued silence to her carping invective, surprised by the venom of her lash out, he unwittingly engineered a supercilious smirk that enraged her rancorous fury to even greater heights of disparagement. He heard her, but not what she said, his mind switched off. What did he care, he listlessly brooded in idle insolence, emotionally self destructive. What the fuck is he doing with her anyway? She's nothing but trouble. Is he less in love with her than he imagined? Skulking around the apartment awaiting the pleasure of her company; always there for her. Oh yes! He did want to be with her. And when they could be away together behaving like illegal immigrants, or, escaped convicts, lying low in out of the way places. Chubby's right, all a load of "fuckery". Rising from the armchair to retrieve another beer from the icebox, his indecorous crapulence rendered him perfunctorily offensive, pouring more fuel on the furnace of her rage, giving her sound reasons to hate him. Relieved to hear the bang of the door as she stormed out of the apartment with an air of maligned righteousness, he threw himself on the bed and slipped into a stuporous slumber.

On Monday, early, she personally hand delivered a note, leaving it propped against Cantillon's woodcut inscription on his desk:

Steve   Monday

I am dropping you this note rather than phoning because I don't know how you feel towards me right now or how you would react if I phoned. I know I won't say everything I want to especially if, as I imagine, you are still hopping mad with me and there is also the possibility that I may not get the chance to as you might bang down the phone. So please, when you get this note, count to ten and "simmer down before answering it.

What the hell was all that about on Friday? I could not get through to you - even had we stayed talking until 5 a.m. it would have made no difference. And your extraordinary behaviour was… well let's not go there. I was so mad – you really have a way of making me see "red" at times. But the next day when I "cooled off" and thought about everything, I regretted having said a lot of things to you. I didn't mean to be so hurtful – that is the last thing I want to do to you because I love you. I don't want it to end this way – I can't just wipe out everything you are to me and everything I feel for you over a row. If we are going to part, let it be because one or both of us want to and as friends.

If you can't meet me this evening, please phone me but don't phone me until you have "simmered down". Honey, please try to make it this evening as I need to talk to you as soon as possible.

Love you - Tina

9

Days, weeks, months, in a kind of concertinaed time-span, passed in a haze of lover's assignations, collusions on togetherness, and a knowing conflation of carnality, interspersed with puissantly finical criticism of each other's behaviour, harsh words said in the exigency of fiery rows forgiven. During this sublime time he received a vitriolic letter from his sister Eileen with whom he did not correspond:

Dear Skunk,

So you did not get home for father's funeral despite all your so called good intentions. You did not even write that letter you so heart-rendingly promised your mother. Too much inconvenience for you – too much bother - you worm.

Did you know your own father was afraid of you – yes afraid of the son he reared. He told me so – crying – the week before he died. An old man, ill and dying and crying he was afraid of you. That you did not take-up his job at Peters yard, a job ready made for you to walk into. That you did not stay home and look after mother. That you were too carried away by fancy wants. How selfish you are. Yes – that old man who feared you in life thought the blackest day of his life was when you upped and left for America, leaving our mother to fend for herself in a house with no heat – no lights as often as not – a house in which she could rarely afford to light a fire. All too much of a burden to you. Such wanton neglect by a son.

Finally and in conclusion I want you to know that I resent the cruel stroke of fate that made you my brother. Down the years I shall point you out as the man my father feared.

That is about all and this is goodbye – not for now – forever. I do not hate as I am – I hope too mature for that. In years I shall probably even forgive but I know I could never meet and be friendly. It would have cost so little to be kind to our parents wouldn't it!!! But then maybe each of us thought it was too big a burden to bear alone. When next you visit a church (do you even bother to darken a church door now?) just say a prayer and think on this for a second or two – that doesn't cost anything.

Ta a lot

Eileen

Distressed, he thought hard about the implications of its content. Such bizarre hate he could not fathom. Did he deserve it, any of it? It was so perversely bitchy. He made up his mind to ignore her and her venomous accusations. However, he would raise the monthly payment to his mother to $100 thereafter.

All of which took its toll on Maca's pit watch at the Stock Exchange, where mistakes are made and errors are to be expected. A simple misunderstanding of a buy or sell hand signal, or, the price semaphored by a trader, meant the bank would have to carry the trading loss, unless the dealer had time to rectify the client's position, the client having bought or sold in good faith based on the opening punt. If the dealer could not rectify the loss, it would be posted to the bank's Error Account and written off against profit. Most such errors clocked up were so small they did not register on the bank's radar. There could be upwards of twenty errors in any one day across the trading floor, but only those that impacted on the client's bottom line had to be reversed or booked. And if the aggregative monthly losses climbed into the red zone ($50,000+ per dealer), only then did the bank's internal auditors start to ask awkward questions of the dealers.

One day during Maca's absence from the Exchange on rendez-vous with Martina, Frank, in covering his dealer telephone, made a mistake in selling in a rising market rather than buying, in con-travention of the order of one of Lehman's longest established customers, Prudential Insurance. On arriving back at head office later that afternoon as usual to assist the back room support staff reconcile the thousands of trader slips and dealer contracts, he uncovered a bottom line discrepancy of $55,000. It took him the best part of three hours to spot the delinquent trading slip, a sale note for twelve contracts signed off under Frank's scrawled sig-nature as pit trader, no sign of the balancing purchase contracts. Frank, obviously with no time to rectify his gaffe, had hung him out to dry, his signature verifying the instructed pit trader's role from the dealer. But he had not been there to issue any such in-struction. The mistake, if uncovered, would assuredly be identified as a dealer error. The client's unfulfilled buy order would have to be made good by buying back twenty four contracts, probably at a higher market price which would still, he calculated at the most advantageous price, leave a loss to the bank of between $20,000 and $30,000. The error (for even if Frank owned up to his improvident act, Maca having abandoned his desk would have to bear full responsibility) could not be hidden and could well result in both of them being fired. With the flawed contract note in hand, he took the elevator to the next floor intending to apprise Chubby of his dilemma, and seek his advice on how best to address it. The office was deserted, Martina's desk clear of paperwork, the seat of her black leather swivel chair retaining an indented impression of her callipygian rear end. Resisting the urge to kneel and kiss the vestigial semblance, he withdrew and walked to Moran's pub, seething with anger at Frank's crass slip-up, hoping to find Chubby there, the brisk cool breeze drifting off the East River invigorating his frenzied thoughts. Even if the loss could be reduced to $20,000, it could also double if the market opened higher again next morning. His vaunted ambition had been trans-formed into a financial nightmare. On stepping inside Morans with tentativeness, he stood by the door adjusting to the ambient darkness and the fug of tobacco smoke. Soon he observed Frank huddled amid some stragglers from the bank indolently sipping their beers. On approach, Frank blushed scarlet and appeared to shiver, a strained look of embarrassment spreading over his face. There was no sign of Chubby or Martina.

'You'll never guess who 'phoned from Chicago looking for ye today,' Frank said in hokum light-heartedness.

'Well! Who?'

'Johnny Cassidy.'

'Johnny! What the fuck's he doin' in Chicago?'

'Workin' as a barman at The Ritz Carlton. He's given up the music business, at least as a source of reliable income. Here's his telephone number. I'm sorry Maca,' Frank then broached through a hangdog grin. 'You obviously found we're in a spot of bother. It was fucken mayhem on the floor.'

'Why the fuck didn't ye phone me instead of lettin' it run?'

'I called the loft I don't know how many times. There was no reply. How the fuck was I to know where you were. I've been waitin' here all evening for ye.'

'Ye should'a left a note. I had to wade through every slip, several times, to find out 'twas you was the culprit.'

'If I'd left a note god knows who else would find out. Knowin' you I thought it best to let the hare sit. To see if there was any way round the problem.'

'Well the hare's sittin' in my fucken lap right now thanks to your fucken recklessness. Has Chubby been in for a beer?'

'No… did ye not hear? He's been drafted to the reserves.'

'What! When?'

'Finishes up on Friday.'

*

That Friday evening a farewell get together in Moran's pub was sponsored by Jeffrey Robertson to send Chubby off on a high note prior to leaving for his stint of duty in Vietnam. Two other staff members from different divisions in the bank had also been drafted but Robertson was intent on looking out for his team by reserving a private room for dinner later in Trattoria Baldovino. This turn of events dictated (to Maca's way of thinking) that disclosing to Chubby Frank's tactical blunder could well prove counterproductive, Chubby not having the time to supervise any corrective measure to be adopted in rectifying the situation. He also decided not to inform Robertson, aware of his punctiliousness and knowing he had little understanding of the *modus operandi* of the markets, his forte being people management. Maca didn't let it worry him overmuch, he and Frank would go it alone and endeavour to solve the problem internally.

The markets had risen next day forcing him to post the

discrepancy to the Error Account under a fictitious trade to the client, a transaction that necessitated him making a balancing entry of twelve contracts fictitiously bought at the same price and booked to Prudential, the Error Account absorbing the variation. As an opening redoubt, he was now playing with twenty four fictitious contracts, the dealing buying him some time to work out a solution. He calculated he had the better part of three weeks to resolve matters before Internal Audit started sniffing around. If alarm bells started to ring in the interim, he would say the Senior Managing Dealer had been alerted, but obviously with all that was going on in Chubby's personal life, the error had been overlooked. That first evening, he had been prepared to come clean with Chubby whatever the consequences of the revelation to his promotional prospects; that way resolution of the problem would, going forward, be a team effort. Having hidden it, it became his problem alone, Frank sitting on the fence. Imperceptibly his outlook changed.

The usual eulogistic speeches were made at Chubby's farewell bash: Robertson assuring him that his position in the bank was secure and there for him on his discharge from the army; that he was a much prized, and indeed virtually irreplaceable, member of staff. Chubby suggesting there were two or three of his colleagues well up to the job, and that he might have a difficulty wresting it back from the chosen candidate on his return, archly winking at Maca as he said so. Martina stayed close-by Chubby the whole evening, the picture of solicitous concern for her boss, a scenario that suited Maca as he was in no mood to frivol with her. Later in the Trattoria Baldovino, he and a nervy Frank sat together at the long rectangular table, promptly joined by the vivacious Myra Johansson flaunting her charms in a see-through blouse and cerise minidress, seemingly intent on scoring. The beer and wine flowed freely, the meliorative effect of which reanimated him in to taking an impulsive interest in the female flesh up for grabs seated next to him. The alcohol loosed his stressed-out frame of mind caused by the unrelenting pressure he had endured over the past few days, and amid howls of laughter he and Myra fairly dominated the discussion at their end of the table. But he knew Myra to be a scatterbrain, her outbursts dragging everything down to flippancy, and was not seduced by her siren play, considering the dalliance with her at the Griswold Inn a false step. Looking down the opposite side of the table where Martina sat between Chubby and Jeffrey Robertson, the usual claque around them, observing her frosty look, her eyes emitting deep disdain of the ostensibly loutish antics he was embroiled in in Myra's company. Not wanting to further aggravate her misconceived notion of resentment, and bothered by the potent diuretic effect of plenteous alcohol, he upped and headed for the washroom where he was soon joined by Chubby at the urinals.

'You know Steve if you play your cards right you're a shew-in for the job. Jeff thinks highly of ya. You fit the bill.'

'As Jeff said earlier Chubby you're irreplaceable. I'm more than happy as a dealer. No way do I need the extra hassle of your job.'

'Just take some time and have a good think on it. I'm only marking your card should Jeff approach ya,' said Chubby, now bumptiously drying his hands with copious paper towels. 'He's a likeable bastard to work for. It's a great opportunity.'

'I will think about it. Thanks Chubby. And you know I never really got to thank ye for your help on the job. Couldn't have done it without ye. And hear me now, when you get over there take good care of yerself. We need ye back here in one piece.'

On exiting the washroom he saw Martina standing stonily shrouded under the shadow of the stairwell tacitly beckoning him to follow her outside. She looked wistfully mournful as he, in portentous unease, followed her steady willowy stride. Once outside they stood for a little in rancorous silence till she turned toward him seeking eye contact, her face expressionless, unreadable:

'We should part,' she said in a firm uninflected tone with seeming irrecusable resolution, her eyes questioning him to gauge his reaction. The blood seemed to drain from his veins, leaving him numbed. He flipped open a pack of cigarettes, lit two and offered her one, which she declined with a minute shake of her head. Taking a deep drag, he sibilantly blew a smoke ring that wafted over her head and watched her face contort in an angry grimace, smothered by suspicion. Please don't let your imagination run away with you he begged of her inside his head. Cockamamie jealously, that primitive emotion, making you crazy, he wanted to bawl out, his heartbeat quickening. She continued:

'I think we should break up. Not one call… no note… not a bleep out of you for well over a week. Everything's a mess. Too much distrust,' she griped, her voice nervily throaty.

'Distrust! I thought we were over distrust by now. I thought we absolutely trusted each –'

'Obviously not. I do love you Steve, more than you'll ever know. But I no longer seem to know myself, my love for you is eating me up. My every waking thought is of you… is about us. I don't think I can do this anymore,' she was speaking in a voice both low and quick, eyeing the profile of his face, now fractiously reddened as he dropped the cigarette butt and ground it out with the heel of his shoe on the pavement. Turning his back on her, not wanting her to see the emotional strain that crept over him, afraid of his own voice, he moved a step or two closer to the street now skimming with a slew of litter in the thick of rumbling post theatre traffic; the stridulant honks of the cabs; dipped headlights refracted by walls of glass of the office buildings seemingly reflecting animistic rage. Had she heard he was in trouble at the bank, he pondered, but immediately dismissed the thought from his mind.

'I love my husband, not as I love you. Never thought it possible to love two people at the same time, but I do. And Tom is deserving of my love – always there for me. When I'm with you

I'm so happy. With you I know I exist, you more than any man I've known make me feel like a real woman.' She spoke in prosodic tones. 'Thinking of you, and all about you, even after the rows we have… no, more so, fills me with being, and a longing to be with you. Yes. I believe that's it. It's the heartache of longing to be with you that eats me up.'

Vacuous bursts of laughter reached them through the swing doors of the restaurant as people began to take their leave, he smarting at the reveller's callous indifference to the human stupidity of his plight. They both lapsed back into silence. He lit another cigarette, embarrassingly not offering her one, dumbly exhaling smoke from his mouth and flaring nostrils, his heart fit to burst in silent anguish, his knees shaking as if about to give way. Tormented by passion's entanglement he could not formulate a response, her words stuck in his craw. There was no answer to make, she holding the trump card – her husband. Any decision to wreck her home had to be hers to make.

'It will cause me a lot of pain. And for you too I know,' she resumed, biting her nether lip, her eyes rimming with tears. 'I meant it when I said I would never forget you. How could I forget you… you're a part of me. And I know I'm a part of you. My heart is yours… yours to the day –'

'If that's true… if ye really believe that then where's the distrust you speak so glibly about?' he said, not looking at her.

'"Glibly?" I said it because it's the truth. When we're apart, I tear myself to pieces thinking of where you are, what you're doing, who you're with. I swear to you Steve I'm at breaking point. My nerves are shattered. I can't take it any more.'

Someone called his name in passing as he watched Martina droop her head in her hands, melodramatic and pitiable. Flicking the cigarette end onto the roadway sending out bitty red embers, he moved to hold her in his arms but she would not meet his eyes and stepped away from his comforting embrace.

'Please don't,' she said, shifting on her feet as her will wilted, anxiety drowning her fears.

'If that's what ye want then so be it,' he said, looking at her questioningly, ineffable feelings welling up inside him in a tumult of emotions. 'I never meant to cause you pain and I hate myself right now seeing ye so... so miserable. I don't want to hurt you. My every instinct is not to hurt you. Just to... to be with you.'

She turned and quickly walked back into the restaurant, leaving him with the familiar knotty emotions, a sense of the futility of it all sweeping over him, his wits fragmenting in the loss of love and fervent regrets of forfeited sensuality. Not having the stomach for the banal craic, the cupidinous jabbering and scumbled laughter from unheard jokes that echoed out onto the street he did not follow her. He needed to be alone, to think. Hailing a cab he left for home, leaving his car at the bank, leaving behind the pitiless bustle of the city.

After a sleepless night mulling over her words, wrestling existential torment in silence, listening to his heart beating in his ears, he rose early and journeyed to the bank to collect his car, picking up a bottle of Jack Daniels, two packs of cigarettes and the New York Times from his local drug store on the return to his apartment. Telephoning his old friend Johnny Cassidy in Chicago, they exchanged a lot of friendly intelligence but nothing in their good-natured banter lifted his spirits. Remembering the big ball game was on that afternoon, he decided to take a catnap on the sofa, setting the alarm clock to go off fifteen minutes before the live television coverage was due to commence. He had no particular interest in either team and no great love of the game, considering the rules the least skilful of any ball game he knew, the players not playing the ball but the man. However, he reasoned the effusive television commentary would for a few hours help dull the hurt of realization that he had separated from the woman he loves, that she had initiated the parting of the ways as much, apparently, for her sanity as for any other reason, and that between the loss of Martina and the pressure at work his own sanity would be sorely tested. *"I love my husband… not as I love you… never thought it possible to love two people at the same time"* he again reflected on what she had said. Bullshit. No two loves could possibly be the same. If she loves him with the same passion she loves me how could she cheat on him. Yes cheat; there is no other word for it. She cannot love him the way she loves me. She may well love him in a wifely way, fussing over meals and laundry, making a home, reaching out for and grabbing security, the kind of love that lovers settle into after years of marriage. But not as lovers love, not like us, he mused, swallowing his despair in assimilable doses. And what of all the lies, the duplicitous scheming, plotting trysts by anxiously working out her husband's plans, her stony-hearted deception. She's twenty seven years old for chrissake. Married now, what, three years. No children. No complications. She can start over, fight the mistake in her life. Her being with me, her wanting to be with me, into whatever the future holds out for us is her call, her choice. I will not take her away from him. She must, must leave him. My body aches for her. I want her. I love her. I love everything about her. Everything.

Wallowing in self-pity, sleep overpowered his restless mind and not hearing the alarm clock ring, he missed out on watching the ball game. Throughout that night and next day he chain smoked and in an intemperate fug polished off the bottle of whiskey. By Monday morning after fitful sleep, perhaps he had never been asleep, he was reduced to digging out and smoking long butts from the cigarette-ends filled ashtrays. Later at work in a state of interminable fatigue, as he exited the bank on his way to the Exchange he bumped into Martina by chance, she having been dropped off by her husband and as she began to mouth some, no doubt, fatuous utterance, perhaps a casual greeting, he, seething with rage, brusquely met the gesture with a plaintive exclamation of "Go fuck yourself". The market prices remained high all day preventing him from addressing the pressing task of rectifying the discrepancy in the Error Account. Tuesday morning he read the missive left by her propped against Cantillon's woodcut:

Steve   Monday

You really upset me the way you treated me this morning. I <u>must</u> see you to talk everything out between us. Please let me see you – I want, so much, for both of us to understand each other and that we don't hurt each other in any way, unnecessarily. What we have between us is too important for that. Please don't let pride, stubbornness, etc. get in the way. My feelings for you haven't changed in any way, so it's just as difficult for me that we have to part. If we can't be together the way we want let us, at least, be close friends, let me phone you, from time to time, and I want you to phone me and see each other sometimes. Am I asking too much?

It's very important that I see you - I don't want to lose everything, so it's up to you from here. Don't leave me this way. I can see you on Friday – perhaps by then you will have had a chance to think things out. If it's too early for that or if you don't want to see me again, I'll try to understand. You know how and where to contact me and if sometime – later on perhaps – you need me, just call me.

Love you

Tina

Before leaving for the Exchange he hastily scribbled a note asking her to try and understand his feelings, that no other woman can touch his very being, can make him be as she can, telling her how much he loved her and of his wanting to be with her – always.

Steve   Thursday

Thank you for your note – I was afraid you were going to ignore mine. I'm trying to understand your feelings which, are similar to mine, but Steve I must see you and talk to you. I miss you so much and am miserable without you.

I also feel very bad about the way I treated you at the weekend – I want to explain why I thought we should part at the time and now I realize it was all so stupid because it just had something to do with something you said. If I hadn't been so stubborn we could have talked it over.

If you are as miserable as I am – apart from each other – then let's not part at all because it's not what I want either. Let's have a bloody good talk and reach some sort of understanding of each other and the situation we are both in.

Right at this moment I just want to hold you and be with you. I miss all we had together, good and bad, so please don't let it go.

Love you,

Tina

10

Two weeks after uncovering Frank's blundering mistake, the loss to Lehman Brothers had mushroomed to $88,000, the market having risen another one hundred and fifty points, so affording Maca no opportunity to buy contracts to replace the twelve fictitious contracts he had booked to Prudential Insurance in the Error Account. In order to get over the hurdle of internal audit's monthly review of all dealer contracts and the bank's liability under the Error Account at November month end, he closed down all the open positions he had been running and posted a journal entry to the Error Account to bring the balance back to zero. To help balance the other side of the entry he surrendered his commissions earned. This slight of hand and Thanksgiving Day would get him past the scrutiny of internal audit that month end, and with the Christmas holiday pushing the next review out to January he had bought himself an extended breathing space of at least six or seven weeks to come up with a solution to the problem.

On Tuesday December 5, Jeffrey Robertson summoned him to his office and on making his way there he fretted the game was up, believing he was about to be fired:

'Ah Stephen, thanks for coming along at such short notice. Take a seat won't you. I've been meaning to have a word with you but you know how it is… busy busy,' said Robertson. 'As you are aware Stephen the bank is committed to holding the Senior Dealer position open for Charles Schweitzer pending his return from Vietnam. Charles is the best dealer, bar none, on the Exchange and I for one will be a very happy man to see him back here.'

'Ahhemm. I second that Mr Robertson,' he said, nervily clearing his throat.

'In the interim, the board has decided to split the onerous re-sponsibility of Charles' position between currently operating key dealers, as fair a division of the responsibilities and indeed the spoils as can be mustered so that one is not thrown in at the deep end. I've already spoken with Richard Phillips who has expressed himself keen to take up the challenge. I would like to think I need look no further than your goodself to fill the other position. Prior to his departure Charles acquainted me with some expressed reser-vations on your part... the "extra hassle" I believe was the remark. But at the time you would I believe have understood him to refer to the full management position rather than the very much appor-tioned duties I am now planning for. And indeed, I intend to take a much more hands-on approach thus hopefully reducing the job-share tasks for you and Richard. Martina Patterson will continue her role of supervising the back room support staff but will henceforth report directly to me. Naturally, in offering you this temporary role it will undoubtedly be seen in some quarters as treading on the toes of more senior, indeed longer serving personnel, who may well consider themselves more deserving of the promotion. I can handle such resentments. I trust you will have no problem doing likewise.'

Recovering his composure he listened to Robertson's faggoty prissiest proposition with intense concentration, meanwhile mentally determining that acceptance of the position could prove advantageous in his endeavour to rectify the Prudential error, hopefully giving him more time to offload the flawed and fictitious contracts; and greater authority with which to cajole the internal auditors should they get stroppy with him.

'So Stephen. What have you to say for yourself? Interested?'

'Very interested Mr Robertson.'

'Of course should you wish to take some time to think it over by all means do –'

'No need Mr Robertson. Subject to sorting out the job-spec and being satisfied with the increase in salary you can count me in.'

'Splendid… splendid. I have here a summary of your additional duties which also contains details of salary and perks commensurate with the position.'

Glancing at the figures and heedful of his boss's punctilious manner he hastily asked with satisfaction:

'Where do I sign?'

'At foot of each page.'

In a swoon of excitement he signed the three pages of the document and handed them back to Robertson who, with a flourish, countersigned as witness.

'Splendid. I'll have it photocopied and a certified copy left on your desk in a sealed envelope. The contract commences Monday next,' said Robertson, moving from behind his desk and shaking Maca's hand with a limp grip. 'I'm so glad we see eye-to-eye on this Stephen. You are a very decisive and impressive young man and I am delighted to have you on my team.'

'Thanks Mr Robertson,' he said, blushing as he made to exit, maladroitly stumbling against a chair close to the door. He felt such a lummox.

'Oh by the way… almost forgot. Of the bank's next batch of Harvard Business School graduates, two will be allotted to the Exchange. I intend for both of them to work on your team. I expect they will grasp the ropes more readily under your astute tutelage than that of Phillips who, if it is not too unkind of me to say, can be a bit of a nit-picker… a stick-in-the-mud. They start with you in January. Okay?'

'Okay.'

*

By this time he was more than ever deeply in love with Martina, his friend Frank perplexed and somewhat cynical about what he perceived as their monomaniacal relationship, an obsessive preoccupation with each other virtually to the exclusion of any other interests. The lovers revelled in being able to spend long weekends *a deux* in cloistered ecstasy at his apartment, and some spent travelling through fulvous forest trails in upstate New York staying at pilgrim and colonial inns. The most memorable had been a trip to Niagara Falls where they stayed at the Asa Ransom House in Clarence having pre-booked The Blue Room with its lulling canopy bed. On the Saturday they got soaked to the skin in the hurled up mists (despite wearing supposedly impermeable cagoules over their winter coats and sou'westers) when visiting the vertiginous cataracts and Goat Island. Unable to hear each other above the deafening roar of the plunging rapids, they delightedly spent the time eyeing each other about the wonder of it all. Cold and exhausted they rushed back to the inn and took a hot leisurely bath, guzzling red wine from a jeroboam bottle cushioned by raffia leaves as the steaming water soothed their fatigued limbs; the white marbled bathroom suffused with the flickering light and aroma of twenty vanilla scented candles. That evening they drove to Lewiston, the street decorations and Christmas lights of the town featuring thousands of coloured bulbs twinkling out their happy message: hand-painted storybook displays of merry anthropomorphic characters; animated Christmas shows; all dusted by a light fall of seasonal snow. Rejuvenated, like excited children they posted whimsical letters to Saint Nicholas in the Santa Claus mailbox, his wish being that the venerated saint (who in infancy refused to suck the breasts on fasting days) would make time stand still and leave them in the blissfulness of the now to spend the rest of their lives together. Later at dinner in the Clarkson House Restaurant, they sat in a booth surrounded by agrestic *décor* of old farm tools and gadgets, the old-fashioned revamped kerosene lamp on the table barely lighting the patrician refinement of a dyspeptic-looking patriot gazing out from the smoke darkened oxidized oil portrait that hung on the wall behind them. A portrait he took to be of Benjamin Franklin but whom Martina insisted was of John Adams, a difference of opinion condescendingly settled by the major-domo in her favour. The mouth-watering aroma of sizzling prime rib beef and lamb chops that emanated from the charcoal grill in the middle of the dining area whetted their appetite already sharpened by the exertions of the day. Embraced by lento time, they ate contentedly, relishing the scrumptious food and earthy French red wine. He felt closer to her than ever this day and seriously pondered asking her to leave her husband and spend the rest of her days with him, for good or ill. However, there remained the thorny prerequisite of divulging the existence of his son, the upshot of his hedonistic spree with Julia, and his own illegitimacy.

'Tina… I need to share something with ye,' he said leaning forward, blushing self-effacingly, elbows on the table, fingers tented like a wigwam.

She regarded him inscrutably and judging the earnest expression and self-conscious manner with which he launched into this divulgence she grew uneasy, knowing he was not referring to a share of the melody of desserts that ornamented his plate. She speared a morsel of cheesecake and unhurriedly put down her spoon and fork, the tines tinkling, and gently laid a hand on the crook of his elbow, her chin resting on the knuckles of her other hand.

'I have a son… Gary. He's goin' on four now.'

Remaining silent, she listened to him with rapt attention, fixing her inquisitive brown eyes on his.

'I didn't love his mother. It was a sex thing… just happened. But I do love my son. This was when I was in Boston.'

'Where is he now?' she asked with intense weightiness.

'In San Francisco. She took him away. I was already breakin' up with her when she got pregnant. I looked after her… in my own way, throughout the pregnancy, money and things like that. She wanted me to marry her, started pesterin' me. On the level her getting pregnant was the last thing I saw comin' down the track. I had been growing to detest being with her. And then I felt trapped. Believe you me she could be a right bitch. I refused to let my name go on the birth certificate. Out of the blue she told me she was taking Gary to California. She was goin' out there with this guy she said she had been involved with while seeing me. Produced the birth certificate with this son-of-a-bitch's name down as the father. All a right load of fuckery.'

'Did you ever see Gary again?'

'No! All I know is they're in San Francisco. She said she wanted me out of her life. When I asked her what she would tell our son if and when he ever asked about me, she said she would tell him she didn't know his biological father, that to her shame she didn't even have a name, that his being... his being born was the out-come of a one night stand. This, in all likelihood, to prevent Gary seekin' me out... ye know, when he's grown.'

'Do you want to see him again?'

'Don't really think about it much to be honest. What's to do about it? 'Tis all in the past,' his voice breaking as tears blurred his vision. Seeing the ardent concern on her face he said: 'I just thought you should know about it.'

'It's sad Steve, yet isn't it, in a way, gratifying to know there's a part of you out there, a son making his own way in the big bad world. If he's anything like you he'll do fine.'

'Yeah! He'll be all right. I know she loves him. It's me she couldn't stand,' he repined with a self-deprecating response.

They both became caught up in an emotional silence. Then, all of a sudden, he blurted out: 'There's somethin' else... I'm illegitimate myself. Only found out a few years ago that my mum and dad are not me mum and dad. I was adopted. My mum's name is McMahon. I was christened Stephen Michael McMahon. Don't know anythin' about me father, who my real father is.'

She smiled understandingly, reassuringly, her mouth pursed in a sympathetic moue. A hunger for contact swept over him. They needed to hold each other, to be alone with each other, away from the ambient hurly-burly of the restaurant. Asking her to leave Tom would have to wait for another day.

Opening the car door for her he watched her beautiful legs swing gracefully in unison as she sat into the Mustang, parting briefly on placing her handbag on the floor revealing the white triangle of her panties. Firing the engine he set the temperature booster on high and as they waited for the hoar frosted windscreen to thaw manically kissed and embraced in the intensifying heat. Driving back to Clarence he noticed she had left her thighs uncovered and began lightly touching her between her legs, both her hands holding his gently encouraging as she leaned toward him softly moaning, her sweet breath entrancing him. Pulling into a lay-by, engine left idling, he rolled over as she exhorted him to hurry and yanking aside the gusset of her panties pushed into her with wild fervency. That night at the inn he again made love to her, slowly and tenderly, spooning her as they drifted into sleep, semi-tumescent inside her – "Don't ever leave me" she sighed as she dozed off.

*

At the office Christmas party Martina was in buoyant mood, recklessly hanging out in his company (something they had agreed should not happen at work), she apparently oblivious to what he took to be the bitchery of some of the tongue-waggers scornful looks. On the dance floor, the live band belting out a sonorant medley of Elvis Presley hits, she dragged her dancing partner over to join him as he danced with Myra to the strains of "You're The Devil In Disguise". Eyeing him with a bewitching stare, her eyes salaciously radiant, her lips silently mouthing 'love you', she coquettishly mocked his clumsy hip-hop movements. When the band segued to "Love Me Tender" she discreetly slipped into his willing arms, dreamily stepping out the slow dance, while he sprung an erection and fought the temptation to randily smooch with her.

'Let me drive you home,' she whispered in his ear. 'I can stay with you the whole night and most of tomorrow.'

Dawn light filled the bedroom. Realizing he had run out of cigarettes he hurriedly dressed without disturbing her, intending to grab some at the local twenty-four hour drugstore. Heading there in the nippy morning breeze, the ground iridescent with frost, he saw that the left rear tyre of her car was flat and following closer inspection found the rim of the right rear wheel was touching the roadway. He rushed back advising her of the predicament; that he would have to jack up each wheel in turn and take it to the nearest garage for puncture repair, or hopefully for pump up only. She snuggled deeper under the bedclothes, a serene smile adorning her sleepy countenance. Having pumped up the first tyre at the garage he established it was not punctured; and when removing the second wheel spotted the chrome valve cap lying under the wheel arch. 'Pranksters, fucking pranksters,' he fumed all the way back to the garage when it occurred to him that the culprit might well have been someone from the Christmas party, perhaps some of the gossip-mongers who took a dim view of their relationship and followed them home. A sense of panic flooded his mind, his mouth drying-up. Being found spending the night together was the *corpus delicti* of the affair. But who would do such a thing? Why should anyone bother? Buying two packs of cigarettes at the garage, her brand and his, he banished that dark suspicion from his mind, sharing it with her would only cause her unnecessary distress.

He could smell a fry-up on re-entering the apartment and called out that her car was now sorted. Moving to wash his hands at the kitchen sink he felt her slim arms tightly embrace him, her velvety lips nuzzling the nape of his neck and, jovially turning to face her, saw she was naked but for the loose fitting of one of his shirts.

"Sorry for not helping out with the bloody car."

"'Twasn't any bother."

"What a night honey…. I loved every minute of it. Where the hell do you find the energy… and then having to get up so early?"

He tenderly kissed her, then gently hoisted her onto the worktop and hungrily tongued her juicebox, she firmly caressing his head desiring him to go deeper. An acrid smell invaded his nostrils. He rushed to switch off the cooker, and then carried her to the bedroom. Knowing they would not see each other over the Christmas vacation added intensity to their lovemaking.

The following Monday was Christmas day. He had made no arrangements to meet up with anyone, to be with anyone, to be anywhere, and for the first time felt dizzyingly claustrophobic in the confines of his bachelor apartment. Grazing on the indifferently bland contents of the fridge-freezer, his melancholic thoughts conjured up images of Martina and her husband animatedly enjoying festive drinks with their neighbours. Had they invited family members to share dinner at their home, nieces and nephews in tow; festive hats worn in cheery jubilation; the festal table strewn with the spilled novelty contents of Bloomingdales Christmas crackers. Endeavouring to banish such huffish thoughts from his mind, languidly he took to reading "War and Peace", indolently turning the pages. But after some thirty pages or so of apathetic browsing and disheartened when realizing there were another eleven hundred pages to go he distractedly threw the book on the floor. Passive misery was his accomplice for the rest of the day, compounded by the god-awful rubbish that passed for festive entertainment on the television. A bottle of whiskey his only solace temporarily easing the haunting loneliness.

In virtual hibernation that week abound in slothful habits he grew a beard. Sunday, New Years eve, he joined the usual suspects from the bank, Frank Connolly, Myra Johansson (Whats with all the facial hair? she taunted him) and Richard Phillips, in Moran's pub from where, after liberal imbibitions of lager, they moved on to the Lotus Garden Chinese restaurant which had been pre-booked by Phillips. Soulless rollicking was the order of the evening, loud-mouthed hair-brained attempts at jocularity upsetting their co-diners necessitating the sourpuss waiter remonstrating with them for more quiet or they would be ejected. Intemperate consumption of alcohol can make a foolhardy hero of a wimp, and Phillips' bold contumelious stance against the waiter's reprimand saw the revellers escorted out of the restaurant in the midst of their main course. Pub crawling all the way down the Lower East Side, they arrived at the East River in time to witness, with the tumultuous crowd already gathered there, the pyrotechnical fireworks display welcoming in the year 1968, the multiethnic crowd greeting each salvo of bright coloured rockets with raucous *"ooohs"* and *"aaahs"*. Hamburgers and hooch were ravenously consumed, quickly followed by ice cream guzzled from plastic cups with miniature wooden spoons; all dispensed by gleeful street hawkers. Except for the roisterers' intent on partying throughout the night, most of the crowd dispersed in an orderly manner following the conclusion of the salutes to the New Year. Maca, having gluttonously consumed the lethal mixture of beer, burger and ice cream, on top of the partly consumed spicy Chinese food, disgorged the nauseous contents of his stomach in the alcove doorway of a bank, some of the vomit spattering his coat and shoes. Reeling on jellified legs it was opportune for him to lean like a lummox on Myra for support, an expression of soppy concern spreading across her face as she wiped his mouth with her extravagantly perfumed dainty handkerchief from which he recoiled gasping for air. He hailed a taxicab for home, she climbing into the back seat beside him. Mid morning he awoke with the "mother and father" of a hangover, buck naked, but relieved to see no sign of Myra. If he had had sex with her last night he had no memory of it. Then he heard the toilet flush and soon she appeared white faced and mascara smudged from the night's carouse, bath towel slung over her naked body, beard rash gracing her slender neck and shoulder, her broad smile signalling the answer.

'The dead arose and appeared to many. How are ya sweetie? I'll make us some breakfast. Juice, cereal, coffee. Okay.'

'Juice? Just the hair of the dog,' he croaked in tetchy dismissal of her offer.

'The hair of the dog that bit ya last night? Doesn't work ya know. I'm a maven... never worked for me. You need sustenance to get over that katzenjammer of yours. Juice to help detox, bowl of cereal for roughage, strong coffee to let ya know you're back in the land of the living,' she mewled in her element.

'Don't bother yer barney. I'll get it meself. Me fucken head's splitting.'

Clambering from the bed and clumsily hopping from foot to foot as he climbed into his underpants, he headed for the fridge, kicking aside his discarded clothes from the night before that lay strewn on the floor, and made himself a revivifying Bloody Mary.

'Ya sure nailed the festive proceedings,' he heard her call out from the bedroom. 'The guys couldn't give a fuck what happened ya, probably too tanked up themselves to give a shit. I took ya home babe, looked after ya while ya were talking on the big white phone –'

'On the what?'

'The crapper,' she answered with a throaty laugh. 'Ya razzed your guts up in the crapper. Where ya got it from I can't imagine for ya'd already dumped a load in a street doorway before we got here.'

Knocking back a fortifying gulp from his glass, he decided he had to be rid of her. 'Thanks Myra,' he snuffled. 'You saved my bacon. For the life of me I can't remember a thing about last night.'

'Not to worry hon... I had a great time.'

'Look Myra,' he said, standing in the bedroom doorway quaffing his drink, 'I have to go in to... to the office today. I promised –'

'On New Years day?' she asked earnestly.

'Yeah I know. Jeff asked me to check over some charts and I didn't have time to –'

'That asshole! To hell with the chinless wonder hon… I thought we might spend the day together.'

'Sorry! I'm already late. I'll drop ye at the station, or, if we make it quick I can give ye a ride home. There'll be little or no traffic.'

'Don't fucking trouble yarself yousonofabitch. I'll see myself home,' she spat out with asperity as she staggered from the bed and began dressing hurriedly.

'Sorry,' he snuffled again, blushing for her.

'Oh yeah! Sorry doesn't cut it sweetie,' she snapped peevishly without turning around as she grabbed her handbag and stomped out of the apartment.

Breathing a huge sigh of relief on hearing the door slam behind her, he finished the Bloody Mary, gathered his clothes that reeked of cigarette smoke off the floor, his coat stained and his shoes flecked with last nights technicolour yawn, and stretched into his shirt and pants. He felt a tightness gnawing at his chest, a smarting dryness in his cigarette-sore throat and made himself a strong cup of coffee. Reflecting on the holiday season he realized it had been a shambles of forced jocularity and fatuous conversations spent in an alcoholic haze, soured by pent up resentments about the current state of his life, his morassic humdrum life, leaving him grappling with inertness. Yes, he was miserable without Martina. That was the true cause of his broodiness, the cause of his despondency. He missed being with her. He missed her now till his body ached for her, the pain charring his heart. He loved her, a love he felt deep in his innermost being. A love tainted by his bitterness at not being able to share her life free of her other life - her marriage. He hurt. He was sore for her. Idly shaving off the beard, he groomed his facial hair to a neat goatee and moustache.

*

186

Seeking out the panacea of work, on January 4 he received a telephone call at the bank from Robert Perotti:

'Everything I hear about you kiddo is hot.'

'All good I hope.'

'Yip! Keep it bitchen. Happy new year by the way.'

'Many happy returns to you and yours.'

'Looka Stephen, I might have a new client for you, could earn you a few bucks. An Irish guy, builder here in Boston. Puts good business my way. Does a lot of trading on the markets on his own account. But you know, he's so busy what with the port redevelopment program, he asked me to recommend a go-getter dealer to handle his portfolio. I put in a good word for you kiddo. What do you say?'

'Sure Bob. Delighted to help out.'

'Great! He's in New York as we speak. I'll give him your direct line. You can expect his call later today. The name is Sean Flannery. He'll want to meet up with you before committing so the new business is down to whether he likes the cut of your jib. As an existing customer he won't need clearance. But assuming he bites I'll talk to Jeffrey Robertson. You should clear it with him as well, the usual protocol. Besta luck.'

He didn't get Flannery's call till he was about to 'phone Martina prior to leaving off work for the day. He could hear the noise of children playfully screaming and laughing in the background.

'Mr MacAlindon, I need to see ye. I believe Bob Perotti filled you in… will ye shut-the-fuck-up back there. Sorry about that. Can't hear meself think. I'm with the wife and two of my kids; dragged out all day shopping at the sales would you believe.'

'That's okay Mr Flannery. I was expecting your call.'

'Good… good. I'm staying at my favourite New York hotel, the Algonquin. Can you come over?'

'Sure, what time?'

'Within the hour, say five thirty. How does that grab ye?'

'Fine, suits me fine.'

'I'm taking Marge and the girls for an early dinner so we should wrap up our parley fairly rapidly. I'll meet ye in the lobby. Not quiet enough to do our business in the suite. I'll be the guy who looks like he can't afford to stay in the place.'

Having replaced the receiver the telephone instantly rang again. It was Martina.

'Can I come round?'

''Fraid not no.'

'Don't like the goatee. Puts years on you,' she said in a peremptory tone.

'Ah! Ye'll getused to it.'

'I like the moustache though. Very *a la mode*. Let's meet for a drink then.'

'Can't.'

'Why not?'

'Meeting a customer at five thirty.'

'Aahh! Where?'

'The Algonquin… new client.'

'How long will you be?'

'Half an hour, an hour at the outside.'

'There's a lovely French restaurant nearby. Can't remember the name of it. Let's just say I could meet you outside the Algonquin at seven and we walk to the restaurant. Deal?'

'Do ye hear me lookin' at ye babe? Deal.'

Walking into the hotel lobby he had no difficulty recognising the new client, as Flannery had suggested. In his mid forties, overweight, curly carrot red hair and eyebrows, his face and hands so covered with freckles they virtually merged, open necked shirt, and the crotch of his well-worn trousers hanging half way between his groin and his knees, his aquiline eyes watching the lobby traffic.

'Mr Flannery.'

'Mr MacAlindon. Glad you could make it,' he greeted by gripping his hand in a double handshake. 'There's a cupila seats in a quiet wee corner of the Blue Bar. Let's go grab 'em.'

They sat opposite each other, Flannery noisily eructating as he settled into a low armchair, twitching his trousers at the thighs before casually crossing his ankles.

'Well now! Bob tells me you might be the man I'm looking for and that unscrupulous bandit is never wrong, not in my experience anyhow. I'll put it to ye this way. I've been playing the markets myself for years, made a packet if you don't mind me bumming me own chat. I'm a builder be trade and no doubt you're aware the business has rocketed over the past locka years. Can't keep up with the demand. Got to keep my eye on me core business, it goes without saying. So that's where you come in.'

'Whatever way I can be of assistance.'

'I don't want to use a broker. Middlemen are grand for the lazy investor. Not for me. And local traders are not on top of the game. I want to be able to instruct a dealer direct… a dealer with balls who's not afraid to take a punt. Of course I'd need responsive feedback. Are you the man for the job?'

'Depends Mr Flannery. You'd have to be putting a serious amount of business my way to make it worth my while.'

'Oh I'll make it worth your while all right.'

'Would you want to settle through us?'

'Lehmans? Yeah, but through the Boston office. I like the idea of Bob Perotti keeping an eye on things for me. And as far as the numbers go, how many contracts would you normally deal in a day?'

'Obviously 'twould depend on the day, how the market was performin' on the day.'

'How many on a good day then?'

'On a good day anything between six and eight thousand. Sometimes more.'

'On a good day I'd like ye to trade upwards of three or four thousand on my account,' he said, blowing his nose like a trumpet and tucking the handkerchief back in the pocket of his trousers, straightening his leg to make room for it.

Maca's brain worked overtime calculating the potential commission on Flannery's proposed business.

'Are you the dealer I'm lookin' for then?'

'Most definitely Mr Flannery, most definitely. I look forward to doin' the business with ye.'

'Sean, call me Sean. May I call you Stephen? Give us your direct line at the Exchange –'

'You already have it.'

'Give it me again. Expect a call from me early next week.'

The meeting had barely lasted twenty minutes leaving him the best part of an hour to kill before meeting up with Martina. Not wanting to hang around the hotel lest he bump into Flannery and his family, he decided to check out the French restaurant she had proposed for dinner. Having come across Le Coq Hardi he reserved a table close to a blazing log fire. Sauntering back to the Algonquin he passed by a seedy sex shop and with time to spare wandered in. Mooching around, bemused by some of the sex toys on display, he picked up an ithyphallic corkscrew as a gift for Martina. Flicking through some of the explicit magazines that quickly raised his blood pressure, filling him with excited anticipation knowing he would spend the evening with her, the shop attendant approached him and in an admonishing schoolmasterly tone of voice requested him to peruse the display materials only, proffering by way of explanation – "You wouldn't care to buy a well thumbed magazine yourself now would you?" Such an off-putting attitude determined him not to buy anything. So, handing the jokey corkscrew to the sleazy attendant, he left and dawdled back at his ease to the hotel. Waiting out front for her, a tap on his shoulder found him confronted by Flannery, his dowdy wife and red-cheeked daughters.

'Hiya Stephen, still here I see. Not spyin' on me are ye?'

'No! I'm waiting for someone.'

'The wife?'

'No no… I'm not married, not that I know of anyhow.'

'But you're havin' a good time I'll bet eh! eh! We're dining at a restaurant just up the street here… what's it called again Marge? Oh yeah, Le Coq Hardi. Very suggestive name don't ye think. You and your friend care to join us?'

'Thanks Sean, but we're goin' to the movies,' he lied, taking in Marge's dowdy attire, she being the kind of woman who dressed for comfort, certainly not out of vanity.

'On second thoughts maybe that wouldn't be such a good idea anyway what with the kids an'all. We'll get together next time I'm down on my own on business. Get you to show me some of the hot spots eh! I'll leave ye at it Stephen, give you a call next week. See ye.'

It was now ten after seven by his watch and as yet no sign of Martina. Having lied to Flannery about his intentions for the evening, he entered the hotel lobby and telephoned the restaurant cancelling his reservation. He also dialled her office number but it rang out. By seven thirty she had not shown up. Approaching the reception desk he enquired if any messages had been left for him. Handed a telephone message, he read with a sinking sensation that Martina's mother-in-law had died, necessitating her dropping everything to be at Tom's family home. "Think of me a little. I'll be thinking of you. Miss you. Love you – Tina" she had signed off.

11

Friday morning before leaving for the Exchange, Maca stuck his head into Jeffrey Robertson's office, noticing Martina's uncluttered desk on the way, his heart sore for her. He said:

'He took the bait. We hooked him last night.'

'We? Him?' asked Robertson quizzically.

'Sean Flannery. Perotti out of Boston cleared him with ye didn't he?'

'Ah yes, the Mick. Met up with him have you? Not one hundred per cent sure about the calibre of the man I must say.'

'Perotti vouched him, says he's good for business. Flannery says on a good day he'd put upwards of three or four thousand contracts on the books. Think of the rake-off.'

'A bit outrageous don't you think. Who does the reprobate think he is, William Randolph Hearst. My gut tells me he's trouble.'

'For fuck sake Jeff why didn't ye give me a heads-up if you had reservations about him?'

'Didn't know you were meeting the blatherskite did I,' rebounded Robertson with a hint of rancour, somewhat taken aback by his staff member's attitude and use of the "F" word. 'Hope you checked him out thoroughly. How-and-ever, Perotti says he's clean, so be it on your heads. My advice to you is to stay alert, watch the guy like a hawk. And watch your back.'

Maca hurriedly retreated before Robertson could descant any further irksome words of wisdom.

Tuesday morning of the following week he was in the throes of buying contracts, albeit at a price he considered on the high side, to set against the Prudential losses which had accumulated to over $108,000, when his outside line rang:

'Stephen, Sean here. What price have ye on March contracts?'

'Stable at three hundred. Are ye buying?'

'Buy two thousand. But if the price drops or remains stable buy three thousand.'

'The initial buy will push it up, and with other trade it will probably reach three fifty.'

'You can buy to that limit. Keep me posted.'

Maca roared for Frank's attention and then semaphored for a talk.

'Buyer for two thousand March.'

'For fuck sake Maca I'm up to me tits, and the liquidity's tight right now. After three twenty she'll move quick.'

'What's the seller numbers like?'

'Steady, about four twenty.'

'Flood sell and flush some of the bastards out. Low-tick any stop loss sellers, then we buy back, limit three fifty firm. Go go.'

The market was in bedlam with the New Year bounce, but Frank had hoodwinked copycat traders pushing it down to two hundred. Maca started buying in blocks of five hundred and by lunchtime his tally stood at two thousand, after which the price tracked upwards. He bought in another seven hundred on spot purchases at higher prices in an inexorably rising buyers market. Then towards close of play, he punctiliously secured a couple of thous- and sell orders at the top end of the market for key clients. By the bell for close, he was charged with energy when telephoning Flannery confirming two thousand seven hundred buys at an average price of two fifty for his account. The yelps down the line sent his eardrum thrumming – 'Atta boy. Keep the cabbage rolling.'

Flannery's trade kept him busy, so busy that, on top of his exist- ing dealer responsibilities including training in the new interns from Harvard and the pressure of resolving the discrepancy in the Prudential account, he hardly had time to talk to, or, arrange to see

Martina on her return to work. So exhausted was he after each days trading he avoided, whenever possible, having to meet with her and deliberately parried her telephone calls. When they did meet at the office his behaviour toward her was perfunctorily dismissive, her presence in his life at this time an added complication he could well do without. Non-working time became of necessity rest-up time.

January 17, on returning to the office late after drinks with the team from the Exchange, the following compelling missive awaited his attention:

Steve   Wednesday

I am writing this note for two reasons:-

I am completely in the dark – I don't know what is happening or why. I can understand if you have decided to end it all but, surely, you are adult enough and you should at least tell me and not just leave me without saying so. Is this your normal form? – I never expected that you would treat me in such a way.

I don't want any bad feelings between us – we will have to meet from time to time at work and, surely, after all this time an explanation is not too much to ask for.

Last week you said you didn't want to see me as you were in bad form and had problems of your own – fair enough – but it would have been nice if you could have talked to me about it and if I could have helped in any way – I would have – but instead you cut me off completely which left me feeling very hurt which also makes me doubt that you ever loved me or needed me. Surely this is not the way you treat someone you, supposedly, love.

I know I banged the phone down on you last week but what could you expect. You had told me I could see you on Thursday evening but when I phoned you told me you had other arrangements which, you said you could get out of; but how do you think I felt when you said one day you could see me, the next day you couldn't? If that is your reason for not contacting me – it is a very limp one and I hope there is a better one. I would rather we part in the way we always promised we would – at least as friends – after all we have been together now for almost two years and we have both gone through a lot together.

That is not the reason for this note – I would have left it as it is – as you appear to want it, but for the second reason which I cannot deal with myself. It concerns us both and I must talk to you about it – I can't talk to anybody else as it concerns us. I am worried sick and don't know what to do. I need some help and advice and you are the only one I can talk to.

Right now, I don't particularly want to see you either. I can let you know my problem by note, if you would prefer, but I don't think it is the best way.

   This note is not just an excuse to see you or trouble you, which you have accused me of doing before. I need help and I hope that you will, at least, help me with this problem.

Martina

Troubled by the anxiety so clearly expressed in her note and apprehensive about the signification of the second reason she had written it, he had to see her and took the elevator to her floor but found it in total darkness. Too fatigued and bewildered to write her a note there and then he left for home, picking up a pizza from Giovanni's Food Emporium on the way. Collapsing in front of the television as he wolfed down the pizza, beer bottle in hand, between mouthfuls he listened to, but absorbed only snippets of, President Johnson's State of the Union address to Congress – "our great nation is being challenged, at home and abroad… troubled and new waters… a tragedy for every American family… the will to meet the trials that these times impose… that America's will to persevere can be broken. Well… the enemy is wrong, America will persevere." Thirteen days later, the Viet Cong and Ho Chi Minh's North Vietnamese army launched the Tet offensive, its timing catching the South Vietnam puppet regime and the American military forces by surprise as the Tet Nguyen Dan festival in celebration of the Lunar New Year is popular with every religious group and social class and was seen as an inviolable holiday period throughout Vietnam. Maca had paid scant attention to the sheer lunacy of the destructive war, an undeclared war, and the impact it was having on America's collective consciousness. But this audacious communist offensive, leading to calls from the Pentagon for conscription (a well-substantiated rumour had it that General Westmoreland wanted another two hundred thousand troops to augment the five hundred and twenty five thousand based there) and a call up of the reserves to reinforce ground actions, brought the human tragedy and devastating consequences of the war to the fore in his mind. Prior to Tet, more bombs had been unleashed over Vietnam than all the bombs dropped in Europe and Africa in the Second World War, the magnitude of such carpet and precision bombing (introducing napalm and fragmentation bombs) supposedly causing the enemy demoralizing losses. And despite President Johnson's declared assurances that America was winning the war and that the enemy would soon sue for peace, the President was rapidly losing the hearts and minds of a formerly indifferent and complacent public opinion. While the military were pursuing the logistics of a major counteroffensive in Vietnam, The White House mounted a public relations campaign on television and in the newspapers to counter communist propaganda, President Johnson declaring that the agents of the enemy were trying to destroy confidence in the South Vietnamese government and its allies. America had pledged itself to defend the free nations (free of communism) and if it betrayed that pledge to South Vietnam, the countries of Southeast Asia would fall like a stack of dominoes. The magnificent rhetoric of John Fitzgerald Kennedy's inaugural address played over and over – "Let every nation know, whether it wishes us well or ill, that we shall pay any price, bear any burden, meet any hardship, support any friend, oppose any foe to assure the survival and the success of liberty". Doubts in the public consciousness about the validity of the war and America's capacity to pay for it were reinforced by news reports that an American army major had said it was necessary to destroy a village to save it from the Viet Cong (Your war, their village). And images broadcast of a Viet Cong prisoner, arms trussed behind his back, still standing in the street as blood and brain tissue burst from his head having been summarily shot by Saigon's chief of police. The effect of such news reports was to further undermine the hawks in the Pentagon by intensifying the people's opposition to the war.

*

The escalation of the war crises in Vietnam coincided with the climacteric events that now erupted in Maca's life. The morning after he had read Martina's note he telephoned her at work and they agreed to meet that evening in his apartment. She was pregnant. The thorny questions were not asked: How? – wasn't she on the pill. Why? – had she come off the pill for medical reasons and if so why didn't she tell him? When? – they had last made love on the morning of December 23. Who? – is it Tom's or his. Her face provided no clue. What to do about it was the issue needing resolution. In asking her what she wished to do he was taken aback, and somewhat chastened, by her overwrought response – "I want rid of it". Did she fear having the baby, or, did she not want it?

'Apart from being against the law, it could prove risky for you. Are ye sure you want a termination?'

'Yes I'm sure,' she softly gasped as tears began to well up.

It was agreed an abortion was better carried out by a medic outside the State of New York. He, aware that a banking conference on legal and securities was to take place in Chicago the following week, assured her the appropriate appointment would be made. They watched a movie on television in sober silence before she left early for home.

He called Johnny Cassidy in Chicago for contact numbers:

'Johnny, how's things?'

'Good. You sound a bit down Maca, what's it at?'

'I have a favour to ask of ye. A friend of mine's pregnant. It's not her husband's.

'Jeez Maca! I don't know – do ye really want to be involved?'

'I am involved. Can ye recommend an abortion service there?'

'Here in Chicago?'

'Yeah! No back-street charlatan mind, a competent medic. I'll pay upfront, safety and confidentiality being all.'

'Hang on a minute Maca – let me think. One of the guys working here told me there's a place hereabouts, close enough to the hotel. I haven't had cause to use it meself but he said it's sound. I'm sure I have the number in me wallet.'

He could hear Johnny fumbling with the wallet and then, with relief, wrote down the number.

'Tell her to ask for Gloria. Has she had counseling?'

'Fuck! I don't know.'

'Be sure tell her to ask for Gloria... and say she's had counselling.'

On hanging up he phoned the number, asked for Gloria and nervously explained the circumstances.

'Are you a cop?'

'No. I'm a friend.'

'Friend or not we don't talk to you. Have the lady phone us and we'll see what shows up.'

'The procedure is carried out by a doctor?'

'Yes.'

The line went dead. The following day Tina joined him at his apartment and put a call through using the alias Luisa Vergallo, asking for Gloria.

'$500. You okay with that?'

Tina searched his eyes and said – 'Yeah! I'm okay with that.'

'You calling long distance. This line ain't good.'

'I'm calling from New York. I'll be in Chicago next week.'

'Where ye staying?'

She searched his eyes again as he mouthed Ritz-Carlton Wednesday – 'I'll be at the Ritz-Carlton from Wednesday.'

'Nice! There's a swank bar a few doors down – Nellos. We'll pick you up outside at eleven o'clock Thursday. Wear a red coat, or a fire brigade red dress under an open coat.'

He suggested they fly there on the Wednesday, offering to make all the necessary arrangements. She considered it prudent they travel on separate flights; she would book a flight for herself and a woman friend (who hailed from the Windy City) whom she intended inviting along as "shopping trip" cover, *vis-à-vis* explaining to her husband the reason for the journey.

When reporting to Jeffrey Robertson on Monday his intention of attending the banking conference, Robertson, despite the short notice, in discerning his willingness to take on the task on behalf of the bank and having satisfied himself that the Exchange team would survive his absence for the few days, expressed himself impressed by his enthusiasm and agreed the bank would cover all expenses. Maca reserved two superior rooms, a twin and a double for three nights, at the Ritz-Carlton. His flights, conference attendance reservation at the Convention Center, and hotel accommodation at the Intercontinental Hotel (which he would not use) were secured for him by Holly in the bank's Personnel Department.

Meeting up with Martina and her married friend Karen that Wednesday evening in their room at the Ritz-Carlton, busily re-examining their successful purchases of the afternoon; trying on shoes and holding up dresses (Martina's a fire brigade red) as they stood in turn before a full length mirror, he was chuffed to find both women in good spirits and raring to go dine at a little Italian restaurant nearby, recommended by Karen, having booked a table for three. The chit-chat over dinner did not, in any way, hint at the purpose for which all three now found themselves there, yet he detected in Karen a gracious spirit of understanding, he in turn wordlessly empathizing with the invidious position she was in. Strolling back to the hotel in animated mood, the two sylphlike women did him proud by linking his arms, their jauntiness attract-ing admiring glances from passing strangers. Over a nightcap in the hotel's Red Devil Bar, he was approached by Johnny Cassidy, whom he barely recognised in his hotel livery and short back and sides haircut. He rose from his chair to have a discreet chat with him out of earshot of the company. Johnny said:

'Did everything work out okay for ye?'

'Yeah. Thanks Johnny. She's in at 11.00 tomorrow.'

'Which one is she?'

He paused before answering, believing his friend had put two and two together. 'That's her with the dark hair.'

'Jeez! She's a fucken smasher.'

He and Johnny agreed to meet the following evening for drinks. Next morning he skipped breakfast at the Ritz knowing the taxicab ride to the Conference Centre could take the greater part of an hour, depending on traffic flow, deciding instead to breakfast at the Intercontinental amongst the conventioneers. Prior to leaving, he pushed a note under Martina's door telling her how much he loved her and of how much he would be thinking about her all day. The conference proved interminably boring, the speakers monotonously voluble. Absenting himself before conclusion of that day's agenda, he rushed back to the Ritz hoping to join Martina and Karen. He knocked their bedroom door which was opened by Karen. No sign of Tina:

'So what's the story?' he grumbled.

'I don't know,' she replied contritely. 'We were outside Nellos when a car pulled up driven by a portly woman… well dressed. I wasn't permitted to travel with them. I don't know where she is. I've been back here all day… waiting, just waiting.'

'Fuck! I'll phone… fuck.'

'That woman said no calls.'

'To hell with that,' he exploded in a low choking moan. Lifting the telephone he began to tremble violently as he dialled the number.

'Is that Gloria? I need to know how Luisa Vergallo is.' Silence at the other end. 'Look, I'm worried about her.' Silence. 'Just tell me she's okay. When can I see her?'

'She's fine,' came the whispered response. 'She'll rest up with us tonight. All being well she'll be dropped back at Nellos tomorrow.'

'When tomorrow? I need to be here for her.'

'Late afternoon.' The line went dead.

Mystified yet somewhat relieved, he turned to face a bewildered Karen. 'So you heard all that.' She nodded. 'It seems she's resting up and will be dropped back at Nellos tomorrow afternoon.'

Later that evening he and Karen met up with Johnny and his girlfriend who brought them to a local jazz club where Ronnie Scott was making a guest appearance:

'Are you in? Are ye legal?' Johnny asked him aside over beers during a lull in the music, the women chirpily chin-wagging.

'Yeah! I took citizenship last year. The bank was of great help… with the paper work ye know. Because of the bank's support it all went hunky-dory.'

'You lucky fucker ye. I'm thinkin' of enlisting. 'Tis about the only way to regularize things for myself. Me visa's about to expire. No point sittin' around waitin' to be drafted or deported.'

'Ye mean to tell me you'd volunteer for that fucken blood-bath? 'Tis nothin' but a warring quagmire, chewing up the GIs, whatever the rights or wrongs of it.' He didn't really care about the war, he was so preoccupied with his own affairs.

'From what I hear those drafted are first in line to the front,' Johnny continued. 'By signin' up I might get PP, a less risky – '

'What the fuck's PP?'

'Preferential placement. And of course get me papers in order. Ye could get the call up yerself Maca.'

'I'm a conscientious objector. Nobody's puttin' me in them there fucken killing fields.'

'CO's don't count for shit. If ye're drafted you're fucked anyway. Despite the protests of the draft resistance movement, the draftcard burners, the army's fillin' its quotas. Anyway, apart from missin' Zara here, I wouldn't mind seein' a bit of the Orient, ye know what I mean. Story has it the women over there are drop-dead gorgeous, two-a-penny.'

''Tis the dollars in yer wallet they'll be chasing.'

'Well ye know what they say about women likin' a man in uniform.'

All through the infinitely desultory discussions at the conference next day he felt wearisome, finding himself unable to concentrate on the technical data, his thoughts otherwise engaged. Mentally abstracted, he eschewed contact with his fellow bankers. He needed to see her. He ordered a finger of whiskey at the bar, no ice, and gulped it down. Then took a leak in the washroom where he had a long hard look at himself in the mirror, studying his face that seemed to reflect an inexpiable dark guilt, tears springing to his eyes. Had he encouraged and facilitated, without demur, the woman he loved in the abortion of their child? Why had she, without prevarication, wanted "rid of it", no hint of remorse, not even a "maybe life could be different for us" if she kept it? Later that afternoon, he again phoned the number and was advised she had been discharged an hour before. Racing back to the hotel, heavily finger buzzing her doorbell, she was not in her room. Fidgeting the key to unlock his own room door, it was opened by Martina, standing there in a white bathrobe, projecting righteous anger, or, confident indifference, or, vulnerable fragility, he could not tell, her gravely inscrutable demeanour not helping him determine which, her face as white as a sheet.

'I did it on my own. I went through this… this nightmare on my own,' she said with temperamental ductility as he entered the room.

After a brief silence, he murmured: 'Where's Karen?'

'At her brother's place,' she replied in an undertone with a slight shrug of her shoulders. 'Left this morning apparently.

'Yes my love, you have been very brave. Are ye okay? What happened? Are you sure everything went well?'

She made no reply and sat on the edge of the bed, her shoulders hunched forward under the weighty mindfulness of the enormity of what had transpired in her life this day, lost in her own thoughts. He made her a long drink of vodka and coke and lay down beside her, looking up at her, looking on her face in profile, discerning a haunting sorrow in her, a distant otherness he could not cross over to, as he reached out and gently pulled her to him, her head then and there buried in the cradle of his shoulder and embracing arm, her enfeebled body all at once engulfed in tremulous convulsions. They lay thus cramped for what seemed hours, her drink untouched, silently watching the shadowy stippled patterns of light swelling like tongues across the ceiling spurred by the streetlights below, the low hum of street traffic an intrusion into that refractory space, till he was obliged to move his benumbed arm from under her.

Realizing she was in a deep sleep, he waited for sleep to overtake him, his mind in turmoil. On waking to the dawn light creeping through the open curtained windows, he found himself alone. Showering and dressing hurriedly, cramming his belongings into his travel bag, he trundled to her room and came by her ready packed, sitting on the side of the unslept-in bed blow drying her hair having already showered. He lay down on the bed happy to watch her perform her morning ritual, the open bathrobe revealing her pert alabaster breasts and the surgical pad that covered her groin. As she vigorously brushed her hair, he playfully cupped her breasts and they kissed, kissed passionately, her hand releasing his stiffening member from the folds of his trousers, her lips sheathing his hard-on, her mouth soon enveloping it. The bedside telephone rang and foolishly he answered it. It was Johnny.

'Hey Maca, checkin' out today. What time's yer flight?'

'Two fifteen,' he lied, it being Martina's flight time. He wanted to be with her throughout the gliding-by allotted span they had together, his flight scheduled some two hours later.

''Twas great seein' ye. I must give ye a shout next time I'm in "The Big Apple".'

'Yeah! Ye have my number… so do that,' he said, a quiver in his voice as he watched Martina work over his pulsating member.

'I might be makin' the trip in the next three weeks or so. How ye fixed for a spare bed should I need to kip down at your place for a night or two?'

The swelling embolus of sperm he fought to hold back ejaculated into her luscious incarnadine mouth, her eyes tantalizingly fixed on his, pearl drops dripping from her lips.

'Maca… Maca. Are ye there?'

'Yeah… yeah.'

'If I get there in say three weeks time can you put me up at your place.'

'No bother Johnny. Just give me a holler when you arrive at La Guardia. I'll come and pick ye up.'

'Thanks Maca. Have a safe trip.'

'Thanks, I will. And thanks for the other night. We really enjoyed Ronnie Scott.'

Deciding to breakfast in her room he called room service and ordered the full panoply of the Ritz-Carlton luxury breakfast, so hungry were they not having eaten the evening before – eggs Benedict with champagne and all the trimmings. On presentation, they both found they had little appetite, merely nibbling the choice fare. In the taxicab to O'Hare Airport, they held hands in a melancholy quiescence, the tranquil mood continuing as he helped her at check-in and the long trek to boarding gate 27, and over coffee while awaiting her flight boarding announcement. What came to pass in Chicago was not discussed, and was not raised by him again, ever, being there for her was all. He watched as she boarded, occasionally losing sight of her amid her fellow passengers. She did not look back, and now out of sight his heart sank in forlorn separation. Their souls were truly as one but would they ever, rightfully, be together as one. Turning away, he checked his watch and adjusted it to Eastern Time. Later she told him she could not look back because of all that was paining her heart.

*

Back with his nose to the grindstone at the Exchange, a baleful looking Richard Phillips apprised him of the interrogation he had endured at the hands of Russell from internal audit regarding major discrepancies he claimed to have uncovered in the Error Account. Certain transactions had been unaccounted for, or, erroneously posted, and the losses debited to the bank now exceeded $250,000 over and above the usual monthly float. Phillips wanted to know if he could shed any light on the problem, which appeared to accrue from a basic screw up back in October. Maca played dumb, expressing himself mystified.

The following day saw saturation coverage on television of the Vietnam Tet offensive and by Wednesday, the newspaper reports were castigating President Johnson and his White House staff for lying to the people about the current status of the war. The North Vietnamese and Viet Cong forces assaulted thirty-six provincial capitals, five of South Vietnam's largest cities, and almost one-third of the country's district centres. In Saigon itself, they struck the U.S. Embassy compound, Tan San Nhut Air Base, the Presidential Palace, South Vietnam's Joint General Staff headquarters, and other government installations. Effective resistance blunted their attacks in Saigon, but most of Hue, the country's ancient capital and site of the symbolically important Imperial Citadel, fell under communist control.

On his return to head office following close of business at the Exchange on Thursday, Martina told him Jeffrey Robertson wanted an urgent few words with him and watched in unease as his physiognomy metamorphosed from the healthy hew of a busy day's graft to troubled ashen grey. Filled with irrepressible antsiness, he made his way slowly to Robertson's office believing he was definitely in for the chop this time, internal audit having more than likely worked out the intricacies of the fictitious transactions he had posted to the Error Account. In trepidation, he entered Robertson's office and seeing the man stand crouching over his desk seeming to study minutely the single piece of notepaper that rested there, his fears were not allayed. When Robertson languidly pointed to the chair indicating for him to take a seat, he observed the bloodshot in his boss's eyes and, ill at ease, said he would prefer stand. Robertson turned his back on him and stood looking out through the window beyond his reflection:

'I'm sorry to be the one to have to tell you this Stephen. I've just received terrible news. Charles Schweitzer has been killed,' Robertson said, his voice wavering to inaudibility as Maca stood rooted to the spot. 'The attack on Hue, he'd only been there a few weeks working preferential placement in storage and supplies administration. His building took a direct hit killing seven U.S. personnel and many more locals. I need you to communicate this frightful news to the staff. Please request Martina Patterson to draw up an appreciative in memoriam memorandum for internal distribution. And I would be greatly obliged if you would assist her in its preparation. You Irish seem to have a way with words. Meantime, communicate our loss of Charles to as many of the team as possible,' he continued, turning back to look Maca in the eye.

'The boisterous laughter I've had to listen to on the floor seems so out of keeping with the necessaries of appropriate behaviour in the circumstances. I wish them to be more silent than Amyclae. You are the first to hear of it Stephen,' he confided, blowing his nose noisily into a large cotton handkerchief, 'and I know you will attend my request with politic empathy.'

'I'm so sorry Mr Robertson. Chubby is a great loss. We'll miss him desperately.'

'Yes. Such is life. Please go now.'

He blubbed out the shock of Chubby's death to Martina, her reaction to which was to resort to silence and step into his arms as tears flooded her eyes carrying streaks of mascara down her sallow cheeks. They shared the responsibility of quietly approaching as many of their fellow workers still at their desks, and relating the sad news. The bustle of routine office noise quickly gave way to a deafening stillness as the shock wave spread, colleagues gathering in groups of grieving susurration. Having spent the greater part of two hours jointly preparing a poignant and humorously worded eulogy for Chubby and leaving it in the post room for distribution next morning, Martina went with him to his apartment where they ordered in a Thai meal. She presented him with a gift of a gold-plated wristwatch by way of thanks for his love and understanding, her words written on the back of a photograph of her looking engagingly demure seared on his heart – "Three days with you were like three minutes, three minutes without you are like three days. Love you, Tina". She stayed with him overnight and together they commuted to work next morning.

Prior to exiting the bank for the Stock Exchange, Robertson telephoned asking him to join him for coffee in his office:

'Thank you for the choice of words and respectful expressions of character used which so epitomize Charles and the qualities he brought to bear while he was here amongst us.'

'Martina Patterson's doing for the most part,' he rejoined, blushing self-effacingly.

'Ah yes Stephen, her sentiment perhaps but your coinage. The humorous inflection has your stamp on it. I've already conveyed my thanks to Martina this morning. I need however to share something with you, a serious matter only recently brought to my attention.'

Robertson's penetrating stare unnerved him. He shifted his buttocks uneasily in his chair, the blush rising from his neck to his brow as he fingered his shirt collar in a vain attempt to seek relief from the inescapable inquisition.

'In strictest confidence, given the circumstances I find it difficult.

Where to start,' Robertson continued, kneading his eyebrows with the thumb and middle finger of his right hand.

'Internal audit have been on my back these past few days. It seems they stumbled on substantial discrepancies in the Error Account, going back to late summer early autumn last year. They have yet to unravel the history of it and find the source of the unauthorised liabilities, perhaps they never will. Russell may have said something of it to you. He is gung-ho pointing the finger at Charles, but he's barking up the wrong tree there. I won't have it Stephen. There is no way I will allow Charles's reputation to be sullied… to be besmirched by such blamestorming, particularly now since he is unable to defend his good name against such charges. His family will hear nothing of such scurrilous allegations. I'll see to that. I've spoken to the executive members of the board and they have agreed to wipe the slate clean. I instructed Russell and his team to stop digging. Let sleeping dogs lie and all that. So there's an end to it. What I just related to you Stephen must not go outside these wallss. The reason I'm confiding in you is that I hope by my doing so you will remain vigilant and on top of the job. If someone on the team is mucking about, you need to flush him out before more serious damage is done.'

By the time Robertson finished this exhortation, Maca had regained his composure.

'You're my key man at the Exchange now Stephen and I needed to put you fully in the picture. Your joint management with Phillips of Charles's portfolio and the bank's proprietary trading will have to run its course. But when the time comes you'll be in poll position for Senior Managing Dealer. You may go now,' he pronounced, offering a limp hand shake.

Maca jauntily picked up his coat from the cloakroom and left for the Stock Exchange with a renewed spring in his step, indomitably striding out, serendipity now playing the game, chance as relentless as necessity.

12

The television was set close to full volume. "With our hopes and the world's hopes for peace in the balance every day, I do not believe that I should devote an hour or a day of my time to any personal partisan cause or to any duties other than the awesome duties of this office – the presidency of your country. Accordingly, I shall not seek, and I will not accept, the nomination of my party for another term as your President".

Maca, listening to President Johnson's live broadcast, knocked the wine glass from Martina's hand to a crash on the floor as he jumped with triumphant glee from the sofa, the red wine slopping the carpet. She upped and ran to the fridge to retrieve the half-empty bottle of white wine left over from their starter course, intent on diluting the ruby pool and rapidly spreading splotches that threatened a stain if left untreated.

'Yippee! That leaves Kennedy with a clear run. Fuck the stain Tina, don't ye see, McCarthy will have to withdraw from the race and Kennedy will end our participation in the war. He'll bring the troops home.'

'Oh yeah! That's if Kennedy gets nominated and wins the election. You're still talking a year, more likely two years, before that begins to happen. Get me some paper towels will you and help clean up this mess you've made,' she chided him. 'And turn that darn thing off.'

In a flurry of excitement they frolicked in celebration. Having fetched the paper towels, he put a Marvin Gaye long play on the record player, pumped up the volume and grabbed her for a jive listening to "Wherever I Lay My Hat (That's My Home)" followed by a smooch to "How Sweet It Is (To Be Loved By You)". She had been sweet to him all weekend but would shortly leave him to drive home, her husband returning that Sunday night from a golfing holiday in Florida. Four days later Martin Luther King, who had dedicated the previous thirteen years to nonviolent protest for civil rights, was assassinated as he stood on the balcony of the Lorraine Motel in Memphis. Many blacks took to the streets in outrage as violence erupted in the major cities across the country, the protests ensuring a turbulent and controversial last nine months for Johnson's presidency.

Spring eased into summer. Maca kept apace with the senator for New York's inexorable push to reclaim the throne in memory of his brother. Illinois should clinch it, he believed, but first the difficult hurdle of the California primary had to be surmounted, McCarthy having stayed in the race. He had never been busier at work, being hailed as one of the top dealers at the Exchange; the millions of dollars profit earned for the bank elevating him to celebrity status with the bosses; the business on behalf of Flannery and others fomenting envy amongst his peers. Flannery's dealings had grown steadily more volatile, driving him to take greater risks gambling for higher stakes, his inscrutable client boastfully triumphal by his successes and enigmatically deadpan on his losses. For a whole week at the end of May the market had soared each day by over one thousand points, building up a serious backlog of trades that had to be accounted for, necessitating him working most nights into the small hours facing the arduous task of reconciling the staff's unresolved dealer contracts, some of which remained unresolved into June. On the night of June 4, he and Martina stayed back in head office to clear the backlog and by 3 a.m. gave up exhausted, leaving eleven trades unresolved. They retired to an all-night diner for supper where, now sitting with his back to the television having learned that Robert Francis Kennedy had won the California primary, he felt obliged to request the waitress to turn down the volume on the broadcast of the result of the count, his head still pounding with multiple dealer slip calibrations. He was about to tuck into a hamburger when Martina drew his attention to Kennedy's victory speech at the Ambassador Hotel in Los Angeles, and cheered loudly on hearing the senator's rousing, rallying parting shot of "and so on to Chicago". Munching on his rapidly cooling hamburger (it had lost that scrumptious sizzle he always relished), she let out a shrill cry that pierced the air amid shouts and screams emanating from the television set causing him to choke on a piece of burger bun which had stuck in his throat. By the time the teary blur brought on by his hawking had cleared from his eyes, he watched in horror the black and white image of Bobby Kennedy outstretched on the floor, his head resting on an election boater streaming blood. An old man in the diner shouted at the television – "What a fucked-up country".

Prostrated by overwork, that morning he called in sick to the bank and spent the whole day in bed. Thursday, still reeling from the shock of Robert Kennedy's assassination, he took a telephone call from Flannery on his outside line at the Exchange:

'Where the fuck were ye yesterday? That bootlicker, Phillips I think he said his name was, wanted to do the business for me. I told you Stephen, I only deal with you. I lost out big time because of your no-show.'

'Sorry about that Sean. How can I make it up to ye?'

'How are ye feelin' by the way? Another Kennedy taken out eh!'

'Gutted. But I'm okay now. Thanks.'

'Good. Looka here now, I want to do a cash deal sellin' the last two seventy calls and buyin' September two fifty calls.'

'How many?'

'Five thousand.'

'Right! That's a big order,' he said, weighing up and mentally calculating the commission the order could reap. 'Did ye check for any offers?'

'I had point one five nine yesterday but held off for ye. The best I can get now is one five eight. Ye need to better it. Don't let me down on this one sonny boy.'

'Ye should have taken it at point one five nine.'

Flannery having hung up, he found he was talking to himself. He signalled Frank to his desk and, when he arrived flushed and sweating profusely, told him Flannery wanted some options.

'Don gobshite! Chrissake Maca, how do ye put up with the smug bollocks? He chewed Phillips out of it yesterday for no reason a'tall.'

'If ye want the business you gotta put up with the flack. He wants to roll over the two seventy June calls into two fifty calls in September. He has an offer of point one five eight and wants us –'

'What the fuck does that mean?'

'– to better it. It means I need to better it if I want to hold on to his fucken business. Someone out there is discounting like fuck to get the trade.'

'I don't like it Maca. You should talk to Phillips.'

Maca needed to know promptly what the market would offer, yet Phillips was the last man he wanted to share his problem with. He called Cyril Hobbs, a dealer for Bank of America he felt he could bank on, on the internal line and related the business and asked if he was interested higher than point one five eight.

'That's a good offer. Anything higher is a bit risky. I'll match it. But the market needs to go down before I'd make a higher offer of say one five nine.'

He called round other dealers at Morgan Stanley, Merrill Lynch, Citibank, and some of the foreign banks, all of whom were prepared to deal at point one five eight but no higher, and any one of whom he knew could be the bidder for Flannery's business. Determined to keep Flannery on the books, he called him advising he had offers at point one five nine but moving down fast.

'Well done ye boy ye. I knew you'd look after me.'

'What's your exact number?'

'At one five nine go for five. No! let's stick the neck out. Go for six thousand.'

'That's pushin' it. Leave it with me.'

He had embarked on a flyer ("legging it" as it is known by the dealers). Having promised Flannery to do the deal at point one five nine he gambled that the market would fall, but even if it did so, as soon as he commenced trading Flannery's roll over the market would begin to move against him. His eyes were literally out on stalks watching the prices, his head throbbing in anger that he had allowed himself be bullied into such an exposed position. The market began to move downwards and by midday had dropped two hundred points. Bank of America was his first call and he told Hobbs the best he could do was point one five nine and talked him into taking one thousand. On the back of that trade, he offloaded five hundred each to Merrill Lynch and Swiss Bank. Before lunch break, the market spotted the trading and started to climb. Citibank and Deutsche Bank declined to bid. Having done two thousand options over the telephone, he told Frank over lunch that he needed a cross trade, and back at the Exchange he joined Frank in the pit. Some interest was shown at point one five nine but not enough, the upshot being he was one thousand four hundred option contracts short. Realizing his continued presence in the pit signalled his intentions to the other dealers he backed away to his station in a state just short of outright panic. Not having bank authority to hold a proprietary position exceeding five hundred option contracts, he was out on a limb sitting on one thousand four hundred. He moved to separate the order, the basis of legging, and by mid-afternoon had sold nine hundred of the two seventy calls at two forty, some way short of the two fifty they had commanded in earlier trading. A hasty calibration of the figures showed point one fifty five. He was way off target. Everyone on the floor had figured out what he was trying to do, and they were still offering the two fifty September calls at one thousand four hundred and bidding one thousand three hundred and seventy. He was gambling big time trying to redress his position. With minutes to go before close the Market started to trade lower, but not low enough and fast enough. He needed to buy two hundred and sixty four of the September two fifty calls to make Flannery good at the ratio of point one five nine. The bell rang to signal the last minute of trading. He semaphored Frank to bid one thousand three hundred and sixty five for two hundred and sixty four contracts in the September two fifty call, and rushed to the pit hoping to take advantage of some other activity in the trading to hide it. There was nothing. His trade at well below market was jumped on by a number of players, both Deutsche Bank and Citibank joining his bid, so he had to sell to them as well.

His mind in a distorted brainstorm, he made a beeline back to head office to help reconcile that days trading slips, separating Flannery's slips so he could establish the final position without any prying eyes looking over his shoulder. Flannery's position turned out all square, and with the options transferred to Perotti in Boston, he breathed a sigh of relief, thankful any threat from that quarter had been averted. However, he had been unable to leg the trade and was left holding five hundred September calls in an open, unhedged position. With the spread between the bid and offer for these options, he calculated a loss of $127,000. Moreover, the open position could swing even further into loss with any adverse movements in the market. Fretful he was on the ride for a fall, that he had no place to hide, he covertly watched Martina assiduously sift through reams of trading slips in assisting the back room staff, her radiant beauty and magnetic, unaffected charm inciting in him a longing to be with her now, be with her away from all this, away from the rat race, away from the lie that was her marriage. The intensity of this ardent desire filled him with a profound sense of isolation and loneliness. Catching sight of the wistful expression on his face, she approached him and concernedly asked if everything was okey-dokey. Without answering, he stuffed the five hundred September calls in his pocket and left for home, his plight a deadweight on his back.

*

Unable to sleep that night, Moran's collar ever tightening, the surge of blood in his brain growing turbulent, his tongue stuck to the roof of his mouth, treading water as he tossed and turned, blinded by a whirlwind of futile scheming as he quested his mind to spill an oneiric solution to his ignominious problem, like Orion hunting down Oenopion. Having gulped neat from the neck the greater part of a bottle of whiskey, towards dawn, while dragging on one too many cigarettes, he remembered Chris Cheaver (one of the Harvard interns) raising with him the identity of an account, apparently long dormant, yet still in the system – why? Why indeed he pondered. He had had no answer at the time and no answer now, but was intrigued enough to try and find out. What was the account number or reference? Had he written it down? Yes, he remembered he had written it down in one of his desk notepads. It was around the time Robert Kennedy declared his candidacy for the presidency. Yes, just before the weekend of the Saint Patrick's Day parade which had fallen on the Sunday. Did he still have that notepad or had it been binned? Hurriedly he showered, sipped from a cup of piping hot coffee while dressing, and sped off to the office arriving there at 6.30 a.m. Emptying out the drawers and scattering the usual office detritus on top of his desk: old investment charts, telephone messages (most ticked indicating follow-up), biros, pencils, defunct calculators, paper clips et cetera; he sorted the well thumbed, dog-eared notepads and waded through the numbers, calculations, calibrations and doodles, honing in on identifying trading slips he had worked on in mid March thus narrowing down his search. Eventually finding the account number – 0097707, all he had succeeded in uncovering in the hours prior to leaving for the Stock Exchange was that the

215

account was still in the system; that there was no title or reference attached to it; and that it would be essential for him to access the IBM mainframe computer. He booked time on the computer for 5.00 p.m. declining the assistance of a programer, insisting he was just checking out some five and ten year performance charts.

Trading that day was slow, the market not moving much either way. After closing, he skipped the few beers with the team and went straight to the office intent on making headway in decoding the obscure account, hoping to gain access to it, and doubly hoping it would prove a suitable medium to hide the five hundred September calls. Being a Friday, the bosses had departed early for the weekend, most of the high-ranking managers likewise absent. Carrying with purposeful poise some miscellaneous files by way of deflecting undue attention, he found himself ensconced in rare isolation at the IBM mainframe computer. Intuitively feeding in program after program from the index files, after what seemed like hours of trial and error with possible entry codes the account data opened up. Tracing back over multiple transactions on the account he could not decipher its genesis, its purpose and, perhaps more importantly, by whom or by which section of the bank it had been utilised. Tracking the columns revealed alternately hundreds of thousands of dollars credit the source for which proved unfathomable, and hundreds of thousands of dollars debit created by cryptographic transfers to account or accounts unspecified.

'How's it going Stephen. Need help with anything?' It was Haughney from the computer management team.

'Nah! Nearly there. Be done in another ten minutes or so. I'll give ye a shout.'

Relieved to see Haughney walk back to his desk, he refocused his attention on the last entries to the account. The final transaction was posted more than four years previous and left a credit balance of $17,386 with no interest accruing. The whole caboodle was a closed book to him, though his gut feeling told him it had been some kind of slush fund, perhaps a political contrivance or tax evasion scheme. Worn out, he was no longer curious enough to find out. Jerking to the puppet strings of impulse, he decided to bury the five hundred September calls in the account, reasoning it would give him greater room to manoeuvre and allow more time to trade out of the problem. Any which way he looked at it, the day of reckoning had merely been postponed. Closing out the program he courteously let Haughney know he had finished and retreated to Morans pub. Arriving much later than usual, Martina, surrounded by the usual coterie, gave him a quizzical look as if to say – where the hell have you been. After a few drinks he left for home, she discreetly following him, they having agreed that she would pick up a Chinese takeout while he prepared table, uncorked the wine and chose and stacked the record player with mood music. Having found what struck him as a jim-dandy means of parking the work problem, he unloosed the violence of his desire in keyed up energy and made frenzied love to her that night with an unrelenting vigour that both shocked and surprised them.

'Fuck! What brought that on,' she panted.

Smoking cigarettes in post coital lassitude, while gossiping and engaging in easy love banter, he, on the spur of the moment, asked if she knew anything about the bank's use of account number 0097707:

'No. What is it?' she muttered softly.

'If I knew that I wouldna asked ye would I,' he said brusquely.

'Okay! I'm all ears. Give me some detail for God's sake!'

'It's the detail I'm tryin' to unravel. I think it's some sort of slush fund, political party support, lobbying, or something like that.'

'What's it referenced under?'

'Don't know. Couldn't turn up any reference a'tall. Just an account number. Seems well camouflaged.'

'Well no, I don't know a thing about it. A slush fund you say. Surely that would be fully disclosed. When was it last used?'

'Hasn't been used in yonks, left dormant with a credit balance of a few thousand dollars. But heavy transactions, some in excess of half a million dollars put through, all encrypted. You'd need a code breaker's brain to decipher the –'

'If it's dormant it should be closed out. I'll talk to Jeff on Monday about –'

'I didn't ask ye to talk to anybody about it. I just wondered if ye knew anything about it, like what it might have been used for.' The conversation had taken an acrimonious turn.

'Why should I know anything about it,' she said ruefully. 'But Jeff should know. If it's dormant as you say, it should be –'

'For fuck sake Tina let it alone,' he raised his voice aggressively.

'What's that supposed to mean.'

'Look! I was only thinkin' out loud. Don't mention its existence to anybody. Forget I asked ye about the fucken account a'tall. I'm sorry now I brought it up.'

'Sometimes you can be an ungrateful bastard,' she bridled in a calm voice. 'If you don't level with me I can't do a frigging thing for ye. I'm only trying to help –'

'I don't want your fucken help. Jesus, just lay off will ye.'

'See what I mean,' she said, climbing from the bed, her fists clenched in anger, and begin to dress. 'You should listen to yourself more often. I certainly don't need this kind of abuse and I have no –'

'Abuse? I'm askin' ye not to mention this conversation to Jeff, or anybody else for that matter. Just forget I ever said anything about the fucken account.'

'You know Steve, at times I find myself frightened of you,' she said with vehemence, stepping into her skirt and buttoning it up in fidgety haste. 'You blow a fuse over the simplest thing. And it's always somebody else's fault, never your fault, oh no! Sometimes I wonder what the hell I'm doing with you, messing up my life for –'

'Messin' up yoouuur life, so that's what you're doin' eh? Heaven forbid I should wreck a good marriage, so go start unmessing up your life by stayin' tied to that fucken Neanderthal husband of yours.'

'See! That just about says it all. If things aren't going your way all you can do is hit out, insult people,' she asserted, fingering her shoe over the heel of her foot.

'Don't fucken annoy the head off me,' he said with insensate impulsiveness.

'I won't. You need have no worries on that score,' she countered without looking at him.

'Go fuck yourself then,' he shouted as she rushed out.

'Fucking bastard', she shrieked, slamming the door so hard that his favourite Turner print – The Fighting Termeraire – hopped off the wall and smashed on the floor.

*

Following close of trading at the Stock Exchange on Monday, he joined the dealers for a beer and then walked to head office deliberating in his mind the kind of reception he could expect from Martina following his outburst the previous Friday night. She was not at her desk and by its tidiness and lack of trading slips he assumed she had not shown up for work. He made no enquiry. Next day he again noticed her absence and on his way to see Robertson barked at the back room support to have the days trading slips sorted by the time he got back.

'We're a body down on the reconciliation team,' he baldly stated on entering Robertson's office. 'Martina Patterson is missing again today.'

'She's been in a motor accident Stephen. I thought you knew.'

'Jeessus! Is she all right?'

'I received a call from her husband. Yes, she's all right, badly bruised but no fractures as far as I know. I believe she is to be discharged from hospital tomorrow. Kept in for observation… the usual battery of tests. No other vehicle involved. Apparently her car flipped over as she drove home last Friday and veered –'

'Last Friday!'

'Yes, by Tom's account her car flipped over and veered across the road on its side. Luckily an oncoming car braked hard… just avoided plunging into her.'

'Holy shit!'

'Yes, bit of a shock right enough but she'll be okay. However, you'll have to do without her services for the next week or so. Moreover I've no stand-in available to help out. I take it you'll manage.'

'Yeah! Shouldn't be a problem. Poor Martina… glad to hear she's okay though.'

For the rest of that week the market soared by over one thousand points each day, the system fragmenting in entropic bedlam. By Friday a great pile of trades had once again built up, Martina not there to ease the burden of reconciling them, and despite Maca working every night till two or three o'clock. He roped in the assistance of Chris Cheaver and insisted he and Belinda Harvey of the back room staff stay late that Friday night to clear the backlog, he doing most of it himself. Nevertheless, the numbers stubbornly refused to balance and by 11.00 p.m. and tired of their kvetching about the lateness of the hour he was obliged to let them go home. By 2.00 a.m. the backlog had been sorted but only balanced when he isolated another crass error. A premonitory shiver went through him. In a cold sweat he realized that in dealing that day he had made a December call but Frank had traded September. He reckoned the miscall shambles, with a two hundred points differential, left him with the one hundred and fifty contracts generating a loss of $65,000. Frank had once again dropped him in the proverbial. Exhausted, surrounded by nights blanket but for the arc of white light from the desk lamp, and knowing he had to work the problem through Saturday, he posted the one hundred and fifty contracts to account 0097707, the account he now designated his "shield account".

Next day he did not make it to the bank having received a telephone call from Martina to say she was on her way over. Finding him still in bed when she arrived she quickly undressed and with panties on modestly insinuated herself beside him, making an elbow-rest among the pillows.

'Hi there sleepyhead,' she said with a hint of hostility. 'Can I be close to you,' she then hankered.

Drowsily he became aware of her serenity, she sporting a new hairstyle – a pageboy bob, eyebrows faultlessly tweezed. Aroused by the intimacy of her closeness he nestled up to her and began to remove her panties.

'I'm having my period,' she sighed, making a wry face at him.

'You know I love everything about ye. I love your very soul,' he whispered while toeing, with her acquiescence, the silky material from her ankles, then fingering the loop of the tampon and slowly withdrawing it. Libidinously hooked by her concupiscent eyes, he inhaled the menstruous flow. 'I want to be with you in everyway' he exhaled, laying the plug on the bedside table.

While making love in awkward intimacy, she occasionally made mild protest when his caresses tweaked her bruised body, the injuries she had sustained in the accident now dark macular patches she showed off with infectious enthusiasm.

'You behaved very badly Mr MacAlindon,' she said laughingly, lighting a cigarette for them to share. 'You oughtna treat me like that. No need to snap the head off me.'

'I know. Forgive me. You do forgive me don't ye.'

'I'll think about it. I cried all the way home that night. That is as far as I made it home that night. My car hit the bloody kerb and I lost control. Everything went black and the next thing I remember is a white light being shone in my eyes, concerned voices asking me all class of stupid questions. Anyway, I enjoyed my rest away from your wacko antics. The medics and the nurses couldn't have been nicer. When the hunk of a doctor signed my discharge he asked me who Steve was. Apparently I was muttering and cussing you to kingdom come when they brought me in.'

''Tis hard to kill a bad thing, or so they say. You're okay now though, just a few bruises here and there,' he said, as he gently prodded her slender body.

'Why do you get so angry with me Steve? You know how much I love you. You know I want to be of help whenever I can. But sometimes you can be so irascible, so unfairly aggressive.'

'I don't mean to be so. Maybe it's because I'm so madly in love with ye – "You have my heart and soul",' he sang jocosely, as she frolicsomely thumped him on the shoulder.

'A strange way for you to show it, giving out all the time and never once –'

'Surely not all the time Tina? I'm so crazy about ye and yet don't have ye… to myself. And work has been a pain in the ass lately.'

'I know honey. And you'll have to do without my invaluable services for another few days you poor thing. But I'll come see you. By the way, what about that accursed account? Did you finally discover what –'

'Please, put that to bed. As far as I'm concerned the account doesn't exist and you're better off not knowin' a thing about it. Trust me Tina. Just forget I ever mentioned it to ye.'

'It's such a beautiful day,' she chirped. 'Whaddoya say we take the Verrazano Bridge to Staten, top deck, go eat at Rico's.'

13

How prescient his comment to Martina proved when on Monday night working late alone in head office, frenetically calculating the losses now stashed away in the shield account, he was flummoxed by the figures the calculator kept throwing up. Having tapped in the figures again and again, no matter how many times he number crunched the same losses showed up. The one hundred and fifty contracts from Friday now stood at a loss of $107,000. That figure he had expected, the market having moved against him. However, by not closing out the five hundred September calls he held in an open, unhedged position, the total losses now stood at $465,000. He paced up and down the floor in the shadows thrown by the arc of diffused white light from his desk lamp, a cloying sense of panic welling up from the pit of his stomach shattering his normal composure under pressure, plunging him into total disarray. He had hidden the rogue trades in the shield account with the idea of trading out the losses then calculated at no more than $200,000. How long could he keep them hidden now that the losses had escalated to just short of half a million dollars. How much time would he have to trade himself out of the problem before internal audit started asking awkward questions, or worse, before the Exchange Regulator moved against the bank. There was no one in whom he could in confidence admit his problem to; Frank seemed unable to control his tongue and would blabber about it in a drunken stupor; it would be an intolerable burden to saddle Martina with however much he wanted to confide in her. No, he must hold his own. Having hidden the rogue trades the problem was his alone. He would do his best to trade out of it.

Next morning he was cheered by Martina's return to work. She telephoned him in euphoric mood saying she had tickets for the "Hair" rock musical at the Biltmore Theater on the Thursday night.

'I don't like musicals,' he replied absent-mindedly, yet agreed to go, lured by her guileless pleading. At the Stock Exchange, staring in disbelief at the cumulative losses, deadening his acuity and stamina for the job, he acknowledged for the first time that the concatenation of incidents had resulted in out and out forfeiture of control. As the losses mounted that week, he had to accommodate increasingly larger figures. Some days he made close to a million dollars profit simply because the size of the position led him to large swings; other days he lost a million plus and was back to the hidden losses of half a million dollars, then $750,000, creeping inexorably toward $1 million. The losses grew because, gripped by necessity, he had to sell unhedged positions to try to bring in a decent premium, leading him to take unprotected risks with karstic investments in a bid to win back the lost money. The fluctuations in the market led him to double and redouble his position in an endeavour to take advantage of any bounce. Surely, he thought, a bounce would come soon. That is what he gambled on. Everything prodded him to impotent rage.

By Thursday, feeling exhausted by the unrelenting pressure to perform, he decided he did not want the distraction of attending the "Hair" rock musical, and telephoned Martina to tell her so. Hearing the exasperated tone in his voice, she did not make an issue of it, saying – 'Not to worry. I'll offload the tickets to a friend'. They agreed to meet that evening in his apartment. Waiting for her, pacing the floor in an intensity of emotions, now and then peering out the window, bodingly alert for the sound of her car, mulling over all he wanted to say to her, all he knew he had to say to her.

While making her way there, she turned over in her mind the refractory turmoil that now bestrode their relationship – What is it with him, he's grown distant, uncommunicative and moody with it, no fun in him anymore. I would do anything for him - anything, even to the extent of leaving Tom to be with him come what may. Now I find his volatile temperament worrisome. How can I leave Tom for a future of passion fulfilled and what? The elusive unknown. Our sporadic hates of each other so eagerly vanquished. But he doesn't help, doesn't even talk about it. It's all so uncertain. We need a heart-to-heart, clear the air, sort things out.

Walking into his apartment, cheerfully striving to hide her disappointment by reason of their no-show at the Biltmore, she remarked his downbeat state of mind and wanted to cuddle him. He remained aloof and abstracted. Disquieted, she noted he did not make for her the usual drink of vodka and coke. Nor did he have a tipple himself. As he paced the floor in ponderous silence, she sat on the sink-down sofa.

'If you love me let me go,' she disbelievingly heard him say.

'No! I can't,' she mumbled, feeling the blood drain from her face, her whole body enervated by the bluntness of his utterance, staggered by this immediate rupture. Falling on his knees before her, she moved closer to him as he knelt between her legs.

'You must let me go.'

She saw in these words a miserable end and suffocatingly brooded, letting her head drop on his shoulder, scalding tears coursing down her cheeks.

'I love you Steve, I love you,' she whispered a *cri de cœur* as she clung to him. Yes. I do love him. I need him, she was saying to herself. What has happened to make him ask this of me? How can I let him go? Why can't we talk this through, like before, take time and space to plan a future together, as we wish to be, break free of the chains of past mistakes.

She felt the firmness of his grip as he held her by the upper arms, spellbound by the glassy stare in his troubled eyes. The words would not come to her mouth, knowing deep down that time had lead to this inevitable parting, rendering her speechless. They held each other in a torturous reticence.

'I'll love you all my life…but I can't be with you anymore. It's a dead end. Let me go,' she heard him say, repeating the very words she had said to him all those times ago. They kissed, she sensing a burning intenseness in him as their tears mingled, sniffling noses pressed against each other's cheeks, arms fastened in a covetous embrace, an irresistible passionate want blotting out the searing pain of knowing she had lost him. He led her to the bedroom, and in the impregnable silence she savoured his lovemaking as if to lock the sensations indelibly in her memory. Afterward, watching him in a deep slumber for a lingering time, his body fitted to hers, she rose in harrowing sadness and left him.

*

He awoke to another day of enervating heat, a scorching dawn light over Manhattan, to find Martina gone. He could not conjure up an image of her leave-taking, love's passion spent. They had lain in an intense conflation of entwined limbs unwilling to be severed, until his body succumbed to oppressive exhaustion prodding him into fitful sleep. And so he had endured a protracted, emotionally charged last parting, last goodbye. Reluctantly clambering from the bed that held the vestigial impress of her body, he did not shave, wash, or shower, wanting to keep her muliebritas redolence, her closeness, with him for as long as possible. Sipping black coffee, he mulled over whether or not to go to work? Weighing up the likely consequences, he decided going AWOL amounted to capitulation. With a heavy heart he hurriedly dressed, picked up the usual barrage of mail from the mail box in the hallway and headed out under a white sun in an unforgiving blue sky. A braise heat hit him as he climbed into the car, throwing the bundle (comprising a blizzard of unsolicited mail shots) on the front passenger seat. Spotting the bald eagle emblem of the military draft board, he tore open the envelope, glimpsed a

226

troublesome future, and falteringly read the directive, ragingly exclaiming as he did so – fuck-fuck-fuck – all the while thwacking his fist against the steering wheel, sweat breaking out trickling irritably down his back, his stomach taut. The directive compulsorily required of him to report to the local draft office for classification, and if marked "Available for Service" to undergo pre-induction tests of his physical and mental abilities. – No fucking way am I up for that – he told himself, but was not assuaged. He sat motionless for a long time, the airflow booster at blue on full blast against the torrid humidity, his mind enmeshed in jungled uncertainty, his life exponentially plummeting into a shambolic morass. Beginning the drive to work, he knew he wanted no part in the red tape and ritualistic escapades of army life. He nevertheless felt menaced, believing that once the military got their hands on him he could well end up posted to Vietnam, any conscientious objection he had to the war given short shrift (as Johnny Cassidy had forewarned). He had no intention of falling into that death trap by becoming one more statistic in fulfilling General Westmoreland's recent demand for an additional two hundred thousand troops, the neoconservative lobby bleating that perhaps seven hundred thousand might finally do the job of winning the war as promised by the generals in The Pentagon. But how to avoid it?

Pulling into the bank's carpark he decided to skip the office and go directly to the Exchange. Frank made a flippant comment about him being in a downbeat mood, which he ignored. He spotted a note left on his console that Tina had 'phoned. He ignored that also, and parried any further calls from that quarter by instructing the girl at the switchboard to say he was unavailable. Having spent the working day in zombifying wretchedness, he was relieved to join Frank, Richard and the Exchange crew for the usual Friday after-close beers, remaining there, thus bypassing a very likely encounter with Tina at Morans. Chris Cheaver and Myra

Johansson soon joined them, Chris handing him an envelope marked <u>Urgent - Strictly Personal</u>. He knew it was a missive from Tina and stuffed it unopened in his jacket inside pocket. Not having eaten that day the alcohol went straight to his head rendering him churlishly unintelligible, and obnoxious company. Yet he remained tight-lipped about the military call-up. Later on, staggering from the hostelry, Myra stood by him and taxied him home, undressed him and put him to bed, naked and dead to the world. Having found the letter in his jacket pocket, she decided to open it. Having done so, she fumed at Martina's lovesick words – 'Maca can do without this shit', she surmised, and crammed it into her bag. As she made to close the door leaving him to sleep off his drunken humour, the telephone rang. On answering it she heard a throaty gasp followed by dragging silence and the hang-up tone. 'Bitch' she muttered on banging the door behind her.

Next morning, gingerly sipping from a mug of strong black coffee, he remembered Tina's letter and searched everywhere for it. Not finding it, he assumed he had inadvertently dropped it in the taxi or on the street. Spontaneously telephoning her home number the phone was lifted, a listening silence at the other end:

'Tina.'

'Who the fuck is this? Is it you MacAlindon', Tom bellowed indignantly.

He cut the line, shrinking into pathetic idiocy. – Fuck.Fuck.Fuck. Surely she'll 'phone over the weekend, he obsessed hopefully. But there was no call. Mulling over his dilemma, he decided to have a meeting with Jeff on Monday, relate how he had been drafted and would probably get called up, and, depending on Jeff's reaction, come clean about the accruing deficit in the shield account and his part in the debacle.

The walk to work that Monday helped clear his head, and first thing he 'phoned Tina's extension. The dial tone rang out. Plucking up the courage to dial Jeff's extension direct, hoping to make the destined appointment, he was surprised when Tina answered. His voice faltered and he had to take a deep breath:

'I've been trying to –'

'Clear the line please.'

'Tina, I need to talk to –'

The line went dead. He 'phoned again. The receiver lifted, quickly followed by the hang-up tone. He slammed the phone down with a growl and took a few steps to go and confront her. Thinking better of it, he returned to his desk and wrote her an admonitory note advising he needed to have an urgent head-to-head with Jeff, that in the event of his not being there to receive calls she should accept them as courteously as possible. To do otherwise is to hurt other people, including herself. He did not mention the military call-up. In haste he delivered it to the post room as he headed for the Exchange. Next morning he received the following missive at work, written in a heavy hand, splenetic and vindictive, plunging him into profound despair:

Stephen,

I want nothing to do with you – be that meeting you at work, in Jeff's office, taking telephone calls or whatever. As far as I am concerned you don't exist – I would rather forget that I got involved with a bastard like you. I never hurt you intentionally before – I have no desire to do so now. You are not worth it, but you are such a small minded, lying, sneak that if I ever come in contact with you again, I will make no bones about it. You think you can use people as you see fit but in this instance, I am afraid you have met your match.

As regards being courteous – I am to everyone – excluding you – so don't worry about me hurting other people – least of all myself. In your note you say:- "As regards me, I'm past being hurt by you"- You don't know what it is to be hurt by me, but, I can assure you, you can start finding out because you have done all the hurt you can possibly do. As regards you – I don't give a fuck what you do or think – I have some nice suggestions though.

There is one thing I want from you and that is my photographs – I can't bear the thought of you having them. I only hope others see you for what you are – sooner than I did. Oh! By the way, glad to see you haven't changed, still thinking about yourself. I can't figure out why you wrote that note –then I never could. Perhaps you were missing me – like a hole in the head.

Martina

He was dumbfounded, his heart racing, and he lost in speculation – 'What kind of metamorphic fuckery is this. What had she
said in that lost letter.' Chimeric doubts, plots, fears and intrigues
crowded his imagination. At his apartment that evening, choking
with rage, he retrieved her photographs from between the leaves of
his favourite books and enclosed them with a laconic note saying,
among other things – 'My despair is like a rabid dog biting into
me.' – 'I will keep our love that will never fade from my memory a
secret.' – 'I will never talk about you. Nor speak to you again.' He
wished her happiness in the future; that for himself he had no
regrets. The telephone rang several times but he was in no mood to
talk to anybody. A three a.m. call panicked him out of drowsy
restlessness and on answering the line disengaged. Lamenting her
loss, he felt stifled by the pounding of his heart, shaken by great
shudders, tears saturating the pillow, taking deep breaths in an
effort to control himself. On Thursday after close, he found another
missive propped against Cantillon's woodcut, but didn't read it
until he was back in his pad that evening. Again, a hand written
letter, but written in a more equably generous vein:

Steve,

I tried to phone you last night but when the phone was answered I
froze – and couldn't speak. I was afraid of how you would react to me
phoning after all I have said.

The reason I phoned was to ask you to disregard everything I said
in my letter – the things I said were written by me because I was
hurt and bitter towards you, but not true, and not what I wanted to say
at all. I regret having written them now. I do NOT regret my love for you.

I would like us to be friends and part in the way we had decided to, on
that last night we spent together. I wish you every happiness too. Take
care of yourself – keep in touch.

Love you,

Martina

He was utterly confounded by this reply, his mind a quandary of
uncertainties and discord incensing his mood. Overcome by a
commingling of surprise, farcicality and bewilderment, he spent
the wee hours mooching around the pad swilling whiskey and

chain-smoking, his health close to breakdown under the stress of it all. All this emotional upheaval was robbing him of sleep – 'Where will it end'.

*

The morning delivered a broiling sun blanketing the atmosphere with suffocating humidity. While hastily dressing he remained un-decided about going to work – 'What's the fucking point?' He didn't bother to check the mailbox on his way out.

Burning rubber as he pulled away from the curb, hacked off and frazzled, he found himself driving east, too late for work, too shattered to think of work, heading for the bridge, heading for Brooklyn. What to do? Where to go? He was gnawed by irresol-ution. An irresistible urge had him divert along Martina's road of elegant brownstone houses, and deliberately dawdling past her house he saw her car standing in the forecourt silhouetted against an arbour of hanging clusters of lilac-blue flowers of a wisteria shrub, her bedroom curtains pulled closed against the invasive sunlight. Is she there? Had she also not gone to work this day? Overcome by the desire to see her, to touch her, to possess her, he brought the car to a halt in the middle of the road, and in that eternal moment his every sinew ached to be bound to her. So deliberating, he knew that should he find her there it would undo all the unavoidable pain of the break-up they had gone through. A tooted car horn startled him out of his frantic reverie. With his heart skipping a few beats, his throat taut with apprehension, he indicated an apology in the rear-view mirror and slipped into drive moving on, slowly, the very movement making the intensity of his feelings all the more agonizing. His predicament at the Exchange flitting out of focus, he drove south to Coney Island, parked the car, and, heeding the muffled roar of the breakers, strode across the stony shingle and corrugated sand on Sea Gate beach where he and Martina had visited on occasions gathering shells and nubbins of fossils; the water slides in the distance crowded with frolicking youths seeking refuge from the high humidity in the city; the sky criss-crossed with jet contrails. The breath of the sea on his face gently cooled his intemperate ardour as he sucked in the clean salty air, sauntering along on pebbles licked by the ebbing tide, the rhythmic white rush of the breaking waves soaking his shoes. He didn't care, the sea held no consolation; nothing assuaged the disharmony of his mind. The heartache of having let go the love of his life was slowly being subsumed by the challenging metanoia as to what he must do to climb out of the baleful voidness. Gazing unseeingly out to sea to the flat horizon where water meets sky he was torn by conflicting impulses, pulling him in different directions: the powerful pull of the will, of love; the worth of everything his time in America had shown him; the trouble now to be avoided. Given one's druthers he would stay, come what may, see if the tide turns in his favour. Yet that hope could be run aground by the current of events. So, with perspicacious acuity, the purview of truth determined him to go home. The uncertainties could no longer be lived through. Yes. He would go back to Ireland; stiffen himself against life's vicissitudes. In that Rubicon moment, the deadweight of torpid unpredictability swiftly lifted from his shoulders.

He began inventorying a mental list of things to do. Reckoning his savings account held over $30,000 and his current account approximately $8,000 he decided he would, that very afternoon, close both accounts following withdrawal of the credit balances in cash. He contemplated authorizing the handing over of the title deeds of his apartment (held by his attorney for safe keeping, the market value of which he estimated at $135,000) to Lehman Brothers Bank in part recompense for his errant ways, the authorization to be posted his attorney with the keys once he had safely left the jurisdiction of the United States. He would pack his Montana leather travel bag with as many possessions as he could carry: his best clothes, favorite books, personal correspondence, inclusive of Martina's challenging love letters and notes (he had binned the gossipy ones), and the pick from his record collection. With a renewed spring in his step, he dashed back to the car, tapped the loose sand from his sodden shoes, climbed in and raced back to the city.

At his apartment perusing his Bank of America account statements, he established the savings account held $34,000 and the current account $7,487 in credit. Sorting out the bills for domestic utility services, he telephoned each supplier terminating the accounts, furnishing metre readings where appropriate, then wrote checks discharging them to the end of the month. Calling American Express, he cancelled his membership and scissored the card. Turning up at his local Bank of America branch, Helen the petite blonde staff member (with whom he always endeavoured to do his dealings and regularly exchanged flirtatious railleries) gave him the disagreeable news that without twenty-four hour prior notice the maximum cash withdrawal from his savings account was restricted to $10,000 per day. Withdrawing in the largest denomination notes available $6,000 from the current account, leaving the balance to cover credit card payments and the utilities checks he had written earlier, and $10,000 from the savings account he then dashed to the next nearest branch of the bank and withdrew a further $10,000 from the savings account. By the time he arrived at a third branch to clear the balance $14,000, the banking system had blocked the withdrawal obligating him to make no further enquiry. That final withdrawal would have to wait until he was on the road. Despite the nefarious losses to the extent of $1 million owing Lehman Brothers, no doubt accumulating, he was more intent on finding a secure way of bearing out of the country the guts of $40,000 in cash. President Johnson earlier in the year had introduced draconian currency restrictions in an attempt to prevent attacks on the dollar and the speculative rush for gold, but primarily to get the massive federal payments deficit in order. Johnson's austere directives to stem the outflow of dollars saw increased surveillance at airports and seaports and created a dollar glut in the country. Brainstorming over where to stash his money Maca kept it close to his person pending his planned departure from New York on Sunday. Friday evening and most of Saturday he spent thoroughly clearing out the apartment; depositing in a local charity shop items too burden-some to hold on to, bulky winter clothing and knick-knacks. Saturday evening he shaved and showered, dressed in the clothes he would wear on the morrow, and dined alone in Giovanni's Food Emporium, obliquely thanking Armando for all the delicious food he had enjoyed over time and evading questions as to when and where he was off to as best he could. Back in his apartment, he secreted $24,000 in four water-proofed bundles of $6,000 inside the lining of his travel bag. Fatigued, yet buzzing with accomplishment, he sat down to plan his route home. Wanting to spend his last night in the United States at a place he had been with her, a place that evoked her memory, he had the idea of travelling to Toronto with a one night stopover in Clarence at the Asa Ransom Inn; then cross the border via Niagara to Canada by bus, slinking amongst the day trippers so hopefully lessening the prospect of a baggage search and confrontation with customs, and from Toronto fly direct to London. However, reckoning the border crossing could prove troublesome (if apprehended and found bearing all those dollars out of the country he could end up in jail on that account alone, not to mention his evading the clutches of military services), he reasoned it was not a risk worth taking. Also, on calmer reflection, stopping over at the Asa Ransom Inn struck him as ridiculous mawkishness, such a yearning totally irrational. He resolved to take his chances on hitching a ride out of the country by boat.

*

On Sunday afternoon, he drove to Boston and overnighted in a motel on the southern outskirts of the city, where he endured another sleepless night due in part to the frolics of the couple in the room next door who, by the sound of it, seemed to run the gamut of the Kamasutra with the whole of the Red Sox baseball team in support spurring them on. Next morning he awoke late. All was quiet. He drove into the city and withdrew the balance $14,000, drawing $7,000 from each of two branches of the Bank of America, and closed the savings account. Back in his motel room, he stitched a further $12,000 in two waterproofed bundles of $6,000 inside the lining of his travel bag.

Over a casual lunchtime chat at a prototypal diner, he procured the address of a nearby reputable second hand car dealership, and having spent the best part of an hour washing and polishing the Ford Mustang in readiness for sale, he pulled up at the forecourt seeking $1,000 cash for the hot rod. After some pretty aggressive haggling he had to settle for $650, handed over in crisp clean $50 dollar bills which he crammed into his wallet. Nearby he spied a marina store and sauntering in purchased a Gore-Tex parka (as protection against the elements at sea) and a lockable heavy-duty waterproof canvas holdall (as a means of staving off prying eyes into his possessions). The balance $2000 cash he had folded tightly and tucked into the money pocket of the parka.

Ready to roll, he took a bus ride south and caught the Woods Hole Nantucket ferry steamer. Passage paid and baggage secured, he slipped into his parka, lit a cigarette and lopped with casual detachment in the balmy breeze at the stern of the steamer, entranced by the churning phosphorescent slipstream from the boat's propellers push its cargo of passengers, vehicles and merchandise away from Cape Cod, a sleepy cluster of terraced and stand-alone houses amidst a dense green forest of deciduous broadleaf trees edging into panoramic view. The metabolic wastes of fatigue (as Freud put it) made him giddy as he watched the spumy spray, seeming to invite him to throw himself overboard. Withstanding its allurement, he was relieved to spot a ragamuffin boy, as freckled as a thickly mottled mistle thrush, join him at the boat's rail. Observing the boy toss an empty coke bottle into the wash, he ground out his cigarette on the deck and scolded him for littering, his rebuke meeting with an impudent "fuck off mister". As Chappaquiddick Island receded into the distance under a crepuscular sky, and the snorting waves of the open water slammed the bows of the ferry-boat, he turned into the bracing brined wind that bedewed his face to marvel at the munificence of Nantucket Sound, submerged in his own self-absorption, alone, his lippy ragamuffin companion having abandoned his watch. Striding along the deck, chain smoking cigarettes in reflective mood of all he had left behind, it seemed no time at all before the marram grass sand dunes of the hillock island of Nantucket with its high-spire churches and picturesque waterfront buildings aglow in a low-angled sun swept into view. Before long, the steamer had manoeuvred its way into the breakwater and dock. Trundling away from the ferry slip, baggage in hand, the soughing wings of a skein of wild geese overhead, the chandlers cries ringing in his ears, he had walked but a short distance when he espied the Jared Coffin House where, chancing upon the rotund innkeeper standing proprietorially on the granite stone steps, he asked about accommodation and took a room for a two night stay, letting the insouciant innkeeper know that he might well prolong his visit should the fishing prove sporting. At dinner that evening he sang the praises of the choice quahog chowder and bay scallops to the harried *maitre d'*, and believing he had secured his serviceable attention enquired if any of the seasonal residents were visitors from Canada:

'Why would you want to know?'

'I'm on my way to visit my aunt Maggie in New Brunswick and crew help is how I plan to get there.'

'You'd be quicker flying.'

'Yeah I know… I know. But I don't want to fly, I want to go by sail. Sailing is in my blood and I'm a bloody good yachtsman even if I say so myself. I'm willin' to work crew for free passage. Can't do much fairer than that now can I?'

The dubious *maitre d'* discreetly moved away, busying himself with obsequious attentiveness to the other house guests. Later, as Maca enjoyed a calming smoke over coffee, the *maitre d'* approached him and advised that Monsieur Jean-Baptiste Mermoz, the suave moustachioed gentleman sitting by the bay window smoking his briar pipe in the company of his son and three friends, would be sailing his yacht back to Quebec, leaving in a day or two. On exiting the dining room, he wished Mermoz and his company at table a courteous 'bawn so-air-ee' in an accentuated Irish accent.

Wearing as befitting a seafaring attire as he could muster from the few clothes he had been able to pack (blue linen cargo trousers with his wallet bulging the thigh pocket, a short sleeve white shirt with his Irish hardback passport prominently on show in the breast pocket, and brown sneakers), he skulked around the marina next day amid the yachts with bristling masts, every so often idly resting on a capstan taking in the view, and in no time identified Mermoz's yacht – "Strongbow" – by its ensign whipping in the breeze. Hovering close by awaiting the opportunity to introduce himself, he came upon Mermoz's son Alain (whom he judged to be sixteen or seventeen years old) down on his hands and knees scrubbing the deck, and while uproariously shamming a trip over the hawser mooring rope, he pantingly called out:

'Don's a lot of work for one fella. Break yer back so 'twould. 'Tis a long handled deck scrubber ye need for the job.'

'Don't have one.'

'Have you a brush? Get me the brush and I'll put together a deck scrubber for ye.'

Having climbed aboard, when Alain handed him the brush he snugly fitted the top palm-end into the scrubber head, tightening it with the torn off top of his cigarette pack.

'There ye are, brush and deck scrubber in one. Listen to me here now, I'll do the scrubbin' for ye and you slosh her down with don bucket there. She'll be spick and span in no time.'

The work proceeded apace, and nearing completion Jean-Baptiste Mermoz returned to his boat to find his son chatting animatedly with the perspiring stranger.

'Holloa Mon-si-eur Mermoz. Just givin' Alain a bit of a hand here. Hope ye don't mind?'

'I do not mind if you do not mind. But I should like to know the reason for such beneficence,' a French inflection on the last word.

'I'll come straight to it so Mon-si-eur Mermoz. Like myself I noticed you're stayin' at the Jared Coffin House. I hail from Ireland. Stephen… Stephen MacAlindon by name. Me friends call me Maca for short –'

'Ah! You are Irish, like your great countryman D'Arcy McGee. Many Irish flee the famine to our country.'

'Yeah, the great hunger.' He knew nothing of D'Arcy McGee.

'Many die in shipwrecks, or of disease.'

'Coffin ships they came over in. Coffin ships, not fit for cattle never mind human beings. Treated like swine they were. Well, I love boats and everythin' to do with them. This yacht of yours is a beaut, a cracker. What is she? A forty footer?' he said, *faux naïf*.

'*Seize metres en fait*,' Mermoz said dismissively.

'And I love the name, Strongbow. We had a great Norman, Richard de Clare, who married the daughter of a high-king of Ireland, who went by the name of Strongbow. Became more Irish than the Irish themselves as the fella says. That was the guts of a thousand years ago. Well now, I see your homeport is Quebec. The thing is me mother's sister Margaret Murphy, me auntie Maggie that is, she lives above in Saint John –'

'St. John's, Newfoundland?'

'No! Saint John, New Brunswick. And sure I've never met the woman but the mother asked me to look her up before I head home to Belfast -'

'Belfast Maine?'

'No! No. Belfast Ireland,' he said, producing his Irish passport for inspection by the Quebecker. 'I was hopin' ye might be in need of an extra pair of hands to crew for ye on your return trip. I'd be willin' to –'

'I would not have undertaken this voyage without adequate crew numbers –'

'Ah yes! Of course you wouldn't. I know ye wouldn't. That's not what I meant. I wouldn't want to be paid or anythin' like that there, I mean, I would help ye all I can in exchange for passage. I have money enough to pay me own way at any stopovers and for food. I could coil the lines, keep things shipshape, help out with the cookin.' I'm a dab hand at the cookin'. And I see ye have radar, I could do night-watch for ye. No bother. I wouldn't be a –'

'My boat is a five berth, three fore two aft, so I do not see how I can accommodate you on board being five already, much as I might wish to 'elp you.'

'I'd bed down on the floor, no bother. I'm used to slummin' it and –'

'Slummin. What is this word?'

'Slumming. I'm used to roughin' it, discomforts like -'

'Used or not I have to consider my colleagues. We are on vacation and intend to enjoy ourselves at each port-of-call. We are not in any great hurry.'

'Nor am I, nor am I. No hurry on me a'tall. Just want go see me auntie Maggie before I head home. 'Tis unlikely I'll be about these parts again. Shure me mother would never forgive me if… if I didn't take the trouble.'

'The bench seat in the cabin pulls out to make an extra bed,' said Alain.

'That would suit me fine and dandy. Just fine altogether.'

And with that admission by his son, the reluctance of Mermoz was overcome, swiftly replaced by a grudging acceptance that the Strongbow would carry an additional crew member as far as Saint John. Having dickered for his passage out of the United States, Maca, apart from seeking confirmation of the date and time of departure, kept himself very much to himself, lest any inapposite encounter with Mermoz caused his deliverer to have a change of mind. Killing time, he enjoyed sauntering round the port town, particularly his visit to the Whale Museum, finding himself gobsmacked by the titanic skeleton of a sperm whale.

On Thursday, as the first long red streaks of the rising sun filled the immense horizon below reefs of clouds that shadowed the morning's blue brilliance of the Atlantic, he stepped aboard the "Strongbow" with his travel bag and parka locked in the canvas holdall. Over the next ten days the yacht would make good speed northward, often exceeding twenty knots, being lashed through the blue-green expanse of the ocean by freakishly variable but mainly backing southerly winds of force five followed by veers to the east and north east, spindrift salting all on board an eldritch white, making stopovers in Plymouth, Marblehead, Newburyport, and along the rugged shores of Maine at York Harbor, Portland, Boothbay Harbor, Rockland, Bar Harbor, before entering the Bay of Fundy, bypassing Nova Scotia to starboard, becalmed close to Grand Manan Island to port necessitating a pull in at Eastport, and eventually reaching the safe-haven of Saint John, New Brunswick on the evening of the twelfth day.

His lack of prowess in the skills of sailing rapidly became evident after the first day at sea, compounded by his inability to make head or tail of the yacht's portolan, it being written in French. Nevertheless, he did his best to make himself as useful as possible by helping out with house-keeping duties; and by cooking hearty Irish breakfasts that left phenolic chunks of grease under the grill, as often as not the fry burned to the proverbial crisp. Being of a willing disposition he joined Serge, in whose jovial company he adopted a more relaxed manner, on watch during night sailing, and on the lookout for submerged rocks as the yacht passed through narrow channels on entering marinas at neap or low tide. Instinctually, he got to grips with the yelled joual commands of "*larguez le spi*" when running before the wind, and the heave to "*abaissez la grand 'voile au premier ris*" when the wind gusted above force five, the sails often at a tangent to swelling waves. Boasting an enthusiastic zest to take over at the wheel, he was brusquely rebuffed by Mermoz with a – "*Non*! You are no helmsman". It may well be that his most positive contribution was the entertaining of the brawny crew with his bawdy humour. The first day at sail was dominated by Mermoz and his colleagues communicating in French, and but for Alain he had nobody to talk to. By day two, sailing to Marblehead, the company begged of him more stories and jokes. So enthralled were they, each evening thereafter Serge insisted at dinner that he regale them with the "missionary" joke, laughing uproariously even before he began its retelling:

'Paddy was in the wife's bad books. She went historical on him, no not hysterical, she listed every blunder and wrong he had done her since they married twenty years before, and that was historical. But worse for Paddy was the wife's repulse of his overtures for sex, she declining to participate in any sexual activity in or out of the marital bed. Despite his cajoling attempts to bring her round to giving him some relief, she would turn her back on him and begin to snore. One night, at the end of his tether and tired of her shrewish ways, he suggested they should try the missionary position. "What position is that would ye mind tellin' me?" she asked, feigning interest. "I'll stay here and you fuck off to Africa".'

So captivated by his company had they become that when mooring the "Strongbow" in Lorneville Harbour outside the port city of Saint John, Mermoz offered to await his return to the boat after his visit to his aunt Maggie, and take him onward to Quebec, where he planned to catch the Canadian Pacific passenger liner to Liverpool. He astounded them by disclosing (dropping the accentuated Irish brogue) he did not have an aunt Maggie in Saint John, that he had lied in order to secure safe passage out of the United States. He heard Mermoz's tongue clicking reproachfully against the roof of his mouth, his eyes fixed on the mooring ground between his feet.

'The truth is Monsieur Mermoz I'd been drafted and as a conscientious objector I don't want any part in that war. It ain't my fight. Anyway I believe it's unwinnable. Johnson is making a terrible mistake. A lot of guys are being blown away in Vietnam for no good reason a'tall. Friends of mine have been killed.'

'The very same mistakes the French generals made thirty years before him. Johnson must learn from those mistakes,' said a subdued Mermoz.

'I'm glad ye see it that way.'

'*Peut-être*! Alas I am not happy you lied to me Maca. Had we been boarded by the coast guard my boat could have been impounded for carrying a draft dodger, a runaway from U.S. justice.'

'Hardly that serious Monsieur Mermoz. But that's the very reason I didn't tell ye. What you don't know can't hurt ye.'

The trust and camaraderie he had built up during the trip melted away. He thanked them for the pleasure of their company and took his leave, making his way to Saint John. Relieved at having successfully arrived in Canadian territory, money and possessions intact, he established at the port shipping office that the "Empress of Canada" passenger liner sailing from Montreal for Liverpool would pick up passengers in the city of Quebec on the Tuesday of the following week. He booked his Atlantic passage in tourist class, and lumbering along carrying the canvas holdall took the long bus-ride to Quebec.

Following a crisp cold lager in the Fairmont Le Chateau Frontenac bar set high above the majestic St. Lawrence River, he took the short ride on the funicular down to the historic quarter with its parade of boutiques and cafes, his mind fixed on exploring Champlain's beautiful city. Long days were spent in a vaporous solitude walking the noble ramparts, the narrow cobblestone lanes, tiring on climbing upward-curving paths and country squares, visiting the must see tourist attractions. Taking a look inside the Basilica of Sainte-Anne-de-Beaupre where, responsive to the abrupt silence throbbing in his ears, he shambled in its hollow expansive stillness in broody thoughts of Martina, lighting a votive candle on the amorphous antiquated iron stand amid others spurting thin black tendrils of piquant smoke, and marvelling at the ogives of blood-red and ultramarine tints of the stained glass rose window. Surrounded by the sepulchral aura of the basilica, the flickering monumental altar candles casting shadowy illumination on the vaulted roof and reflecting gleamy light off the stone columns, the stupendous organ pipes emerging dimly from the gloom, she had again come to monopolize his every thought after he had only fleetingly entertained reminiscences of her during his odyssey out of the United States. He could not find solace in this strange city, its romantic charms weighing down his sensibilities freighted with yearning for her and their unthinkable, unbearable parting. Judging he had loved her too well but not wisely, his body ached for her, potent images of the symmetrized fulfilment of their coupling incessantly scorched his brain, such resonances inflaming his sense of desolation. Wretchedly and sentimentally absorbed in the pain of her memory, knowing he would never see her again, that it was all over, he saw the city through her eyes and would sit in vacant melancholy for hours in the afternoon crystalline sunshine at pavement cafes on Dufferin Terrace overlooking the sparkling river, composing in his mind the explanations he owed her for his sudden departure. Passing the time so, on the Tuesday afternoon before embarking on the "Empress of Canada", while sampling a bowl of poutine (the provincial dish), he wrote her a long letter confessing all: the complications imposed by his being called up by the military, necessitating him to flee the country; the mistakes he made at the bank leaving a debt liability of one million dollars or more hidden in that infamous account (the repercussions of which he believed she would probably be alerted to by the time she read his letter, the consequences from which he had sought to protect her); the handing over of the title deeds of his apartment to her for delivery to Jeffrey Robertson, this being his only means of partly redressing the debt, otherwise leaving it to her good offices to deal with the property as she saw fit. Page after page were taken up with recovered memories, some anecdotal, and expressions of his undying love for her; of how fate brought them together, then cruelly severed the bond, they both knowing their hearts were as one. He placed the sealed letter in an envelope addressed to Bill Crosby, his lawyer in New York, enclosing the keys of the apartment with authority to have it delivered with the title deeds to Martina Amorosino Patterson at her Brooklyn home. He then wrote his mother alerting her to expect his arrival home for good in ten days, or so, time. Having posted the letters, he felt self-composed having put his affairs in order.

*

The transatlantic crossing on board the "Empress of Canada" he found to be agonizingly long and mind-numbing, due primarily to wet weather conditions; every few hours it would rain cats and dogs, and then the sun breaks through again. Wearied, his mental apathy made him shrink from contact or participation in small talk with his fellow passengers, exchanging a few words in passing, monosyllabic courtesies for the most part; spending monotonous periods in the garish shopping arcade buying presents for his mother and sisters; most evenings sitting moodily in the caco-phonous Sky Lounge drinking beer and smoking cigarettes, the dissonant live music deadening his senses. On arrival in Liverpool, and on ascertaining that the ferry boat would not depart for Belfast until late that night, he decided to kill the waiting hours by visiting the much vaunted modern design of the Roman Catholic cathedral. Later, dropping into the Cavern club, he let it be known to all within earshot that he was personal friends with George Harrison and the rest of the fab four having played saxophone on their first record to hit the charts. He was not believed. He was ignored. Entangled in self-consciousness as he wrestled with his demons he felt like a nobody pondering the stain of invisibility, his sense of incompleteness, wallowing in drink-fuelled self-pity, asking himself – Where do I come from? Who am I? He had never felt so alone. He was alone, like the derelict boat he had seen drifting rudderless in mid-Atlantic. By degrees, a new sense of freedom disrupted such downhearted thoughts, easing the chafing that irritated his spirit. Am I alive? I am alive. He would start life over, look to himself, be himself. What other choice did he have? As Walt Whitman said – "I exist as I am, that is enough".

On a misty grey morning, he torpidly traipsed the deck as the ferry boat, klaxon blaring, approached Belfast Lough. Fastening the hood of his parka at the neck against the chilly breeze, he blearily eyed the shadowy moraine of Black Mountain, Cave Hill to the fore, standing, it seemed to him, ever ready to dump slabs of basaltic rock on the dreary confines of the city below. Now what had seemed an interminable journey home would end? Now he was returning to the back of beyond, back to the mediocre life he thought he had escaped, having believed he had kicked over the traces. As the boat slowly edged into dock, he watched the gantries shift freight. He could hear the clunks of pile-drivers and the clangorous hammering of iron on sheet iron and steel echoing from the Harland and Wolfe Shipyard. Mushroom clouds of inky smoke belched from factory chimney stacks rose and merged in the murky penumbrae of a loury cumulonimbus sky before falling back to cover the city's cheerless architecture in a cloak of smeary drabness. With only fleeting remembrances of happier times, tears sprang to his eyes as he grappled with a deep convolution of feelings: the uneasy joy of his homecoming; the readiness to be with family again; the loss of Martina and all that America had to teach him about life. A deep presentiment of forlornness overwhelmed him. What days were lying in wait for him? He had reached that fork in the path and would now take the road less travelled; endeavour to be at ease with the world; rid himself of the malaise of melancholy.

Having disembarked, while standing on the terminal concourse, canvas holdall at his feet, waiting to hail a taxi to take him on the final leg of the journey, a pretty girl attracted his eye as she approached the shipping office, and in the exchange of an evanescent smile he glimpsed at the edge of vision the anomalous presence of a shadowy figure and a blurring movement before a blow to his head pitched him into blackness.

Part 111

14

Emerging dazed from a dragging tortuous blackness into the incandescent strip-lighting of a hospital corridor, its walls exuding disinfectant, he felt the jolt to his head as the wheels of the gurney speedily traversed the floor divide as it entered the lift shaft. Imperative voices surrounded him. He didn't like those voices.

'No name tag. Who we got here?'

'Found no ID. Victim of assault, possible robbery.'

'Appears stable. Any assessment?'

'Trauma to the head, perhaps internal bleeding.'

'Who's on duty?'

'Dr Desmond.'

'Ask Sally to alert Mr Tindall ASAP.'

The elevator bell pinged and once more he felt the jolt to his head as the gurney exited. Ceiling lights whizzed by, the cruel brightness blinding him, some respite as he underpassed blown light bulbs or bulbs deliberately not replaced, perhaps a cost saving measure he surmised mischievously. The gurney came to an abrupt halt under the glare of sunlight streaming in from a high walled window, the ceiling fluorescent tube stuttering arrhythmically, and as the green screen curtain swished closed along the u-shaped rail he sensed the blood throb-throbbing in his head. He could hear an agonized cry of – "I don't wanna die… help me… I don't wanna die", the petrified groans of a wretched old man unnerving him. Hoisted and arm-wrestled shoulder and leg both sides onto a softer bed, a rosy-cheeked nurse with bushy eyebrows firmly holding his head (viewing her contrariwise she reminded him of his double-faced kiddie toy - a bald man with a long beard and turned about a shaven man with wild stand-up hair), gently positioning it in a brace that held the dense coldness of a marble slab.

'Well hel-lo there. What's your name?' she fawningly asked.

This perplexed him, his mind a blank.

'You do have a name. You understand English don't ye?'

'Yeah! I'm in Belfast amin't I. This is my home.' My name, why can't I remember my name, finding himself getting worked up in baffled agitation.

'Where were ye going, or coming from then? The ambulance picked you up at the port terminal.'

'From America. Liverpool. What happened? Why am I in hospital?'

'You had a bit of an accident. The doctor will see ye soon. Tell me your name. Is there any reason ye won't tell me your name?'

'What have we here nurse?' a somewhat imperious voice demanded, an expression of snobbish ennui on her face.

'Blunt force trauma to the head. Won't tell me his name but says he's a local.'

'Any medication administered?'

'Aspirin, two shots.'

'Let's take a look then. Steve! Why Steve, I thought you were in New York.'

Steve. She calls me Steve. He fixed her gleaming blue eyes with an intensive questioning look, suspecting he had wobbled under her entrancing gaze before. But when? And who is she, this beauty who called him Steve in an overly haughty familiarity. Pushing his mind into memory overdrive, it refused to take cognizance of any past meetings. Of course she's a doctor, yes, checking me over with demonstrative professionalism, he weighed up. But how does she know me? Do I know her?

'Steve, its Deirdre, Deirdre Desmond.'

'I... I like yer face. I know yer face from somewhere.'

'As well you should,' she said, noting his quizzical expression.

Following a cursory examination of the head injury she said:

'Nurse! Contact neurology and book a slot in X-ray. I know this man. I'll notify Mr Tindall. You'll be okay Steve. You're in good hands.'

'I should hope so. I feel I know ye. I hardly know –'

'Shush now. I'm giving you an injection to help you relax. We'll talk again. Plenty of time to fill in the gaps.'

Her triaging helped him jump the queue, the old-timer's croaking complaints of "I don't wanna die" beginning to recede as he slowly slipped into a hypnagogic peacefulness before losing control, plunging him back to blackness that gradually engulfed him in emptiness. In that dark void he did not dream. In sleep he knew he sometimes dreamed, a subconsciousness that could sublimate his darkest impulses or impose the unfathomable horrors of a nightmare. Consciousness returned him, after a time-lapse of how long he knew not, yet his mind remained ready to absorb new information, now aware of muffled gobbledegook about him. Groggily, his sight wavering, he watched her face in profile as she earnestly conversed with a portly bespectacled man of indeterminate age sporting a bald spot like a monk's tonsure, massaging his eyebrows with thumb and index finger as a blue haze of aromatic smoke flared from his briar pipe. The red-faced nurse was first to welcome him back to the land of the living, her heedful smile prompting him to bestir himself.

'Mr MacAlindon. Stephen. How do you feel?' Tubby asked, leaning over him while shining a light in both his eyes, his garlicky tobaccoy breath stimulating the patient to muzzy alertness; then, in subdued tones discussing anatomical details with Deirdre.

He felt his heart skip a beat as he watched her. Her slim figure appeared slimmer than ever, her lustrous ice blue eyes conveying concern, she standing dauntless behind Tubby who was now insalubriously rubbing his hand across his bristled chin. He weakly leaned out a trembling hand toward her, spotting the cannula in his wrist, Tubby taking a firm hold of it:

'How you doing there young man? I carried out a simple procedure which I'm happy to say should rectify the problem. You should make a full recovery. Do you recognize Dr Desmond here beside me?' Maca nodded and in doing so became aware his crown was heavily bandaged. 'You know each other I believe. We'll keep you here for a week or so for observation. My name is Tindall, Mister Tin-dall. My colleague Dr Desmond will be looking after you during your stay with us. I'll keep an eye on your progress, drop in to see you on my rounds. Okay?'

'Okay. Thanks Mr Tindall,' he muttered as he watched the surgeon leave. Effortfully raising himself on one elbow he sought to clasp Deirdre's hand:

'Hi Dede, how's things,' he said, slyly looking for a wedding ring and not spotting one. He felt blood rush from his neck to the top of his head and realizing his face must be the colour of beetroot was vexed by his inability to suppress it. 'How long have I been here?'

'Nurse, leave us a few minutes please.'

'Of course doctor.'

'Three days,' she informed him, her lower lip alluringly quivering as she plumpt up his pillows and gently laid him back. 'The blow to your head aggravated the previous fracture. You've been in an induced coma to allow the swelling subside. We drained the occipital lobe, cleaned out the congelation. All going well you'll be as right as rain in no time.'

'Thanks Dede. Thanks a lot. When can I go home?'

'Mr Tindall says a week, maybe ten days. You've had a pretty nasty shock to the system.'

'The mother expected me home. Can ye get a message to her, maybe phone Dempseys, or give Eileen a shout at the office.'

'I'll swing by the house when I finish duty. Don't want her unduly alarmed.'

'Would ye Dede. That'id be great.'

'You're a lucky man. Had the blow been a centimetre to the left you could have sustained brain damage.'

'Might be an improvement eh! ha ha.'

'Seriously! A bone chip broke along the line of the previous fracture, got imbedded near one of the cranial nerves. Mr Tindall says you had a lucky escape. What were you doing there anyway?'

'Whata ye mean? I was on my way home, waiting for a taxi. Shit! Is my bag here. Where's me stuff?'

'Stuff? As far as I know all you had were the clothes on your back when they brought you in. No wallet, no ID, your wristwatch appears to be missing too.'

'Ah fuck!' he exploded, observing the white band of skin on his wrist.

'I alerted Mr Tindall to your previous –'

'Dede, they took the bag, they took me fucken bag. What am I goin' –'

'For God's sake Steve –'

'– to do.'

'– forget the stupid bag. You have more important things to worry about. You may need rehab and –'

'Everything I worked for in America was in that bag.'

Growing more and more agitated, the colour once more rushed to his cheeks.

'Nurse… NURSE. Give him a diazepam shot and keep an eye on him. I have to go now Steve. I'll look in on you before I knock off for the day. And don't worry about your mum. I'll call as promised.'

After the nurse jabbed the injection into his rump, he asked her about his clothes, his parka. She mooched about in the narrow wardrobe at the head of the bed and retrieved the jacket.

'Is this what you're looking for?'

'Give us it here, the trousers as well. And pull don curtain …

tight... TIGHTER,' he said brusquely. The nurse did his bidding and left with a huffy shrug of the shoulders, her squelchy rubber-soled shoes irritating him to boot.

Enervated following his discussion with Deirdre, feverishly he checked the back pocket of his trousers - no sign of his wallet. He searched the inside pocket of the jacket - the passport was missing. Nimbly running his fingers along the lining over the money pocket he could feel the outline of the roll of notes and practically tore off the flap button in his nervy exertion to recoup the dollars secreted there. With trembling hands he counted the stash, $2000, and then recounted it. All I've left to my fucking name is $2000 – he cursed to himself – the bastard even nicked Tina's watch.

The following afternoon his mother and Monica found him propped against a bank of pillows, attired in one of those flimsy colourless hospital gowns, marasmic with medication, desultorily perusing a magazine given him by Deirdre. No sign of Eileen.

'You've lost weight son. I brought ye some of yer father's things, didn't have time to buy for ye. Hope they fit, pyjamas, slippers, some toiletries. We'll make a note of what ye need and –'

'Not to worry ma. They gave me hospital gear to tide me over. Ta anyway.' His mother appeared to be only a shadow of her former self, she had become smaller, shrunken, her face creased and mean looking, as if not best pleased to see him, almost a stranger to him.

'Did ye get me letter?' he asked.

'I did. Worried sick I was when ye didn't show,' she peevishly replied behind the haggard mask of the careworn.

'You miss Dad. Sorry I couldn't get home to be with yis,' he said, disheartened as he watched his mother's tentative expression in seeking Monica's stay on comment. In the resulting silence the customary hospital clatter seemed progressively heightened, ne-cessitating them to raise their voices. 'How are ye all doin'? Here... give us a cuddle.'

Holding his mother in a bear hug, he observed Monica (dressed as a trendy young woman and not as a schoolgirl) remain aloof, perhaps alarmed by his condition, greeting him with shy deliberation.

'You're in a nice ward anyhow, just the five beds,' his mother said in a bit of a fluster, not being one for physical manifestation of affection, not in public anyway.

'Aayyeee! Right beside the jacks,' he curtly replied. 'Ye can hear every bleedy thing that goes on in there. How are ye Monica? How's the job at the… the tourist office?'

''Tis all right!'

'Do ye get to travel a'tall?'

'No, not 'specially. A cupila trips across the water, Scotland mainly.'

'And how's Eileen? Still beaverin' away in uncle Peter's office.'

'Aye! She is that. Got engaged week before last.'

'Jeez! That's brill. Who's the lucky guy?'

'Ronnie… Ronnie Sullivan. You don't know him.'

'Well hopefully I'll get to know him now I'm home for good.'

'Aayyeee! She caught her man. I hope the pair of dem will be happy together,' his mother said, giving the eavesdropping patient in the bed opposite a brash smile. 'And how are ye now son. The doctor says the operation went well. Have ye any pain a'tall?'

'None ma. Me head's a bit sore. But shure I'm doped-up to the gills. I'll get over it. Hard to kill a bad thing, or so they say.'

'Ye look like a survivor from the wreck of the Hesperus. Tell me now… what happened ye a'tall? Not a one told us about that there.'

'All I know is that as I was stood there waiting for a taxi,' he commenced hesitantly, a hot flush creeping across his face, 'some bollocks sneaked up on me and struck me on the head, with what I don't know, knocked the seven bells out of me. Made off with me bag. Everything I had in the world, money I had saved to make life here a bit easier for us, me clothes, and the presents I had for yis. Gone. 'Fucken disaster… sorry… excuse me French.'

'That's terrible Stephen. All yer money?'

'The bloomin' lot. Save for a cupila hundred dollars I had stashed in me jacket pocket. Makes me want to puke just thinkin' about it.'

'Jesus Mary and Joseph but isn't that a dreadful how'd-ye-do. Did they catch the culprit at the least bad luck to him.'

'Shure I only found out meself yesterday. If he'd been caught on the spot wouldn't the peelers have made contact by now.'

'Well when ye had it you were good to us, sendin' home those dollars helped keep me head above water. You'll just have to put it behind ye son and make the best of things.'

'I know ma. That was a pittance to what's lost to me now.'

*

Over the period of recuperation he saw a lot of Deirdre, she acting more than as his attentive physician by tending his every need. The challenge of neurolinguistic programming she had him undergo satisfied Mr Tindall that the initial memory loss suffered had been remedied once the swelling on the brain receded. The hours spent in rehabilitation permitted him to reflect on their past friendship, some home truths being freely discussed between them which heartened him in that he now understood his adolescent despondency (where she was concerned) was primarily due to personal neurosis, a kind of juvenile paranoia. In time he confidently entertained the notion of a future with her, a future he hoped would embrace their getting together again, as lovers. On discharge from hospital, under clouds darkly gathering, being collected by Monica by arrangement, he was jubilant when Deirdre said she would drop in on him at the house that evening to ensure he had all the necessary paraphernalia for his continued recovery.

The drive home to Bombay Street in pelting down rain proved depressingly familiar for the most part, he embarrassed by the litter strewn streets which seemed narrower, the houses smaller. Passing through the Loney area he was gobsmacked by a new high-rise development:

'Holy shit! What's don bleedy colossus?' he enquired of Monica, craning his neck upwards, glaring through the rain bespattered windscreen in disbelief.

'Divis flats.'

'Flats! They expect people to live there?'

'Yeah! Our lot were pleased to move in for the most part. 'Tis so close to the city centre. Father Macken encouraged it.'

''Tis a monstrosity. There must be what… twenty floors at –'

''Tis modern… and clean. I wouldn't mind movin' in meself.'

'Just wait till the fucken lifts start breakin' down. Trust me Monica, there'll be people throwin' themselves off the balconies.'

'There's been a jumper, about two months ago. They say it was an accident but mammy says she committed suicide.'

''Nough said.'

St Peter's Cathedral appeared dwarfed following the shock of the Divis monolith. Passing by St Mary's junior school, Monica commented that it was now a school for girls only – 'God help them. I couldn't wait to get out of the place.' The twin spires of Clonard church loomed incongruously out of the murky drizzle like gigantic devil's horns. Old memories crowded his mind.

Pulling up outside the home place he was struck by its paltry lowliness. The house has shrunk… it's a hovel, he thought. Once inside he began to regret Deirdre's plan to call in on him, finding the house dreary and oppressively pokey, filled with the gimcrack and tawdry bric-a-brac of working class comfort (not his homesick memory of it); a television now dominating the living room whipping up mind-numbing white noise; the air permeated with freon cherry blossom fragrance. Such a flurried fuss was made by his mother in welcoming him that her good intentions only further raised his hackles causing him to grow grouchier. He felt worn out, crushed, conscious of nothing but overwhelming tiredness and craved to be left alone. Ploddingly, he climbed the narrow stairs. As he reached the top stairs he noticed chipped paint on his bedroom door and the bottom panel kicked out. What the fuck? Disconsolate, he flung himself on the bed without taking off his clothes, his mind absorbed by self-pity, the hopelessness of his situation. Forlornly he looked back at the stream of his life: What had he ever done but drift, living the drifting moments, chasing abstractions? Always a stranger in this city, and now, now a stranger to himself. What could he make of the situation, the ivory tower having crumbled, his luck a busted flush. No money. Not, as far as he could make out, the remotest prospect of a job with the earning power he enjoyed at Lehmans. His circumstances were absolutely analogous to those prior to leaving for America. Had he not virtually exhausted all possible avenues in search of a good job, only to end up barely eking out a living as what? – a sorting office postman, working with bigoted so-and-sos. Another of life's fucking jokes. And the joke was rapidly wearing thin. Is this the destiny he'd assigned himself to, the nothingness of his way of life, remaking himself invisible? All the promises now thwarted and ridiculed by the tawdriness of his existence. The sheer impulsiveness of his exit from America. Had he been precipitant. Breaking out in a cold sweat, his mind racing, he conjured up an image of Martina's wretchedness on the night they parted and pondered what she might now make of it all having, no doubt, read and reread his letter. In hindsight he regretted some of the things he had written in that letter: the vain apologies for the pain he had caused her; the torrid consequences of the military call-up; the inflated excuses for the trouble he had left behind at the bank (had it got into the papers?). Would she keep the apartment for her own use, perhaps as a love nest, or, as a welcome source of income, a means of furthering her independence? Independence from what? From whom? She had to have comprehended the inescapability of their parting. Besides, she had done nothing to make matters different between them; had never as far as he knew explored the possibility of sharing the future with him; had not considered a choice for happiness with him. Or had she? Perhaps, so avoiding a life-wrecking choice, torn between two lovers – "a tit for Tom and Steve" she had once said jocosely as he champed engagingly at her breast. Cowardly, driven by uncertain compulsion she had behaved cowardly, lacking the courage to take on the challenge of being with him, whatever the future might hold. Yet maybe that future would have proved constrained, a sense of purpose yes, their togetherness, but the certainty in life given up, the certainty she had clung to. How foolish he had been. Her's had been a selfish love, a needy passion; his for her a misallied obsession. Still, he could not forget her, and deep down he knew she would not forget him. Such thoughts kept running at random through his head, imbuing intense exhaustion, his spirit now drifting in an emotional dissipation. How could he escape from this consuming introspection?

Monica roused him from slumberous unease. She said:

'Dr Desmond's downstairs. Will I send her up to ye?'

'Jeez no! I'll be down in a minute. Is she here long?'

'Just arrived. Mammy's making her a cuppa.'

Hastily getting ready, taking a last fidgety glance in the mirror atop the oversized tallboy while fingering his heel into his shoe, he lost balance, falling with a resounding thud to the floor, raising a floc of dust that made him sneeze. Pulling on the bedspread in a scramble to raise himself, emitting uric farts, he could hear rumbling footsteps racing up the stairs before being intrusively confronted by Deirdre and Monica's return seeking to know if he was all right.

'Yeah yeah!' he bleated dismissively, the blood invading his face as he finger combed his rumpled hair. 'Fell on me arse steppin' into me shoes. Beat's me why the fuck I was in such a hurry.'

'You're running a temperature,' Deirdre said, sitting on the bed beside him, the palm of her hand flat across his forehead. 'Let me get my bag-of-tricks and check you out. Monica, here's the key. It's in the boot.'

'Jeesus! You're as bad as the rest of them, fussin' over nothing,' he tersely remarked in Monica's absence.

'I'll go now if you want Steve. But you need –'

'No Dede. I didn't mean it like that there. It's just my whole world's falling apart.'

'Look… you have to get back on track,' she said restively. 'You're a little out of sorts just now. But the injury is not long-term debilitating. I'll check your blood pressure and give you something to lower your temperature. I don't want to see you moping about the place like a lost sheep. You'll be looking at the lid long enough (he smiled at that). You just need to take it easy for a few weeks, give yourself time to adjust to your new circumstances. Then you must get back into the stream of things.'

'I had a loada money in that bag Dede,' he said, slowly turning to look at her. 'Enough to start over, build a house, a business maybe. All my plans gone up in smoke 'cause some bollocks knocked me cold.'

'You'll get over it,' she said, giving him a piercing look. 'As soon as you get back to your old self you can make a fresh start. I'll help you Steve.'

'You'll help. How? In what way help? Why would you bother?'

'Because I want to.'

He thought he glimpsed a yearning look in her ice blue eyes, like the mystical ache he had gleaned there that last term in Queens when she had settled a marbled stare on him. Had he been a fool for not acting on his love for her, his want of her all those years ago? But she was the one who avoided him then. A sense-memory of that first innocent kiss floated around his head. Overcoming his diffident pride he greedily kissed her, his tongue deep in the wetness, the warm avidity of her mouth an affirmation as her hand gripped the nape of his neck pulling him to her. Their frantic intimacy was interrupted by Monica's noisy clambering up the stairs with the medical bag-of-tricks.

Weeks later, having made a full recovery, by way of thanks for her affectionate care of him he invited Deirdre out for a meal, leaving the choice of restaurant to her. She collected him in her car, a custard-yellow coloured Fiat Bambino, and brought him to an upmarket restaurant on the Lisburn Road. On sighting the *table d'hôte* menu he began to fret about the steep prices (set to dissuade the riff-raff no doubt, he brooded). Relieved when she selected a main course only from the *a la carte* – 'I'm not a big eater. As often as not I just have a starter,' she said, a fussy little smile on her face.

'So that's how ye get to keep so slim and trim!' he teased.

Mollified, he did likewise. She discouraged him from ordering wine suggesting a jug of iced water would be better for both of them – 'I'm not much into alcohol either,' she cooed. She ate slowly, pausing often, her knife and fork placed in an X on her plate. Over his coffee (she declined any beverage) he pulled out his cigarettes and offered her one which she rejected with a rictal lour of disapproval:

'I don't smoke. And you should quit,' she said in brazen admonition. 'Apart from the fact it's bad for you, it's a disgusting habit.'

'Yeah I know, but I enjoy the kick of nicotine,' he said, sucking deep on the first drag and blowing twin cones of blue smoke from flared nostrils. 'So ye made the course at Queens?'

'Well I got through. Doing my houseman year at "The Vic". What I'll be doing this time next year God only knows. Why'd you flunk out? When was it… after second year.'

'I didn't flunk out. I dropped out. No choice. Dad couldn't work, MS you know, and the mammy was put to the pin of her collar tryin' to make ends meet,' he replied, sensing a blush break out on his cheeks. 'The job with the post office helped keep things afloat and had things turned out right I'd probably still be there, 'cept for the bigotry. Got the shit kicked outta me in the Pepper Canister after a difference of opinion with a right gouger on the sectarian political system we put up with. That fiasco made my mind up for me to join Frank in Boston.'

'How is Frank?' she asked with one hand supporting her chin.

'Well, you know Frank better than anybody. Couldn't make a decision if his life depended on it.'

'Ah! I like Frank. He was always nice to me.'

On hearing her indulgent words about Frank the heat of his blush withered away. 'Frank's fine. Probably makin' more money than he knows what to do with.'

'Eileen told me the pair of you had great jobs at Lehman bank.'

'Yeah! Great while it lasted.'

'You're not going back then?'

'No. Can't. Drafted by the effin military. The very same day I decided to come home for good. No way was I goin' to end up in the killing fields of Vietnam. Not my fight. Some of my bank colleagues got themselves killed over there.'

'Oh God! I can't bear to watch the news now, those pictures, horrendous. Imagine what must be happening on the ground, the pictures we don't get to see.'

'Like I said, not my fight. You'll never guess who I bumped into in Chicago,' he said, anxious to change the subject.

'Chicago? I thought you were in New York. Well... who?'

'Johnny Cassidy. I was attending a bank conference there.'

'Johnny. What's he doing in Chicago?'

'Barman at the Ritz Carlton. Hardly recognized him with the short back and sides. He's put the music on hold, for the time being anyway. Gung-ho to enlist, no visa and believed it would help get him documented. Lost touch, don't know if he did.'

'Just like Johnny to do something crazy.'

The waiter sought to know if they needed anything – 'a liqueur for mademoiselle perhaps?' He watched her effortless beauty as she demurely shook her head and then flashed a vestige of her former haughtiness as the waiter pointedly ogled her. All the messianic zeal of past thoughts and dreams of her during those angsty teenage years pressed against the front lobe of his brain.

'We're fine,' he snapped at the waiter with a barefaced grin, placing his elbows on the table and making a tepee of his arms and fingers. 'Yeah! Believed the uniform would work wonders for him with the women over there.'

'So what will you do now?'

'I'm tryin'… lookin' around at this and that. Had I not lost me savings when that bollocks creamed me I'd be sittin' pretty. Couldn't see much further than settin' myself up in some small enterprise or other.'

'Like what?'

'Well, haven't worked it out yet. Have to do a rethink.'

'There's a meeting tomorrow night Steve, in Clonard, about the housing problem. Why don't you come along.'

'Ah jeez! I hate parish-pump politics. What the fuck would I know about that kinda parochial stuff.'

'I seem to remember you were big into "that kinda stuff", one-man-one-vote, The United Irishmen and all the rest of it. Things haven't changed much hereabouts while you were away. If anything, it's all taken a turn for the worse. And anyway, if we get a meeting of minds it won't remain parochial for long. People are coming from all over.'

'What! To take on the dinosaurs above in Stormont. Give me a break,' he said sardonically.

'Look what the Negroes have achieved under Johnson.'

'They still can't vote in the southern states.'

'They have the right to vote and the oppressive barriers of bigotry and white supremacy in those states will be torn down in time.'

'Oh! I don't think so. The blacks are in disarray since King was taken out. The civil rights movement is up against obscurantist blood and thunder.'

'Hopefully not. Their just cause has achieved recognition, world-wide recognition. There's no going back to the old ways, even should it take another generation to fulfil King's dream.'

'Ye think so.'

'I know so. We have our own share of sectarianism here. Come along tomorrow.' And observing the wry smile that creased his face she told him – 'I'll call at your place at seven. We can walk there together.'

Surprised how reasonable the bill total came to, he settled with the waiter and received effusive thanks, probably for over-tipping (old habits die hard). As they sauntered back to her car he helped her into her cardigan, the while eyeing the firm contour of her bust.

'So where're we off to my little woman?' he jested as she turned the key in the ignition.

'Little? I'm as tall as you are,' she retaliated.

'Not in yer bare feet you're not. You've three inch heels on ye.'

'To my place,' she guffawed. 'I want to give you something.'

'Sounds intriguing. You have a place of yer own now eh, away from the mammy.'

'Intriguing! What? The fact I moved out or the something I want to give you.'

'Both,' he blustered, twiddling his thumbs.

'Yeah! Moved out last year. Made sense to get a flat closer to work. Renting… I didn't buy it… not on my salary. As for what I want to give you, it's a new tonic drink that's being promoted at the hospital. Not yet available on the market. I believe it'll be good for you. I'd like you to have a go taking it anyway, see how it goes.'

'And what, be your squiffy guinea pig,' he crooned to a popular advertisement jingle, at which they both chortled.

Her flat was located adjacent to the Royal Victoria Hospital, on the third floor, facing south-west.

'Very nice,' he quipped as they exited the car,' the howl of an aircraft screaming overhead. 'And ye get the sunshine all day.'

'Yeah! Nearly all day when the sun does shine and I have the time to enjoy it. Only a short walk to work. Dodge the hassle of traffic jams,' she breezily yapped as they ascended on the lift.

On entering her flat, his olfactory nerves immediately reacted to the captivating smell that pervaded its space, redolent of the scent she wore when he first knew her. The *décor* and furnishings were suggestive of a doll's house, delicate and tempered by evocative colours, predominately pink, the soft lighting unveiling lumin-iferous exquisiteness. This imbuing feminine touch he found heart-warming, if not a little intimidated by the girlie accoutrements scattered about her cosy lair.

'Make yourself a coffee, instant only I'm afraid. You'll find it in the top press to the right of the sink, the sugar too. No coffee for me… I'm into tisane. Back in –'

'What the hell is tisane?'

'– a jiffy. Herbal tea, better for you than coffee. I'll fix my own.'

He ran the cold water tap as he emptied the dregs from the electric kettle and then filled it to the max mark. A coal-black cat rubbed itself against his legs, mewling for attention. He could hear wardrobe doors opening and closing in what he took to be her bedroom. Finding the coffee jar he noted it was Italian, a brand not known to him. Searching for cups or mugs, he spotted some photographs loosely stacked at the back of the kitchen press. Teased by curiosity, he couldn't resist having a dekko. Most were holiday "having fun" shots of Deirdre with her friends, obviously in sunnier climes. A photo planed to the floor and bending to pick it up discovered to his amazement it was a box camera black and white arresting image of he and Deirdre smooching, he grinning at the camera, obviously taken years ago at a dance in Clonard

Community Hall. On hearing her opening the adjoining room door he rushed to put them back.

'Did you find the coffee?' she called out on her return, carrying two packs, six bottles in each, of the wonder tonic.

'I did. You okay with a mug for the tis... tisane? Here now, if you'd given me a shout I'd have helped ye with that,' he said, moving to assist, and in his haste standing on some part of the cat's anatomy resulting in an unmerciful yowl and bared claws.

'Poor Bobby, he's such a pet. Not to worry, it looks heavier than it is. See, plastic bottles. Yeah I prefer a mug. Well this is it, this is what I want you to have. Take the lot.'

'What about for yourself?'

'There's plenty more where this came from. Here, have a read. If the claim for its medicinal properties is only half true this could prove the elixir of life.'

'"Stimulates the mitochondria in the brain cells while cleansing the plasma membranes". Jeesus Dede, is this stuff safe? Meself and Frank smoked a fair amount of pot in the States which had a hell of a kick in it, but at least we weren't guinea pigs.'

'Unlike street drugs this is scientifically developed by Cosmo Inc. It has just received a US FDA license.'

'Have ye been takin' it?'

'Only for a week or so. Much too soon to know whether I'm the better for it. But early analysis of monitored results at the hospital is extremely positive. Here... try it. It has a sweet taste, like a mix of cranberries, coconut and honey. One a day. The best time is last thing at night before bed. Seems it works best when the metabolism is in low gear.'

Is that a subtle invitation to her bed he asked himself as he eased a bottle from the top pack and released the cap to a fizzy sound. 'Well here goes,' he guffawed in a fake ghoulish voice, emptying the contents in one draught. 'Be it on your head if I turn into Mr Hyde.'

266

'I should be so lucky,' she chuckled.

He grabbed her in an ogreish embrace, pulling her close to him, and as the squeals of merriment petered out, the fun embrace led to sensory togetherness. They kissed, his tongue probing deep, her body eagerly responsive to his touch. While losing himself in the snugness of her muliebrity, a key could be heard slotting into and turning the door lock. In the twinkling of an eye, she moved away from him, an antsy look spreading across her face.

'Richard! I wasn't expecting you.'

'Well Dee… here I am.'

15

They sat three rows back from the raised platform. Although seating had been arranged for over one hundred, approximately thirty only were occupied; people dispersed in small groupings around the hall, some engaged in low and terse conversations, backsides shifting uneasily awaiting commencement of proceedings. Having draped their jackets on the back of the chairs, he ogled the intricate filigree of her black laced bodice as she leaned into him and suppressed the urge to nuzzle the perfumed hollow between her breasts. Perhaps later, he told himself.

'See that man just about to sit down.'

'Yeah! Four eyes.'

'That's Gerry Fitt,' said Deirdre, pointing out the opposition MP and leader of the Labour Party. 'And see the fella to his right.'

'The guy with the fuzzy beard?'

'That's Ronnie. Ronnie Sullivan.'

'Eileen's man. Jeez! Bit long in the tooth for her isn't he? Big noise is he?'

'A staunch republican. Interned in fifty three. I'll introduce you later.'

The meeting got off to a haphazard start under the impatient watchfulness of the gathering, the MC fretfully shuffling papers at the podium and testing the audio equipment, amplified booms and squeals ricocheting around the hall, sounds that grated on Maca's nerves. The opening speakers proved pedantically dull and human, some patchily inaudible as they shambled too far from the microphone, or failed to readjust its height, haltingly muttering as every so often they had recourse to check or recheck some data in their notes, housing quota statistics and the like. After the warm-up speeches, in a burble of background noise and intermittent applause, Ronnie Sullivan took hold of the lectern in both hands and delivered an enunciation in a plosive sonorous voice, without notes, snippets of which rekindled Maca's mindfulness of government sponsored sectarianism:

"The root of the problem is our justifiable resentment of the unionist manipulated voting system which deprives us of any possibility of governing our own constituencies even where we are in the majority and the corrupting influences that flow from its sectarian foundation. And the siege mentality of that governing cabal that any concession made to nationalists is but a stepping stone to a united Ireland" – "Unionist hegemony is an anachronistic absurdity and its denunciatory proclamations against civil rights for all is blatantly undemocratic" – "The success of the civil rights march at Dungannon is the spark for renewed hope that non-violent demonstration will achieve reform. We encourage those who can to join the civil rights march to Derry".

'Well! What do you think?' asked Deirdre, turning to gauge his reaction as the meeting terminated, seeing the answer on his face.

'What happened at Dungannon?'

'The local MP organized a peaceful march, despite police erecting barriers, against the inequities of eviction and council housing policy.'

'Did the peelers not try to break it up?'

'The protesters, about four thousand of them, halted at the barriers and there listened to a battery of speakers air their demands. The police could find no cause to intervene, other than what had already been achieved in blocking the marchers from entering the town centre.'

'And what, pray tell, were the protesters demanding?'

Deirdre retrieved a pamphlet from her pocket and with stentorian panache read him the list of demands: '"One-man-one-vote in local elections – The removal of gerrymandered boundaries – Laws

269

against discrimination by local government, and the provision of machinery to deal with complaints – Allocation of public housing on a points system – Repeal of the Special Powers Act – Disbanding of the B Specials." So you see, nothing very revolutionary in that now is there? Come on, I'll introduce you to Ronnie.'

The urbane effectiveness of Sullivan's podium performance now revealed an unflappable magnetism on personal introduction.

'Howdydo? So your Eileen's brother. Heard a lot about ye.'

'All good I hope.'

'For the most part. You wouldn't expect Eileen to speak ill of her brother now would ye?' This caused him to straighten up and look his future brother-in-law in the eye. 'You're just back from the States I believe. Great country. What brings you back to this neck of the woods?'

'Avoidin' the draft. Conscientious objector.'

'More power to your elbow, not your war eh!'

The exercise of that charm on Maca did not persuade him to make up the numbers at the forthcoming march to Derry scheduled to begin on the first Saturday in October, despite Deirdre's insistence that she was going and pleas for him to join her. Excusing himself, he left the hall for a smoke, saying he would wait for her at the entrance. He had smoked two cigarettes by the time she joined him there, appearing wilfully moody and upset by his absenting himself. Striding back to Bombay Street, where she had parked her car at the house, he asked her what was uppermost on his mind:

'Who's this guy Richard... when he's at home?'

'Richie, ah he's nice. He's a genial soul.'

'He's knowingly nice, all that smirking politeness,' he stridently retorted, wondering what she meant by genial. 'Watchin' him being so nice makes me want to throw up.'

'He's my friend.'

'A friend... with a key to yer flat,' he persisted callously.

'It's really none of your business.'

Two days before the mass rally the Minister for Home Affairs, William Craig, issued an order banning all marches, the effect of which galvanized moderate middle class nationalists to take up the cudgels for civil rights, the burgeoning support encouraging the organizers to defy the choleric minister's contrived ban. Watching the news on television on the evening of that day's march, Maca felt nauseous on viewing the violence that erupted, trusting Deirdre had heeded his advice not to attend. The marchers faced a cordon of tenders and well armed police, and he heard, in a state of sober apprehension, megaphonic voice warnings that women and children should depart. Uneasy about Deirdre's safety had she participated willy-nilly, he hoped she had had the good sense to get the hell out of there, as he hesitantly moved closer to the television to see if he could spy her amid the throng. Voice-over informed that the marchers had tried to avoid the police by taking a different route, but that route was also blocked so they ended up virtually surrounded by the forces of the northern statelet. After a short meeting amongst the penned in protestors, the leaders instructed them to calmly disperse. The police then, it was reported, broke ranks and used their batons indiscriminately, water cannons also being deployed at close range. Seventy-seven civilians were injured, mainly bruisings and lacerations to the head, including Gerry Fitt, and Eddy McAteer, leader of the Nationalist Party.

*

Having agreed to meet up with Sammy "Mugsy" Dixon for a drink and catch-up chat in Dempseys that evening, but having no means of contacting Deirdre to find out if she was unharmed (he had petulantly telephoned the flat numerous times, his calls unanswered), he now found he did not have the stomach for such a meeting with his old school buddy. Grabbing his coat and cap he walked to her flat but got no response to his many heavy fingered presses on the doorbell. With racing heart, he ran the short distance to the

271

hospital hoping to find her there, or, the staff might have news of her whereabouts. The receptionist advised him that – 'Dr Desmond is on a week's leave – have you an appointment? NO! I've no idea where the good doctor is.'

Next morning, after attending mass with his mother and Monica in Saint Peter's Cathedral, he rushed back to her flat and again finding no sign of her, slipped a note expressing his concern through her letterbox. The television news that evening showed some students from Queen's University protesting outside the home of William Craig where they were met with a hostile reception – "Go home you silly bloody fools", the minister had barked at them. By Monday, the student numbers swelled to approximately eight hundred as they marched to City Hall only to be confronted by a counter demonstration led by a burly cleric, Ian Paisley, the heavy police presence separating the two groups provoking a three hour sit-down.

Not having heard from Deirdre over the next few days, trepidatiously he made his way to her parent's elegant house, its stuccoed walls ornamented with virginia creeper, (what if her mother slams the door in my face?) and was gladdened when Deirdre opened the door to him, although disquieted on sighting the yellowish-black bruise that bedecked her right eyebrow. She was smiling, an embarrassed tigerish smile.

'Are you okay Dede? I was worried about ye,' he said on being invited to enter the hallway.

'I'm fine fine. Got myself a little souvenir for my troubles,' she ruefully replied as she pointedly finger-rubbed her forehead. They kissed and hugged like long-lost sweethearts, she palpably glad to see him.

'Seein' the melee on the telly I tried to contact ye at the flat and The Vic. They told me you had a few days off. All that trouble. Looked bleedy awful, bleedy frightenin' altogether.'

'Well it was frightening,' she affirmed, tucking a tress of her blond hair back in place behind her ear. 'But there's no going back. Craig's henchmen have blood on their hands. The media are involved, beginning to see the light. The BBC is giving no holds barred coverage. Come, Richie's here, and someone you may remember from uni days. You need to hear what they have to say.'

He followed her into a room that bore the ostentatious simulacra of middle class opulence, and was again introduced to Richie. The other man he had no memory of meeting before. After brief convivial chit-chat about college days, the conversation about protest strategies was taken up where presumably it had left off on his arrival. From what he could make out, a lot of heated meetings had taken place on the university campus following Paisley's intimidating blocking campaign at City Hall the previous Monday and steps were afoot to better manage the inchoate nature of the civil rights movement by pulling together the various "ad hoc" groups: agree the adoption of a name that would appeal to all sections of the nationalist community; reach some kind of unison on a constitution and procedure; and arrange the appointment of overseeing officers to establish co-ordinating committees. Although he saw merit in all of this, he was troubled by the pace of events, and uneasy about Deirdre's involvement. Hearing them laugh at something he wasn't in on, he sought to have a quiet chat with her:

'What's this guy Paisley hammerin' on about?'

'The so-called Rev Ian Paisley. Calls himself Dr Paisley. He's a bigot, a narrow-minded bigot… a sterer-up of hatred. Publicly excoriates Catholics and the very idea of civil rights,' she explained.

'How can a dog collar get away with that? A turbulent priest yes, as that bollix Henry said of Beckett, but he's a Christian evangelist isn't he?'

'He's a proselytizer of Brookborough's "Protestant Parliament for a Protestant People". Doesn't countenance any truck with political reconciliation or religious ecumenism. Caused a riot insisting a tricolour be removed from the Sinn Fein election office in Divis

Street. Organizes stupid protests like the one last Monday, and at Stormont when O'Neill met with Lemass, making catcalls denouncing him as a "Fenian Papist murderer". Referring to the Pope disparagingly as "Old Red Socks".'

'Ha ha! Not far off the mark there then is he? About the Pope I mean.'

'You think so Steve? You find it amusing do you?' she queried haltingly, giving him a searching look. 'He spouts his hate with rhetorical savagery, went to Rome to protest against Archbishop, I can't think of his name, the Archbishop of Canterbury's visit to the "scarlet whore of Rome", "the Antichrist". He's not a proper clergyman at all, bought his doctorate through a correspondence course from Bob Jones University in South Carolina. The so called Free Presbyterian church is his foundation.'

'Well! what's to worry about then? People will see him for what he is,' he riposted, while inertly keeping an eye on Richie who appeared totally absorbed in indepth conversation with his colleague, parts of which on overhearing alarmed him. 'Let's go to a movie this evening. The new James Bond is on,' he said, wanting to be close to her, believing she was too wrapped-up in the hubbub of the campaign. He froze as the door opened and Mrs Desmond entered carrying a tray of tea and sandwiches. It seemed she did not recognize him as she fussed about placing the china cups and saucers on the low table.

'Don't go getting that daughter of mine in any worse trouble with all this malarkey and loutish cudgelling that's brewing,' she cheerfully reprimanded as she left the room, quietly pulling the door closed behind her.

'You'll come to the cinema then,' he said, a slight tremor in his hand as he raised the cup to his lips.

'The pictures! Not this evening, mebbe tomorrow. Call round to the flat about five. I'll make us a chicken casserole and we'll take it from there.'

On pouring more tea for Richie and his colleague, she rejoined their earnest discussion. Feeling left out of it, he made his excuses and departed the scene, saying he would see himself out and asking her to thank her mother for the tea.

And so the following evening he arrived at her flat with a chilled bottle of Chardonnay. She was wearing a light blue button-through dress that emphasized her figure, the top two buttons left undone, a rope of jet black glistening beads nestling between the curves of her breasts.

'The necklace goes well with the bruise,' he quipped.

Following a languorous hour or so over a scrumptious meal, her favourite music playing softly the while in the back-ground, amid gossipy refrains he blurted out:

'I don't like that friend of yours, Richie.'

'Rich, you don't know him.'

'True. But I'm pretty good at sizin' people up.'

'Are you now?'

'He's the one got ye mixed up in that whole hullabaloo to Derry. And listenin' to some of the things he was on about yesterday… he's a bit of a hothead, much too radical, could land ye in a place you don't want to be, a place you can't get back from.'

'Meaning?'

'All that guff about acquirin' guns to protect the ghettos. Utter madness.'

'Oh! I don't think so. Look, the six counties are saturated with armaments, all in the hands of the so-called forces of law and order. And now we hear that some hardliners, the UVF or whatever they call themselves, Protestant Volunteers, have imported arms, the authorities turning a blind eye, the B Specials a law unto themselves. Remember that murder at the Malvern Arms. No you weren't –'

'So! What? A few nationalists get guns in their hands in hope of takin' on that lot.'

'No! The civil rights movement will succeed. The nationalists will get equal rights and fair play. The world is watching.'

'Why's he callin' for guns then?'

'Because the other side is out of control. Threatening to burn Catholics out of their homes. If they can't protect their homes and their families they face Armageddon.'

'Jeez Dede! Your boyfriend's fillin' yer head fulla shite, and you're fallin' for it hook line and sinker. Get real will ye. As you know I did a stretch in industrial school havin' fallen foul of the bastards. 'Twas no picnic I can tell ye.'

'He's not my boyfriend,' she said, a quiver in her voice as she lowered her head. They remained quiescent for what seemed an eternity, the silence buzzing in Maca's ears. He felt conflicted between the elation that overcame him following this revelation that freed him from curiosity and the anguish in watching her descend into sombre cerebration, as if holding in a secret sorrow.

'Look, don't get me wrong on this but why hang out with him then?' he said in a hushed tone after what he considered a seemly time-lapse.

'He's a good friend.'

'For the life of me I can't see it meself.'

'It's the key thing that's bugging you isn't it? I gave him a key so he could look after Bobby, like if I'm working late or away somewhere.'

'Ah! The cat. That sorta friend.'

'No. He's been very good to me. Earlier this year I broke up with someone. It was rough... a tough decision. Broke my heart. He was always there for me, an empathic listener, not finding fault, not censuring me. He was the only one I could confide in.'

'Sorry Dede,' he said, his heartbeat quickening. 'Look, I don't mean to pry, are ye over this guy, this relationship?'

He could hear the phlegm catch in her larynx as she straightened her shoulders. 'It wasn't... she wasn't a guy,' she said falteringly, clearing her throat.

'FUUCCKKK!' he whistled through his teeth with a sinking feeling, sensing the blood curdle in his veins, draining from his face. Pouring the last of the wine, half filling their glasses, he mumbled insinuatingly:

'Are you… are ye one of –'

'I don't know. Am I?' her intense eyes burning in to his.

'Do ye want to talk about it?'

'Not particularly. Do you need to know?'

'I'd like to know everythin' about ye, eve-ry-thing,' he said, gulping the last of his wine.

'It's not possible to know everything about someone. We like to think we know everything about someone, but it's not possible.'

'I want to know everythin' about you. I thought I knew ye. I've long been obsessed by you.'

'Obsession can be menacing.'

'I always thought we had somethin' going between us,' he said, noisily fiddling with the food stained cutlery on his plate. 'We do have somethin' don't we? Or am I a fool for thinking so. Do you mind if I smoke?' he bleated, compulsively reaching into his jacket pocket, to which she made no reply. As he lit up a cigarette he rose from the table and filled the empty wine glass with water from the cold tap, Bobby the cat wary of his every movement. Leaning infirmly with his rump against the sink, exhaling plumes of tobacco smoke that served to emphasize the umbrageous space between them, he observed her sit with her head propped in her hands, unmoving.

'I love ye Dede. Always have. You were the flame, you are the flame,' he said, his voice breaking, afraid the bond that linked them would be broken. 'Please… please tell me it's not in vain, that yer relationship with her was just somethin' that happened, somethin' you went through.'

He watched as she unhurriedly rose and walked towards him, tears rimming her eyes. Moving to hold her in his arms he fought to restrain the convulsions that seized his every muscle, the weight of expectation, inured to disappointment where she was concerned, his mind conjuring the image of his first sight of her. Silently, they clung to each other, her feminine warmth passing through him, slowly at first, and then in waves. She said:

'If I have feelings for any man like the feelings I had for Olivia then I know I too love you.'

A tear drop broke free and slowly traversed her cheek in soulful expressiveness. Audaciously looking into her eyes, looking into her soul, he then kissed her hard on the mouth, his tongue probing deep, urgently seeking answers to the myriad questions that flooded his mind like a maelstrom. Plunging a hand into her unopened bra he released her breast and maniacally bit on the nipple, sensing its engorgement under his tongue. Lifting her onto the kitchen worktop, he released her other breast, nuzzling her voluptuousness, lustfully tonguing her cleavage, her sweaty breasts moistening his burning cheeks. Shifting position, stepping back to look on her beauty, he deftly removed her panties and gently fondled the labia and clitoris of her blond hair crowned pudendum, his fingers sucked in by her wetness soothingly stroking the neck of her womb he knowing the iconography of the cervix, her libidinous moans arousing him to fever pitch. There being no brake on heightened passion, right there and then they slid to the floor where she moved to please him, her hands nimbly unbuckling his trouser belt, her fingers caressing his stiffening penis, her mouth warmly sheathing the swollen head. A surge of tricky tremors pulsed through him as he eyeballed, disbelievingly, her expertise in pleasuring him. Virgin, or fingered only he weighed up as he manoeuvred her onto her back and straddled her. Hurriedly he entered her and after some moments of blissful coupling, much to his chagrin ejaculated like a bungling novice.

'Dede. Sorry,' he gasped as he lay breathlessly on top of her.

'Beautiful… beautiful,' she whispered, her eyes clear, her high cheeks sensuously radiant.

Remaining priapic inside her he rotated his hips in rhythm with her ecstatic wiggling, bringing her ignited body to orgasm. Looking into her ice blue eyes he saw love light shining through, engulfing every part of him.

'Jeez Dede, how long have I dreamed… dreamed of being with ye, wantin' you like this. I had almost given up hope of it ever happenin',' he murmured in euphoric lassitude.

He stayed the night. They would spend many suchlike nights together at her flat.

*

Over that time, their love reached a degree of better understanding and waggish familiarity with their respective foibles. Despite the escalating streams of violence that peppered the political horizon engineered mainly by hardliner Protestant groups led by Dr Ian Paisley and the B Specials as a counter to the civil rights legitimate marches in many cities and towns (the crises had brought matters to the attention of the Westminster government, resulting in the dismissal of Craig as Home Affairs Minister), Deirdre, at Maca's urging, began to distance herself from the hothouse of political reform, they becoming more and more absorbed in each other. She gave him a key, Richard's key, he promising to look after Bobby in her absence. And shortly thereafter, following her seductive entreaty, he moved lock, stock and barrel into the flat. Concurrently, his endeavours to procure meaningful employment had proved unavailing, leaving him at a loose end.

He telephoned Nellie saying he would like to come visit her (it's been so long) and hearing the warm tremor in her voice and finding her ever gregarious and cheerful agreed to call on her at the farm next day. Borrowing Deirdre's car, he arrived under a clear pellucid sky to discover the old place well maintained; the annexes to the stone farmhouse recently painted a sunburst yellow. Two fine chestnut horses whinnied in the garden field. The Volkswagen, now of a gleaming vintage, was parked outside the front door, a door that stood wide open in expectation despite the chilly air. He heard her weakened voice in greeting before entering and finding her alone, hunched by the range fire, was momentarily shocked how the hand of time had rested heavily on her, she, frail and shrunken, cumulating the insidious afflictions of old age. Time had taken its toll, presumably due to the burden of aloneness in destined isolation. Yet her eyes exuded a youthful radiance and joy on seeing him. Slow moving, she rose from the chair and embraced him, uttering tender words of welcome. He said:

'The door was open, lettin' all the heat out.'

'I heard the car. Knew it was you… and opened it.'

'You have the place lookin' great Nellie. How do ye manage it?'

'Ah Robbie's a pet give him his due. Robbie Goss you know, who has the land rented from me. He keeps everything shipshape. If I remember rightly I told ye about that before.'

'You did indeed. And ye still have the Volkswagen I see.'

'Aayyee, me trusty old jalopy. I'd be lost without it.'

'You've no trouble at the driving.'

'Divil-the-bit. Only in to the town on pension day mind, to do the shopping and pay bills and the like. Sure where else would I be gallivanting off to at my stage in life?'

He watched her maundering about the kitchen making tea, the table preset with her best china, and while the tea brewed, amid ongoing idle chatter, she heated some scones in the oven.

Over cups of strong tea ("You could trot a mouse on it" he told her, chortling), he scoffing sultana scones with lashings of melting salted country butter and dollops of blackberry jam, she nibbling, they nattered and gossiped, he updating her on how Eileen and Monica were getting on, answering her eager questions about his time in America, eliciting her hearty laughter on telling her how he had conned his way to the job with Lehman Brothers bank; relating how much he loved that great country. During a lull in the conversation, he asked her jocosely if she had a man in her life:

'A man!' she giggled. 'After Barry no man could hold my interest for more than a nagging need or the necessary want of somebody or other to do odd jobs about the place. He was the love of my life, if love it can be called for it sprang from the darkness of hate. Having lost him I've lingered on too long, my dog days full of time; nothing but time. I pray to God every night to take me in my sleep and let me join him above in heaven. Ah! But the journey to a distant God is very long; dying can be a slow business.'

So taken aback was he by her frankness (what did she mean by "a nagging need?"), he sought further revelations about her love for the old man, who, when all is said and done, had killed her father.

'Stephen, have you ever loved? I hear you're living with your sweetheart of yesteryear. But do you love her? If ye do you have no need of explanations from me.'

'I do love her, wholeheartedly I love her. But in truth I wouldn't have known the power of that love had I not loved another before, painfully loved another.'

'She wasn't free to love you, this other, but love you she did. I see it in your eyes Stephen. You've been hurt. But now you're content with a love you've grown to understand, a love that gives meaning to your life.'

'I believe so,' he said, ruffled by her acuteness in getting so close to the bone. His mind inopportunely conjured up that intimate bedroom scene from all those years ago.

'Nellie, I saw ye with him, with grandpa, when he came back from the hos –'

'Ye what? I'm deaf in one ear,' she said holding the tip of her index finger to her right ear, 'and bothered in the other.'

'I saw ye in grandpa's bedroom,' moderately raising his voice.

'Ye did? You saw what?'

In answer to her inquiring look he stated firmly – 'Profound intimacy. I didn't understand at the time but now I think I do.'

'Ah! The old man leching. That was at the end. All doubt flown.' Nellie leaned forward and clasping the poker in her papery hands riddled the fire, red embers spitting a shower of sparks. 'He was a possessive lover your grandfather. Ah yes, love, finding love, although sometimes tormented by misunderstandings, the suspicion and needless jealousies that love provokes. To delight in the joy of togetherness that's the secret. And respect, respect for each other. That shared truth carefully nurtured proves the key to our happiness. And no matter the outcome of a loving relationship we keep the memories, good and bad.'

'Really sorry for the way the family treated ye Nellie, all that petty backbiting, givin' ye the cold shoulder, grandma a bit of a battleaxe. How did you put up with it? How did ye put up with the small town mindset?'

'Och! Your grandmother had a lot to contend with immured as she was on the farm. As I said memories, the treasured memories strengthen us, equip us to withstand anything that life throws at us. Truth is everything, being true to yourself. The cruel gossiping of simple minds can't hurt the happy soul.'

'I'm not family, found out a few years ago I was adopted. Eileen and Monica too. Did ye know about that Nellie?'

'I did surely.'

'Ye never said anything to me about it.'

'"Twasn't my place. I mind me own business.'

'And can ye tell me anything about my birth mother?'

'No Stephen.'

'Mammy told me I was given her by the nuns in Armagh, that she knew nothin' about my birth mother Agnes McMahon. There's no entry for my father on the birth certificate.'

'My advice to ye is to leave well alone.'

'But 'tis only natural to care to find out.'

'I understand that, I do. But curiosity killed the cat. Should your birth mother seek you out, that's different. I can't be of help to ye Stephen 'cept to say that your mammy and daddy did the very best they could for ye. You've always been family.'

On leaving and thinking over their conversation and Nellie's touching send-off – "Go n-eiri an bothar leat", he stopped off at her old haunt The Market Bar. There was no sign of Bill or the bull's pizzle in the revamped premises. The spry barman, nosy-parkering about his journey, served him a shot glass of whiskey and a tumbler of water. Not knowing anybody there he gulped the whiskey straight and left. On unlocking the car he heard a woman's shrill voice berating the bad-tempered bickering and sobbing of a toddler and could not help but stare at her (did he know her?) as she strode toward him on the pavement dragging the red-cheeked boy along by the hand, her other hand pushing a pram that held a pink bundle with a snotty nose that lay bawling to the high heavens. The commotion attracted the attention of some other inquisitive pedestrians nearby; across the street a matronly porcelain-faced woman washing down the pavement outside her shop stood resting on her brush wryly watching the ado.

'Dorothy, is it you?' He felt a knot in the pit of his stomach.

Dorothy Ryan gave him an equivocal glance (had he changed so much), a blush rising to her cheeks as she lackadaisically walked on up the street.

On return to Belfast and being offered his old job back in Dempseys, he accepted, the meagre income enabling him hand his mother a few pounds every week. He briskly resigned himself to the dailiness of his work. After a short while he became aware none of his Protestant neighbours frequented the place, their absence especially noted during the Saturday night music sessions. The odd evening he was free he would prepare dinner at the flat, and then wait outside the hospital entrance to walk with Deirdre the short distance back. It would take her the best part of an hour, as often as not, to unwind after her hectic schedule at the hospital, the cat questingly trailing her from room to room.

One afternoon, finding he was alone at work, he telephoned Bill Crosby's office in New York. Advised by his secretary Crosby was tied up at a meeting but would be free in about an hour, he agreed to call back at 2.30pm NY time. Informing Mr Dempsey of his need to make a long distance call to New York – 'Don't worry I'll pay ye for it,' his kindly boss answered – 'Fire ahead son.' He made the connection at 7.32pm.

'What the fuck man, what happened ye? Where are you?'

'Hi Bill. I'm back in Ireland. Got called-up. Had to fly the coop via Canada, from where I posted the letter. Did ye do as I asked?'

'Exactly as instructed.'

'Have ye heard from her?'

'Not a dicky bird. Not even an acknowledgement. I had the title docs, keys, along with your correspondence, delivered by courier and signed for, so I know she got them. Do ye want me to do a follow-up?'

'No! No, that's all right. As long as I know she received it. Did ye hear anything on the grapevine… about Lehman Brothers.'

'No! Should I have?'

'No! I just wondered if there was any news.'

'Look buddy, don't fucken weird me out here. What news were ye expecking?'

'Take it easy Bill. It's just… I miss the place.'

'Yeah! Well ye did right to dodge the fucken draft, nothin' but a passport to hell. Nixon's turning up the heat over there. This whole war thing's a fucken shitstorm.'

'Right Bill. I'll let ye go. And thanks. Do I owe ye anything?'

'Get away with ye. Glad to help ye out buddy. Here! Give us your address. If I hear anything I'll drop ye a note.'

*

That Christmas they exchanged presents: for her an emerald ring (her birthstone); for him a collection-set of some of Charles Dickens's classic novels, she having once heard him say he had only ever read the one – David Copperfield. Earlier that month they agreed to rent a television from the local TV rental shop, and already enjoyed lounging together on the couch of an evening watching movies, especially Humphrey Bogart movies. Late on the Saturday night before Christmas they watched Casablanca which brought tears to Deirdre's eyes and evoked in him a want to tell her about Martina. But that was something he wasn't yet ready to do. Instead, as soon as the film ended, they slipped quietly to bed and gently canoodled, embracing sleep. That morning he had bought a small noble fir tree and while he was at work Deirdre decorated it with fairy lights, baubles and tinsel, the coloured lights suffusing the flat with an ambient romantic hue as they watched Casablanca. Their joint effort at cooking dinner on Christmas day proved a right foul up, she having left him to keep an eye on the turkey crown as it roasted in the oven while she attended mass. On her return, solid black smoke billowed from the oven, the acrid smell of burnt fowl flesh pervading the flat. She found him enthroned on the toilet, reading, oblivious to the calamity. Having roundly upbraided him for his remissness, she managed to retrieve some inner breast cuts. What they missed out on turkey meat they made up for with double helpings of pudding doused with cheap brandy and smothered in custard.

Two days later, on returning to the flat after work, he found her in deep conversation with Richard over coffee, Richard sprawled in his favorite armchair with his legs crossed and one arm resting on the back cushion, his mug leaving milky opaque rings on the table. Listening to their talk cured him of his envy.

'Rich and his buddies have set up Peoples Democracy. He's one of the officers' co-ordinating tactics.'

'Well good for him,' Maca drawled derisively, giving her a peck on the cheek and pointedly refusing to shake hands with him.

'They've organized a three day march from here to Derry starting out on New Year's Day. He wants us to join them.'

'But shure… that's sheer madness, crazzeee stuff! Three days, no doubt passin' through Protestant towns, protesant strongholds. Isn't O'Neill already conceding our demands, that list of –'

'He's yet to repeal the Special Powers Act, disband the fucking B Specials,' Richard belligerently interjected, his darting eyes filled with disdain. 'You've seen what happened in Armagh and Dungannon? Paisley and that ally of his, Bunting, with their B Special lynch mobs.'

'Yeah! But Craig's gone, sacked by O'Neill. What more could ye ask for now that –'

'I've been trying to dissuade him,' interposed Deirdre. 'Not having much luck though.'

Maca, fearful Richard was doing his damnedest to embroil her back in the civic ferment was relieved to hear her say that and now stood facing his foe.

'Craig has now aligned himself with Paisley and Bunting. O'Neill's ability to hold on to the leadership is precarious to say the least. I'll bet he's ousted by Faulkner and the zealots of the right before Paddy's day,' said Richard, warming to his subject.

'I don't need a punt at your omniscient speculations. The man's doing his best. He should be given time. Didn't ye see him on the telly? Isn't that all he asked for, the time to put things right. Look Richie, I know you've been good to Dede. There when she needed a shoulder to lean on.' Out of the corner of his eye he saw, or suspected he saw, Deirdre cringe in revulsive dismay at the latter comment, so confusing him and stalling the conversation. A funereal quiet filled the room.

'I believe you've been instrumental in persuading Dee to abandon the cause as demonstrated by your reluctance to get involved,' Richard went on. 'I know you prevaricate. You're not disposed to political action, or even to think in terms of social change. In fact, America, instead of incentivizing you to fight for change seems to have blinkered you into complacency. Time to get off the fence.'

'Listen you smart-assed fuck,' he was surprised by how loud he said it. 'My politics is my business. I want the same things you want. The only difference is I don't like the way yer goin' about it, imperilling people's lives, puttin' the life of the woman I love at risk. You go ahead with yer march but leave us out of it.'

'Dee can speak for herself,' Richard retaliated, springing to his feet in a hissy fit.

She sat with head bowed, haughtily impassive, Bobby on her lap purring contentedly. Maca saw Richard smirk a sheepish, bodeful smile, and felt the heat rushing to his face. 'I reckon you should go now,' he said as he moved to open the door. In leave-taking Richard, glowering with suspicion, again sought eye contact with Deirdre but she demurely upped and busied herself bringing the used mugs to the sink where she cursorily rinsed them under the cold tap. In Richard's absence a surreal tranquillity filled the flat.

'I feel shamefaced, like I'm letting him down,' she said matter-of-factly.

'Don't. You've no reason to feel that way. The high moral ground is a lonely place and he seems to spend a lot of his time there. If I'd thrown a bone to the fucker he'd have gnawed at it all night. And thanks for doin' that for me, puttin' him straight. I was a little afraid he'd –'

'I did it for me, for us. I'm pregnant.'

A lusty paean of emotion washed over him. Flushed with pride he stooped and took hold of her, kneading her buttocks, then lifting her above him, his face buried in the warm solidity of her fecund womb. Slowly he let her slide the length of his body until her lustrous eyes met his, his filled with warmth.

'That's the best Christmas present ye could ever give me. Oh my love, me darlin' Dede. Now… now you're really mine.'

He carried her to the bedroom and after making sweet-tempered love, as they wallowed in the sleepy afterglow of sex, their sapped bodies entangled in a serpentine embrace, her precious head tucked in the cradle of his shoulder, he spoke in a soft whisper:

'Our first date, after we'd walked to the bottom of your road and kissed, oh so innocently and thrillingly kissed, and I watched ye, I stood there watchin' ye walk away, yer nylon stockinged legs gleamy under the yellow circles of the streetlights, I made a promise to meself… if you looked back I would marry ye.'

'And I did.'

'That look back is forever fixed in my memory.'

He turned to look her in the eyes and saw that she was weteye-lashed, holding back the tears.

16

Having worked all through the Yuletide and New Year celebrations, he had the weekend after New Year's Day to himself. That Saturday morning, he went over to his mother's house to spruce up the garden and help her dispose of the collected waste from the festivities. Eileen and Ronnie arrived while he, with shirt sleeves rolled up above the elbows, was spading and turning the soil of the rose beds out back.

'You didn't go then?' Ronnie called out to him with a censorious, supercilious grin as he stood at the back door, a Humphrey Bogart hat nonchalantly pushed back from his forehead, a lighted cigarette in his left hand, the fingers of his right hand jingling some loose changes in his trouser pocket.

'To Derry? Mugs game if ye ask me. I know some of them Queens blokes in Peoples Democracy and they're a bit too radical for my liking. A bunch of leftist hotheads encouragin' young fellas to behave like hooligans. Ye didn't go yourself.'

'No. Tied up at meetings. Might get there this evening. Have to hand it to them though, there's been a lot of progress made these past few weeks. Ah well! better tottle on so. I'll leave ye at it.'

As he watched Ronnie retreat into the house he said to himself – 'I don't like that fucker, there's something priggish about him. What's Eileen doing with him anyway, the smarmy bollix? Fucking hell! he's way too old for her. But then most of her friends had gotten married before they were twenty five. Maybe she's panicky about her biological clock counting down. Just then Eileen appeared carrying a mug of tea for him.

'That's a grand job yer doin'. Mammy'll be pleased.'

'You're cheery in yerself?' he said, hesitantly, almost adding –

You fucking snarky bitch – but he didn't, as he condescendingly accepted the mug from her and leaned inertly on the spade.

'And why wouldn't I be? I am gettin' married ye know! The mammy's inside havin' a good cry. With excitement I hasten to add, or, relief.'

'That's great news altogether. When's the big day?' he tentatively asked, giving her a lukewarm one-armed hug and keeping tight-lipped about Deirdre being pregnant.

'Ninth of May. So be sure and tell that girl of yours to put it in her diary. She'll have to take the day off. Maybe she'll be a bridesmaid.'

'I will. You never came to see me at the hospital, or after.'

'No! Up to me fucken tits with all that was goin' on. I thought mebbe ye wouldn't want to see me.'

'Because of that letter ye mean?' he had gone one step beyond where he had thought to go.

'That… and other things,' her face tightened.

'I didn't understand yer letter, nor the reason you sent it.'

'Ah! Yer head was so far up yer arse ye didn't know what was goin' on at home,' she grinned contemptuously. 'A pretty kettle of fish no doubt. I was in a bad place at the time, hangin' out with fucked-up people. Not that that excuses ye.'

'What? On the booze were ye, or was it drugs… or both?' She made no reply. 'Did daddy really say all that about me?'

'Yeah! Fucken sure he did.'

'I did me best to help ye know.'

'We all did our best. But 'twasn't enough don't ye see… 'twasn't enough. Mammy didn't tell me until long after that ye had been sendin' her the few bob.'

'I don't believe I gave daddy any cause to be afraid of me. It doesn't make sense. I was honest in sayin' I didn't want to work in the coal yard. I needed to get out of… I needed to get away –'

'Well! That's all water under the bridge now so let's skip it.'

290

' –from this fucken wasteland. Huh! Easier said than done.'

She turned on her heal and hurried back into the house.

As soon as he heard Eileen and her husband to be take their leave he began to think about Deirdre, knowing she would finish her morning shift by late afternoon. So he tidied up and got ready to go meet her. Washing his hands at the kitchen sink, he observed his mother sitting straight backed by the range fire, chain-smoking in neurasthenic preoccupation with her hypochondriacal ills, seemingly unaware of his presence. He said:

'Well that's great news altogether.'

'What?'

'Eileen gettin' married. 'Tis hard to believe.'

'Och! 'Tis and it 'tisn't,' she quarrelsomely replied.

''Twill be a big day out for ye.'

'I'm glad for Eileen's' sake, for 'twas about time he saw fit to make an honest woman of her. But shure they've to move outta the flat… savin' for a house I'm told. He says rentin' is just like pourin' money down the drain. She's awantin' for Ronnie and herself to live here for a year or two. In on top of me they'll be.'

'Well! Wouldn't that be an agreeable arrangement, a bit of company for ye. Monica tells me she applied for a job with Bord Failte in Dublin. So looks like she'll be movin' out.'

'Aayyeee! So she informed me. And what about yerself. When are ye goin' to put yer mind to gettin' a daycent job?' She said bad-temperedly, leaning back in her chair.

'I'm tryin' ma, but there's sweet fuck all work for the likes of me around here. Ye know rightly I'm tryin' me damnedest.'

'Och! I don't know Stephen, since ye came back from America there's no get-up-and-go in ye a'tall. Look at Monica, never stops striving, tryin' to make things better for herself.'

'Oh yeah! Well if she gets that job she'll be headin' off to Dublin. You'll be here all on yer own-e-o then.'

'If that happens I'll be happy for her. But 'tis this idea of Eileen's that's botherin' me. We all know how long 'twill take for them to get their act together… have their own place. She says if they don't get a house within two years or so they'll use their savings to build a home of their own somewhere, maybe at me home place. The lord only knows… I could be pushin' up daisies by the time that comes about,' she hypothesized.

'But they would pay ye a few bob for the privilege. And Ronnie could help out with the chores. The few bob would come in fierce handy for 'tis about time ye gave up work at the monastery.'

'I don't believe the same fellah is much of a handyman. I dread to think of him loafin' about under me feet all day while Eileen's at work. From what I see he hangs out with some very shady characters, and the last thing I need is to have to make pots of stew for the likes of that lot. She says 'twill have to be this house or his mothers, and she can't abide the woman. So there i'tis.'

'I went over to see Nellie a few weeks ago. She's all on her own but in great form and still drivin' the Volks –'

'Don't mention that nasty piece of work's name in this house,' she snorted, shifting in her chair.

'–wagen. It's just… if ye could let bygones be bygones ye could go live with her on the farm, leave the pair of them to get on with it, livin' here I mean. It's not as though you'd be movin' to a strange place. 'Twould be like movin' back home. Well ye would be. All I'm sayin' is –'

'Aye! Back home to what? Don one prancin' about the –'

'She's a good woman mammy,' he rebuked her. ''Twasn't all her doin' the house and farm being left to her.'

'That's what she told ye is it? Well I know the better of it. Ye don't know the half of it.'

'You'd have no work to do apart from helpin' her keep house. She's still drivin' the Volkswagen and sure wouldn't yis be great company for each other, slippin' away to the town to do the shopping and meetin' up with some of yer oul cronies. The land is let on conacre returnin' a hefty income she tells me. I know Nellie would love to have ye back there.'

'Is that so? Listen here to me now… I don't want to hear another word about it. Leave it for –'

'I'm only tryin' to be of help. 'Twould solve your scruples about havin' to put up with Ronnie loafin' under yer –'

'What! And go from the fryin' pan into the fire. Is that yer solution son? Well 'tis not for me. Don woman… vile vile woman. Wormed her way in to my father's affections with her immoral charms, inveigled her way in to our house, causin' me mother such heartache and pain she nearly ended up in the loony bin. Don't talk to me of don one, no better than a street walker despite her fancy ways of carryin' on. And don't dare tell me she didn't have an unholy influence on me father… persuading him to leave the homeplace to her. Bad enough me mother havin' to suffer her in the house, but to lose the roof over her head to the trollop.'

'Grandma didn't lose the roof over her –'

'Don't talk nonsense son. Ye were but a coddy when all this was goin' on. Surely ye remember yer father stoppin' ye goin' back to help on the farm after yer grandfather passed away. She's a cuckoo wasp. May the devil take her.'

Realizing his efforts to come up with an answer to her dilemma only further aggravated the conniption, he left her mithering herself about Nellie and headed off on the hoof to await Deirdre at the hospital. On the way he dropped into the library and picked up The Naked and the Dead by Norman Mailer, a book he had wanted to read for some time. On exiting the library he bumped into Eddie Atkinson and heartily asked – 'Haven't seen ye in Dempseys lately.' His friend gave him a surly look and marched on. – 'Whats with the brush off,' he mused. 'Ah fuck 'im.' He had a long wait for her outside the hospital entrance, to-ing and fro-ing, mulishly grumbling to himself (what the hell is keeping her) and smoking one cigarette after another. Yet when he saw her rush through the exit and race toward him, her long blonde hair swept back in the breeze, his heart skipped a beat. What had he to bellyache about?

'You've heard?'

'What?'

'About the mayhem… at Burntollet,' she cried out, gasping for breath, and knew by the blank look on his face that he had not. 'Did you not have the radio… or TV on? They're on-and-on about it … all afternoon.'

'No. I was at mammy's helpin' out in the garden, doin' a bit of tidyin'-up. Eileen was there. She's gettin' married on the ninth of May. She wants ye to put the date in your diary.'

'Are we going? I thought… thought you couldn't stand her.'

'We'll talk about it later. On me way here I dropped into the library,' he said, showing her the book. 'Why? What's goin' on?'

'The bastards ambushed the marchers at Burntollet Bridge, hurling bricks, stones… bottles down on them. Then the heavies, most of them off-duty B Specials by all accounts, burst through the hedges on the hillside carrying iron bars, nail-studded clubs and bicycle chains… and laid into them, beating them senseless. The RUC did nothing… nothing, just stood there looking on. Turned their backs on them as if they got what was coming to them. Terrifying… badly injured people left lying all over the place. No help offered. Come on… see for yourself.'

'Jesus fucken Christ! Fucken animals,' he muttered, as they dashed to the flat.

Turning on the television, they sat close-to on the couch in muffled silence, not taking time to doff their coats as they watched the flickering black and white pictures in shocked disbelief, her tremulous hands clutching his, her finger nails digging into his wrist. He saw for himself all that she had before breathlessly related. The reporter seemed to speak with a lump in his throat as the relayed pictures showed some of the felled marchers floundering on the ground, others in confusion striving to flee the onslaught. Suddenly, she bolted upright from the seat and stood transfixed in front of the television:

'Rich! Oh my God Richie,' she screamed as his bloodied image filled the screen, the camera homing in on an unfurled flag on the ground beside him bearing the legend Peoples Democracy. His gallant efforts to comfort and calm her were in vain, she reflexively pushing his hands away. Rising from the couch he prepared and cooked an Ulster fry, the sempiternal bacon, sausages and eggs done sunny side up, slices of loaf bread cut thick like planks (door stoppers she glacially nagged). In restrained reticence they ate a vespertine breakfast, Bobby lazily stretching out its front paws and twirling at their feet scrounging food.

For Sunday dinner he had planned to cook for them a gastronomic meal having bought in all the ingredients on Friday (prawn cocktail starter, fillet steak garnished with a pepper sauce, French beans, garlic mushrooms, roast potatoes, and Black Forest gateau for dessert). 'You're eating for two now,' he had jokingly chided her. 'That's an old midwife's tale,' she chaffed, her face beaming, being spoilt by him now that she was expecting his baby.

However, matters took a turn for the worse when, awakened by her radio alarm that morning (set for her to attend mass), they heard the reportage on overnight events in Derry.

'What the hell's going on?' she cried, as in her dressing gown and he pulling an old cardigan over his pyjamas they rushed to the couch and turned on the television. The first flickering images showed live pictures of people erecting barricades across the main entrances to the Bogside. The voice-over related how in the early hours of the morning groups of RUC policemen and B Special auxiliaries had run amok, roaming through the streets of the Bogside, shouting, singing, throwing stones, dealing out arbitrary punishment with their black billy clubs, tenders crashing from time to time into the tiny terraced houses, even a department store.

They broke in windows, kicked doors and shouted to the terrified inhabitants to "come out and fight yis Fenian bastards". Anyone who did come to his or her door was grabbed and beaten up.

'Mebbe Richie's right. It's time to get our hands on some guns and teach the fuckers a lesson,' he heard himself say.

Deirdre felt unable to tear herself away from the blanket TV coverage, having made up her mind not to bother attending mass. And so he rustled up some toast and a mug of coffee for himself while pouring a herbal tea for her. Then he fed the demented cat. The television was again showing images of the attacks at Burntollet Bridge and the aftermath scenes in Guildhall Square in Derry city centre where thousands of angry protesters had gathered to hear the reports by bloodstained marchers of their experiences.

'This changes everything,' she edgily intoned. 'We can't not be involved. We can't leave it to others to bear the brunt. We have to play our part.'

A bombshell of misgivings peppered his brain, and, without answering, he held her close endeavouring to calm the trembling motions that pervaded her body. They sat uncommunicative for what seemed an interminable time, she flushed with burning tears, he whey-faced and drained by anger; the voluble reportage of the chaos now blunting his mind. Where would all this trouble and strife lead? he brooded. Where would it lead him?

'I'm dead beat,' she said, slowly rising to her feet. 'I'm going back to bed. Don't wake me. I'll get up when I'm ready.'

He switched off the television, his sensibilities bloated by the images that had bombarded him. Having partaken only of coffee and toast for breakfast, he wolfed down a bowl of cornflakes. Although he remained hungry, knowing the meal he would prepare for dinner later that evening he refrained from further grazing from the fridge. Lethargically opening the French window, he stood on the narrow balcony and could hear, above the hum of traffic, a whole clatterer of sirens in the distance (ambulance? fire brigade? police?). He shivered as the cold crisp air filled his lungs, its penetrating rawness persuading him to retrieve his coat. Having done so, he returned to the balcony and in reflective mood smoked one cigarette after another while watching jubilant squealing youngsters playing football on the wintergreen grass common, their boisterous shrill cries and prelapsarian bravado causing him to become even more downbeat – 'What did the future hold for them?' Flicking a cigarette butt to the damp black tarmac below, as he followed its zigzag course he noticed a young woman hurriedly approach along the pavement clasping her coat collar tight to her neck, the winter sunlight revealing the sleek sheen of her blue-black hair bobbing in the breeze. She looked up at him, a flinty grin spreading across her winsome face (probably in reproach of his littering, he brooded). Casually making eye contact, she reminded him of Martina. His heart throbbing, he felt an icy shudder darting through him, as he gaped at her bustling along, prompting him into reverie. Is he over Martina? Their love had given way to social reality. Should he seek her out and try to make things right between them. Would she seek him out, ever? Such thoughts he had strived to occlude, yet sometimes, as now, his inner demon stung him with aching reminiscences, questing consolation in his memories of her. Had she been the one to bring about their parting he would hate her. Yes, deep down, he knew he would HATE her, his anima swamped by a paranoiac enmity. Did she hate him? Her animus beset by loathsome illusions of ways and means of getting even with him, perhaps of sweet revenge. How quickly love turns to hate. A gesture, a word, once revered in intimate familiarity now anathematized in neurosis, exposed to the full hostility of a woman scorned.

Intoxicated by his introspections, he retreated and closed the French window, his body all of a tremble (anxiety? the cold?) surrendering to the suffocating heat of the flat. Heavy-hearted, he removed his coat and needing to escape to another world asked himself where he had put Mailer's novel. Having searched to no avail through an untidy heap of tattered medical journals and old newspapers on the kitchen worktop, he concluded it must be in the bedroom. Unwilling to disturb Deirdre, knowing she needed to be alone, he retrieved from the pile a November issue of the Belfast Telegraph, and stretched out on the couch to read it. How innocuous the coverage of old news struck him, the editorial extolling O'Neill's proposed five-point package of reforms and emphatically critical of the treachery "our Leader" faced within his own party.

He awoke, with what felt like a hangover, to the discordant sound of sirens and realized the television was again broadcasting, the cathode tube's electromagnetic waves bouncing lances of diffracted light off the French window panes that held at bay January's rapidly fading twilight, the volume set uncomfortably high. And there she is, deshabilled, the magnesium flares lighting up her joyless face, standing statue-still over him, hands on hips, in what seemed to him in his disorientation her impudent imperious air, coupled with an accusatory attitude:

'What?' He felt a stab of self-consciosness on hearing the irritability in his voice.

'Richie's dead.'

'Holy shit! How the fuck did –'

'A cerebral aneurysm. While undergoing treatment in Altnagelvin hospital.'

'Christ Dee, I'm so –'

'Strange, that's his… was his affectionate name for me,' she petulantly interjected.

'– so sorry. A Freudian slip. How did ye hear?' he asked, scrambling from the couch, realizing he was still in his pyjamas.

'His mother phoned. That's what woke me up. You could at least have answered the cussed thing.'

Sensible of her whole body quaking in shock he moved to hug

her, but she sidestepped his essayed canoodle and shuffled back to the bedroom. Dawdling to the French window, he peered passed his reflection in the glass to the common, now deserted by the footballers, the grass wavering in the rising wind blanketed with the ferruginous embrace of the amber street lamps, the odd passing vehicle casting elongated shafts of coned whiteness into the distance. Bewildered, feeling out of sync, he grew more and more conflicted by the relative calmness of his outsider world and Deirdre's inscrutable state of mind. All this played out against the dinning turmoil that emanated from the television. Switching on the cooker he readied the potatoes on a baking tray and stuck it in the oven, then crushed a garlic clove in butter heating on the pan.

'I'll put the steaks on,' he called out to her.

'Are you out of your mind? I can't eat knowing all this is going on,' she replied, exiting the bedroom dressed in her best suit, his favourite – a plain grey tweed in a fashionable slimline cut. 'Anyway I have to go over there. His mum expects me.'

'But I've everythin' ready for eats. Turn the bleedy TV down will ye,' he bellowed agitatedly.

'Sor-ry' she crooned vexedly as she did his bidding. 'I've no stomach for it. Don't see how you can possibly think of –'

The telephone rang and she rushed to answer it.

'What! How… how many? Oh my God… I'll be there as quick as I can… about ten minutes.'

Having heard one side only of the baleful conversation, he stood beset by total confusion, compounded by her hasty action in racing to the bedroom and arriving back loosely attired in her coat.

'I've been called in. Horrendous! Injured people jamming up Emergency.'

'Holy shit! I'll walk ye there.'

'No need,' she snapped in antsy cold comfort.

'I want to. Let me get my coat. Nobody'll notice me pyjamas.'

When they reached the pavement, dusk switched gloomy dark, a gibbous moon shading through patchy cloud, she began to walk so fast he had difficulty keeping pace with her, his sockless feet pinched by the dry leather of his slip-ons. The yammer of sirens could be heard soaring on the wind, the sky over Clonard aglow with blazing fires.

'Sorry... about dinner. We'll have that... that steak of yours tomorrow,' she said in short, quick breaths.

'Right. That's okay then.'

'You do understand Steve. I have to go in.'

'Yeah! 'Course I understand.'

On reaching the hospital forecourt they hastily kissed, the merest brush of the lips, and then he watched her go. Turning away in ovine vacillation, raising the collar of his coat against the rawness of the freshening wind, he heard the screech of tyres on tarmac followed by the deadening thunk of metal on flesh.

'Oh my God no... No! No! No!' he cried in gagging intonations, swinging round and moving towards the chaotic happening, his legs like lead weights recalcitrant to his charge. He fought to get there – *there – I must get there*. Approaching as fast as his legs could carry him, the ambulance driver, his face warped by the flashing blue light, held up his arms to block him getting any closer. 'Hold off fella,' he gruffly commanded, stumbling back-wards with the impact of Maca's momentum but managing to hold on to him, before long assisted by a burly security guard who held him in an armlock. A paramedic on his knees leaned over her unmoving, mangled body. A nurse raced down the hospital steps, her starched white cap carried off in the wind, and straight away lowered Deirdre's skirt to below the knees. In striving to speak, to call out, to yell his love for her, with mouth open attempting to let them know he was her man, he dry retched on gulped air.

'She came outta nowhere,' he heard the throaty voice of the ambulance driver. The paramedic shifted uneasily on his knees and, with a pathetic look at the nurse, discreetly shook his head.

Epilogue

Stephen MacAlindon's panglossian view of being had been crushed, his personality immolated, leaving him in a state of psychological myopia, of conscience wrestling with the meaning of it all. His tribulatory relationship with Martina during his years in New York had been the love affair that can never be. On retreating to Belfast fate brought him together again with Dede, the woman he always loved. Now his hollow existence was being gnawed by inexpressible grief. What was there to live for? His life seemed to him not worth the candle.

Throughout this period of pain and loss, Maca sought diverse interests and failed to find any in mitigation of the misery, his being continuing to drift in and out of a dark dysfunctional tactility that often led him to contemplate putting an end to it; putting an end to the loneliness. Dede's family wanting nothing to do with him, he was back (with Bobby the cat) at home with his mother in Bombay Street. She proved unshakable in her belief that had her son listened to her sound advice all those years ago, none of these mishaps would have befallen him – "Family is the strongest bond of all… unbreakable. The family that prays together stays together" – she relentlessly harped with a hardhearted scowl. Should he track down his birth mother?

He continued working in Dempseys, perceiving himself a serviceable dogsbody with no prospect of getting a better job. If anything, his sense of exclusion from the jobs-market was exacerbated by the intensifying troubles, the latent sectarianism now rampant. Peaceful street demonstrations over Divis Flats and the housing policies of the Housing Trust were brutally put down by RUC baton-charges, ending in widespread rioting in the area.

The protesters had no protection against these onslaughts which sometimes led to civilians being killed or seriously injured.

The Peoples Democracy campaign for civil rights for all had been paralysed by the continuing savage attacks of Bunting, Paisley and their henchmen of mobilised B Special militias, including rogue RUC officers; and by the collusion of the state forces in failing to protect its involuntary subjects as police let the allochthonous brutes get on with their dirty work. All O'Neill's attempts at legislating for a fairer society had failed, as the hoped for confluence of ideological affinity and political ambition fell by the wayside. The increasing polarization and divisiveness of the social order made life a living hell.

Maca, recognizing that amidst all this turmoil there was no way of improving the circumstances of his reality, seriously considered returning to the States. Reckoning he could travel on a tourist visa and feasibly disappear into the diaspora of the needy wishful thinkers and the great unwashed. But not having heard from Frank, or indeed Johnny in Chicago, where would he pick up the threads of a life in America? The risk of arrest by the Federal Authorities for evading induction into the army and/or in consequence of the banking chicanery seemed insuperable. Be that as it may, in lighter moods it seemed like a risk worth taking if it meant getting together with Martina again. Would such a coming together be possible? Would it be sensible? Maca would never know the answers to these questions unless he did something about it. Should he write his old frenimies to establish the lay of the land? If positive responses were forthcoming he might then write Martina, or, perhaps wait until he was back in America to seek her out. The recrudescent destructiveness of the local violence encouraged him in this endeavour. There was no good reason to hang around, life itself on the edge of an alarming precipice.

Following the 'Battle of the Bogside', the febrile atmosphere that had pertained in Belfast during the months of his return turned apocalyptic, visiting pogroms on nationalist ghettos, including his own tiny enclave of Bombay Street. A loyalist mob, including many members of the B Specials, armed with rifles, revolvers and sub-machine guns had marauded along the streets leading to the Falls. They petrol bombed Catholic houses that lay on their route, beating up their occupants and shooting at fleeing residents, the RUC in tenders later evicting those residents who refused to leave. About 150 Catholic homes had been torched leaving the landscape of his childhood gutted. The retreating residents began to erect barricades at the entrances to adjoining streets to prevent further penetration by the ravagers into the area. There were TV reports from the Republic stating the Irish army would be dispatched across the border to protect beleaguered nationalists and in support of evacuation plans for the fleeing refugees. The Westminster Labour government of Harold Wilson, in an effort to avoid direct rule, agreed to send British troops in to Belfast and Derry to assist the RUC in keeping the peace, on the strict understanding that the B Specials would be stood down. Suchlike earnest efforts to procure peace proved to no avail resulting in a thirty year conflict commonly known as "The Troubles".

Throughout these cataclysmic events, Maca remained riven by Deirdre's death, grief mirrored in his psyche, bereavement unmanning him, feeling her absence as an amputee feels the missing limb, the searing pain of her loss and the loss of his child forever stamped in memory. In those dark days of the soul, amid the escalating and seemingly unending violence, he was haunted by her, her words coming back to him like a distant echo resounding in his head – "We can't not be involved. We can't leave it to others to bear the brunt. We have to play our part."

Author's Note

A book which provided valuable insights into the modus operandi of a stock exchange is *The Man Who Broke Barings Bank* by Neil Leeson. Another work which assited in establishing some facts relating to the Vietnam War during the administration of President Lyndon B. Johnson is *Flawed Giant* by Robert Dallek.

Special love and thanks to my wife Elizabeth and our children, to whom this book is dedicated.